RANDOM
HOUSE

LARGE
PRINT

# The Spies of Shilling Lane

Also by Jennifer Ryan
Available from Random House Large Print

**The Chilbury Ladies' Choir**

# *the*
# Spies
# *of*
# Shilling
# Lane

A Novel

## JENNIFER RYAN

RANDOM HOUSE
**LARGE PRINT**

This is a work of fiction. Names, characters, places, and incidents either are the product of the author's imagination or are used fictitiously. Any resemblance to actual persons, living or dead, events, or locales is entirely coincidental.

Copyright © 2019 by Jennifer Ryan

All rights reserved.
Published in the United States of America by Random House Large Print in association with Crown, an imprint of Random House, a division of Penguin Random House LLC, New York.

Cover design: Laura Klynstra
Cover image: © Stephen Mulcahey/
Trevillion Images
Spine image: © hoverfly/Shutterstock

The Library of Congress has established a Cataloging-in-Publication record for this title.

ISBN: 978-0-593-10285-5

www.penguinrandomhouse.com
/large-print-format-books

FIRST LARGE PRINT EDITION

Printed in the United States of America

10  9  8  7  6  5  4  3  2  1

This Large Print edition published in accord with the standards of the N.A.V.H.

To my mother, Joan Cooper,
with gratitude and love

# The Spies of Shilling Lane

*1.*

ASHCOMBE VILLAGE, ENGLAND
MARCH 1941

How do you measure the success of your life? Mrs. Braithwaite wrote determinedly in her notebook as the train sputtered out of the little station. She hadn't left her village for a year; hadn't been to London since the war began back in 1939. The journey to see her daughter was long overdue.

Every so often the train would hurtle through a station, now nameless because all the station signs had been taken down at the beginning of the war to confuse any invading Nazis. None had come over yet, thank heavens. For now the Nazis were content sending planes across every night to bomb

British cities to pieces—the Blitz, they called it, "lightning." Their intention at first was to take out factories and docks, but now they were bombing at random, trying to exhaust the Royal Air Force and break the spirit of the people.

Mrs. Braithwaite muttered to herself, "Well, my spirit has well and truly been broken, but **not** by the Nazis."

The previous morning, Mrs. Metcalf and the village matrons had demoted her from her rightful position as head of the local Women's Voluntary Service.

"It was a joint decision," Mrs. Metcalf had said, two ladies on either side of her. She had placed herself at the center of a folding table in the village hall while Mrs. Braithwaite was required to stand before them. "You have been in the top position of the Ashcombe Women's Voluntary Service since the war began, and now we feel that it's time to pass the baton to a more"—she paused, thinking of the right word—"a more thoughtful and considerate leader." Naturally, she meant herself.

Mrs. Braithwaite had a sturdy frame, which she felt gave her lack of height more gusto. Her short hair was still a rich brown despite her fifty years, her face large and uncompromisingly oblong, her mouth drawn effortlessly into a frown. She narrowed her eyes at her old neighbor and so-called friend. "I've put my all into this group and **this** is how I'm repaid?"

"The truth is, we're fed up with you bossing everyone around," Mrs. Metcalf's daughter, Patience, stated with far less subtlety than her mother. A twenty-two-year-old who had married well and stayed in the village, Patience was the opposite of Mrs. Braithwaite's own Betty, who had vanished off to London at the first whiff of war. Mrs. Metcalf's children—both Patience and her son, Anthony—were practically perfect, according to their mother. Anthony was an exceptionally bright student at university, while Patience had already produced three children, much to Mrs. Metcalf's pride and Mrs. Braithwaite's infuriation; why did Betty have to be so bookish?

Patience glanced sideways toward the other ladies and added, "And with the end of your marriage, we wondered if there was a more reputable leader—"

"So that's what this is about!" Mrs. Braithwaite roared. "Am I an embarrassment to you all because I'm divorced?"

A sharp intake of breath echoed around the hall. Divorce was rare in these parts. It was a word that quickly conjured up ideas of carelessness, loss of control, depravity.

Mrs. Metcalf raised a condescending eyebrow. "Now, let's not get beyond ourselves. It's not only to do with that. It's also because of the events on Saturday evening."

Mrs. Braithwaite felt the blood rush to her face.

The events alluded to had occurred around dinnertime, when Mrs. Metcalf, in the midst of entertaining Lady Worthing, the ceremonial head of the WVS, had spotted Mrs. Braithwaite's podgy, pale face looking through her dining room terrace window. Excusing herself politely, Mrs. Metcalf opened the French doors and looked out into the cool night air. There hadn't been any sign of Mrs. Braithwaite, only a stubby shadow behind a potted ornamental bush.

"I know you're there," Mrs. Metcalf called, and eventually Mrs. Braithwaite had no choice but to come out. It was a mistake to pretend she'd been looking for a lost brooch; they both knew that she was spying. She'd suspected Mrs. Metcalf's butler of stealing the pig that was missing from a local farm, and she was now waiting in full expectation of seeing a large pork joint—a victorious apple in its mouth—as the centerpiece of Mrs. Metcalf's table. The food rations had hit Mrs. Braithwaite especially hard, with her love for roast beef, pork, and puddings. When she'd heard about the missing pig, her love of mysteries had got the better of her: she'd become intent on uncovering its whereabouts.

"I was helping the police with an important investigation," she explained to the committee, adopting the self-righteous air of one doing a service for the community.

"You were trespassing on private property." Mrs. Metcalf sniffed victoriously.

"But the pig is not a WVS matter. You can hardly expect me to stand down under such circumstances."

"You will have to let the committee decide that," Mrs. Metcalf said. "Until then this meeting is adjourned."

The ladies stood, discussing the matter among themselves, while Mrs. Metcalf came forward to have a quiet word with Mrs. Braithwaite.

"I would also like to remind you that I know about that little matter you've kept hidden all these years." Mrs. Metcalf gave the smug smile of one who knows a secret and acknowledges its power. "I think your daughter, Betty, would be very keen to hear what you've been keeping from her."

Mrs. Braithwaite expelled a great snort of breath. She loathed the fact that Mrs. Metcalf knew the one thing she dreaded leaking out. Goodness knows what effect it would have on her reputation, not to mention how it would affect Betty. Mrs. Braithwaite had tried over the years to forget about it, to sweep it under the rug. But Mrs. Metcalf always reminded her, like a ghoul from the past wagging a condemning finger, always ready to seal her doom.

She noticed Mrs. Metcalf's son, Anthony, moving some chairs at the back of the hall, hiding a smirk. He was a slim, ferret-like young man who was a little older than Betty; they'd been great friends, getting the bus to the grammar school in town every day. Occasionally he would visit from university, and yesterday, annoyingly, had been one of those days.

**Had Mrs. Metcalf already told him her secret? Would he tell Betty?**

Furious, Mrs. Braithwaite snapped, "You can't get away with this! You've been after the top position for months, and now you're forcing me out—"

"Not forcing you out, exactly," Mrs. Metcalf interrupted. "You are still welcome to help out with the other village ladies."

Mrs. Braithwaite contained a howling bellow, the sound sticking in her throat like an unerupted missile. The WVS was all she'd had since Dickie left. Without her ladies to lead, she would have no one.

But it would be impossible for her to attend the group as a normal volunteer, not the group leader. She had noble blood in her veins, after all, even if she lived in a small house these days. She could never lower herself.

Regaining her composure, she brought herself up to attention. "If you don't want me here, I'll find other people who will appreciate my energies."

With that she threw Mrs. Metcalf a final look of disdain and stormed out, her proud exit sabotaged by a pile of folding chairs lying against the door, which clattered to the floor, pulling Mrs. Braithwaite down with them. After sprawling around like an upended beetle, she scrambled to her feet, straightened herself, and marched through the door with as much dignity as she could muster.

Mrs. Braithwaite remained in her sitting room for the rest of the day. As the setting sun cast a golden glow onto her chintz sofa, she realized that drastic measures were needed. With her husband gone, her village peers tossing her aside, and Mrs. Metcalf threatening to expose her secret, there was nothing else for it. She had to go and see the person who still mattered in all of this.

She needed to see Betty.

She needed to tell her everything.

Otherwise, every time Mrs. Metcalf needed more power, she would remind Mrs. Braithwaite about what she knew; that she could drop it over the small community like her very own incendiary bomb. She couldn't let Betty hear about it from Mrs. Metcalf or Anthony.

Betty, who was now almost twenty-one, had sent her five letters since she'd been in London, and as she sat in the train to London, Mrs. Braithwaite pulled them out of her sturdy brown handbag and flicked through them. The first was short, letting her mother know she was living in a boardinghouse in Bloomsbury. The next had a new address: Three Shilling Lane, Wandsworth, sharing a house with two girls. The other letters were also concise, telling her about lunchtime concerts with girlfriends, a play she'd seen at the theater—"a murder mystery, you'd have loved it, Mum!"—and a marvelous new film, **Gone with the Wind**. She seemed to be incredibly busy, enjoying her job filing in a sewage works, and keeping herself safe from the bombs.

The train began to slow. Outside, the fields turned to houses, then to the back gardens of the suburbs, many growing vegetables for eating, some with chickens or rabbit hutches, one with a couple arguing on a terrace. Mrs. Braithwaite speculated as to whether they were having an affair, her forehead wrinkling in abhorrence. She had been born in the age of Queen Victoria, when sex wasn't discussed, let alone performed with people other than one's husband. In fact, Mrs. Braithwaite had been rather horrified to discover after marriage the kind of bestial activity that was expected of her, although she mused that the Queen herself must have done it at some point. She'd had nine children, after all.

She scowled at the occupants of the carriage as if expecting them to concur with her private grievances, which caused the old man beside her to shift to a farther seat in a bit of panic, catching the sympathetic eye of another passenger as he did so.

Mrs. Braithwaite's trusty notebook lay open on her lap. It was usually reserved for WVS memoranda, notes, and the taking down of people's names when their knitting was below par or they'd missed a meeting.

Today, however, she had more important matters

to consider, and her mind returned to her question. **How do you measure the success of your life?**

She jotted down the things that came to mind first:

**Social standing. Reputation. How the world sees you.**

These had been Mrs. Braithwaite's guiding principles. She had been taught that her birthright bestowed upon her an innately higher status than the other women in the village. "Blue blood," her dearly departed Aunt Augusta had instructed, "is running through our veins." One need only look at that matron, with her strict rules and stiff upper lip, to recognize a member of the upper crust. The daughter of an earl, Aunt Augusta had made sure that her straitened circumstances were never confused with a lowering of standards. Mrs. Braithwaite had been brought up in the certain belief that the pair of them were more worthy than just about everyone else.

But as the vile memory of the previous day's humiliation came hideously to mind, tiny strands of doubt began to worm into Mrs. Braithwaite's mind.

Outside the train, the buildings began crowding in, disorderly and grimy with dust and ashes, some broken apart by the bombs. Busy streets flashed by with pedestrians scuttling among the buses, trams, and cars. The noise and smell of smoke and fumes seeped into the compartment, jarring and suffocating. The train began to slow down to a trot and then to a walk as it went over the great gray River Thames before heaving to a halt in Victoria Station.

Mrs. Braithwaite had forgotten that you had to stand by the door if you wanted to be first off the train, so she had to barge past the old man and some younger women, swatting them out of the way with her handbag.

"What's the hurry, love?" said one of the young women, letting out a jeering titter.

Mrs. Braithwaite swung determinedly back at her. "I have a daughter to find."

Grasping her handbag close and striding purposefully down to the yawning station forecourt, she drew a deep breath as she surveyed the massive information board for Wandsworth Common, the quiet South London suburb that was Betty's new home.

## 2.

Exhausted by her exertions, Mrs. Braithwaite got off the small commuter train at Wandsworth Common and demanded from the nervous station-master how to find Shilling Lane.

"Down the road, opposite the common—that's the large stretch of grass. Can't miss it." Then he hurried into his office just as she was hinting that her suitcase was excessively heavy. How frustrating of him! It wasn't as if anyone else were trying to buy a ticket, after all.

She walked slowly, lugging the suitcase the full half mile to number three, a detached Victorian house opposite the green. It looked pleasant enough, with windows in the attic for a maid or two, a luxury only the rich would have these days, if they could keep them, that is. She'd heard that Lady Worthing had lost half of her maids to a bomb factory that was paying three times as much—apparently they'd been delighted to get away.

Mrs. Braithwaite had once had a woman who came in every afternoon to clean and cook, but after Dickie began traveling around the country for sales meetings, he'd insisted they do without, as money was short. Keeping house was certain to bring on a headache if nothing else would.

As did the notion that it hadn't only been meetings of the sales variety that he'd been attending.

She strode through the tidy front garden to the porched front door and knocked loudly.

Much to her surprise, a diminutive, middle-aged man opened it. "How can I help you?" His voice was as thin as he was, a theme repeated in his face, his gray wire spectacles, and his hair, through which Mrs. Braithwaite could see his scalp, shiny and mottled with pink like a very large marble ball. His eyes were the pale blue of a startled rabbit.

"May I come in?"

She barged past him into the narrow hallway, bumping her suitcase against a hall table, upon which lay a shallow dish housing someone's matchbook collection, a small carriage clock, and an assortment of model elephants, which she shoved to one side to make way for her handbag.

"I've come to see my daughter, Betty Braithwaite."

"I'm afraid she isn't here," he said politely, bending around her to reposition the elephants. His spectacles had fallen slightly over a hump in his long, bony nose, and he jerkily pushed them back up with a clean, soft hand. Mrs. Braithwaite wondered if he had previously been a member of the clergy.

"Isn't here?" She tried not to sound alarmed, but of all the things she hadn't expected, it was that she'd get to London and find Betty not at home. Yet how like her: busy, hardworking. "When will she be back?"

"Well, that's the point," he said worriedly. "We don't know."

"What are you talking about?" She looked him up and down. "Where is she?"

He made a small, embarrassed cough. "I'm afraid we don't know where she is. She hasn't been home since Friday."

She felt the blood drain from her face, her eyes piercing this ridiculous man. Her arms wanted to reach up and give him a jolly good shake until he changed his tune. "It's now Tuesday. Friday was four days ago. At what point did you think you should call the police, contact her mother?"

"Well, I wasn't sure—"

"Who are you anyway?" She was getting louder, looking around for someone more knowledgeable to speak to. "Where are the girls she told me about?"

"I'm her landlord." He put out a limp hand for her to shake. "Mr. Norris." She eyed the hand, which looked clean, and shook it cautiously.

"I thought Betty lived with some girls of her own age."

"Yes, there are two other girls, Florrie and Cassandra."

"One of them must know where she is. Would you be so good as to fetch them for me?"

"I'm afraid they're not in."

"Well, where are they? I hope they're not missing, too?"

Mr. Norris was quietly clasping his hands together with discomfort. "No, not missing. At work. Cassandra is usually back around now, unless she stays out."

"What do you mean?" Mrs. Braithwaite opened her notebook. "Would she go out in the evening without coming home to change first?"

He smothered a laugh. "Life in London is unspeakably hectic, Mrs. Braithwaite. We're working long hours, doing extra voluntary shifts, and fitting in sleep between the bombs. Coming home to change has become a bit of a luxury, especially for those who like to go out a lot."

"Really! And is Cassandra one of those types?"

"Well, she does seem to enjoy social events, if that's what you mean."

Mrs. Braithwaite wrote an addendum to Cassandra's new profile in her notebook.

"And at what time are we to expect Florrie?"

"Oh, Florrie. She works late, so she won't be back until ten. You'll have to come back tomorrow."

"Come back tomorrow?" Mrs. Braithwaite was getting cross. "Betty is missing, and since no one else seems to be looking for her, I'll jolly well have to find her myself. And if that means staying here, then that's precisely what I'll do." Mrs. Braithwaite picked up her suitcase with the expectation of being shown in.

"Don't you have a hotel room booked?" he said nervously. "There's a place in town that has a few nice, if small, rooms—"

"I'll stay in Betty's room," she announced. "She's paid her rent, hasn't she?"

"But you're not Betty, and she's only paid until Saturday," he said fretfully. "After that, well, I'll have to offer it to someone else. Rooms are scarce with the war, you know. All the bombs are leaving a lot of people homeless. I've got a waiting list in case anything comes up."

A frown furrowed her forehead. "Well, I shall stay until Saturday. By then I trust we'll have found her."

"And then you'll go home?"

"Why yes, of course I'll go home. Where else do you expect me to go?" With that, she began climbing the stairs. If the ridiculous little man wasn't going to show her to her daughter's room, then she'd simply have to find it herself.

He hurried to catch up with her, leading her to one of the doors on the landing. "It's this one."

The room was basic and rather gloomy. A bed ran down half of it, tidily made with a washed-out blanket. On the other side, a dressing table was wedged between a chest of drawers and a shabby brown upright armchair that looked as if it hadn't been reupholstered this side of the last war.

"It's the smallest bedroom, I'm afraid." Mr. Norris looked embarrassed. "The other two were here before Betty and naturally took the larger rooms. Betty never complained though."

Mrs. Braithwaite looked despondently around the room.

**Is this what her daughter's life had amounted to?**

The dressing table had a tall pile of books, her hairbrush—the same black one she'd had since she was a child—and a few clips tidied to one side. Otherwise there was nothing else on show. It was as if she were a shadow of a person.

Mrs. Braithwaite considered one's living space a canvas on which to display one's success, style, and breeding. Her own elegant, although aged, furniture, her antique piano (now badly in need of a tune), and her small but carefully used collection of crystal scotch whisky glasses and Royal Doulton teacups all glowed with the very best of taste. Betty, on the other hand, seemed to be doing the opposite. A kind of obscure secrecy pervaded her things;

or was it privacy? An attempt to conceal any tiny detail of herself.

"I knew I should never have let her come to London."

A window looked out onto the gardens behind, the roofs of some houses fractured by bombs—then the horrific possibility that Betty could have been killed in the Blitz shot through her. "Were there any bombs on Friday night, after Betty left?"

Mrs. Braithwaite knew that many people never came home after air raids. They were bombed on the roads or buried in rubble. She'd read about it in the papers. Unless you went searching for them, checking bomb sites and the London hospitals, you wouldn't know whether they were dead or alive unless some authority found a body and sent a letter. If they didn't have an address—or one couldn't be found—the name would be printed in the newspaper. If it was known.

"No, there were no raids on Friday or Saturday," Mr. Norris assured her.

Mrs. Braithwaite found that she'd been holding her breath; that Betty could have been killed before she got to her was beyond bearing. How she longed to see her!

"Perhaps she went away?" Mrs. Braithwaite took a quick look under the bed and on top of the narrow wardrobe. "There's no sign of her suitcase." She turned to Mr. Norris. "Did Betty mention any trips?"

"No, but the girls often don't tell me when they'll be in or out. If her suitcase has gone, she probably went to stay with a friend. The girls do that sometimes, especially if they have a few days off work."

"Do they?" Mrs. Braithwaite plumped herself down on the bed, a feeling of impatience overtaking the worry. "Typical of Betty to go away when I need to see her. I wonder where she's gone."

Mr. Norris stood beside the bed wringing his hands, and she looked up at him with exasperation: he was clearly completely unable to deal with the situation. No help at all! Judging by the look of him, he must have been over fifty, too old to join up. But why was the poor man still in London? He looked a nervous wreck.

"Tell me, Mr. Norris. What is it that you **do**?"

"I'm an accountant with a city law firm. It's a reserved job, so I have to stay put here in London. I'd rather not, frankly." Then, as if he realized he was being unpatriotic, he added more cheerfully, "But the worst seems to be over. We had bombers coming over for fifty-six nights in a row at the beginning. I took to sleeping in the local shelter so that I didn't have to get up in the middle of the night. You get used to sleeping on concrete floors after a while, you know."

It suddenly seemed unthinkable to Mrs. Braithwaite that an entire city could live like this, bunking down in shelters or running to them in the middle of the night. But now that she **was** thinking about it, the lack of sleep, the whole population in peril night after night, not knowing where anyone was, must be utterly appalling. It was no wonder the poor man looked exhausted.

Mrs. Braithwaite eyed him with a little more respect. She hadn't spent a lot of time thinking about the Blitz. It had started last September and punished the cities through the long winter. Now it was spring, and although the planes were still coming over, it wasn't all night every night. She'd heard about the bombs on the wireless, of course, but with the divorce and her position at the Ashcombe WVS, she hadn't been paying as much attention as perhaps she should have.

Silence hung in the air for a few moments, and then Mr. Norris looked at his wristwatch. "Well, I have to get some dinner and prepare for the morning. You should be able to get something to eat at a restaurant if you walk to the other side of the common. If you want to see Florrie, you might have to wait for her in the hall as she tends to go straight up to bed."

"I shall take dinner here with you," Mrs. Braithwaite said determinedly.

"The rations!" Mr. Norris gasped, glancing over her large form as if she might eat more than a person of his size. "I can't possibly share our rations! Each person has a correct portion, and there won't be enough if we share ours with you." Then he added pointedly, "Since you'll only be here until Saturday, you'll have to eat out."

**What a nuisance!** She was stuck with a rule-following, number-obsessed nitwit. She got up, tied on her beige and maroon head scarf, and pushed past him to the door. "Could I bother you for a front-door key?"

"I only keep one spare, and that's for emergencies, and—"

"This **is** an emergency. My daughter is missing, and since no one else appears to be doing so, I intend to find her." She put her hand out, palm faceup, giving him little choice but to comply. He brought out a large bunch of keys, selected one, and slid it off the key ring.

"Thank you," she said, clenching the key in her fist.

And with that, she turned and marched out into the darkening dusk to find some dinner.

## 3.

Mrs. Braithwaite was waiting by the front door when Florrie came home at around ten o'clock that evening. Mr. Norris had retired to his bedroom, which appeared to be in the maid's quarters on the uppermost floor of the house. Having closely inspected the sitting room, dining room, and kitchen, she'd found a stool and carried it into the hall, placing it between the front door and the stairs so as not to miss anyone.

The girl who rushed through the front door looked as if she could do with a thoroughly good brush. Her auburn hair curled around her neck and shoulders, any attempt to pin it up had woefully failed. As she stood up straight, Mrs. Braithwaite noted how striking she was, with her height and curvaceous figure. She was wearing a cheery lilac summer dress that spread out from her waist over her hips, the material swaying with her movement. Over the top, a tan mackintosh was perched around her shoulders, as if she hadn't had the time to put it on properly. Her face was heart shaped with a pert little chin and a wide smile. A smattering of freckles sprinkled the bridge of her nose, a small mole charmingly set on one cheek. Her hazel eyes were flecked with an orange-brown that danced energetically in the dim hall light. Pretty, and alluring, too.

"Good evening." Mrs. Braithwaite got up and stepped forward.

Florrie immediately leaped with fright, dropping a newspaper, a paper bag full of potatoes and carrots, and her handbag, the contents of which sprawled noisily in an arc across the dark wooden floor.

"Oh, clumsy me!" She laughed nervously while bending down awkwardly to pick up everything.

"I'm Mrs. Braithwaite, Betty's mother." She got down to help Florrie collect the array of paraphernalia that had fallen from her handbag: two lipsticks, a compass, a torch, two small padlocks, a silver-colored ring, two small bottles of pills, and no less than five pens.

Florrie straightened up and looked at her incredulously. "**You** are Betty's mother?"

"Yes, that's what I said. I'm Mrs. Braithwaite. And **you** must be Florrie?"

Florrie laughed, the whole of her body moving, making Mrs. Braithwaite step back, bumping into the hall table and toppling the elephants.

"Yes, that's me, although some people call me Rita, after Rita Hayworth," she mused, giggling and tidying her hair. "Are you here to visit Betty?"

"Yes, and I've come all this way just to find that she's missing." She eyed Florrie pompously. "But I'm hoping that you'll be able to solve the riddle of where she is?"

Florrie shrugged. "I'm afraid I don't know. Let me see, the last I saw of her was Thursday night. She's been seeing this chap, and I gather they'd had a fight, and she came home late, rather upset."

"Who is this man?" Mrs. Braithwaite felt a flurry of emotions: fierce protectiveness, then annoyance (why hadn't Betty told her any of this?), then concern as to what they'd been fighting about (could Betty stand up for herself?), and finally an undeniable relief that at last Betty was finally attempting to court a young man. She'd never been interested in boys, apart from Anthony Metcalf, of course. Betty and Anthony had been inseparable as children, but in more of a sister-brother kind of way (not that Mrs. Braithwaite would ever want to be conjoined to his mother, the nefarious Mrs. Metcalf, in any context). Anthony had shared Betty's love of science. Yes, they'd both loved biology, something called genetics, wasn't it?

"I don't know the boyfriend's name, or rather ex-boyfriend now. I gather she was greatly disappointed in him," Florrie said in dramatic tones. "He'd been keeping secrets from her, another girl, perhaps. She decided it wasn't going to work out, but I didn't get the full facts. You see, we were both on our way to bed after the air raid on Thursday night. It was about three in the morning, and she had some special event early the next morning."

"Did you see her in the morning?"

"No, I work the late shift at the telephone exchange, so I usually sleep in. She was gone by the time I came down."

"Did you expect to see her Friday evening?"

Florrie tried and failed to conceal a yawn. "We all live our own lives these days, Mrs. Braithwaite. Life's always a bit hectic with me." She giggled at herself. "But I love a bit of chaos."

An ideology she clearly adopted while dressing, Mrs. Braithwaite thought, eyeing her lilac dress that could do with a good iron. "Yes, I can see that."

"Well, I'd told Betty about a party on Saturday night, trying to cheer her up after what had happened with her boyfriend, but she said she was busy and may not be around. I didn't know what that meant, but I did wonder if she was going away somewhere."

"Where do you think she could have gone?"

"She often goes away. I think she mentioned a good friend who lives in Sevenoaks. Perhaps she went to visit?"

"Sevenoaks? That's a town just south of London, isn't it?" Mrs. Braithwaite's lips descended into a fierce frown. "I've never heard her mention anyone from Sevenoaks. Was it another young man?"

Florrie shrugged. "It might have been."

Mrs. Braithwaite inhaled fiercely. How confounding Betty was! She'd come with the express purpose of sharing her secret, and Betty had gone to Sevenoaks to see someone she clearly didn't even know terribly well.

"Honestly!" she exclaimed. "Tomorrow morning I'll go to the sewage works and see what they can tell me. The special event may have gone on longer than anticipated, and if it wasn't that, she must have asked for leave." She felt her spirits burgeon with the conciseness of this approach. "They'll be able to let me know when she'll be back."

Florrie pursed her lips. "Good luck with it," she said and then quickly added, "I'm sure she'll turn up soon."

*4.*

As Mrs. Braithwaite sat on the train to the Bexley Sewage Works the next morning, she couldn't help wondering why her only daughter hadn't chosen a more upstanding place to do her clerical work. She was a clever girl, had done well in school. She could have taken a job anywhere.

With the war, thousands of young women had flocked to London to take on the typing, administration, and driving jobs usually done by the young men who were now fighting on the front. Mrs. Braithwaite couldn't work out why the girls were so keen to leave their homes to face a city that was likely to be bombed—half of London's population was headed the other way into the safety of the countryside. But apparently the pay was good, the work was interesting, and London was a hotbed of parties, debauchery, and other frivolities.

Annoyance spread through her. It seemed so unlike Betty to get excited about parties. She'd always preferred plain clothes to pretty dresses, much to Mrs. Braithwaite's frustration. As a girl herself, Mrs. Braithwaite had been considered quite a beauty. She remembered her cousin's wedding, where she'd met her future husband. He'd asked her to dance, and she was careful to keep quiet, reining in her exuberant nature. There'd be plenty of time for that after they were married, Aunt Augusta had told her.

In hindsight, that didn't seem as good a suggestion as she'd thought at the time.

She let out a long groan. All her problems could be sourced to her former husband, Mr. Richard Braithwaite—Dickie. A moderately handsome man, what Dickie lacked in looks he made up for with charm. His bonhomie and easy manners had completely won her over, as they had for all the other women, too, including the one he'd decided to marry after her.

Following the divorce, the village shunned her, and precisely at the time when she needed friends. The WVS was **her** success. The jumble sales raised good money. The sewing bees and knitting groups ran like clockwork. Evacuees were housed and schooled. Her canteen was the best run in the country. She had been at the helm of it all.

And now it had been whipped away.

She was left with nothing, nobody.

Betty was the last tangible thing in her life.

She remembered her only daughter as a baby, the way her small back arched as she sat on the living room floor. And as a little girl, with her mop of brown curls, Betty had danced around the house singing, filling it with magic. And when she'd been older, the games: dominoes, crossword puzzles, the endless card games. Occasionally they'd sit at the dining room table together, shuffling and dealing. At some point—Mrs. Braithwaite couldn't pinpoint precisely when—she'd stopped letting Betty win, and at some other point, Betty had begun letting her win, making sure of an even draw at the end of every game.

Mrs. Braithwaite would say, "Goodness, another draw, Betty!"

And Betty would give her a shrewd half smile. "Well played, Mum!"

But as Betty grew, she hadn't needed her mother so much. They'd had less in common. Mrs. Braithwaite had been busy with the village ladies and caring for Aunt Augusta, who'd come to live with them when Betty was nine. Somewhere along the line, Mrs. Braithwaite had decided that the girl was old enough to look after herself.

She had her own life to lead.

Then, when war became imminent, Betty had left for London. It was with a deep pang of regret that Mrs. Braithwaite recalled that day. Betty had quietly organized her things and come down to the hallway, her battered brown suitcase in her hand, its broken handle tied up with string.

"Good-bye then, Mum," Betty had said in that thoughtful, rather serious way she had. She was wearing a black felt hat over her brown curls, her gray mackintosh belted tightly around her narrow waist.

"You will stay out of trouble, won't you?" Mrs. Braithwaite snapped, thinking about the stories of young women becoming pregnant, abandoning their morals "just in case a bomb had their name on it." Not that Betty seemed overly keen on men, but one could never tell.

"Of course I will!" Betty said, tilting her head to one side as if to say "you silly old thing."

Then there was that awkward moment when Betty turned to Mrs. Braithwaite, waiting for something else, a kiss on the cheek perhaps, an arm around her shoulders. But Mrs. Braithwaite wasn't keen on that kind of sentimentality. They'd never been a very demonstrative family, Mrs. Braithwaite preferring not to touch other people.

There was a word for that look on Betty's face: **forlorn**.

"Don't you remember how I used to run up for a cuddle when I was young?" Betty had said, out of the blue, taking a few steps toward her, trying to lighten the moment with a little laugh.

Mrs. Braithwaite took a step back. "Children do

that, you know," she said dismissively. "Wait until you have your own; then you'll find out."

"Maybe I won't have any." Betty turned to the front door, a strangled sadness twisting in her voice. "I'm not sure I want to be a mother. It seems so hard and exhausting. Sort of pointless."

Mrs. Braithwaite knew what Betty was implying, that Betty's experiences of her own mother had been chilly and distant, but she chose to ignore it. It was too late, she felt. The sooner Betty was out of the door, the less she'd have to think about it. Taking a deep breath, she watched as her only child, suitcase in hand, let herself out.

Betty's departure marked the beginning of the end of the marriage. Without Betty at home, Dickie's work trips became more and more frequent. Then one day he simply didn't come home. The divorce papers arrived the following week.

Betty had been in London throughout the divorce, so she'd missed the brunt of the bad times: the pointless arguments, the bitterness, the abysmal chill of what had been home. It hurt that Betty had stayed keenly in touch with her father. She took after him, with her narrow frame, her continual arm folding, the half smile. It became easier for Mrs. Braithwaite to turn her back.

As the train pulled into Bexley Station, Mrs. Braithwaite felt a twinge of discomfort. How could she have been so cold?

And that was when she became resolved.

She had to make amends.

Whatever Mrs. Braithwaite had been expecting of the Bexley Sewage Works, she found the building far more ostentatious and dramatic than its title warranted.

"It was the Victorians, madam." A nasal young woman walked her from the reception desk into the heart of the voluminous, cathedral-like palace. "They saw sewage treatment as revolutionary, a monumental change for the better." She turned and smiled. "Funny, it gets a bit whiffy in here, but it always looks glorious."

"Quite," Mrs. Braithwaite said, thinking the opposite.

The interior was decorated like a cross between a parliamentary state room and an ornate public toilet, and as their footsteps echoed around the high-ceilinged corridors, they came to the most opulent part of all: the head offices.

"This is Mrs. Braithwaite," the young woman told an older woman behind a desk. "She's come to see her daughter, who works here."

"Name, please?" the older woman asked, without smiling.

"Her name is Betty Braithwaite," Mrs. Braithwaite replied clearly. She always pronounced her words properly. Aunt Augusta felt that it immediately put one above everyone else.

"We don't have any Bettys here." The older woman gave Mrs. Braithwaite what could only be described as a withering look.

"But you must have! She told me this is her place of work." Mrs. Braithwaite took out the small pile of letters. Selecting one of them, she thrust it, open, before the woman. "You see, it says so here."

The woman snatched the letter and studied it, then handed it back with irritation. "This letter was written in September 1939. She must have changed her job since then."

If there was one thing Mrs. Braithwaite could not abide, it was someone getting the better of her, but for once she controlled an impulse to raise her voice at the insufferable woman, to tell her to simply find her daughter. She realized with unusual insightfulness that this wasn't going to get her anywhere. In fact, what she needed to do was to be polite and, most of all, patient.

"I wonder," she said with a smile, "would it be possible to look over the files and tell me when she left?"

The woman glared up at her. "Oh, all right." She let out a great sigh, pushed her ledger to one side, and went slowly to a filing cabinet.

After going through four drawers, she returned with a single sheet of paper. "This is the only record we have, from the very beginning of the war. It states that Betty works in the Records Office, but this is the Records Office, and we've never had a girl called Betty working here."

"If it says so, you must have."

The older woman crossed her arms. "Well, I say that we haven't! It's only old Mrs. Allen and me here. No one else is allowed to touch the files."

"Maybe she works in another part of the building, but they didn't change her record?" This woman's attitude was beginning to aggravate her. Muscling forward over the desk, Mrs. Braithwaite put her large, snarling face in front of the woman's.

But the woman pursed her lips and snapped back, "I'm afraid, madam, there are no other records of her, no one called Betty or Braithwaite at all." She softened slightly. "Perhaps you should try St. Thomas's Hospital. A lot of missing people are found there these days, injured from the bombs." She took her ledger out and went back to her work, only saying, "Good day to you."

"Well, I should like to be able to say the same to you," Mrs. Braithwaite said in a huff, and throwing a final menacing look at the woman, she headed outside.

It had begun to rain, cold, fat drops plunging at her feet as if the sky were slowly falling down around her. She retied her head scarf.

**Betty had lied to her.**

But why?

And where was she now?

## 5.

Mrs. Braithwaite didn't like going to hospitals. The first time she'd been in one was when she was six, awakening shivery with pneumonia, close to death, her parents nowhere to be seen. But she couldn't think of that now, and she quickly pushed the muddled sequence of images to the back of her mind, as Aunt Augusta had told her to do whenever they surfaced.

But ever since then, she'd felt a foreboding that made her gasp for breath at the mere mention of a hospital. And now, today, she knew that she was going to have to brave one again.

Betty could be injured, dying, or worse. She had to find her.

Dithering before she entered the massive Victorian building, nausea welled up inside. But taking a deep breath, she strode forward. Memories crowded into her mind: the freezing chill, the smell of antiseptic, the sound of nurses whispering, "Is she still alive?" The images were ungraspable, but instead of shutting them out, Mrs. Braithwaite had to get used to them. She couldn't let this age-old fear get in the way of finding Betty.

Aunt Augusta had always warned against thinking too hard. "It's not how the Empire was won!" she would insist. Death was a subject particularly to be avoided, especially the death of her parents. Hence, it was rarely referred to, **they** were rarely referred to, and when they were, it was always quickly, brusquely.

As she took her first steps into the hospital, the huge, galleried entry began to spin. Clasping hold of the front desk, she tried to get her bearings.

"Do you need any help?" a girl behind the desk asked, getting up to put a hand underneath Mrs. Braithwaite's elbow for support. "The Emergency Department is through the doors on your left."

"I've come to find out if my daughter's here," Mrs. Braithwaite explained, still jittery. "She's been missing since Friday."

"I'm afraid you'll have to join the queue over there." The girl pointed to a solitary desk with a line of people that reached back to the door.

"Thank you," she replied, scowling at the line, which at least had the effect of distracting her from her nerves.

Mrs. Braithwaite didn't hold with queues of any sort. Surely the significance of her quest gave her the right to go to the front, notwithstanding the importance of her time.

So she barged forward.

The man she knocked out of the way looked annoyed for a second before encountering Mrs. Braithwaite's sternest face, and then seemed to slip aside, unsure how to react.

"No pushing in!" another woman called from farther back in the line, a few others muttering, too.

But Mrs. Braithwaite was already at the desk, jabbing a fat finger on a list and demanding that her daughter be found.

"There's a B. Braithwaite upstairs in Ward 10," the woman at the desk said in a dismissive way.

Shock hit Mrs. Braithwaite. Had she really expected Betty to be here, in the hospital? What on earth had happened to her?

Head pounding, she strode for the stairs, forgetting about her phobia, climbing quickly up and marching off to find Ward 10, which was on the second floor.

At the entrance, she drew to an abrupt halt. The long, darkened hall of beds was deathly silent.

"I'm looking for B. Braithwaite," she said to the nurse at the desk by the door.

"Shh," the young nurse whispered back, a kindly look about her dark eyes. "She's in the eighth bed on the left. You can let her know that you're here by touching her hand."

A cold chill stirred inside Mrs. Braithwaite as she walked cautiously into the interior of the ward. The windows were covered with curtains that allowed only a shadowy dark light through the black fabric. Amidst the gloom, on either side, lay casualties of the bombings: women with bandages and casts glowing white in the dank, antiseptic air. Beneath the veil of sterility there lingered an underlying stench of burned skin, burned hair. Some of the bandages seeped with fluids, possibly the source of another putrid smell. An amputee's leg stump was darkened with blood. Plastered limbs were held up with chained contraptions, likening the scene momentarily to a torture chamber. One woman had so much plaster on her that it was difficult to see whether she was really a person at all.

The air was lifeless. Still as an empty church, silent as a mortuary.

Mrs. Braithwaite's feet echoed on the polished wooden floor as she walked slowly down the aisle. Eyes followed her, even though nothing else moved.

She was petrified. What had happened to her daughter? She hadn't been expecting this. No one had warned her.

Carefully counting the beds, she stopped just before the eighth one. On it was a mound, a body with a heavily bandaged head lying motionless on the pillow. Below the sheets, the mound was diminished at the other end, indicating that one of her legs had somehow come away from her body.

Mrs. Braithwaite let out a small, hollow cry, "Betty!"

She rushed forward, stopping before she went to put her arms around her, suddenly conscious that she couldn't do that. It would be too painful, possibly even harmful. She ended up turning her hands back on herself, gripping them together, kneading them into a tight ball.

"Betty, are you there?" she cried.

She peered over, through the dim light, at the small portion of the face showing between the thick bandages. Her eyes were tightly closed, her nose and mouth scarred with scratches, a deep gash coming from the side of her lip, closed together with two reddish-brown stitches. Her neck was held up with a stiff collar, and Mrs. Braithwaite wondered if all of her hair had been burned because nothing protruded from the bandages around her scalp. Not a single wisp.

But one thing was immediately clear.

This was not Betty.

She was older, although not by much, and her nose was too small, her mouth too full. Even with the injuries and bandages, it was plain to see.

Mrs. Braithwaite felt her whole body go limp with relief, putting a hand on the bedside table for support. The thought of Betty going through all that pain was beyond comprehension.

She quickly looked down at the face to be sure. Yes, it definitely wasn't Betty. This B. Braithwaite must have been a Bertha or a Beryl. She wondered what she had looked like, who she'd been. Whether she was aware of what had happened to her, where she had ended up.

"Touch her hand, to let her know you're here." The nurse had come up behind her.

"But she isn't my daughter, after all," Mrs. Braithwaite whispered.

"It's all right." The nurse smiled, as calm and serene as could be. "You can still let her know that you're here."

"But I don't know her."

"I'm sure she'll enjoy the company." That smile again, enticing—or was it coercing?

Even though Mrs. Braithwaite would rather not—it was awkward enough as it was—she didn't want to cause offense.

And she didn't want to seem heartless, not to this kind young nurse.

One of the injured woman's hands lay outside the sheet. It was half covered with bandages and mottled with blood and small wounds.

"She doesn't have burns on this hand," the nurse said. "So it's all right to hold it. I think she likes the connection. It must be terribly lonely for her in there, not being able to see or speak or hear."

"What happened to her?"

"She's a hero. Saved eleven children from a fire in a bombed school before the roof collapsed on her." She gave a small shudder. "They had to amputate one of her legs to get her out. They didn't even have time for pain relief, which is probably why she went into a coma. Absolutely dreadful if you think about it."

Mrs. Braithwaite decided she'd rather not.

"She worked at the school, you see," the nurse went on. "A teacher." She sighed. "Some people have so much love in their hearts. They'd do anything for anybody. They're the real heroes of this war."

"What about the men fighting on the front?"

"They're heroes, too, but not like this courageous woman. No one told her what to do; she simply saw someone hurt, someone in trouble, and found the bravery to go into the chaos, help in the best way she could. It didn't matter whether it put her own life in danger."

"And look how she's repaid," Mrs. Braithwaite murmured, looking at the tumbledown brutalized body.

The nurse smiled calmly. "But think of the children she saved. They owe her their lives! They'll always remember her. It must be wonderful to know that you made so much difference to so many people's lives. You enabled them to live! Can you imagine that?"

Mrs. Braithwaite let the idea roll around her mind. "Yes, I do know what you mean. But it'll be a difficult life for her when she comes out of the coma."

The nurse looked sadly at the woman. "**If** she comes out of it."

Mrs. Braithwaite looked aghast. She hadn't realized it was **that** drastic. The poor woman was wavering on the border between life and death, waiting for one to come, the other to gently recede. "Does she stand a good chance?"

The nurse shook her head, a movement so fragile that it was barely perceptible. "We don't know how much she can hear, how much her thought processes are working. That's why we keep touching her hand. We want to make sure she knows we're here."

"What about her family? Do they come in to visit?"

"We haven't been able to reach them. She was brought in straight from the scene. It was the ambulance drivers who told us what had happened to her, wrote her name down as B. Braithwaite. We don't even know what the B stands for."

Mrs. Braithwaite shook her head with incomprehension. "You mean you've had her here without knowing her full name or where she comes from? How long has she been here?"

"Two weeks."

"And there's no way to reach her mother? She must be beside herself with worry. There must be some way of finding out?"

"We haven't the time to find families. It's hard enough keeping up with the casualties, let alone finding out who they are. Most people have some form of identity on them, thankfully. I know it's a bit morbid asking people to wear identity bracelets or carry their names and addresses just in case they're bombed, but it would make it far easier if they did."

Mrs. Braithwaite silently hoped that Betty was doing so, wherever she was.

"It's a pity her family hasn't come in to find her," the nurse continued. "Visitors can make a tremendous difference to patients. I know one woman who came around after being in a coma for months." She suddenly looked sad. "And I've known patients who died after their families came in, as if they'd been given a blessing to go, had a chance to say their good-byes."

"Why would they want to die?"

"Sometimes the body simply has too much damage. It can't heal, and it has nowhere else to go. The brain tries and tries to keep it alive, but then one day it feels it's all right to let go. It finds peace."

Mrs. Braithwaite looked sadly at the injured young woman, alone and half dead, without her family even knowing where she was. She imagined how it would be if it were Betty lying there without anyone to console her. What would she have felt?

Putting her fingers out, Mrs. Braithwaite touched the hand on the bed.

"It's warm," she said sharply, surprised by it.

"She **is** still alive," the nurse whispered.

Mrs. Braithwaite stretched out her hand and took the still, slim one in hers, holding it as she might hold a child's hand, and for a moment, she remembered Betty when she was young, her little hand hot and restless as they walked into the village together, the tiny fingers slipping in and out as she skipped down the pavement, joyous to be outside, amazed to be alive.

## 6.

Mr. Norris arrived home from work at a quarter to six. He took off his bowler hat and put it on the hat stand, then he placed his gas mask box and briefcase on the shelf beside the door and walked through to the kitchen to put on the kettle. Taking his newspaper out from under his arm, he sat at the kitchen table reading while the kettle came to a boil.

The day had been good, apart from a worrying incident when the cafeteria had run out of his usual cucumber sandwiches; he'd had to settle for Spam, which had set him off balance.

As the kettle started whistling, he couldn't help thinking that it wasn't only the sandwiches: the whole war had put him off-kilter. At least he hadn't been required to fight. He didn't know whether he would be able to kill someone, let alone live in ever-moving compounds with no idea what was going to happen.

After tea, Mr. Norris always did a little tidying up before making dinner, and today he went to the hallway to reposition his model elephants. They were arranged in order of height: the white marble one on the left, and then descending in order to the smallest, a blue pottery one, seated like a child. They had been especially out of place since that Mrs. Braithwaite had shown up. She reminded him of a marauding hippo charging around like she owned the place.

**Perhaps she'll have left by now**, he thought hopefully.

Funny, though, Betty was such a pleasant, level-headed sort of girl, quite unlike her mother. He'd always had good conversations with Betty. Interested in science, she was.

He'd been worried about where she'd gone. It was unlike her to go away without saying anything, and to be gone for so long. Although he would never admit a word of this to Mrs. Braithwaite, her disappearance concerned him.

**Where could she be?**

Deciding to go straight to his bedroom, in case that woman was lurking in one of the main rooms, he crept up the stairs, peering over his shoulder to make sure she wasn't following—

When, **crash**! He ran straight into her as she steamrolled down the stairs toward him.

"Oh, there you are, Mr. Norris." Her voice had a squawking quality that could only be likened to a parrot's.

He put his hand to his head involuntarily, as if a headache were coming on, if it had any common sense.

She went on impatiently, "I have news. Come and sit with me in the kitchen. I bought some Spam for dinner."

"But I don't like Spam. I have some sausages."

She threw him a menacing look. "Sausages are made from bread and sawdust these days. I haven't touched one since 1939."

He hurried down the stairs ahead of her, lest she attempt to squeeze past him, a situation he felt certain would not serve him well. With luck she could be dispensed with quickly, and he could get back to his evening routine: the meticulous ironing of his shirt for the morning, the careful making and then eating of dinner, the letters he quietly composed, yet never sent, to Enid Tuffington.

His hand instinctively went to his heart. His weak heart.

Thus it was with mild vexation that he put off his plans in order to find out what Mrs. Braithwaite had to report about Betty.

Mrs. Braithwaite plumped her ample behind on

the chair at the end of the table, indicating that he needed to sit down on the adjacent one, and took out a notebook that looked as if it had already served a long, vengeful war.

"Did you go to the sewage works?" Mr. Norris asked, taking this all in.

"I did, and do you know what I discovered? That Betty wasn't there! Never had been there!" She marked something in her notebook with a small cross. Mr. Norris hoped it didn't have anything to do with him.

"She wasn't there?" he asked.

"I forced them to double-check. Betty has never worked at the place. They had a record that she had been hired, but nothing about her employment." She took a few deep, rapid breaths. "Do you know what that means?"

"That she changed her mind and got a job somewhere else?" he suggested.

A furious frown came over her face. "That she was lying to me."

**Oh good heavens, now the woman was cross.** That was all he needed.

"Maybe that's a sign that you should stop looking for her," he said cautiously. "Perhaps she doesn't want to be found."

"Of course she wants to be found," she snapped. "Why shouldn't she? In any case, I need to see her, especially now that I can see how much tragedy the war has caused here in the city." She looked at him accusingly. "Did you know that she didn't work there?"

"No, although to be honest, I can't remember her ever talking about her job. I try not to interfere, you know. If she can pay her rent on time every week, why should I pry?"

She tutted, then carried on. "I went to the hospital afterward to see if Betty was there, but she wasn't. But I did find a Miss Braithwaite, who was barely alive." She lost a little of her usual verve as she said, "But it wasn't Betty."

He wasn't sure what to say.

"The poor girl had had her leg amputated to get her out of a burning building," she continued in an uncharacteristically desolate voice; then she raised her head and met his eyes. "And now they can't find her family, so she might even die without anyone coming to bid her good-bye."

Mr. Norris hadn't thought Mrs. Braithwaite capable of feeling sad for anybody, so he watched curiously, wondering what had happened to her. "I'm afraid that kind of thing happens a lot in London, which is why it's so important to use air-raid shelters when the sirens go. You can't be too careful."

Mrs. Braithwaite frowned. The air-raid shelters didn't have the reputation of being the coziest of places. With a grimace, she went back to her notebook.

"I've been thinking . . . Florrie mentioned a boy-friend. If we can find him, he's bound to know where Betty is, or where she really works. One of the girls **must** know him. I have yet to meet the other girl, Cassandra." She made another note, then added crossly, "She didn't come home last night at all."

"I'm not sure you should be pinning your hopes on getting much out of Cassandra. She keeps to herself a bit more than the other two."

"What do you mean?" Mrs. Braithwaite began, but was stopped by the sound of the front door opening.

They both stood up, hurrying into the hallway to see the entrance of Cassandra, a glamorous blond woman looking terribly à la mode in a dark red suit with matching pillbox hat, tan stockings, and high-heeled black shoes. She was about the same age as Betty but looked completely opposite. Her dyed hair was perfectly curled. Her good-looking features were even: luxurious eyelashes, a straight nose, a rather ruthless square jaw, and a full, sulk-ing mouth heavily embellished with a deep red lip-stick. Her eyelashes were so thick, they could have scurried off her face. She looked almost Germanic, and Mr. Norris once again fought off an image of her goose-stepping in full Nazi regalia.

"Cassandra," Mr. Norris stammered. "This is Mrs. Braithwaite, Betty's mother."

"How do you do," Cassandra said dismissively. Her voice was low, surprisingly upper class, and had that practiced raspy quality, as if she'd just woken up.

"How do you do," Mrs. Braithwaite replied, putting a hand forward, which was reluctantly taken by Cassandra. "We wondered if you knew Betty's whereabouts?"

"Sorry, I can't help you there. I've been busy the past few days. Hardly time to breathe, let alone speak to anyone." She yawned dramatically to support this statement.

"Well, when did you last see her?"

Her eyes flitted around the hall, indicating that she was thinking about it while also communicating that she thought it a complete waste of her time. "Friday morning. She said she had to leave early for a special occasion. No end of fun in the sewage works." She pursed her lips to one side to cover a smile. Mrs. Braithwaite got out her notebook, and Mr. Norris saw the words "Piece of Work" added.

Mrs. Braithwaite glared from Cassandra to Mr. Norris. "When might it have crossed one of your minds to contact me, her mother?"

"I hate to say it." Cassandra smirked, beginning to enjoy herself. "But she never seemed too keen on you, if you get my meaning."

"No, I do not get your meaning!" Mrs. Braithwaite squawked, blood rushing to her face, a force of rage building beneath her hefty bosom. "What did she say?"

"Oh, nothing in particular. One simply got the

impression that she, well, didn't get on with you, that's all."

Mrs. Braithwaite looked livid. "Did you know that she doesn't work at the sewage works?"

"No, I'm afraid I never spoke to her in much depth." There was a challenging look on her face. "Betty wasn't really my cup of tea, or me hers."

"Well, that can only be considered Betty's great fortune," Mrs. Braithwaite snapped back.

Mr. Norris took out a large handkerchief to mop his forehead. Confrontations were not his strong point. He tended to stand down quickly, terrified of someone becoming cross with him. It was too much like his childhood.

Cassandra opened her tiny handbag, took out a compact mirror, and began to inspect her lipstick. "Betty did seem to be working around the clock. Who knew that a sewage works could be so busy! I mean, what are they doing down there? Even through the air raids, she was never home. She was either working late or staying with her boyfriend."

Mrs. Braithwaite let out an audible gasp. "I'm sure she'd never do that!"

Cassandra sneered without saying a word.

"Do you know anything about this 'boyfriend'?" Mrs. Braithwaite pronounced the word as if it were a dubious monstrosity.

"Not very much." Cassandra slid the compact back into her handbag and took out a packet of cigarettes. Her practiced fingers with their elegant red nails flipped one out and lit it from a matchbook that may well have been pilfered from Mr. Norris's collection on the hall table. He'd noticed it dwindling in size; especially missing were all his favorites, such as one from the Charing Cross Club; even the one from the Savoy had gone.

Cassandra took a long drag as she lit the cigarette, turning her head to blow smoke dismissively away from them. "I met him once. He didn't warm to me, which is unusual. Seemed to like boring Betty much more. I remember that he lived next to that big old pub in Clapham, the Pendulum. It's beside Clapham Common."

Mrs. Braithwaite was too busy writing—and possibly too grateful for the precise information—to make a rejoinder about the "boring Betty" remark. "What was he like?"

Cassandra laughed elegantly. "I bumped into them quite by accident, as it happens. It was late at night, and Betty obviously wasn't expecting to see anyone she knew in Clapham. She seemed nervous, trying to hurry him along. He was a bit shady, to be perfectly honest. Rather rough for my tastes, but I should think Betty can't afford to be fussy." She sucked in her cheeks to stop herself smiling. "If she's missing, I wouldn't put it past him to have, well—you know how easy it is to dispose of bodies in the Blitz."

Mr. Norris grimaced with horror, and Mrs. Braithwaite looked venomously at Cassandra.

"I'm sure he wouldn't have done any such thing."

Cassandra headed for the stairs, turning as she put her elegant high-heeled shoe on the first step. "He wasn't the sort of man **I** would be hanging around with."

With that she swung around, mincing upstairs as if she were in a fashion parade, hips and behind swaying back and forth as she disappeared out of sight around the bend in the staircase.

Once the sound of Cassandra's footsteps had faded, Mrs. Braithwaite tucked her notebook in her handbag with deliberation. "Shall we go then?"

"Go where?" Mr. Norris asked.

"To find this young scoundrel, in the building beside the Pendulum."

"But it's dark outside. The blackout makes everything so very difficult, not to mention dangerous." He went over to the small hall window, adjusting the blackout curtains to ensure that not a crack of light spilled out into the night. He'd hate to be fined, let alone have locals accusing him of letting the Luftwaffe see a good spot for a bomb. "Civilians aren't supposed to be out wandering the streets at night, Mrs. Braithwaite. There's the blackout, and there may well be a raid. Why don't you leave it until the morning?"

"There's a good moon tonight." Mrs. Braithwaite briskly began putting on her coat. "In any case, I want to meet this young man, and he might be working tomorrow."

"Well, why don't you go on your own? I also have work tomorrow. There's a lot of things I need to do before bedtime, I'm afraid, and if there's another air raid, we need to be ready—"

"I couldn't possibly go by myself! I don't know the way. How am I supposed to find this place on my own, and in the dark, too?"

He felt a flurry of panic as she opened her handbag and brought out a handkerchief. Her eyes did not appear to be teary, but the threat was there.

"As you so rightly pointed out, there's moonlight tonight," he said. "And it's quite a direct route. I'll show you on the map."

The handkerchief was brought up to the eyes, where some cautious dabbing took place. "Is it a dangerous area? It's rather frightening, being a woman alone, in the blackout, not entirely sure of where I'm going or whom I might find."

It was said dramatically, with a slight quavering in the voice.

Mr. Norris knew he was in deep water.

"If it's protection you're looking for, I won't be any use to you, Mrs. Braithwaite. I'm not much of a fighter, you see."

"That won't be a problem. I'm rather skilled with my handbag, and if we meet trouble, I'm sure you'll be able to help us out of it with your quick thinking. Or maybe you'll know an escape route." She tied her head scarf on, as if the matter were settled.

Mr. Norris flustered. "But—"

She looked at him crossly. "I've been thinking, Mr. Norris, that you lack oomph. If you asserted yourself a little more, then perhaps you'd feel quite pleased with the result."

"We all have our own ways of tackling life. I'm a peacekeeper at heart."

"You are a coward at heart."

He felt the blood rush to his face. He usually avoided quarrels, but Mrs. Braithwaite was not someone you could avoid. "I pride myself on turning the other cheek. Being patient—"

"Running away instead of standing up for what's right," Mrs. Braithwaite broke in. "Well, this is your moment to change all that, to step up and do the right thing."

"This boyfriend might be a lunatic. He might kill us if we rile him. And there could be an air raid. We could be bombed!" Mr. Norris had started to tremble, his fingers working through and around each other nervously. He hated feeling like this. If only he could go and hide in his bed, pulling the blankets over himself, wait for it all to go away, as he had done when he was a boy, hiding from his father, listening to the shouts downstairs.

"Sometimes, Mr. Norris." Mrs. Braithwaite broke into his thoughts. "Sometimes you just have to take a deep breath and give something a go. Think of poor Betty!"

"I know she's in danger, but—"

"Precisely, Mr. Norris," Mrs. Braithwaite said.

"Betty's in danger, and who knows what we'll find out from this man. Aren't you curious? Don't you want to find out?"

Drawing a deep breath, he found himself reaching for his hat and gas mask box.

"I'll come, but let's try to keep it quick. I have to be organized for the morning."

Thus it was that Mr. Norris trudged out after Mrs. Braithwaite, for the first time in years leaving his shirt unironed and his newspaper unread.

*7.*

As they stepped out into the cool spring night, Mr. Norris whimpered at the sight of the almost-full moon—a "bomber's moon" shed light over the city and usually heralded a big air raid. It spilled a milky glow over the streets and rooftops, eerie in its silent splendor.

They walked in silence, watching their feet through the faded beams of their torches. Wandsworth Common was a middle-class neighborhood, its streets lined with Victorian terraces, behind which were rooms kitted up with good furnishings and maybe an occasional piano. But as they moved into Clapham, the area felt rougher, meaner, the houses less well kept.

Hearing the noise of an approaching engine, Mr. Norris pulled Mrs. Braithwaite into a front garden as a delivery van swung into sight, ghostly in the moonlight. Only two narrow slivers of light escaped from the van's headlights, covered because of the blackout restrictions, which meant that it was winding all over the road, onto the pavement a few times and narrowly missing the garden where Mr. Norris and Mrs. Braithwaite had taken refuge.

"We should report him!" Mrs. Braithwaite said with conviction.

"I warned you it was dangerous," Mr. Norris replied. "Let's hope there aren't many cars about tonight. Most people don't drive at night anymore, especially with the petrol rationing."

The Pendulum was a large, ragged Victorian public house. It overlooked Clapham Common, historically common land where the locals formerly grazed livestock, but now parklands, dotted with vegetable patches since the war began. The pub sign hung in front of the mangy building, depicting a grandfather clock with a long pendulum swinging to the right. No lights could be seen through the blackout shades, but the chatter of voices and shouts could be heard a few streets away.

Mrs. Braithwaite and Mr. Norris stood outside, looking at the neighboring buildings to work out which could be the home of Betty's young man. To the left of the pub was a row of small shops, and because it was unlikely to be there, the pair walked around to the right, finding themselves in front of a small, shabby-looking house.

If he didn't know any differently, Mr. Norris would have thought the house was abandoned. It looked dark, hollow, unloved. The front garden was dominated by a large, unruly bush, which almost completely concealed the downstairs front window. The front door needed a new coat of paint, and the gate to the path had been propped open to prevent it from collapsing off its hinges.

"Let's see if he's in," Mrs. Braithwaite said, striding ahead. Mr. Norris followed behind, walking in her shadow, wincing as she rang the bell and an unnecessarily shrill sound echoed through the interior.

Mr. Norris was nervous. He didn't like asking other people questions, especially people he didn't know. He knew that Mrs. Braithwaite was likely to make her inquiries sound like accusations, which was bound to cause trouble. Surely if this man really had been Betty's boyfriend, he couldn't be all bad.

**Could he?**

They waited for a few minutes, but there were no sounds from inside.

She rang again.

Nothing.

"We'll have to ask at the public bar," Mrs. Braithwaite said—she wasn't even whispering! "They might know him, or know when he'll be home."

Mr. Norris stood still, looking over at the old

pub gingerly. "They say the Pendulum caters to a not entirely respectable crowd. Maybe we should just come back tomorrow?"

She eyed him irritably. "And what if the man knows where Betty's gone? She may be in danger! Do you always give up so easily, Mr. Norris?"

"Well, I suppose ledgers don't pose too many perils on a day-to-day basis." A rueful smile came across his face, which made Mrs. Braithwaite utter a small laugh.

"Come on, let's see what they can tell us inside."

The noise inside the pub was raucous. Shouting, singing, and whistles cascaded around the wide-open innards. A fight was taking place in a far corner with a crowd rowdily urging on the combat. Men sat or stood around tables laughing and arguing. The grubby wooden floor was littered with dust and debris. The air was dense with smoke, and the smell! Spilled yeasty beer combined with tobacco of various types, all mixed with the particularly vile odor of unwashed bodies.

Mr. Norris, not a frequenter of public houses himself, grimaced at the recollection of his few pub experiences. As a child, he had occasionally been sent to find his father in the local hostelries, a task that would invariably end with his receiving a hot slap or a sharp boot.

It was evident that Mrs. Braithwaite had never been to such a place in her life, and she looked stunned for a brief moment, breathing through her mouth to avoid taking in the noxious fumes and frowning in a highly disapproving manner.

But then she recovered, saying, "Come on, Mr. Norris!," and pushed her way through to the bar, with much use of her elbows and only a rare and abrupt "Excuse me!"

The men (there were no women in sight) parted, most of them ignoring her and continuing with their banter, others turning with a laugh. One man nudged her, saying, "Oi, you, missus. D'you want a bit of fun?"

"No, thank you very much," she said sharply, her chin tucking in with revulsion. Mr. Norris stifled a little smirk at her discomfort, although he acknowledged that Mrs. Braithwaite was not to be underestimated. She had not come all this way to be thrown off course by a ribald comment.

"Do you know the man who lives to the right of this establishment?" she asked a young man behind the bar. He was scrawny, wearing a shirt that possibly had once been white.

"No clue. We don't usually serve the likes of you here, so if I were you, I'd scarper before you get a mouthful of something else, if you get my gist?"

Mr. Norris came up behind her. "He's right. We'd better leave, quickly."

"I'm not leaving until I have at least a name." She glared at the few men nearby who were beginning to look at them, sensing fair game.

Then, just as Mr. Norris thought she was about to

retreat, she opened her mouth wide and screeched, "Does anyone know the young man who lives in the house next door?"

The noise did not abate, but a burly bald-headed man who looked like a leader of the criminal underworld barged through the crowd to her. An angry snarl issued from his gold-toothed mouth. His shirt was ripped, showing browned blood from an earlier altercation.

His heart pounding, Mr. Norris slid behind Mrs. Braithwaite, but she stood firm. Although she was small in stature, her frame was solid, and her ample bosom created a formidable presence.

"What are you doing here?" the man snarled at her, pulling up a fist.

"I don't know who you are, my good man, but I suggest you put your hand away. My friend"—she indicated Mr. Norris, who had slunk even farther behind her—"and I are on an important quest to find my daughter, who is missing. Now, if anyone here knows the identity of her young man, who lives beside this very establishment, then I'd be very grateful."

"How grateful?" the bald man said, eyeing her clothes and her handbag, looking for jewelry, money, expensive trinkets.

"I'll give you a shilling," she said, as if it were an absolute fortune.

The bald man's face glowed red with anger. "Are you joking?"

Mr. Norris began quaking, looking for the nearest exit. What should he do? Mrs. Braithwaite clearly had no clue of how vulnerable they were. The crowd had suddenly gone quiet, watching to see what would happen next. How could he get them both out of there?

The bald man took a step forward, towering over Mrs. Braithwaite, who was finally taking in the full danger of the situation. He shot out a hand and grabbed her by the scruff of her silk cream-colored blouse, while his other hand began reaching across for her handbag.

But just as he went to yank it out of her grasp, it became clear.

She was not letting go.

"Let him have your handbag," Mr. Norris whispered urgently. "We can make a dash for the door. Save ourselves!"

"Don't be ridiculous!" Mrs. Braithwaite said from the corner of her mouth.

Mr. Norris took a deep intake of breath as the bald man brought his face down to Mrs. Braithwaite's. His nostrils flared, and a deep throaty growl emanated from his crusty mouth.

Another man warned, "Bobby Mack here has a bad temper. You'd better not cause any problems, missus, or you'll be found in the Thames tomorrow."

"And you," she said with equal venom to the man apparently called Bobby Mack, "need to learn some manners. I only came here for some information, and I'm not in the mood for bathing, especially in the river."

There was a pause. Only the sound of the men breathing could be heard through the tense silence.

Then something extraordinary happened.

Bobby Mack's mouth opened, but instead of a snarl, he let out a low chuckle, following it with a loud laugh.

Gingerly, the rest of the crowd began laughing, too.

He took his hands off Mrs. Braithwaite, dusted her down a little, then stepped back.

"Gentlemen!" He addressed the large room loudly. "We have a comedian on our hands. Would anyone know anything about the young man who lives next door?" He pointed a bony finger at Mrs. Braithwaite, a look of merriment on his face. "The lady doesn't want to bathe tonight."

More laughter. Men began hollering. "You don't get a better bath than the Thames these days, love!" shouted one. And "Nothing like a little dip!"

"It's a little dirty and cold for my liking," she said with an uncertain little chirp of a laugh.

And among the catcalls, a man called out, "The man's called Baxter."

"Thank you," Mrs. Braithwaite said, primly taking out her notebook. "Do you know when he'll be home?"

"He ain't around much," another man said. "Bit of a lad, comes and goes."

"Oh, really!" Her eyebrows shot up. "What precisely do you mean by 'a bit of a lad'?"

"Look, if you want more," the bald man said, his eyes narrowing menacingly, "you have to pay."

She narrowed her eyes. "How much?"

"Five pounds." A muscle pulsed in his jaw. He meant business.

But he didn't realize that he was dealing with Mrs. Braithwaite.

"You can't possibly be serious. I'll give you ten shillings, no more, no less."

"I believe you need the information more than I need the money."

Their eyes held each other's for a ruthless moment.

"All right, twelve shillings."

"Thanks but no thanks, duchess." The bald man gave her a smart smile, then turned his back on her, heading back to his table.

Giving in wasn't Mrs. Braithwaite's practice. But as she stood there, her chance of gathering valuable information walking away, her face fell.

"Perhaps we should just give him the money," Mr. Norris whispered out of the corner of his mouth. "It's quite a sum, but he does seem to know a thing or two about Baxter and his dealings."

Mrs. Braithwaite turned to him, appalled. "We

can't be seen as weak," she whispered furiously. "I was taught never to step down."

Mr. Norris, feeling that the adventure was already somewhat lengthier and more hazardous than he had been expecting, put his hand into his pocket and took out a neat, black leather wallet. Bending over to cover his actions from the assembled company, he peered inside.

"Oh dear," he muttered. "I only have two pounds."

However, he clutched them in his slightly trembling hand and tapped the shoulder of Bobby Mack.

"I say, would two pounds do the job?"

Mrs. Braithwaite, too late to intervene, looked furious for a moment, but then, as Bobby Mack whipped the notes from Mr. Norris's hand, her face lit up with surprise.

"Well done, Mr. Norris," she whispered.

Mr. Norris looked sternly at the man. "What do you know about Baxter?"

"He works behind the bar sometimes, and always wants stuff from the black market."

"What kind of stuff?"

"Passports usually, and ration books. Don't know why he needs them. And he always has meat to sell or exchange. No idea where he gets it, but it's good stuff, pork chops and sometimes even a bit of sirloin."

"Fascinating!" Mrs. Braithwaite said sharply,

writing in her notebook. "Tell me what else he wants to buy."

"Once he was asking round for a handmade bomb. Wanted to see how we did it. Funny thing, though, he seemed to know already, just wanted to see how **we** did it. The bloke what showed him was a bit of a novice, so he got a novice bomb all right. Not sure if it'll work even. Might blow a hole in a shed door at best."

"Interesting," she said, taking a note in her book.

"Other times he come in 'ere wantin' a heavy to follow him somewhere 'in case it gets nasty.' All very hush-hush, know what I mean?"

"I do," she replied, eyes wide with dismay.

**Could Betty really be involved with a man like this?**

"What do you want with him anyway?" Bobby Mack asked.

"He's courting my daughter," Mrs. Braithwaite retorted. "Who has been missing for five days. And now that I see what kind of a man he is, I'm starting to wonder if he might have done something horrid to her."

"I don't know, duchess. I wouldn't put it past him—"

But then, from outside, the air-raid siren began, starting low and quickly building pace to grow piercingly loud and high.

Immediately, people began to leave, some

pushing and running off into the night, some staying behind.

Mr. Norris stepped out from behind Mrs. Braithwaite and led her away. "We need to get underground."

Once outside, he turned to the bald man and asked courteously, "I say, could you tell me the location of the nearest shelter?"

"We don't bother with no shelter," Bobby Mack said, his tongue planted in the side of his mouth. "Better to stay aboveground. See what's going on."

"Absolutely," Mrs. Braithwaite replied, following his gaze.

"That's not what he means," Mr. Norris whispered, urging her toward the main road. "They're only staying aboveground to see where the bombs are falling so that they can be the first scavengers at the bomb sites." He was determined to get her into a shelter before the raid. On this kind of night, the place could be flattened in moments, everyone mutilated where they stood.

But Mrs. Braithwaite stood gazing at the horizon, South London spread before them. The whir of aircraft engines, at first a barely audible buzz, grew louder and louder into a craze of engines and throttles powering through the sky.

Searchlights scoured the skies above the city, striking the clouds, catching glints of metal as the aircraft soared overhead.

A deafening pounding began from somewhere

nearby, the antiaircraft guns, nicknamed "ack-acks" to try to make them seem friendly. In reality, they were thirty-foot cannons, manned by groups of young women—hairdressers and shop assistants trained to watch, coordinate, and fire.

"So, this is what it's like!" Mrs. Braithwaite gasped, amazed.

"Yes, now let's get to a shelter. I think I saw a public one on the way up. Please will you **hurry**!"

But she was now scrutinizing the little house beside the pub. Baxter's house.

"This is our chance," she said eagerly. "We can peek through the windows. See whether Betty's been there, what kind of man he is." Then she added haughtily, "I'm sure I'll be able to tell."

"But what if he comes back and catches us?" He looked around, panicking.

"Don't you see? He won't come back now that there's an air raid. It's perfect. Oh, for goodness' sake, Mr. Norris. Where's your gumption?"

"I like to think I have more sense than gumption," he replied. "Now, **come on**!"

Suddenly the sky lit up, like a huge white lamp switched on from above.

"What on earth is that?" Mrs. Braithwaite bellowed.

"It's a parachute flare. The Nazis send them down to see the targets better. We need to get under cover." Panic was creeping into his voice.

Another bank of planes roared low across the

South London skyline, and Mr. Norris watched as dark shadows were released into the night sky, bombs raining down randomly over their heads. He flung himself against the wall of the building, hoping against hope it would protect him in some measure.

Then suddenly an almighty explosion came from behind them, a direct hit on a neighboring building, the blast throwing them to the ground.

Quickly pulling themselves to their feet, Mr. Norris dragged Mrs. Braithwaite around the corner. They collapsed against the wall, peering out in time to see the house behind them burst into flames, fragments thrown into the night air with a force as great as a volcano. Instantly they could feel the heat from the blaze, the air alive with sparks and smoke.

People were screaming inside—or was it outside?—and through the fire, Mr. Norris saw the roof collapse inward, a wrenching thud sending out a billowing stretch of flame that quickly filled the air with the burned scraps of someone else's life.

The patrons of the pub had come around to see, some of them running off in case the police showed up, others offering to help, organizing a bucket line from the pub's kitchen until the fire crews arrived.

"We should leave," Mr. Norris shouted over the din, hooking his hand into her elbow and pulling her away. "Let's go to the shelter. We'll be safe there."

But Mrs. Braithwaite stood resolutely. "Not on your life. I'm keeping my eyes peeled for Baxter."

And with that, Mr. Norris gave up, unhooking his hand and praying that the bombs wouldn't strike the same place twice.

## 8.

Mrs. Braithwaite watched the fire in horror. Within minutes, a fire engine arrived on the scene, and tired, grimy firemen began shooting water over the blaze from a large hosepipe.

"I hear screaming," Mrs. Braithwaite said, haranguing one of them. "You have to go in and rescue them."

"It's too dangerous," he said in an exhausted voice. "The building could collapse."

Mr. Norris knew Mrs. Braithwaite sufficiently well now to realize that no excuse was going to be adequate, and sure enough, within minutes, the fireman was disappearing into the flames.

At last the fireman emerged, carrying a body over

one shoulder. It was a teenage boy, unconscious and stick thin in old pajamas. The crowd watched as the fireman laid him on the ground and tried to revive him until an ambulance arrived, and two young women trotted out with a stretcher.

"He's still alive!" one called to the other in a very upper-class voice—ambulance driving had become an aristocratic occupation since only wealthy women had driving experience.

A cheer rose from the crowd, like a bellow of relief. An everyday miracle in a city where lives were lost and saved each night.

The two ambulance girls, with meticulous efficiency, sat him up, put a thick blanket over his shoulders, and brought him a cup of hot tea.

Mrs. Braithwaite and Mr. Norris remained rooted to the spot, eyes streaming with soot, watching as the fire was put out, leaving a smoldering half-burned wreck. The fire crew left, and soon afterward a large van appeared. Men of all ages jumped off the back and ran in to lift fallen beams and remove the remains of the roof.

"Who are they?" Mrs. Braithwaite asked.

"That's the Heavy Rescue Team," Mr. Norris explained. "Their job is to come in after a fire and look for anyone trapped underneath the rubble. Alive or dead."

Tonight it was only the latter. Two bodies were pulled from the cellar, where they'd probably been sheltering from the bombs, thinking they were protected. Safe from the blasts, but not the roof collapsing.

Mrs. Braithwaite caught her breath as the body of a woman was carried out on a stretcher, a man from the rescue team following with her cleanly decapitated head. He held it between his two hands, his face stoic as if he'd done this job a thousand times, though he'd never quite become used to it.

Just as Mrs. Braithwaite was thinking it couldn't get any worse, the men began to bring out the second body, a man's, in parts. First one leg, then a torso, a head, the arms, and finally a foot. No one could find the other leg, like a gruesome jigsaw with one piece missing.

Until now Mrs. Braithwaite had been protected from the effects of bombs. She lived too far from the cities, and well clear of the coast or any factories or airfields the Nazis wanted to obliterate. She'd heard about the Blitz, of course, and even expressed a keen interest in seeing it for herself, but now, here, she realized its horrors had never truly sunk in. These were real people, normal families. Amid the debris, she spotted the familiar rung of a half-burned wooden clothes rail, the same model she had at home. Drying laundry was strewn across it, now coated with grime. The remnants of a kitchen—a broken pan, a lone fork, a jagged fragment of blue crockery—lay haphazardly around, never to be used again.

The decapitated woman had been alive and well only a few hours before, living a normal life. Mrs. Braithwaite wondered how she'd spent her evening. Did she cook a nice dinner, then tidy up, prepare for the next morning, put her son to bed, with no idea that by morning he would be an orphan? Would she have done anything differently if she had known? Were there prayers still to be said, secrets to be shared?

Meanwhile, the teenage boy, who had barely survived himself, now faced a world without parents or his home. He sat alone, watching with a vacant look, as if in a dream. A neighbor tried to put her arm around him, but he shrugged her off. He looked like the loneliest person on the planet.

"What will he do? Where will he go?" Mrs. Braithwaite asked Mr. Norris.

"He's old enough to be taken in by family or friends, especially since he looks quite tall, which could come in handy on a farm or in a shop. The younger ones are trickier. Everyone's too busy for them, and there's often nothing left but to ship them off to orphanages."

She shuddered with memories. There had been an orphanage near the village where she'd grown up. Tall gray walls separated the small space from the outside fields. Some days she heard the shouts of the children from inside and couldn't work out whether they were laughing or crying. Aunt Augusta had told her not to worry about them; they were from a different class.

She had never been reminded that she, too, had been an orphan. She was only told how she had been lucky enough to be taken in by Aunt Augusta. How grateful she must be.

"It's rather dramatic, being an orphan," she said, almost to herself, as she watched the desolate boy.

Mr. Norris looked at her grimly. "It's a bit of a shock if you've never seen it before."

Mrs. Braithwaite, disliking the implication of weakness, pulled herself together. No one was going to accuse **her** of being shocked. "We can't let the Jerries think they're getting us down," she said briskly. "The British aren't going down easily."

"That's the spirit." He put a hand on her arm, just at the crook of the elbow, and instead of instinctively pulling away, as she usually would, she left it there, feeling something like relief from the unfamiliar warmth of the gesture.

The siren went up again, but this time it was the all clear, the siren played once to let everyone know it was safe to come out. People began to appear from cellars and shelters to see what damage was done and to get a few hours of sleep before morning. Some stood speechless before the ruins of their homes, unsure what they were supposed to do, where they should go. She wondered if the practical problems—a bed to sleep in, a place to cook—took precedence over possessions, your favorite coat, a teddy bear, old letters, the valueless treasures worth so much now that they wouldn't be seen again.

"Let's go home," Mr. Norris said, and he pulled her arm gently toward the road back to Wandsworth.

But remembering why they'd come in the first place, she yanked her arm away. "Let's have a quick look around Baxter's place first."

"Haven't we had enough for the night?"

But she was already scouting the building from behind a bush, waiting for Mr. Norris to catch up.

"He's definitely out for the evening. He's left the curtains wide open." She moved to the window, bobbing her head up and down. "You have to understand, Mr. Norris, that the police have been known to come to me for help when they're faced with difficult investigations."

"I think I can hear another plane coming low overhead."

"Nonsense, it's miles away. In any case, I can see something interesting." She beamed her torchlight into the window. "Look on top of the cabinet to the side. Is that a pistol?"

Mr. Norris took a sharp intake of breath. He crept over and peered in next to her. "It's a cigarette lighter, one of those modern types."

"It's a pistol, I'm sure of it. Illegal probably, too; I bet he doesn't have a permit."

"You can't throw around aspersions like that. We don't even know the man."

"He frequents what can only be described as a criminal's public bar, deals in the black market, and is an acknowledged member of the underworld."

The reminder of this fact did nothing to ease Mr. Norris's sense of foreboding. But before he could lead her away, she'd hurried off through the overgrown shrubbery. "Let's look around the back," she called.

Behind the house was a long window looking into a dining room. Shining their torches through the window, they saw a pile of books on the table. Some of their spines were visible: European history, philosophy, a few novels. Beside the books, a typewriter sat next to a framed photograph of a young, pretty woman with shoulder-length dark brown hair and a wide-eyed smile.

"It's not Betty, is it?" Mr. Norris asked.

"No, Betty's hair has always been light brown, and she doesn't smile in that way, does she?"

"No."

"But why would Baxter have a photograph of another girl in his house if he's courting Betty?" Mrs. Braithwaite said.

"It could be his sister?"

Mrs. Braithwaite looked at him impatiently. "Would you have a photograph of your sister in your dining room?"

"I suppose not." Mr. Norris's sister, who was six

years older than him, lived in Sheffield and hadn't spoken to him since she'd left home when he was thirteen. He didn't like to dwell on it. After all, what else did they have in common apart from a terrifying childhood? No one had come out of the situation well.

Mrs. Braithwaite was rounding back to the front of the house, eager to see what else she could spot, when she heard footsteps coming down the road.

"It must be Baxter," she whispered. "We have to hide."

"You said he wouldn't come," Mr. Norris said frantically.

"No time for that now, come on." She pulled him into the bush.

A tall man in his late twenties came striding around the corner. He had dark hair and gaunt good looks with a confident, cocky air about him, even though he was wearing rather shabby clothes and a cloth cap, like a market seller.

He took out a bunch of keys, the sound jingling in the night air, but as he put them up to the door, he sensed something and paused.

Then, slowly, he turned around.

Mr. Norris and Mrs. Braithwaite both held their breath, not moving a muscle, and Mrs. Braithwaite was just beginning to feel that perhaps they'd got away with it when suddenly the side of the bush was pulled aside, and Baxter's face came nose to nose with hers.

"I see I have some visitors." He stood back again, holding the branches aside for them to come out.

Mrs. Braithwaite wriggled out, followed by Mr. Norris.

The man had an uncompromising sneer across his face, as if he'd found a dirty nest of rats.

"Now, explain to me what you're doing here." He pointed at Mrs. Braithwaite. "You first."

"I believe you know my daughter, Betty Braithwaite."

His breath caught for the briefest of seconds; then he pulled back and said in a more upper-class voice, "What's that to you?"

"I've come to London to see her, and—she seems to have vanished."

"And you thought you might snoop around my house for her; is that it?" Baxter frowned, taking a step forward. "What exactly is your game, 'Mrs. Braithwaite,' if indeed I can call you that?"

Mrs. Braithwaite continued, undaunted. "How dare you? I **am** Betty's mother, and I can prove it."

"How?"

Mrs. Braithwaite thought fast, thinking what a good thing it was that she'd read so many murder mysteries. "I know that she detests carrots, prefers calculus to geometry, and doesn't get along with her mother." She said the last part rather brashly, almost challenging it to be true—knowing inside that it probably was.

The man watched her evenly for a moment, and

then with a brisk nod said, "Then why are you trying to find her?"

"She's missing, and we"—she indicated Mr. Norris, who was standing just behind her—"are anxious to find her whereabouts."

Looking them both over, he said flippantly, "Well, I'm sorry, but I don't know where she is."

He took his keys out again, as if that were all he had to say on the matter.

"I know that you were romantically attached." Her voice took on the edge of a strict schoolma'am. "And I think you should tell us what you know. We have proof of your dealings with the black market. I'm sure any magistrate would be interested to hear about that."

He looked crossly at her, then glanced around. "Let's have a little chat, shall we?" There was a serious edge to his voice. "What I'm about to tell you is highly confidential," Baxter began, stepping forward. "You must not tell anyone under any circumstances. Do I have your word?"

Mrs. Braithwaite nodded eagerly.

"The truth is that Betty and I work for the police, looking into black-market activities in the area. It has to be very hush-hush, you understand. Betty has been **pretending** to be my girlfriend. She is a colleague and is currently away on a special, secret mission." His voice was different, professional and confident, as if this were the real Mr. Baxter, leaving the casual, suave Baxter aside. "I shouldn't be telling you this, naturally, but you could do more damage if I don't. My job means that I have to be in contact with black marketeers, and my position would be compromised if you reported me to the authorities."

"What job is she doing? When will she return?" Mrs. Braithwaite said determinedly. "I need to see her!"

He opened his hands. "Unfortunately, I can't tell you that. It goes against protocol to tell you as much as I have. You will have to forgive me for keeping silent, Mrs. Braithwaite."

He took his keys out again, indicating that their meeting was at an end. "Now, I ask you to take yourselves home, put this to the back of your minds, and I'll make sure that Betty contacts you as soon as she returns."

His demeanor and frank politeness were such that Mrs. Braithwaite took a step back.

"Thank you for your honesty, Mr. Baxter," she said. "We'll treat this conversation with complete secrecy. You won't have to worry about us."

"Thank you."

**And that**, Mrs. Braithwaite thought, her face falling as they stepped out onto the road, **was that**.

## 9.

The road back to Shilling Lane was still and silent in the cold night air. Neither of them said a word for the first five minutes, and Mr. Norris basked in the comfort that the woman's search was finally at an end. He began planning the following day. She'd be leaving tomorrow, and when he'd return home from work, the house could go back to its usual order. Things had been moved around. The kitchen was in turmoil, the salt and pepper left on the table, and the food she'd brought in—turnips, brussels sprouts, tins of Spam—was everywhere.

As they walked, he could sense Mrs. Braithwaite thinking, her mind like the insides of a clock, spinning with tiny frictions that were barely perceptible.

He worried. It wasn't that Mrs. Braithwaite didn't usually think; she was only too good at getting into the nitty-gritty of something.

No, he was worried because she was upset.

But it wasn't until they'd reached the spired church that Mrs. Braithwaite came to a sudden halt, looking over the gravestones.

"I say, are you all right?" Mr. Norris said, praying that she indeed was.

"I'm fine," she said, giving him her torch to hold while she got out an embroidered handkerchief. "It's just that it was rather thrilling, our little adventure, and for it all to come to such an end, so suddenly, and without even being able to see Betty, it feels like a bit of a disappointment."

"But at least you'll be able to go home now, get back to normal."

"Well, that's the thing." Her voice sounded frail—most unusual. "I don't especially want to go home."

"Well, I know these things are rather hard. I gather that Mr. Braithwaite isn't with us any longer." He made a meaningful gesture at the graveyard. "But we all have to carry on, especially with this war taking everyone from us. He'll be in heaven right now, willing you to strive on."

Mr. Norris was not comfortable talking about death. It brought back too many memories, especially those of his brother. Especially of that day.

No, he stopped his brain quickly, forcing it to

switch to mathematics, as he had done as a child: thirteen times thirteen is—

"But Mr. Braithwaite didn't go to heaven," Mrs. Braithwaite said. "He went to Hemel Hempstead." She suddenly began to laugh, peals of mirth cascading around the dark buildings. "Did you think he was dead?"

"Well, yes." Mr. Norris didn't find it funny.

"No, he went off with a woman we met while on holiday in Dorset. Edith Falcon was her name. I liked her, and I thought she liked me, too. We stayed in touch, letters, that sort of thing, and all the time she was meeting Dickie, having lunch with him in different places around the countryside, staying in hotel rooms."

"How did you find out?"

"I didn't." She heaved a great sigh. The laughter had petered out. "I didn't know a thing until that awful morning. There was a knock at the door, and when I answered, expecting the postman, there was a strange little man. He was wearing a suit and bowler hat. I remember wondering if someone had died, but he doffed his hat, handed me an envelope, wished me good day, and left. I took the letter, surprised that it was addressed to me— all the official-looking envelopes were usually for Dickie—and sat down at the kitchen table to open it." Her face fell, her eyes scrunching, as if she still couldn't quite work it out. "It was fortunate that I was sitting down."

"Was it asking for a divorce?"

"Yes," she said quietly. "And then it all came out. Their long-term affair, their wish to marry, their love for each other." She said the word **love** as if it were a dead rat found in a corner of a shed. "There was nothing about me, how I'd built my world around the marriage. Nothing about how I'd be ostracized by the village, a divorced woman, destroyed by my husband's indiscretions. I didn't factor into it at all. It was as if I were simply an inconvenience."

"Has it really been as bad as all that?"

She paused, thinking it through, and he could see her eyes, her brow, and the corner of her mouth twitching. "No," she replied simply. "It's been far worse. Do you have any idea how society punishes divorced women? I am an outcast, socially, economically, and even morally, which anyone can see is absurd. Just because my husband goes off with another woman, it doesn't mean that I'm a monster."

They continued walking in silence to the house. For once Mrs. Braithwaite was taking her time. There wasn't anywhere pressing for her to be.

"He had more than one affair, you know," she said quietly.

"He wouldn't be the first man." Mr. Norris remembered a moment from his own childhood, and before he knew what he was doing, he said, "My father had an affair with a younger woman. I saw them together in the summerhouse in the garden when I was a boy. They were, well, you know, together."

She looked at him. "How old were you?"

"I was twelve. He was forty. Old enough to know better. They saw me. I remember both of their faces, white and pink, blinking at me above their clothes, all rucked up above their pale, naked legs." Had he just used the word **naked**? He felt a blush swallow him up. "Sorry, I didn't mean to say that."

"Affairs are like that, I suppose. All breathless passion and no thought."

"My father **did** think. He just didn't care." Memories flashed back into his mind: his father hitting his mother, his sister cowering while backing him up—her own set of preservation tactics. "My father always treated us as if we were possessions or slaves to do with what he liked, which mostly meant that he could ignore us or occasionally taunt us or hurt us. The more he bellowed, the more anxious we became, and the more anxious we were, the more he despised us."

"Even when you left home?"

"I thought that as soon as I was away, I'd feel free. But, you see, I didn't. There was always a tutor shouting at me, a colleague, even friends." He pursed his lips in thought. "He died a few years ago, my father, but even now I cringe at the thought of him. Heaven knows how my poor mother dealt with him. She probably would have considered the adultery one of his lesser evils. If he was busy, his focus elsewhere, he was less likely to strike out at us."

They'd reached the house, but before Mr. Norris could get his key out, Mrs. Braithwaite had taken the emergency key out of her capacious handbag and was inserting it into the keyhole.

"Let's put the kettle on." She opened the door and led the way to the kitchen.

Mr. Norris followed her, pleased to be back in his familiar surroundings. "Yes, we could both do with a nice cup of tea."

"I'll stay here another day or so, see if Betty reappears, and then I suppose I'll have to go back to Ashcombe." Mrs. Braithwaite made it sound bleak.

Although Mr. Norris silently prayed that her stay wouldn't be prolonged more than necessary, he smiled to cheer her up. "I'm sure you'll feel better about it when you're back at your own home. There might even be a letter from Betty waiting for you there. And at least you'll be away from the bombs again." He set the milk jug on the small kitchen table and put the salt and pepper back on the second shelf next to the mustard, where they belonged. "It must feel good to know that your daughter's doing something worthwhile for the war effort. The black market is such a blight on morale. I always knew she had some sense."

"Yes," Mrs. Braithwaite replied stiffly. "I'm glad for her. She's young, has her life to look forward to.

But me? I'm just an old has-been. She doesn't want to see me. Just as Cassandra said, she's probably forgotten about me completely."

"Of course she hasn't." Mr. Norris sat beside her at the table. "In any case, I'm sure that poor girl in the hospital hasn't forgotten about you."

Mrs. Braithwaite folded her arms in thought. "I could try to find her parents before I go back to Ashcombe. The nurse told me the name of the school where she was working. If I go there, I'm sure someone will be able to tell me where she lives."

Mr. Norris looked up at her. "That would be very thoughtful of you. What a kind gesture!"

"I know," she said unself-consciously. "I feel so sad for her. The nurse told me that if her mother could be found, it might help her come out of her coma."

"That would be a miracle."

"I suppose it would be." Her forehead furrowed in thought. "To think that a mother's mere presence could make such a difference. She was just lying there, damaged and in pain. The nurse said that if a family member would come, she might allow herself to live or to die. Her soul would be set free."

"How very profound," Mr. Norris said, taking a seat beside her.

"If the same thing happened to Betty, I would hope that there would be a similarly caring woman who might do the same thing."

As if from nowhere, in breezed Cassandra, looking extremely alluring in a shimmering purple dress, well fitted around her curvaceous form. Her eyelashes were thick with mascara, her lips a deep, dense red. Her blue eyes flashed from one to the other.

"You're both looking frightfully downhearted. Any news about Betty?" A wry smile tugged at her beautiful lips as she found a cup and saucer and helped herself liberally to the tea in the teapot. "Did she come a cropper?"

Mrs. Braithwaite glared at her. "No, and I must ask you not to use that term in here."

Mr. Norris was just beginning to wish that Cassandra would go away when the door opened and Florrie came in.

"Fresh tea? Just what I need!"

"And a good hairbrush," Cassandra said snidely.

Florrie ignored her and turned to Mrs. Braithwaite. "How's the hunt for Betty going?"

"Her friend, Mr. Baxter, informs us that she's on an important work trip." Mrs. Braithwaite folded her arms with impatience.

"Well, that's good news, isn't it?" Florrie said affably.

"Why?" Mrs. Braithwaite replied.

"Well, it means that nothing bad has happened to her. You can go home now." Florrie looked delighted with the notion.

"What kind of work trip?" Cassandra asked. "She never mentioned a work trip to me."

"Well, she wasn't exactly your best friend, was she, Cassandra?" Florrie said.

"If she were such a close friend of yours, why didn't she mention it to you?" Cassandra snapped back.

"I hadn't seen her for a few days," Florrie said. "And I'm so forgetful these days. So little sleep with all these bombs. Perhaps she did say something, and it went in one ear and out the other." As she gestured at her ear with her finger, she dropped her handbag, lipsticks and eye pencils scooting across the floorboards. Everyone helped pick things up, except for Cassandra, who took out a cigarette and lit it.

Mr. Norris, exhausted by the emotional pressures of the evening, decided that it was time to clear up the tea things and get to bed. After all, tomorrow would be here soon enough.

And he had his accounts to get back to.

## 10.

**H**eart was a word that usually made Mrs. Braithwaite cringe. It represented the kind of sentimental rubbish that lower-class people bandied about when trying to garner attention or sympathy. A heart was not something that she would ever admit to having. Indeed, Aunt Augusta had been very firm upon the matter, describing heartfelt emotion as a leech that winds its way through the veins, incapacitating if given the smallest opportunity.

But as Mrs. Braithwaite walked into St. Thomas's Hospital, she became all too aware of her heart.

That morning she'd paid a visit to the bombed school, where the headmistress, Mrs. Churley, informed her that the B. Braithwaite whom she had been visiting in the hospital was called Blanche. She'd been pretty, energetic, and as kind as the day was long.

Having been given a home address, Mrs. Braithwaite then went in search of Blanche's parents, only to find the house deserted. A nosy and somewhat malicious neighbor informed her that only a few weeks before, Blanche's mother had been killed by an explosion in the bomb factory where she'd worked. Blanche's father, she'd sneered, had been taken before the war by cancer.

There was no one left to visit Blanche.

Poor Blanche. She probably didn't even know about her own mother's death. She quickly decided that she, Mrs. Braithwaite, would have to tell her.

Whether she could hear or not.

As she walked up the stairs to Ward 10, her feet slowly dropping onto each step, she thought about what it was that she wanted to say.

Death was difficult for anyone to swallow, even a young woman who was so very close to death herself.

Could the blow tip the balance for her, cause her to give up hope? Let herself collapse into the certainty of death?

"I'm not sure that that would be a bad thing," the nurse whispered as she explained all this. "The doctor says she's getting worse. He said it could be a matter of days."

"Well then, perhaps it would be kinder if I didn't

tell her about her mother?" Mrs. Braithwaite said with relief.

"No, I think that you should. If she doesn't know that her mother is dead, she might be waiting for her to come in to visit."

Mrs. Braithwaite trod carefully down the ward, stopping at Blanche's bed. The shallow hump under the sheets was in the same position as it had been on her previous visit. Two of the bandages on her face had been taken off to show nasty burns, one of them slowly seeping. Her eyes were still closed.

The nurse brought a chair over. "Touch her hand to show her that you're here. Talk to her. If she can hear, it'll do her some good, and if she can't hear, well, it'll do no harm, will it?"

She patted Mrs. Braithwaite's shoulder with sad encouragement and walked quietly back to her desk at the end of the ward.

Mrs. Braithwaite sat for a moment before putting her hand out to touch Blanche's. It felt cold, and panicking from fear that Blanche had already died, Mrs. Braithwaite quickly felt her wrist for a pulse.

There it was. A weak and sluggish pump, like the slowing wing beats of a butterfly at the very end of summer.

She put her hand back over the slim, bandaged one, holding it tightly to warm it up.

It seemed like the very least that she could do.

"Hello, Blanche, this is Mrs. Braithwaite again. I didn't introduce myself properly last time, but I came to see you a few days ago. You might remember." She paused. It wasn't easy having a conversation with someone who didn't talk back.

"I'm not related to you, even though we have the same last name. The thing is, I've been looking for my daughter, who is about your age. I came to London to see her. Only now that I'm here, I found that she's missing. I thought she might be injured, so I decided to look in the hospital, and they thought that you might be her." Mrs. Braithwaite's fingers had begun stroking Blanche's hand to comfort her.

If she felt anything.

"Then the nurse told me that no one had time to find your mother, so I went to your old school and found your headmistress—Mrs. Churley—who told me about how brave you'd been, how much they've missed you. She gave me your mother's address, and so then I went and found your house."

She'd been talking quickly, the words spilling out as if she were talking to herself. But now she ground to a halt. How was she going to tell her the next part?

She pulled the chair closer to the bed.

"I'm afraid, Blanche, that I didn't find your mother. You see, she has been killed in the factory where she was working." She paused, waiting for a reaction. There was none. She felt her pulse. Slow, as if it were petering out. Her face was as white and as blank as it had ever been.

**Was it already too late?**

Had she already gone, slipped away gradually through time? Was she destined to die not knowing that her mother hadn't visited because she couldn't?

Mrs. Braithwaite held her hand tighter.

"Whatever happens, Blanche, you know that I'm here now. I might be the wrong Mrs. Braithwaite, the one who isn't your own mother. But I am a mother, and right now you are the only daughter I have."

Before she knew what was happening, a little sob escaped from Mrs. Braithwaite. She began to cry, her breath coming in sobs as she lowered her head down to where her hand clutched Blanche's.

"I don't know where my Betty is. She came to London to work, as you did. But I don't know where she is, and I can't help worrying that . . ." The words caught in her throat. "I'll never see her again."

She looked at Blanche through her tears. What was she saying to the poor girl? She had been through precisely the type of disaster that Betty had avoided.

"I know that what you went through was appalling," she said quickly, "but I've been told that you're a hero." She snuffled, thinking of the children she'd seen at the school. "You've helped so many people."

Mrs. Braithwaite sat upright, taking her handkerchief again. "I don't know whether I've ever helped anyone. Not really helped them. I tried to organize the WVS in my village, but then they got rid of me. They told me I was hindering more than helping. I suppose I could have been a little more patient."

She went off into her own thoughts, feeling herself blush as she remembered holding up Mrs. Harris's sewing as an example of "how not to make a pair of pajamas." And the time she'd forced three of the canteen ladies to reclean the makeshift kitchen in the village hall in case Lady Worthing showed up for an inspection. She hadn't.

How much kinder she could have been.

"I need to tell you how your mother died, my dear," she said, and proceeded to explain, kindly, the details she'd got from the neighbor.

"Your mother's house looks just the way she left it. It belongs to you now."

She watched for a response.

There was none.

"If you don't make it," she said, then checked herself. "I mean, if you can't use it, it will probably be given to people who've lost their home in a bombing raid." Then she put on a gentle voice. "I'm sure it will be loved and enjoyed, just as your family enjoyed it."

Blanche's childhood must have been a good one. The neighbor had said that her mum had been "too nice for her own good." The house looked lovely, clean and neat with a carriage clock on the mantelpiece, ticking down the minutes until dinner or bedtime—or was it death? If a woman knew the moment of her death, would she live her life differently? More wisely, undoubtedly. More frivolously, perhaps. But would she be more full-hearted, less selfish?

**After all,** she thought as she looked down at the young body in front of her. **What else is life for?**

Mrs. Braithwaite thought of Betty, the girl who had exuded independence, always so focused on the future, as if she could hardly bear the present. The image flitted through her mind of Betty on the stage of the village hall, tap-dancing to that Fred Astaire song about putting on a top hat. She looked so small, but brave enough to fly to the moon and back, smiling that half smile of hers as she dashed across the stage.

She turned back to the young woman in the bed. "I'm sure you loved to sing and dance. Such a joyous thing to do."

An overwhelming feeling came over Mrs. Braithwaite, a crush of pain that life was so fleeting, that the dance was over almost as soon as it had begun. She thought about her own life, how she'd wasted so much of it marching, staying on the footpath, when she could have been dancing. Aunt Augusta hadn't approved of dancing, after all.

She thought of her notebook, her ponderings in

the train: **How do you measure the success of your life?** Could it be calculated by how much you enjoyed your life? How much singing and dancing you did? How much joy you had?

She gazed at Blanche, and a sorrow for the young life came over her. Tears slid from her eyes again, this time for the unknown girl, the innocent victim of the war, like many others already dead and more to come. Who was left to remember her?

"I'm sorry that this happened to you, Blanche." She squeezed her hand. "I gather you were a happy, kind person. And the world needs more of those, with so many vile people around." She thought of Blanche's mother's nasty neighbor, of that horrid Cassandra, and then, unwillingly, of the disdainful woman she herself had been in Ashcombe. She shuddered, quickly saying, "I'm leaving for my village in the morning, and so I won't be able to see you again. I would like to have met you," and then, sensing that she should be more positive about poor Blanche's chances, she added, "Well, met you properly, I mean. I'm sure you'll have a good life, perhaps with children of your own, a husband—the right kind, of course—and a home, full of love."

Love.

Mrs. Braithwaite stopped, dropping Blanche's hand, pulling her hands back to her own cheeks in dismay. It had struck her like a massive thump on the temples. Love was the one thing missing from her life. She had never had it, hardly knew what it was, but the more she thought, the more she knew that it was love that Betty had always been trying to get from her.

That's why Betty had left, and Dickie, too.

She sat in silence for a long time, until the nurse touched her on the shoulder.

"Visiting time is up, I'm afraid."

Mrs. Braithwaite coughed slightly and got up, feeling the stretch in her legs, her arms.

Then she bent down, took the slim hand again, and bid Blanche good-bye.

"Don't worry, I'll come to London again, just to see how you are, and have another chat." She suddenly felt like giving the girl a hug—the hug she hadn't given her daughter when she'd left for London. But she couldn't, what with all the bandages. In any case, she wasn't even her daughter— she didn't even know her.

But still, she patted the hand. "We're all each other have, after all."

She backed away, still looking for a movement, a sign.

But there was nothing.

"Did you get any response?" the nurse whispered, as she led her out of the ward.

"No," Mrs. Braithwaite said, thinking that perhaps it didn't matter anymore. Blanche knew about her mother, if she could hear. "What was important was that I came."

"That was extremely kind of you."

"I'll come again to see her when I can," she said, writing hastily on a page of her notebook and carefully tearing it out. "Would you take my address, just in case something happens?"

They both knew what she was referring to.

"We're not supposed to contact people who aren't related to the patient," the nurse said, but then, as she took in Mrs. Braithwaite's anxiety, she added, "but I can drop you a line myself."

Mrs. Braithwaite thanked her, and then, with a glance back at the still form on the bed, she bid a silent good-bye and headed out of the hospital before tears overwhelmed her.

## 11.

Mr. Norris arrived at his house a full hour earlier than usual, as it was Mrs. Braithwaite's last night before heading back to Ashcombe. By catching the 4:09 train instead of his usual 5:09, he'd had time on the way home to queue up at the butcher's to buy some chops (using his meat rations for the week). At home, he began peeling the potatoes, after he'd found a small bottle in which to place a sprig of forsythia that he'd snipped from the railway border.

He couldn't work out whether he was pleased that Mrs. Braithwaite was leaving, along with the drama she'd forced him into, or whether, as he found himself confessing, he might actually miss her.

He went into the hallway to rearrange his elephants. He wasn't especially fond of elephants, but they'd been a legacy, his only brother's pride and joy. Gordon hadn't been killed in the last war; he'd died of heart failure in an institution when he was thirty. Mr. Norris visited the institution following Gordon's short, efficient funeral, an affair attended only by himself and the institution's registrar.

Gordon's few possessions had already been boxed up by the man at the desk.

"Here you are then, Mr. Norris," he'd said. "The end of a long journey." The words **painful** and **awkward** were not used, but they were there, as always.

He'd wept. Gordon was one of his favorite people, always ready to comfort him with a hug or cheer him up with a smile. They'd played cards together, Mr. Norris letting him win, and talked about their days. Gordon had added a unique layer to his life, and somehow, when they were together, Mr. Norris experienced a kind of clarity, one so fragile that if he put his fingertip up to it, it would dissolve into a million stars.

Born when Mr. Norris was ten, Gordon had stayed in their house only one night before the midwife came to take him away. He could still hear the echoes of his mother's screams when he remembered that day, her arms clutching her older boy as she watched the baby depart, grasping at his flesh, wetting his hair and his face with her tears, until he ran down the stairs, out into the rain.

**Why did the baby have to leave?**

The institution wasn't nearby, but they'd visited him every few months, and then only Mr. Norris after his mother had died of heart failure. The brothers' close relationship remained strong, only broken by the end of Gordon's life, although Mr. Norris was aware that the time between visits had stretched further and further. What **had** he been so busy with?

In Gordon's box he'd found an old photograph of the family that his mother must have given Gordon: their father proudly upright, arms folded; their mother smiling shyly, concealing her unhappiness; their older sister frowning angrily; and Mr. Norris, age ten, his eyes as large as coat buttons, anxiously looking into the outside world.

It also contained a few basic items of clothing, and the elephants. That was all. Mr. Norris recalled bringing other gifts over the years but deduced that these may well have been pilfered by the institution staff.

No one had wanted Gordon's elephants.

It was Mr. Norris who'd helped Gordon with his collection. He had brought one in every year or so, whenever he'd come by a nice one at a shop or a jumble sale. Often he'd gone out of his way to find them, searching in market stalls and antique shops, scouring the city during his days off. There were carved wooden ones, ceramic ones painted gray or blue and glazed, and Gordon's favorite: the white marble one, larger than the rest, with his trunk held high, invincible.

Since Mrs. Braithwaite had been staying with him, the elephants had been in a continual state of disarray.

"Yes, everything will go back to normal once she's gone," he told himself.

The sound of the key in the lock echoed through the house, and he found himself trotting to the front door to meet her.

"What happened, then?" he asked eagerly as he took her coat.

"Much, alas!" she said with a dramatic flourish.

Hurrying her into the kitchen, Mr. Norris pulled out a chair for her and began the final preparations for dinner.

"Did you find her parents? Did you go back to see her?" he asked, as he chopped up a few large, floppy cabbage leaves.

"I did, but it was rather more difficult than I had expected," said Mrs. Braithwaite.

The story began to tumble out of her.

And Mr. Norris, leaving the cabbage and the chops on the counter, came to sit down beside her to hear the full account of her day.

## 12.

After a restless sleep, Mrs. Braithwaite woke early, lying for a while in Betty's narrow bed, feeling utterly distant from her only daughter. Betty had lied about her work and about Baxter. What else might she have been keeping from her?

Which is why she decided to have a look through her dressing table drawer. One rarely got an opportunity such as this, and it seemed almost neglectful to let it pass.

**It's for Betty's own good**, she told herself as she pried open the stiff drawer.

Inside there was an assortment of documents, many of them letters from Mrs. Braithwaite, two of which hadn't been opened, for some reason. She put those to the side. One by one she pulled out other items of interest.

The first was a letter from Anthony Metcalf, Mrs. Metcalf's perfect son and Betty's old friend. Mrs. Braithwaite suspected that they might have been more than friends at some point—she'd seen the way Anthony had looked at Betty and had even heard rumors that they'd kissed, but Betty was far too secretive to let her mother in on anything like that.

Dear Betty,

I trust you're keeping away from all those nasty bombs. How is your job in the sewage works? I hope not too dull. I've been lucky to escape since my college was evacuated to the South West. You'll be glad to hear that I decided not to take the government job— they told me I was more useful studying because I have such exceptional aptitude.

That's wonderful news that you're smitten with this new chap. I confess I have been feeling awkward, as I, too, have found a new girl, a beautiful young lady who has completely captured my heart. You can imagine my relief to hear that you, too, have found true love.

I heard from my parents in Ashcombe

that your mother is having a devilish time.
The divorce seems to have unsettled her, and
so the ladies have decided that she should
stand down. She has yet to be informed, and
expectations are that she won't go without
a fight. It's a good thing you got out when
you did.

Keep in touch, and do let me know how
conversant you're becoming in sewerage
systems. I can't wait to hear about it.

Much love,
Anthony


How dare Anthony Metcalf gossip about her to
her own daughter! She reread the letter a few times,
dwelling on the paragraph about her, pondering on
the flippant way he wrote: **It's a good thing you
got out when you did.**
**Is that how Betty felt on leaving?**
On a different note, however, she couldn't help
but chuckle smugly that "exceptional" Anthony
had obviously been passed over for a government
job, while Betty was doing important secret police
work. She thought of how keen Mrs. Metcalf had
been to tell everyone—while **not** "telling" them—
that her clever Anthony could not join up because
he'd been selected for a special government job.
But that wasn't the only part that drew her attention. The letter suggested that Betty must be truly

smitten with Baxter, especially if she'd written to Anthony about it.

A frown came over her brow. Why had Baxter told her they'd been pretending if Betty was busy telling her friends that she was "smitten"? She tucked the letter back in its envelope and went on to the next one.

It wasn't a letter, only a single sheet of folded paper with five or six jumbled words. **It must be a code,** she thought, tucking it into her hand-bag. Probably something to do with Betty's police work.

The third was another letter, this time from Baxter. She hurriedly opened it, then let out a gasp.

It was a love letter.

Darling,

How are you, my sweetheart? I can hardly describe how much I miss you and that sumptuous feeling of your warm velvet skin. When I think of your naked body under mine . . . Oh, I can't bear for us to be apart! Do you remember the night of the meeting? How outrageous we were! I replay it in my memories every night.

Everything is dull here, the training, the people, even the configurations. I need you here to make my life worth living. When I return, I'm praying that you can dedicate an entire day to me. I need you so badly, my darling.

In the meantime, I dearly hope you're missing me, too. Please don't give your heart to anyone else!

All my love, my dearest darling,
Baxter

Mrs. Braithwaite blushed hotly.

She'd never known her own daughter. Who was this other Betty? Who was this woman who allowed her velvet skin to be enjoyed by a man to whom she was not married? Who was this person who went on work missions, not knowing when she'd return, not telling anyone where she was going?

But there was something more pressing.

When they'd met him, Baxter informed Mrs. Braithwaite that Betty was only a pretend girl-friend. Yet this letter explicitly indicated that this was very far from being a pretend romance.

This was as hot-blooded and genuine as it got.

There was nothing else for it. In spite of its con-tents, she had to show it to Mr. Norris.

She dressed quickly and hurried up to the attic to knock on his door.

"Oh, isn't it a little early?" he asked as he reg-istered that it was indeed Mrs. Braithwaite. He was wearing blue-and-white-striped pajamas with a respectable brown dressing gown. Without his glasses, he blinked a lot.

Mrs. Braithwaite was taken aback by his tone. "I have very important news, if you must know."

He rubbed his eyes, giving her the opportunity to barge past him into the room. It was a typical attic with sloping ceilings on two sides, windows protruding into the outside world. It took up almost the entire top floor, but its white walls and meticulous tidiness, with a single bed pushed into a corner, made the place feel like a monk's retreat. A small nightstand sat beside the bed with a few books on top. Various odd pieces of furniture were dotted around, including a purple velvet chaise longue and a card table with four chairs.

"It's a bit of a storeroom," he said, by way of excusing the oddments, while he pulled up the blankets on the bed. "The previous owner left a few items, and I wasn't sure what to do with them. I used to sleep in one of the rooms downstairs, but the girls came, and Cassandra insisted on a double bed—"

"Did she, indeed!" Mrs. Braithwaite frowned with annoyance. "That girl really is far too big for her boots!"

Mr. Norris offered her a seat at the card table and sat down opposite. "What is it?"

Stern faced, she pulled out the letter and handed it to him.

Opening it with his long, bony fingers, he then

put on his glasses to read it, pulling his chin back with alarm at one point. Why on earth Baxter felt it necessary to put such graphic descriptions to paper, she had no idea.

"So, Baxter was lying about their just being work colleagues," Mr. Norris said with a frustrated sigh.

"Indeed." She narrowed her eyes in annoyance. "This only proves one thing."

"What's that?"

"That Baxter cannot be trusted, and wherever Betty is, she may well be in trouble."

"You can't be serious." Mr. Norris was awake now, fully. "I know you love your mystery novels, but don't you think you're taking this too far, Mrs. Braithwaite? Just because he lied to us about the nature of their relationship, it doesn't mean that she's in danger."

"But the whole thing points in that direction. In any case, if he's serious about Betty, then who is the brunette in the photograph in his living room? I knew there was something fishy about him right from the start." She sniffed loudly to support this statement.

"But what do you intend to do about it? You can't go to the police with a love letter and a photograph. Aren't you being a bit melodramatic?"

"You saw the European history books on Baxter's shelf. And the philosophy!" She stood up, leaning across the card table. "Anyone who reads philosophy is bound to be suspicious."

"Why is that, precisely?" Mr. Norris said, affronted. "I'm partial to a spot of philosophy myself. Just because someone wants to consider other ways of thought, it doesn't make them evil."

"It's unbiblical, not to mention un-British."

Mr. Norris sighed audibly. "Many great philosophers have been deeply religious, you know. The one does not exclude the other."

"But how many have been British?" she said victoriously.

"Well, actually—"

"Quite! That's because it's dangerous."

A tinny bell sounded from across the room, and it took a moment for Mrs. Braithwaite to realize that Mr. Norris's alarm clock was heralding the day.

Mr. Norris stood briskly and opened the door for her, saying, "Let me get dressed. We can discuss it downstairs before I go to work."

She stood rooted to the spot. "But you can't go to work after this!"

"What are you proposing to do?"

"Go to the police, of course. We'll show them the letter and take a policeman to Baxter's house."

"The letter concludes nothing, Mrs. Braithwaite."

Her mind struck on something. Riffling through her handbag, she pulled out the scrap of paper covered in gibberish.

"What do you make of this, then?"

He took it.

## YFU gdvmgb-vrtsg xsrogvim xsfixs vrtsg

"It's coded. Looks as if we might need a cipher machine to work this one out." He looked up at her. "Where did you find this?"

"In Betty's drawer, with the letters."

He glanced back down at it, as if it were a rather nasty winged insect. "I wonder where she got it?"

"That's precisely why we need to find out more."

He put the paper in his pocket and stood for a moment, ushering her out the door, glancing at his clock. "Well, I suppose we can quickly go to the police station before I go to work."

With that, he used a little flicking motion with his hands to move her out of the doorway so that he could close it, and she found herself trotting back down the stairs to see what food could be found for breakfast.

## 13

But you have to believe us!" Mr. Norris watched as Mrs. Braithwaite stood in front of the desk at the Wandsworth police station and brought a thick fist down on the counter.

"I believe you all right," P.C. Watts said stiffly. "It's just that we have people going missing all the time. Thing is, all our young policemen left to join the war effort, so we're a bit short on staff. I don't know nothing about this bloke Baxter, nor any secret police work in Clapham—but there's a lot of black-market activity up there, so it wouldn't surprise me."

P.C. Watts was a large man with a thick, dark mustache graying slightly around the nose; a few extra hairs protruding from his nostrils mingled with the mustache hairs in an unseemly fashion. Probably once athletic, capable of outchasing any robber, he now embraced a commendable belly that strained beneath the belt of the black police uniform.

He gave a shrug. He had the look of a man who hadn't reached this age and status to be continually pestered by petty requests. "Everyone's got ideas about secret organizations and spies and things these days. Every day I have someone in here with some crazy story about what might have happened to someone gone missing."

."And do they usually turn up?" Mr. Norris said hopefully.

"Well, they're usually found dead in a raid or they're making the most of the chaos to do a disappearing act. Only last week a woman missing for six months was found to be happily married in Bognor Regis."

"Well, that's rather a good story," Mr. Norris said optimistically to Mrs. Braithwaite.

"Her husband didn't think so." The policeman laughed grimly. "Dragged her back home faster than you could say 'bigamy.'"

Mr. Norris's smile vanished. This wasn't helpful. He had been banking on the policeman to take on Mr. Norris's role in the search for Betty. He had to get to work. The end-of-year financial accounts were half finished, and he could hardly bear to think of them, lying there in their tidy pile, incomplete.

So many figures hovering on the brink of reconciliation.

"Well," announced Mrs. Braithwaite in her forthright manner. "This missing person very definitely exists, and I've searched the hospitals and every other place she can be. Her boyfriend is up to something, and I know it." She drew in a fearsomely large breath. "So it's about time you pull your finger out and do something about it."

"I'll take down the details and let the head office know about Baxter," P.C. Watts said, sweeping the form he had filled to one side. "That's all I can do until I get more evidence."

Mrs. Braithwaite scowled, then she took Mr. Norris's elbow and began pulling him gently away. "I think we should let the constable get on with his work, don't you?"

"Er, do you think so?" Mr. Norris had the unsettling feeling that she had a plan of her own and remained clutching the police desk in front of him.

Then Mrs. Braithwaite did something very unlike her. She winked at him. It was a surreptitious kind of wink, the type that criminals might give each other. She motioned toward the door with her head, then did it again: the wink.

Weakened by confusion, he allowed her to drag him through the door.

"What are you thinking?" he asked when they got outside.

She began walking briskly back to the house. "If **they** aren't going to do something about it, then **we** most certainly will." Stopping dead in the middle of the pavement, she turned to him. "Mr. Norris, if no one else is going to save Betty, then it'll have to be us."

"But P.C. Watts is going to inform Scotland Yard. They'll be certain to stop Baxter, whatever he's up to."

"You heard the man! He said that they have reports like this every day, that most of them don't amount to much. He doesn't take us seriously." She put her hands on his upper arms, giving him a small shake. "It's up to us to find out what's happened to Betty."

The day was gray. Thick clouds sat in a windless sky, going nowhere, and Mr. Norris couldn't help thinking that everything was closing in on him. Becoming too much.

He began plodding back to the house.

Mrs. Braithwaite came hurrying after him. "Where are you going, Mr. Norris? We need to go back to Baxter's place, see if we can follow him again. Maybe try the Pendulum. Perhaps we can get a lead from there. We have work to do. We need to get on with it!"

But Mr. Norris hardly heard a word. He was

exhausted. He'd had enough of this darting around on wild-goose chases.

"We can't just leave it, Mr. Norris. Where is your sense of duty?"

He stopped, opening his hands. "I have none." He reached out and took one of her hands in his, imploring her. "You have to believe me. I'm simply not the kind of man who does these things."

"But you **do** do these things, Mr. Norris." Her hand began squeezing his. "You could be so much more. You only have to try it to see. You are a very skilled and dexterous person. You just have to point all that cleverness in the right direction."

He let the words flow into his mind, weave around like snakes trying to poison him. "It's no use, Mrs. Braithwaite. I have to go to the office. They need me there. Accounts are my rightful place."

They walked home in silence.

Mrs. Braithwaite went to the kitchen to try to rouse him with a very hot, very strong cup of tea, but Mr. Norris took his briefcase, his gas mask box, and his bowler hat, and plodded to the front door.

He was going to work.

## 14.

Mrs. Braithwaite watched his departure with utter frustration. How could he abandon her like this? Then, with deliberation, she stood up, tied on her head scarf, and headed for the front door.

"I'll jolly well find Betty on my own."

There was nothing else for it: Baxter was her last link to Betty. Mrs. Braithwaite had to go back to his house and follow him from there. He would lead her to Betty at some point. She was sure of it.

Many thoughts surged through her mind as she marched up the hill to Clapham, most of them relating to Mr. Norris.

"I'll show him," she muttered to herself.

But as she got to the top of the hill and stood in

front of Baxter's house, it was Betty who crept to the forefront of her mind.

The worst hazard in life, her own experience had shown, was joining oneself to the wrong kind of man.

And Baxter was that, without a doubt.

She eyed his front windows. They were still blacked out from the night, and yet she had a suspicion there was something going on inside, shadows moving behind the shades. Someone was inside the house, and that person would have to come out sooner or later.

She propped herself against the wall around the darkened corner from the front door. Time passed, and her shoes began to pinch a little after the first hour, but she was determined to wait it out. Betty's life depended on it.

Then, just as she was about to nod off, someone came out of the house.

By his lilt and stature, she knew it was Baxter. She pinned herself to the wall, hoping he wouldn't turn her way. Eyeing his broad shoulders and re-membering his aggressive stance when he'd found them in the bush, she shuddered. He was probably a trained fighter.

**Let's hope I'm not his next victim**, she thought as she held her breath.

He strode off in the other direction, obviously in a hurry, and headed toward the telephone box

on the common in front of the Pendulum. Tiptoeing out, she watched him pick up the telephone
receiver. He stood for a few minutes speaking to
someone before replacing the receiver to leave.

But he didn't go straightaway. As he came out
of the telephone box, he stooped down to retie his
shoe, and as he did so, he seemed to wipe his hand
against the door, low down, close to the ground.
After that he walked swiftly off.

She tailed him at a distance. He was striding
toward central London, following back streets
lined with terraced houses, turning quickly and
often.

Because it was quiet once he'd left the main road,
with fewer people on the streets, she had to let him
go farther ahead of her so that he wouldn't become
suspicious.

Suddenly he seemed to have heard something—
her footsteps perhaps—and he turned around
sharply. He blinked into the daylight as Mrs. Braithwaite leaped into someone's front garden, crouch-
ing down and praying that he wouldn't come and
drag her out.

He stood for a few moments, watching, listening. Then a bird fluttered out from behind her, giving Mrs. Braithwaite a fright.

Baxter turned and carried on walking. He must
have thought it was the bird.

Winding through the back streets, he came out
at a high street. It was crowded with queues from

bakeries and grocery shops spilling out onto the pavement, people trying to buy food before it ran out for the day. Women with baskets on their arms hurried from place to place, some with small children trotting to keep up. A blind man with a stick tapped his way through the chaos. Beside a red telephone box, an aging policeman looked around superciliously, probably missing crimes being committed right under his nose.

Just past a butcher's shop, Baxter paused slightly, looking around before vanishing into a door tucked between the butcher's and a closed florist's. It clunked shut behind him, leaving Mrs. Braithwaite standing, watching it.

The door, a battered wooden one with chipped black paint, did not look appealing. A bomb had taken off the upper floor of the butcher's shop, but a sign in the window proclaimed BUSINESS AS USUAL, MR. HITLER. That would mean it was a door to a basement or cellar.

But what, or who, was inside? Although Mrs. Braithwaite prided herself on her toughness, she considered carefully whether to try the door or wait for Baxter to come out.

In the end, curiosity got the better of her, and she decided to ease the door gently open, if she could, and listen. She felt quietly confident that she would know something was amiss if she heard it.

The handle clicked down surprisingly easily,

and she pulled it open with a jerk. The interior was pitch-black with stairs leading down to a cellar. Muffled voices were coming up, but there must have been another, closed door at the bottom of the stairs.

Dare she tiptoe down and open the next door a fraction?

Before she could decide, the lower door flew open, and a beam of low light stretched across the lower stairs. The voices became clear.

"There can't be any sabotage or assassinations." It was Baxter, loud and clear.

Another man said something too quiet for her to hear, but she made out the name Fox, and he finished by saying slightly louder, "Eight on Saturday at the church."

She strained her ears, but there was a lot of movement, someone kicking or moving boxes perhaps.

And that's when she heard it.

"What shall we do with her?" It was a thuggish voice, thick and deep.

A man—was it Baxter?—replied something that she couldn't quite hear.

**Did they have Betty locked up down there?**

Mrs. Braithwaite hardly had time to think before the sound of heavy footsteps came echoing up the stairs.

Pulling away quickly, she dodged back into the street, horrifically exposed, unsure what to do.

She could feel her heart pounding in her

throat. She glanced around frantically for a hiding place. A stairwell or a side alley? But there was nothing. She simply had to stay and hope he didn't see her, or—

A heavyset man in a boiler suit pushed the cellar door open and strode past her without looking twice as Mrs. Braithwaite, retying her head scarf, hurried down the pavement as if she were a normal woman, on a normal day, on her way to the grocery shop. It was the best disguise she had. Hiding in plain sight. No one would ever suspect a middle-aged housewife.

As she went past, she saw Baxter come out and stride off in the other direction.

"Who are these people?" Mrs. Braithwaite murmured, keeping her head down. Baxter could recognize her, after all.

When he was out of sight, she stopped, her heart racing.

**What am I going to do?**

That Betty might be held down there seemed possible, probable even.

She looked around for the policeman she'd seen earlier, but he'd gone, and she knew she didn't have enough time to return to the police station to explain everything.

Drawing a deep breath, she was certain of only one thing.

She had to go in herself.

A niggling worry that it was, perhaps, a little

foolhardy, made her think twice. What would happen if she was captured, too?

With this in mind, she walked briskly to the telephone box, found a few coins in her purse, and dialed the number to Mr. Norris's house.

One ring, two rings, three rings. Mrs. Braithwaite imagined the sound echoing in the empty house. Mr. Norris was probably still at work, of course, and the girls, well, she didn't know whether they'd be there.

Four rings, five, six.

Would one of them come home for lunch?

Seven rings, eight rings, nine.

If only she'd taken down Mr. Norris's work telephone number.

Ten rings, eleven.

There was a loud click as someone picked up the telephone.

Mrs. Braithwaite held her breath, hoping for it to be Mr. Norris.

"Hallo." It was the haughty voice of Cassandra.

Mrs. Braithwaite sighed, wishing it had at least been Florrie, although her flightiness would have lessened the chances of Mr. Norris's actually receiving the message.

"This is Mrs. Braithwaite," she said clearly— Mrs. Braithwaite always spoke clearly on the telephone. Good diction was the sign of good breeding. "Would you take a message for Mr. Norris, please?"

There was some clattering as Cassandra found

the pen that Mr. Norris always left beside the telephone. "What's the message?" Her voice was curt to the point of rudeness.

The awful thought crossed her mind: Was Cassandra trustworthy?

She certainly was unconscionably rude.

Thinking quickly, Mrs. Braithwaite decided to encode the message, hoping that Mr. Norris would have the presence of mind to work it out.

"Tell him that I had to go to the high street to find some sausages," she said crisply.

"Is that all?" Cassandra said, the sound of jotting coming through the telephone.

"Tell him 'Business as usual.' He'll know what I mean."

**Well, I jolly well hope he will!** Mrs. Braithwaite thought as Cassandra bid her a brusque good-bye and put the receiver down.

Outside the telephone box, she collected herself for the task ahead, and headed for the door.

She turned the handle, but this time it was locked.

Putting her head to it, she thought she heard a noise inside, and felt herself edging back. Who was in there? Who might come to the door? Could it be a thug like the one who'd just left? He would kill her if he saw her. She'd be found dead in the river next week. Her clothes would be eaten by fish, and she'd be found on a beach bloated and naked. How Mrs. Metcalf would laugh victoriously.

Mrs. Braithwaite deliberated about whether to run for it or face this dreadful, humiliating death head-on. But after a full five minutes, no one came out of the door.

She tried to open it again, attempting to budge it as much as she could. But it was locked fast.

She was going to have to break in.

Digging around in her handbag, her fingers closed around her trusty hairpin. She'd used it before to open various entry points: her own back door when she was locked out, the neighbor's shed when a cat went missing, Mrs. Metcalf's terrace French door. It could take some time, but she knew she could do it. The street was crowded—who would pay attention to a middle-aged woman having difficulty with her key, after all?

**Hiding in plain sight**, she thought to herself, taking out her own set of keys, to jangle around convincingly.

Looking both ways, she tackled the lock, concealing the hairpin within her keys.

"I'm from the WVS looking for potential housing for the bombed out," she muttered, quietly rehearsing the story she'd tell if she was spotted.

It took a few minutes of careful tinkering, nudging the end of the hairpin against the insides of the lock, before she felt a small click, and suddenly the door pushed open.

She was in.

Straightening her coat, she quietly closed the door behind her.

The landing was dark, but she recalled the location of the stairs heading down into the basement, and feeling her way with each step, she began creeping as quietly as the rotting stairs would allow. At the bottom, she felt around the walls for a door handle, and then tried it. It opened straightaway, and she found herself inside another dark space. She struck a match—borrowed surreptitiously from Mr. Norris's hallway collection—the little flare settling into a steady, bright flame, illuminating a long corridor, three or four doors leading off on each side.

That's when the noises began.

First there was a light scraping, which could have been made by a mouse or a rat, only then it turned into a rhythmic kind of banging, the kind that could only be made by a person. It was coming from behind one of the doors.

Taking a few steps backward, she retreated into a cupboard under the stairwell, pulling the door closed behind her. She rummaged through her handbag for a lethal kind of weapon, like a knife or a bottle, but the only pointed item she had was a ballpoint pen, and she was loath to use that as it was her only one.

From her hiding place, she waited, sweating. But after a minute and then more minutes, she realized that no one was coming after her. The muffled banging had gone back to a slight scratching. Maybe it was a mouse after all.

Creeping out of her corner, she decided, bravely, to try one of the doors.

The scratching was coming from the second door on the left, so she decided to start with the first door on the right.

Easing the door open, she struck another match. The flame fired and simmered, showing some kind of meeting room, uneven chairs crammed around an old wooden refectory table. The chairs were in disarray, as if a meeting had come to a sudden end, everyone leaving their chairs wherever they were.

She went back to the corridor and tried the next door on the right. Inside she struck another match. She'd run out of matches the way things were going.

But then she stopped in her tracks.

She quickly tried to piece together what it was she was looking at. There was an old worn, backless wooden bench in the center of the room. Some areas close to the four corners were rubbed bare of the varnish and dirt that was covering the rest of it, exposing the raw wood beneath. A metal bucket lay next to the bench, empty.

On a table at the side were a number of chains and a bottle with a clear liquid. She went over, opened it, and sniffed. The smell was so pungent that she was almost sick. Was it pure alcohol? Meths? Something worse? Beside the bench on the floor was another metal chain.

She looked at the chain. At the bench.

Had someone been chained here, wearing down the corners as they struggled to be released?

Was this some kind of interrogation room?

The match went out.

Feeling the wall behind her, she backed out of the room into the corridor.

There was that scratching sound again, small scrapes on the floor or wall coming from the door opposite.

She'd try the door. The noise could be anything, after all, but she was ready to run for her life, even though she couldn't remember the last time she had.

The lock clicked, a minuscule sound that seemed to carry around the empty corridor, making her stand stock-still for a moment, waiting for someone to fly toward her. But there was nothing. Only the sound of scraping, which had become louder, faster.

She peeked inside.

It was black with darkness, but she knew there was someone inside, could smell the sweat and dirt of another human. Suddenly she heard the distinctive sound of someone moaning, muffled.

Lighting a match, she made out a gagged figure in the corner, tied to a chair. Mrs. Braithwaite's heart stopped, then beat a thousand times a minute. Even dirty, her hair scraped back, her eyes red and wide with terror, Mrs. Braithwaite knew.

It was Betty.

## 15.

Betty watched, incredulous, as someone who looked exactly like her mother darted across the room and flung her arms around her.

"Darling! Betty! What happened to you?" Her mother tore off the gag and began trying to untie her.

"Mum? What are you doing here?" Not cross, precisely, but Betty was unquestionably miffed. This was **her** operation, and although, yes, things had become a little sticky, it was imperative that civilians not be put in the line of danger.

Especially her mother.

"I'm rescuing you, of course!" Mrs. Braithwaite whispered hoarsely, untying her hands. The rope was thick and strained. "You have to slacken the rope so that I can undo it."

Betty thought quickly. Even with her wrists and ankles free, there was little chance they'd get out before Briggs and Marty caught them.

"You'll have to work fast. What are you doing here?"

"I simply had to save you, of course!" Mrs. Braithwaite said distractedly. "I didn't come all the way to London to find you'd been, well, done away with."

"You shouldn't be here. HQ will have sent someone. They're probably on their way."

"Who are HQ? Why aren't they here rescuing you now?"

That was something that had crossed Betty's mind, too. Where was her rescue party?

As her mother wrestled with the knots in the darkness, Betty wondered what on earth had happened to bring her mother here.

All those years of not caring at all what Betty got up to, and she suddenly decides to show up, save her life, and potentially mess everything up completely.

"Don't you want to know how I found you?" Mrs. Braithwaite asked, proud of herself.

"No time for that. Focus on the ropes."

"You're moving around too much!" Mrs. Braithwaite snapped.

Betty sighed and stayed as still as she could. Even while being rescued, she, apparently, wasn't doing anything right.

Mrs. Braithwaite pulled something from her handbag—**who brings a handbag on a break-out, for heaven's sake?**—and murmured to herself while working at the knot, finally loosening it with the help of a ballpoint pen. Betty wriggled her hands free, and then they both set to work on her ankles, which were damp, it turned out, from blood.

"Did they torture you?" Mrs. Braithwaite demanded angrily.

"Yes," Betty replied simply. Then seeing Mrs. Braithwaite looking horrified, added, "It happens in this job, Mum."

Utter determination was set on Mrs. Braithwaite's face, the corners of her mouth pulling down. "What job is it precisely? Certainly not filing in the sewage works, that's for certain."

Finally released, Betty stretched and stood up.

"I can't tell you. You're in enough danger as it is, without knowing anything about what's going on."

"You're not involved in anything criminal, I hope," Mrs. Braithwaite said, disgusted at the notion.

"Mum, look." Betty drew a deep breath. "I'm on crucial government business, that's all you need to know."

"You couldn't think of anything a bit less life-threatening? Code breaking too easy, was it?"

"I wanted to do my bit for the war."

"Without a care in the world for the fact that you are my only family?" Mrs. Braithwaite struck a match, looking Betty up and down. "How long have you been here?"

"I don't know. I was unconscious for a while." She shook her head briskly. "Look, there's no time for this. We have to go."

Grabbing her mother by the hand, she headed into the corridor and together they raced to the stairs and began to creep up. Noises from the street traveled down to them: a woman shouting at a child, a man whistling through his teeth, the **tap tap tap** of a blind man rapping his stick on the pavement. One step at a time, she crept forward, listening intently.

"Act normally," Betty whispered. "Pretend we're just women on everyday errands."

With a silent "One, two, three," she opened the door.

Bright daylight blinded her for a moment, the grimy street air flooding in, smelling of fresh meat and sawdust from the butcher's shop.

Taking Mrs. Braithwaite's arm, Betty yanked her mother out from behind her as she darted into the street.

Then she stopped dead.

A great dark mass in a boiler suit was standing motionless in front of her.

"Where do you think you're going?" Briggs towered over her, his arms wide, ready to grab her.

"Run!" Betty whispered urgently to her mother, pushing her away.

Briggs seized Betty's arm. She attempted to twist herself out of his grip, but he was ready for her, and a lot stronger, bundling her back inside the black door.

Quickly scanning the pavement as she was pushed inside, she watched as Mrs. Braithwaite, trotting away toward the butcher, went straight into Marty, the scrawnier of her captors who'd disguised himself as a blind man. He threw his stick down and took hold of her, leaving her handbag on the pavement, abandoned.

"Come on," Briggs said, pushing Betty down the stairs before him, steadying her as she seemed to fall forward. His fingers squeezed into her wrists, pinning them together so hard that she winced.

He had switched a light on, a bare bulb hanging from the ceiling at the bottom of the stairs. The door to the corridor was open, and the men thrust the two women forward, back into the room where Betty had been held.

"I knew we should have done her in from the start," Briggs growled as he stood the chair back up and retied Betty to it. "She blabbed all she knows already. Nothing left."

"Boss don't think so, thinks she knows them codes."

Betty put on an inscrutable look, gazing at the floor in front of her without saying a word as Briggs pulled the knots tight.

Her mother was intent on jabbering away.

"You put me down, young man. Do you know who I am?"

Briggs grinned at Marty, jerking his head toward Mrs. Braithwaite. "What shall we do with her?"

"Don't know what use she'll be," Marty said, tying Mrs. Braithwaite to another chair. He'd taken his glasses off to show heavily shadowed eyes, bloodshot from drink.

"I'll have you know I'm the head of the Ashcombe WVS, as well as being Betty's mother, and if anything happens to her, then—"

Betty winced. Was her mother really expecting to shove these men around as she did with the village ladies?

Briggs put his face in front of Mrs. Braithwaite's, grinning sarcastically. "Gonna tell us about a secret jam-making conspiracy?"

Both men laughed, opening the door to leave.

"Leave you two alone for a little family reunion, shall we? See what the boss wants us to do with you."

The door thudded closed behind them, plunging the room into darkness, while footsteps, mingling with laughter, disappeared down the corridor and up the stairs. Then the sound of the black door clunking shut echoed through the empty passages.

They were alone.

"This isn't good," Betty mumbled, trying to loosen her knots. "And they know their knots, which is highly aggravating."

"How did you come to be here, dear?" her mother asked, as if they'd just shown up at the wrong tea party.

Betty paused, wondering how much to tell her. "I'm sorry, Mum. I'm not allowed to say. Government secrets and all that. Basically, though, I was abducted. I was on an assignment when Briggs—he's the large one in the boiler suit—came out of nowhere and dragged me into the back of a van. Next thing I knew I woke up here. They must have knocked me out."

"Why do they want you, though?"

She paused again. "Let's just say I might know something they want, and if they get it out of me, they'll kill me."

"Then don't tell them, Betty," Mrs. Braithwaite said gruffly. "Don't tell them a word."

"Don't worry, Mum. I know how to handle them."

"I knew we had to find you," she added with determination. "We've been working night and day trying to figure out where you could have gone."

"Who's 'we'?"

"Mr. Norris and I, of course."

"Mr. Norris?" Betty let out a weak laugh. "My landlord, Mr. Norris? The one who wouldn't say boo to a goose?"

"Well, he's been a tremendous help, actually," Mrs. Braithwaite said huffily. "He's been all over the place with me to find out what happened to you."

"Oh? Where is he now?" Betty said, still amused. "Is he going to come to our rescue?"

Mrs. Braithwaite's voice trickled away. "He thought it was too dangerous to come today, and I suppose he was right."

"Don't worry, Mum," Betty said, adopting her plucky voice. "I'll find a way out." Annoyingly, the ropes around her wrists were too tight to loosen. She carried on talking while she thought of another plan. "But tell me, Mum. Why are you even here? In London, I mean. I've hardly heard from you since I came here, and now, in the midst of a big operation, you barge in here trying to save the day."

"We would have escaped if it hadn't been for that Briggs fellow," Mrs. Braithwaite said grumpily. "But to be honest, dear, things haven't been going well for me in Ashcombe. Since the divorce, the village women have seen fit to ostracize me. They say that it's my fault that your father left. That I was too hard and cold. That I've sullied the village's good name." She let out a sigh. "I can't see why, though. If anyone should be ostracized, it should be your father. He's the one who was unfaithful for all those years. Do they really think that **I** wanted him to divorce me?"

"Anthony Metcalf mentioned—"

"I know, dear. I read the letter," she said without remorse. "I can only conclude they feared I would try to steal their husbands. Can you imagine? Mrs. Metcalf seriously thinking I might have secret yearnings for that slimy oaf who's been fiddling his books for the last decade? Why should I need another man anyway? I'm perfectly fine without your father. Better even!"

"Yes, I'm sure that you are, Mum. I was sorry to hear you were to be demoted."

Silence hung in the darkness for a moment.

"They said that as a divorcée I was immoral, and thus unsuited to a position where others would be looking to me for guidance."

"Immoral? Of all the things you are, Mum, immoral would not be the one I'd pick to describe you."

"It was your father who was immoral. All his affairs. And yet he gets off scot-free while I am vilified, vilified I tell you. Betty, there is a lesson to be learned here."

Betty thought of Anthony's letter, and then the last time she'd seen him, the silly mustache he'd grown, the way he was supporting his mother against hers, confident that Betty would join him. She blushed as she remembered all those times she'd complained to him about her, cried on his shoulder when she was hurt by an unkind remark her mother had made, ranted about how unlucky she'd been, growing up without a kindly mum. She felt a blush as she thought of her disloyalty, her mother here, now, come to rescue her. Betty decided that should she get out of there alive, she would write straightaway to Anthony, tell him what had happened, and recant every nasty thing she'd said.

"I realized what a fool I've been, wasting all my time on those silly ladies," Mrs. Braithwaite continued. "I should have been paying more attention to the real war. To you." She took a deep breath. "I've been thinking. There have been a lot of things I wanted to say to you, a lot of things I should have said years ago. I know I haven't always been the best mother—"

"Well, apart from that time when you—"

"I know, I know. Do you remember when you left? You said that perhaps you wouldn't have children of your own? I've been thinking about that, and I wondered if it was . . . if it might have been because of me. Because of how I was toward you."

"It's all right, Mum. You were busy with the village," she said bitterly. With her father away philandering and her mother never terribly interested in her only child, Betty felt that she had been lonely at best, neglected at worst.

"Those women in the village are merciless! It was crucial to maintain our reputation."

"More crucial than your daughter? Is that what Aunt Augusta taught you?"

"You may have disliked her methods, but Aunt Augusta was wise in her way."

"She thought she was Queen Victoria. I've spent half my life under that harridan's rule."

"All right, I acknowledge that perhaps she was a little behind the times, but that made her wisdom all the more valuable."

"Was it wise of her to consider herself—and you—as descended from lords, when we lived in a semidetached house in Ashcombe?"

Her mother was shocked by her tone. "She and my mother were daughters of the Earl of Mulcaster, no less. They were brought up in Faversham Hall, the rightful heirs, had they been male. Aunt Augusta was nobility. It pained her greatly that she was reduced in the eyes of the world, that she had to move in with us in her twilight years."

"You're starting to sound like her now, Mum."

"Well, she did me a great service, sacrificing everything to bring me up after my parents died."

"She was a bitter old lady. Don't you remember those horrid things she said about your mother?"

"Aunt Augusta was only looking after my best interests," Mrs. Braithwaite said. "Which is why she brought me up the way she did, with proper values."

"Outdated values."

"Betty! I know Aunt Augusta wasn't fond of you—"

"She hid my science books in the cellar. She tormented me from the moment she moved in when I was nine until she died when I was eighteen."

"She wanted you to act like other girls, like Mrs. Metcalf's daughter, Patience. Why couldn't you be normal like them, not such a bluestocking, your nose always in a book?"

"You were always too busy listening to Aunt Augusta. You never thought about what it was that **I** wanted. Even after she died, you couldn't let go of her ridiculous beliefs—you even started pontificating about them as if they were your own."

"I thought that I was doing the right thing, making sure we were respectable."

She heaved a sigh. "If only you'd had faith in me, Mum. Do you see Patience doing this kind of crucial war work?"

Mrs. Braithwaite stopped and sniffed. "No. I never thought that your education could lead to your being, well, special." Then she quickly added, "Not that it matters, but wherever you go from here, you will always be special to me." She sniffed again and then added, "And now I heartily wish that I had my handbag with me, as I need to find my handkerchief."

Silence reigned, and then Mrs. Braithwaite said, "Betty, are you all right?"

"Yes, Mum," she said, trying but failing to mask the tears. "I always felt that I'd let you down for not being perfect like Patience."

"But you haven't let me down at all," Mrs. Braithwaite said. "You're worth a thousand of that trumped-up nincompoop. You truly are the very best daughter I could ever have had. I just didn't realize it until now."

"And I know you want me to marry well, to have children, but I want to do other things, too. My kind of work, well, it's incredible. It's so incredible to stretch my mind, to do something so utterly worthwhile." With frustration Betty tried to wriggle her hands free again. "And these days, Mum, just because a girl is clever, it doesn't mean she can't get married."

"Well, in my day it did," Mrs. Braithwaite said. Then she added stridently, "When I was growing up, the only woman who had a job and was married was the Queen. Our success was judged by the men we married and the social circle we found ourselves in afterward. My mother married beneath her, and Aunt Augusta never let her forget it."

"And look where that way of thinking got you," Betty said cautiously. "Dad hardly ended up being a good catch, did he?"

She breathed a huge sigh. "Maybe I could have been warmer to him, too."

"Oh, Mum, don't listen to anything Mrs. Metcalf says! Especially now that we both need a healthy dose of your ruthlessness."

## 16.

Finding Betty hadn't been the unqualified success Mrs. Braithwaite had anticipated. True, they had had a good chat, their best in years, but Betty remained miffed at Mrs. Braithwaite for getting herself entangled in her business at all. Even worse, she wouldn't say a word about where she worked and what she was doing that had got her abducted in the first place.

"Come on, dear. You could at least tell me which side you're on."

An abrupt noise came from the corridor, heavy footsteps on the stairs echoing harshly through the darkness.

"They're coming," Betty whispered hoarsely.

"Whatever happens, try to save yourself, Mum. Don't tell them anything."

But before she'd even finished, the door had swung open and the bright white beam of a torch swept over them.

Mrs. Braithwaite felt a frisson of fear as the torch-light flashed from Betty to her.

"Right, you," a voice bellowed at Betty. It was Briggs, angry and aggressive. "I'm to take you to— well, never you mind where." He stormed over to her. "Fox wants to see you."

Untying her from the chair, he started yelling at her to stop squirming. "You're lucky, 'cause if it was up to me, I'd do away with you right now."

"But what about my mother?" Betty said.

"Who cares about her." He laughed. "I'm sure Marty will play bridge with her if she gets bored." Then he added with a poisonous sneer, "And then kill her afterward."

"But, Mum—"

He put a hand over her mouth and pushed her out of the door ahead of him. "No funny business on the way."

"Don't tell them anything, Betty!" Mrs. Braithwaite called.

But she had gone.

The beam of light left the room, and the door slammed with a heavy thud. A key grated in the lock, and then the voices disappeared.

There was nothing.

Mrs. Braithwaite was alone. But she wasn't thinking about death or how they were planning to kill her. She was thinking about Betty and how wonderful it had been to see her. Tears came to her eyes again as she sat back and began remembering, as if a movie reel were playing out behind her eyes: Betty's childhood, every precious moment they'd spent together since the very first instant she'd laid eyes on the tiny baby, all arms and legs, wriggling as she cried, already desperate to get out into the world.

It struck her that this, surely, was how one should measure her success in life. It was family, the time spent with them, helping them, making your way through the world alongside them.

And then a new sound: a door opening, footsteps coming down, slowly, purposefully, and Mrs. Braithwaite knew that this, surely, was going to be the end.

## 17.

Mr. Norris arrived home from work at a quarter to six. He put his bowler hat on the hat stand, then walked through to the kitchen, putting on the kettle. Taking his newspaper out from under his arm, he sat at the kitchen table reading while it came to a boil.

**A peaceful evening**, he mused, listening to the gentle stirrings of the water beginning to heat.

And yet he couldn't shake the feeling that all was not as it should be.

It was all because of Mrs. Braithwaite. She'd messed up his routine. He had become like the water bubbling in the kettle, frenetic and chaotic.

It wasn't that he hadn't grown rather fond of her, but more that she kept appearing and demanding things of him. Things he didn't want to do. Things no one should ask a person of Mr. Norris's sensibilities to do.

He picked up his newspaper to carry on where he'd left off. Since the beginning of the war, he'd felt compelled to read the obituary pages, just in case. They kept getting longer and longer. A pointless list of souls marching out of the world every day, some of them heroes, others just ordinary people caught up in someone else's war. He was caught off guard by a sudden wave of sadness, a lump forming in his throat. It occurred to him that the events of the last few days had made this war something that involved him, too.

The kettle came to a boil. Taking out two cups, expecting Mrs. Braithwaite to appear as usual for a summing up of the day, he felt a vague shiver of emptiness when she didn't appear.

How quickly he'd become used to her. Or was it that he'd become so used to the silence of his world that it was only after she'd been there that he realized how lonely he'd been?

He decided to go upstairs and knock on her door, but as he reached the hallway, the notion struck him that perhaps she wasn't in.

Had she left this morning and never made it home?

Hurrying, he climbed two steps at a time and ran to her door, rapping furiously. "Mrs. Braithwaite. Mrs. Braithwaite!"

When there was no answer, he tugged out his keys and opened the door himself. Inside, the room was tidy, smelling vaguely of her lavender perfume. It appeared she'd been out all day.

He sat on the bed.

What had happened to her?

Perhaps Mrs. Braithwaite had been right. Perhaps Baxter was a nasty piece of work, after all. And, more importantly, perhaps he had now done something horrid with Mrs. Braithwaite, too.

He had to find her. He would go to Baxter's house. He was sure to lead him to her sooner or later.

But it could take forever, and who knew what kind of danger she was in?

Glancing around the room for inspiration, he looked at the dresser and remembered the coded message sitting in his pocket. He'd told Mrs. Braithwaite that he'd work it out, but he had planned to leave it to the weekend, enjoy it over a nice cup of tea.

### YFU gdvmgb-vrtsg xsrogvim xsfixs vrtsg

Sitting at the dressing table, he tugged out a notepad. Two of the words were the same: **vrtsg**. The code must be a single pattern.

He wrote down some possibilities. Mr. Norris prided himself on his crossword abilities, so he knew which letters most commonly sat together:

**t** and **h, w** and **h, g** and **h, e** and **a,** and so forth. Because this was a brief message, surely they'd avoid superfluous words such as **the** or **that.** But why have the same word twice?

And why were the first three letters of the note in capitals? Perhaps it was an abbreviation—everyone seemed to reduce groups, jobs, or places to initials these days. It made it sound more official and important. The Women's Voluntary Service had become the WVS, the British Expeditionary Forces was the BEF; even in letters home, soldiers were using coded acronyms to tell their loved ones where they were: Friendship Remains And Can Never End stood for France; Be Undressed Ready My Angel was for Burma. He felt sheepish at that one.

Then he looked at the note again. Why the hyphenated word? Could that be a number? After all, it was unlikely that someone had added a hyphenated adjective into a coded note. If it was a number, and the second part of the number was repeated at the end and had five letters, each one different from the other, then that number would have to be—

Eight.

From that moment, he knew he had it. The first five letters done, he quickly went through the other possibilities, and slowly the meaning of the note became clear.

But then, as the acronym became apparent, his enthusiasm fell with a thud.

"BUF," he said under his breath. "The British Union of Fascists."

Whatever Betty was caught up in, it wasn't only far more serious than he'd thought; it was also incredibly dangerous.

And Mrs. Braithwaite had walked right into the middle of it.

Striding down the stairs, deliberating whether to actually knock on Baxter's door and demand to know what he'd done with Mrs. Braithwaite, or simply to follow him, Mr. Norris bumped straight into Cassandra.

She was wearing a slim-fitting maroon dress, her heavy eye makeup making her look almost feline. With the new information that Betty was somehow involved with the BUF, he felt a little sickly as he realized that Cassandra could be involved, too. He'd always thought her rather Aryan, with her blond hair. And all that anger.

"Did you get your telephone message?" she snapped in her upper-class drawl. "The Braithwaite woman called to let you know what's for dinner." She let out a laugh, sliding past him up to her bedroom.

"Eh?" Mr. Norris turned back to her, startled. "She telephoned? When?"

"This afternoon, about three o'clock. I don't know why it was so urgent that she couldn't wait until you were home. It's only sausages, too."

Mr. Norris quickly said, "She must have thought

that I would go out and buy some." Then he smiled, as if this were a very reasonable message to leave, which it wasn't at all. Why on earth was Mrs. Braithwaite telephoning him about dinner? And sausages, too. Mrs. Braithwaite hated sausages. She hadn't touched one since 1939.

Cassandra was looking at him pitifully. "I hardly thought she would be your type, Mr. Norris."

He shrugged, trying to be nonchalant. "If she does the shopping and cooking while she's here, then why should I say no to that?"

"I suppose you're right, although I don't think she should be encouraged to stay." She gave him one of her smirks, then pointed down at the telephone pad beside the elephants in the hall. "She said something else about business as usual, which definitely means that she's moving in."

Mr. Norris went to get the pad, thanking Cassandra as she continued to her room.

Reading the words "Business as usual," he grimaced, walking slowly into the kitchen. "What an odd thing to say," he muttered under his breath.

Perhaps it had a double meaning. After all, Mrs. Braithwaite would never have left a proper message with Cassandra, given her mistrust of the girl.

He sat down at the kitchen table, pad in front of him, and read the message in its entirety.

**Had to go to High Street for sausages. Business as usual.**

Something else tugged at him. Mrs. Braithwaite was partial to that vile tinned meat known as Spam; she'd probably walk for miles to find a grocery shop that had a tin in stock.

Was it a code explaining where she was? For Spam, she would need to go to a grocer's shop, but for sausages, it would be a butcher. Was that why she had chosen to say sausages? Had she said sausages because she knew he'd find it odd—how could it not be when she loathed them so much?

There was a butcher's on Wandsworth High Street, but if she had started at Baxter's house, she may have gone to Clapham High Street. There must be a butcher's shop there, if not two.

But why "Business as usual"?

**Could it be an anagram?** He began to jumble the letters around in his mind. "Nasal issues . . . sinus bases . . ."

The more he thought about it, the more it seemed to indicate a minor health ailment in the ear, nose, and throat department. Having suffered as a boy from enlarged adenoids, Mr. Norris was all too familiar with the severity of such complaints.

Pocketing the note, he headed into the hallway.

The only way he'd find out for sure was to go and have a look.

## 18.

As Betty was thrust into the back of a delivery van, two things crossed her mind. The first was an abject fear that her mother was in grave danger. Did anyone know that Mrs. Braithwaite was there? Betty had been locked up long enough to know that these men were not only brutal, they were also clumsy: Their kicks and punches were apt to go too far.

The second thing to cross her mind was that she had to get out of the van. It had been waiting on the side of the road for Briggs to throw her inside, but it took off instantaneously with a screech, indicating that someone else was driving. Briggs, no doubt, had returned to the basement to watch her mother.

Heaven only knew who was driving the damn thing, or where she was headed.

Another basement where she would undergo more torture, perhaps by a more professional team? She wasn't afraid of the pain—they'd trained her to withstand it—but she was aware that she was relatively new to the game. A more experienced extractor was bound to put her determination to the test.

She knew precisely what they wanted from her, too: the name of the other mole and the agency that had sent them. They'd worked out that the BUF had been infiltrated by two moles, and somehow—she couldn't think how—they had discovered that she was one of them.

Even though she'd been exposed, Baxter remained undercover, and she was determined, no matter how much they tortured her, not to give him away.

He was imperative to the operation. But, more crucially, Betty knew what the thud in her stomach meant, the flurry of butterflies, the warm yearning for him.

She was in love with him.

The inside of the van was dark, except for a narrow line of daylight coming from the door, and she made her way across to it, trying to stay upright as the swing of the van threw her from side to side, along with a number of large boxes that, from the smell, seemed to contain large joints of raw meat.

Her hands were still bound by the rope behind

her, and she had to turn around to try the latch, feeling it give under her fingers.

**Was Briggs stupid enough not to lock it properly?**

Trying to make it catch, she worked to force it open. It wouldn't budge.

"Come on!" she yelped, tugging with her fingertips.

Suddenly unbalanced by the swing of the van, she fell heavily onto her side, her hands unable to stop her fall.

"What's going on in there?" a gruff voice yelled from the front.

As the van lurched to a brief halt, she was able to get to her feet again. But then the van jerked forward quickly, sending her slamming against the door.

Suddenly, the door swung open, the old lock giving beneath her weight.

Within seconds, she landed on the road, bumping slightly, her arms and legs grazing as she skidded forward on the ground.

The van, its back door flapping open, careered on, disappearing around the next bend.

**He hasn't realized that I'm gone.**

As she rolled to pick herself up off the ground, a black motorcar came up behind, the brakes screeching, stopping inches away from her.

Gaining her balance, she leaped up, dodging the driver, who had come out of his car to find out if she was all right. She said hastily, "Don't tell anyone you saw me," and then added "please!" in an urgent way, before running as fast as she could down a side street, and then another, again and again until she was sure no one could have followed her.

In a quiet, tree-lined road, she stopped to catch her breath.

She was free.

She found a rusty gate post and quickly shaved through the tired rope, her mind working fast.

She should really go to HQ, report what she knew, but first she had to rescue her mother. Or should she find Baxter, tell him what had happened?

Baxter knew that Betty was being held captive. She'd heard his voice in the basement, after all. Once again, that strange friction coursed through the back of her mind—an uncertainty—but Baxter couldn't possibly be a double agent.

**Could he?**

No. She knew that he wouldn't have been allowed to come after her—MI5 couldn't risk compromising his cover—but Betty still felt somewhat vexed that it hadn't been Baxter who'd saved her.

It was her mother.

Now Betty had to return to the butcher's and rescue her.

She huffed impatiently.

Her mother, as usual, had stormed ahead without thinking twice about what she was doing. It was ludicrous! She was completely out of her depth.

And now she was imprisoned and helpless, and Betty—instead of getting on with the proper work of national importance—had to risk her own freedom by going in to rescue her.

Briggs would still be there, watching. And now the van driver would have alerted him to the fact that Betty had escaped. They'd be looking out for her, ready and waiting.

She took a deep breath, gritted her teeth, then headed back to the butcher's basement.

However risky it was, she knew she had to do her best. After all, she owed her mother her life.

*19.*

Mr. Norris strode up the hill toward the Pendulum. It was that time of day, when workers wearily arrived home, closed their blackout curtains, and prepared for another hectic night. There was a full moon, and those were always trouble. The Nazi bombers almost always came over in droves, using the moonlight to guide their bombs to the docks and factories. At first they were just after the targets that would hamper the war effort—factories, airfields, government buildings—but after whacking the living daylights out of London's docks in the East End, they'd begun a new mission: bombing the public. Offices, homes, schools, churches, they struck anything that would crush the spirit of people. They weren't aiming to weaken the ability of the British to fight back; they were trying to break their will.

The skies were empty so far, and as Mr. Norris paced quickly through the streets with his torch, he looked up at the tiny dots of stars in the deepening dark blue, congregating on the horizon to watch the night unfold from light-years away.

"What difference does it all make?" Mr. Norris said to himself, looking at the moon, which had no idea what its light meant. "We're only here for a fraction of time."

But he knew he was frightened. All his life he'd been certain that dodging harmful situations was the best course of action, and he was now walking directly into one.

And yet he found himself walking faster, then running, something inside him urging him on. He couldn't disappoint Mrs. Braithwaite, with all her bravery, her comment about him lacking "oomph."

No, he had to show her, show the world, that he could do something, too.

Clapham High Street consisted of a long row of shops, now closed for the evening. Mr. Norris began looking for a butcher's shop, wondering if he'd know the right one. How many could there be, after all?

The answer was many. The terrace of shops seemed to have at least three butchers, four if he included one that looked empty.

"What did she say?" he murmured to himself as

he walked up and then back down. Sausages at the butcher on the high street.

The street was busy, people scurrying home to prepare for the night. A woman brushed past him, almost knocking him into the road, and a blind man tapped a stick, trying to get through the crowds.

"Are you all right?" Mr. Norris asked him, touching his elbow to indicate that he was there to help. "It's a bit busy tonight."

"I'm fine," the man said, flinging his hand away, turning as if to look at him through his darkened glasses. "Leave me alone."

Mr. Norris shrugged and carried on. The bomb raids put everyone out of sorts. If he wasn't here, looking for Mrs. Braithwaite, he'd be at home, pacing his room, deliberating about whether to stay put or make his way to a shelter in order to get a good spot for the night.

That option would now be gone.

He carried on walking, looking up and down the shops. There was a large butcher's shop that advertised a list of meats, including sausages; could it be there? Or was it the next butcher? It had a blue-striped awning and seemed like a place Mrs. Braithwaite might patronize.

But then he saw it.

A small butcher shop sat in the middle of a terrace, its roof damaged by bombs, a sign below saying BUSINESS AS USUAL, MR. HITLER!

Mr. Norris couldn't help grinning. How clever she was!

As he approached, he saw something else, something in the window of the butcher's shop.

His heart started pounding as he raced forward.

Sitting on the counter, through the large pane of glass, something brown reflected in his torchlight.

Mrs. Braithwaite's handbag.

## 20.

Mr. Norris gazed at the handbag on the butcher's counter. It looked dirtier than usual, battered, as if it might have been dropped, trodden on, and kicked, before being dusted off and put in the window in case its owner returned.

But Mr. Norris knew it meant far more.

Mrs. Braithwaite would never have left her handbag unless she'd been dragged kicking and screaming away from it. If he hadn't already known that he was in the midst of something horrific and dangerous, the handbag, sitting abandoned on the counter, made that demonstrably clear.

Mrs. Braithwaite had somehow been snatched off the pavement and taken, he had no doubt, into the butcher's shop, or the tatty-looking black door beside it.

He looked at the door. His insides were curdling with the inevitable decision he had to make. On the one hand, he could go to the police station, tell P.C. Watts about the situation, leave it in his hands, and go home. If he left now, he'd have enough time to make it underground in case of a raid. He might even get a choice spot in his preferred shelter, the crypt of a local church. But P.C. Watts would probably leave the problem until the morning. There was no proof that Mrs. Braithwaite was actually missing, and perhaps it would be easier to leave it until daylight, especially if there were bomb raids tonight.

On the other hand, he could take matters into his own hands. Mrs. Braithwaite was definitely in some kind of trouble. The thought of her stuck somewhere—and without her handbag—made him go hot and cold.

**How could he leave her like that?**

They'd become friends over the last few days. Granted, she was bossy, overbearing, and quite unable to see the precariousness in situations that, to him, were veritable death traps. But she was kind and companionable and really rather fun. The sad thought crossed his mind that she had become the closest friend he'd had in many years.

He tried the butcher's shop door. Of course it

was locked. Even after a little budging, it didn't give way.

Then he turned his attention to the tatty black door.

It, too, was locked.

Unsure what to do next, Mr. Norris decided to walk down the street, just in case someone inside had heard him trying to open the door. They might leap out and pull him in, too. What use would that be?

Looking back at the building, he started to wonder if there was another way in.

Then it occurred to him: There must be a back way into the butcher's, where the larger cuts would be unloaded. Could there be a stockroom, perhaps with a door into a back alley?

He trotted quickly to the end of the row and headed down an alley to the small road running behind the high street. It was lined with houses. He'd have to estimate which house the back of the butcher's shop would be behind, and then sneak through the back garden to get into the back of the shop.

Climbing was not one of Mr. Norris's strengths. His bowler hat might come off, or he might rip his mackintosh. Mr. Norris had a reasonable salary, but his wages would not accommodate the sudden loss of an expensive raincoat.

He found the house that seemed to be in the

right location and made a running jump to get over the gate.

Two tries later, he'd managed to get a foot on the top, and he heaved himself up and over, jumping down onto the ground on the other side and feeling rather pleased with himself. He'd lost his hat in the process but decided that he could pick it up later.

The back garden wasn't long, and soon he found himself facing a large back wall that separated the garden from the butcher's backyard. He found a few footholds and managed to get up and over on the first try, landing on the hard ground behind the shops.

By the state of the yard, he could tell that this was indeed the butcher's shop. A clammy stench of blood curdled through the air, as well as the giveaway mound of sawdust, tainted brown and pink from the day's bloodletting. Mr. Norris was not one of those people who liked to dwell on where his food came from.

He took stock of the building.

There was a back door, which most likely led into the butcher's chopping room behind the shop, but it was locked. He looked around for some other entrance into the building.

The only other opening was a window. He tried that, but it was also locked. Through the pane, he could see the bolt on the inside. If only he could get to it. But how?

The answer came to him in a flash, and then was discarded in the next flash. He couldn't possibly break the glass. It would be loud, not to mention damaging to the building. And it could hurt.

But then he pulled himself together.

**Isn't Mrs. Braithwaite more valuable than an old back window of a butcher's shop? Or my hand?**

He looked around, found a fist-size rock, and carefully covered his hand with a corner flap of his mackintosh. After a quick prayer, he hurtled himself toward the window, throwing the rock into the glass. It shattered loudly, echoing through the neighboring yards. Mr. Norris rushed away and hid in the shadows of the fence.

Then silence.

Mr. Norris bobbed his head up. Glittering fragments of glass lay around the window, giving it an ethereal glow in the moonlight. In the center of the pane, a large hole was livid with shards of sharp, spiky glass jabbing inward like daggers.

He went toward it cautiously, particles of glass crunching under his feet. Feeling the point of the largest jagged spike, he pricked his finger, a drop of bright red blood oozing out of the tip. He took out his handkerchief and wiped it away, and then, quick as a flash, enveloped his hand in the handkerchief and punched the spike in, then again for another one, and another, until the whole glass had been punched out of the window.

The handkerchief was covered in dots of blood, and when he took it off, dozens of tiny cuts grazed his knuckles.

He then put his hand through and unlocked the small window, but as he tried to budge it open, he realized that some idiot had painted the window shut.

"Well, that wasn't terribly clever," he murmured, sweeping the fragments away from the windowsill with his handkerchief.

He was going to have to squeeze through the space.

Pulling himself up, he managed to get one foot on the windowsill, and then pushed himself through. It was fortunate that Mr. Norris was a slight man, his shoulders oval, and that they slipped through quickly without touching the splintered edges.

On the other side, he found himself on a large wooden table, which turned out to be a butcher's block. On it, menacingly, lay a massive hacking axe. A few joints hung to one side, then a narrow doorway into the main shop.

Otherwise, it was empty. No captives, no fascists, and no Mrs. Braithwaite.

Perhaps he'd been wrong.

Perhaps this wasn't the right butcher.

Then he remembered the handbag.

She had to be here somewhere.

He began looking for a door to the basement, opening cupboards and larders, even a small lavatory that smelled worse than an abattoir. Then he came upon a narrow door that wouldn't open.

"Another locked door," he fumed. There wasn't a keyhole, which indicated that there must be a bolt on the other side of the door.

Mr. Norris took a deep breath. There was only one thing to do.

He went back to the butcher's block where the axe sat, dense and unwieldy.

All it would take was one blow.

The axe was heavy; it could murder a man in a single strike. With effort, he carried it to the door. Trying to control it so that it made as little noise as possible, he pulled it back behind him and, using all the strength he could muster, brought the blade down hard on the door.

It split open like a tree trunk, a wide strip opening to show a dark stairway leading down. He eased the axe to the floor and put his hand through, feeling for the lock to open the door. It was at the top, and as he pulled it to one side with an echoing clank, he listened hard, petrified that someone might come storming up the stairs toward him.

Just as he was clambering through the doorway, the sound of a scuffle came from below.

At the base of the stairs, a door was yanked open. A great hulk of a man appeared, a deep, throaty growl emanating from him. He charged up the stairs like a locomotive intent on mowing down the small fragile man in his path.

That's when Mr. Norris made the split-second decision that would save his life.

He bent down and picked up the hefty axe.

The rest seemed to happen in slow motion. The man's face flashed from anger to fear, his bottom lip protruding and moving to the side with horror, his legs almost buckling underneath him.

Mr. Norris held the axe up and took a few steps down the staircase, bringing the axe over his head and down as fast as he could over the man.

He missed, of course, but the man, in a bid to avoid the blade, lost his balance and went cascading down the stairs, wheeling over and landing at the bottom, motionless.

The dust settled around them.

Mr. Norris stood stock-still, the axe blade slicing the stair where it had landed. He let go and walked slowly around it down the stairs, waiting a moment or two before approaching the man—he had to be sure he wasn't going to spring up and grab him, after all—and gently put his fingers on his neck.

There was still a pulse.

But it was clear that the man had been knocked out.

Leaping up, Mr. Norris knew that he had only a few moments to see if Mrs. Braithwaite was there before the man began to regain consciousness.

The open door at the bottom of the stairs led into a corridor. He crept through, silently trying each door. When he got to the third door, the bare lightbulb from the corridor sent in a shaft of light, and there was a muffled noise coming from the corner.

A shape emerged as his eyes got used to the darkness, and as he stepped forward, he recognized the groans.

"Mrs. Braithwaite," he whispered, his hands stumbling over the knots of her gag in his haste to release her.

"Mr. Norris!" Mrs. Braithwaite cried as he tugged it off and untied the ropes around her wrists and ankles. She put her arms around him and burst into tears. "I thought you would never come!"

Mechanically patting her shoulder as she hugged him—Mr. Norris was not a dab hand at hugging—he spoke softly to her. "Of course I was going to come. What do you take me for?"

"Well, you didn't seem too brave this morning!"

"That was this morning, wasn't it? Come on, we have to hurry."

Stepping over the unconscious man, they hurried up the back stairs, Mrs. Braithwaite eyeing the axe on the stair. "Did you . . . ?"

"Yes, but no time for that right now."

Inside the back room, Mr. Norris hurried through the narrow door into the shop, returning a moment later with something very familiar in his hand.

"My handbag!" Mrs. Braithwaite sighed, collecting it from him and placing it in the crook of her elbow, as usual, before eyeing the broken window.

Mr. Norris already knew that this might be the place where they got stuck, both figuratively and literally. She was a great deal wider than him.

"Up you go!" Mr. Norris helped her up to the butcher's block, and she sat for a moment glaring at the small hole, running her finger across the prickly edges that encased it.

"You mean **I** have to get through **there**?"

"Yes, and the quicker you do it, the better."

She took a deep breath and stuck her head through, shuffling around to get her shoulders in, and then swallowing hard to ease her enormous bosom through.

But the hole wasn't large enough.

Mr. Norris leaped as he heard a noise from down the stairs. The man was waking up. They had to hurry.

With not so much as a word, he lunged himself at Mrs. Braithwaite's behind, which was protruding from the hole, sending her thrusting through, crashing down on the paving beneath.

"Argh! Mr. Norris!" she cried.

"Hurry," he yelped, clambering out after her. "We have to run."

Off they went, over the wall into the garden, and then over the gate, where they finally stopped for breath. Mr. Norris spotted something familiar and stooped to pick up his hat, giving it a quick dusting down and placing it back on his head.

"We've made it!" he gasped. "Well done, Mrs.

Braithwaite, and my apologies for having to help you through that window."

He looked at her, her hair all higgledy-piggledy, and there was a red smear from a graze down one cheek.

"Mr. Norris, I never would have thought you'd have it in you, but"—she took a deep breath—"I'm so terribly glad you did."

"What's going on here then?" A stern voice came from behind them, the flash of a torch beam blinding them for a moment.

Mr. Norris grabbed Mrs. Braithwaite's hand, ready to run for all they were worth, but then the voice said, "What are you doing in my garden?"

It was the owner of the house, come to see what the commotion was about.

Mrs. Braithwaite was the first to start laughing, a small peal of hysteria coming from her. The joy of being alive, of being back in a world where people got cross with trespassers in their gardens.

Mr. Norris joined in, a sense of the ridiculous coming over him. And as they stood there, bent over with their hands on their knees and laughing uncontrollably, the man began a tirade about private property, privacy, the war, and ended with "If you don't stop laughing, I'll call the police."

And why that made them laugh all the more, he would never know.

## 21.

Betty tidied herself before entering a small restaurant, a handful of locals seated around little round tables for dinner.

"I'm afraid I'm most terribly lost," she said in her best voice. "I'm looking for Clapham High Street."

The waitress, who was noticeably pregnant, was kindly but tired. "Not far, love. Keep on up this road, and it's left at the junction. About twenty minutes."

Betty paused at the door. "I don't suppose I could have a glass of water? I'm completely parched and forgot to bring my handbag with me."

The woman disappeared into a back room and came back with a glass of water and a bread roll.

"Looks like you need a bit of food, too, love. Is it the air raids?"

"Oh, thank you! Yes, it's the raids. I was up all night." She smiled sweetly, drinking the water and trying not to eat the roll too fast.

As she walked briskly up the hill, the sky darkening around her, she couldn't help thinking how the war often brought out the very best in people. That woman didn't need to share the food, especially as she would have another mouth to feed soon.

Reaching the high street, Betty headed to the butcher's, hiding nearby to watch for a moment. Marty was usually positioned outside most of the day, pretending to be blind, and she didn't care to run into him.

After checking for any sign of him or Briggs, she rushed up and tried the door handle.

Surprisingly, it was open.

Creeping in, she tiptoed down the stairs, feeling her way in the darkness, until she reached the main corridor, then one, two doors on her left. This one was where she had last seen her mother.

She gasped. The door was open.

She rushed inside, but it was empty.

**What had happened to her mother?**

She began running from room to room, and then she began calling, "Is there anybody here?"

But there was nothing.

Everyone had gone.

## 22.

Walking slowly back down the road toward Wandsworth Common, Mrs. Braithwaite looked at Mr. Norris and smiled. "You're a true friend indeed, Mr. Norris." She squeezed his hand. "You've quite surpassed yourself today!"

"Yes," he replied, blushing. "Who'd have thought it, eh?"

Mrs. Braithwaite gave a long sigh. "But they still have Betty," she said, exasperated. "I saw her. They were torturing her, trying to get information out of her." She turned to look at Mr. Norris. "She's a spy of some sort. I knew it."

"Makes sense," he said. "Couldn't let such a good mind go to waste. But where is she?"

"They took her away, not long before you came.

I think they're going to torture her some more, then get rid of her, kill her." She heard her voice sounding different, panicked. "They're ruthless monsters, Mr. Norris."

"That puts you rather in danger, too," Mr. Norris said, shaking his head. "If you know who they are—can recognize them—they'll be bound to want to get rid of you, too."

"There were two of them: a large one, Briggs, and the small weaselly one, Marty—he's the one who was staking out the place, acting like a blind man."

"But . . . I offered to help him!" Mr. Norris stammered peevishly. "No wonder they knew I was coming. He must have tipped off the big fellow." Then he gulped, looking over at Mrs. Braithwaite. "What did they do to you?"

"They tied me up. I think they were planning to kill me."

"This war. It brings out the very worst in people."

Mrs. Braithwaite looked up admirably at him, taking his arm. "And the very best! You were incredibly heroic, Mr. Norris. When did you work out that something was amiss? Did you get my message?"

He told her the whole story, from when he'd got home from work, to decrypting the code, to bumping into Cassandra and piecing together the telephone message that Mrs. Braithwaite might be in a butcher's shop.

"You broke the code from Betty's dressing table? What did it say?"

Mr. Norris immediately began rummaging in his pocket and brought out a crumpled piece of paper.

### BUF twenty-eight chiltern church eight

"But what is BUF?" she said, frowning.

"British Union of Fascists, if I have that correct," he replied evenly. "A repugnant band of fascists who think Hitler's the bee's knees. Strange that they're still around. The group was made officially illegal at the beginning of the war. All of their leaders were arrested and put in prison. But some of the followers are still out there, operating as fifth columnists."

She looked at him crossly. "Fifth what?"

"Fifth columnists are Nazis working here in Britain," he said quietly. "That's the term used for a group **within** a country who align themselves with the enemy. They try to bring the country down from the inside."

"What kind of a person would do that?" Mrs. Braithwaite snapped with irritation. "Why would anyone want to help Hitler?"

Mr. Norris spread his hands open. "Some of them have German connections, German blood; some think it's the right side to be on when the invasion happens. Around Europe, people who follow Hitler are being handsomely rewarded, a Polish castle here, a work of art there. Then there are those being threatened by the Nazis, their loved ones put on the line. They aren't given much of a choice. And then there are others."

"What others?"

He shrugged. "They believe his rhetoric about some new world order. They think the world would be run better by people who have **their** interests in mind, who bring wealth and power to them, especially if they feel they've been hard done by. They're grabbing hold of this master race idea as if it's the answer to everything."

"How could they be so unpatriotic? It's despicable!"

"Before the war the BUF would hold meetings where there was a lot of ranting and railing against foreigners, saying that they had to bring back the last king, Edward. A lot of the gentry were—or still are—on Edward's side. I've heard that they're all keeping their photographs of Hitler hidden in drawers, ready to bring out the minute we're invaded."

"But you said the BUF became illegal when the war began."

"Most of the followers jumped ship when the BUF was banned. I went to one of the meetings back in the thirties just to see what it was about, and it was a lot of nonsense, if you ask me. Lots of youngsters enjoying the black uniforms and fighting talk. The economy was in pieces, so they were all desperate to get one back on their parents, or on society, for their sorry lot. That's what all the speeches were about, how the pure British people had been hard done because of outsiders. They'd whip up a frenzy of hatred toward Jews and foreigners, blaming everything bad on them."

Mrs. Braithwaite looked down at the decoded message. "This looks as if it's a meeting," she said. "Twenty-eight would be the twenty-eighth of the month, which is Saturday—that's tomorrow!—and eight is probably eight in the evening."

"That's what I thought," Mr. Norris said with a grin. "Which is why I had a quick look through my set of encyclopedias and found Chiltern Church. It's a disused church on a quiet lane close to the village of Knockholt in Kent, not far from Sevenoaks."

"We'll have to join them, Mr. Norris," she said eagerly.

"Well, I don't know about that," he said weakly. "Perhaps we can hide outside and just watch them go in, see who they are, tell the police. I'm sure P.C. Watts would be a lot more interested once we have some names."

"Of course he would. But we need to find out where they've taken Betty." She tugged him along faster down the road. "Don't you see? We have to rescue her. She's in danger, and don't tell me that P.C. Watts will help. You know he won't."

They began to hurry, even though they were still

quite far from home, and Mrs. Braithwaite began to tell him about her chat with Betty.

"She told me that I'd been, well, not a terribly warm mother, and that Aunt Augusta held too much sway in our house."

"I gather Aunt Augusta had very strict notions."

"She brought me up after my parents died," she told him. "She was the daughter of an earl, along with my mother, and even though she didn't inherit anything, she was always insistent that there was a right and a wrong way to do things. We were nobility, regardless of where we lived."

"She sounds rather forbidding."

"Every time we went to someone's house, she'd say, 'What appalling taste! We have far more class.' It probably made her feel good—after all, she lost any wealth or privilege when the title went to her despicable cousin Cedric. She said it so very often, 'We're better,' when, I suppose, we were really just the same as everyone else." She gave a little sniff as the realization struck her that Aunt Augusta, who had always loomed so large in her life, was just what Betty had said, a bitter old woman clutching hold of past glory.

"Why did Betty dislike her so much?" Mr. Norris asked.

"When Betty was nine, Aunt Augusta came to live with us as she had to move out of her house—she'd always lived beyond her means, of course, and could never cut corners. Dickie complained that she turned over our whole world with her rules and judgments, but it was what I was used to, I suppose, so I didn't see it."

"What did Betty say?"

"She said that Aunt Augusta had tormented her with her staunch rules." Mrs. Braithwaite grimaced. "And she said that I perpetuated her outdated standards."

"I'm sure you didn't."

"Well, that's just it." She sighed. "Perhaps I did. Aunt Augusta was all I knew. It never crossed my mind that she could be wrong. She died shortly before Betty moved to London. She'd always spoken of death as if it were a plight suffered only by the poor. She was so adamant she'd never succumb to such baseness that it was a shock when she finally did."

They were coming to Clapham Common, South London in front of them. The full moon spread light over the rooftops, striking the telephone box and pub with a silvery glow.

Suddenly Mrs. Braithwaite drew to a halt. "Goodness! I forgot to tell you about the telephone box. That one, outside the Pendulum. After Baxter came out of his house, he went into the telephone box and made a call. But as he left, I saw him wipe his hand on the door. It seemed odd to me, but maybe he was leaving a signal?" She suddenly caught her breath. "You don't think he could have left something in the telephone box, do you?"

"Well, I'm not sure—"

"But it's just the place, don't you see?" She looked at him, an excited glint back in her eye. "It's a drop!"

"What exactly is a drop?"

She was pulling his arm, turning him back toward the old pub. "It's a place where a spy leaves something for another spy to collect. A kind of secret conveyance system. You see them all the time in murder mysteries—I knew all that reading would come in useful one of these days. He must have marked the door to tell his colleague that he's left something there. We have to go and see!"

He hesitated. "But will it get us anywhere?"

"We have to," she said determinedly. "Even more now that we know what Betty's embroiled in." She took a deep breath. "I may have been a neglectful mother in the past, but it's time to make up for it."

He watched as she stalked away, then she paused, turning around expectantly.

Her eager eyes met his.

With a long sigh, he muttered, "Oh, all right then," and scurried after her, noting a tiny flicker of delight on her face.

## 23.

Unsure where next to look for her mother, Betty decided that first she should report to HQ in Piccadilly. It was protocol, after all. Baxter would have to wait.

A bus took her quickly out of Clapham, and she nestled in a corner seat in the back, hoping that the ticket inspector wouldn't pester her.

The bus's movement made her tired. The world outside blurred and faded as her eyes closed.

But she couldn't sleep.

Her mind restlessly mulled over the danger her mother must be in.

"They've taken her to one of their other hide-outs," Betty muttered to herself. "They must have moved her quickly to stop me from coming back to rescue her."

But where? And what did they mean to do?

Her mother didn't have secret information—or none that Betty considered valuable—so there was no point in torturing her. In fact, there was very little point in keeping her captive at all.

Unless they were intending to use her as bait.

"They know I'll come to get her, and they'll be ready and waiting."

But what would they do to her mother in the meantime? She'd seen their faces, so they'd never let her go.

The vicious thud of reality dawned on her.

If Betty didn't show up quickly, they'd most probably kill her.

As the bus jolted and jostled her, she sat there, her eyes closed, first one and then another tear slipping down her cheek.

She'd almost always had an ambivalent relationship with her mother. When she was little, it had been warm, if rather traditional, but as she grew older, the temperature seemed to drop. By the time she'd left for the war, it had plunged into freezing.

The whole situation had not been helped when Aunt Augusta had come to live with them. Betty had loathed the old witch. She was manipulative, self-serving, and spiteful.

"You need to be tough, or else you'll be a laughingstock," Aunt Augusta was always bellowing at her mother. "The riffraff of the village will walk all over you if you let them." Or sometimes, "Where's your family loyalty? You will be trampling our family name in the dirt. Do you want to live with **that** on your conscience?"

Aunt Augusta had Mrs. Braithwaite caught up in her moral strictures. Betty had been trapped by them, too, if she was honest, until she'd left home for London. She recalled how she'd played Aunt Augusta in a classroom exercise at the start of her training with MI5. When Betty found herself parroting, "Women of our status should never stoop so low as to converse with a child," she realized how much influence the sharp-lipped old lady had had over their household. Her Victorian priggishness and outright snobbery had smothered Mrs. Braithwaite's life with aggression, haughtiness, and appallingly misplaced pride.

After the class, Betty had gone for a walk, gazing at the architecture, quietly unpeeling the unwanted influences of the woman from her mind. The class instructor had told them, "To understand how people are manipulating you is halfway to ridding yourself of their power." These words reverberated around her head until she'd exorcised Aunt Augusta for good.

As she sat on the bus, Betty felt that her mother had, at last, begun to reassess Aunt Augusta and her malice. It was a shame it hadn't happened earlier.

Betty had always been fonder of her father—perhaps it was because she took after him. She had his brain and looked a little like him, too, with her light brown hair and hazel eyes. The narrowness of her features stood in complete contrast to Mrs. Braithwaite's squareness. While her mother was more physically imposing, Betty was mentally dominant, silently standing back, shrouding herself in the superiority of her sharp mind.

Her father had been her inspiration and joy. Even though he'd only been a manager in a food company, in his heart he was a scientist. When she was a child he'd fascinated her with his understanding of the stars and planets, the secret lives of animals, the way that every river meanders down to the sea. She'd relished those days. They'd go to the beach, and he'd explain how dunes are formed, or those little ripples of sand that wriggle along parallel to the sea, like tunnels beneath the surface furrowed by some extinct sea creature. He was enthralled by waves—they both were—so they watched the mechanics and tried to create a formula to explain it all, to measure it.

To him, everything had a purpose, an equilibrium.

And as she sat on the bus, her head now resting against the window, she knew that he had been wrong.

Equilibrium was a myth.

The world was a frenzy of chaos and opportunism.

**Perhaps he'd known that all along.**

Perhaps he'd created chaos in his world in order to seize the opportunities that came out of it.

She'd looked up to him, idolized him even. It had hurt when he stopped visiting her so often; the monthly dinners after the divorce quickly fell away. One of the reasons why she'd been so keen to join MI5, to make a mark on the world, was to make him proud—or was it just to make him **see** her?

Betty didn't even know where he was now.

And today, when she had been trapped in that basement, it was her mother who had come to find her. Whatever it was that had come between them, Mrs. Braithwaite had never given up on her.

And today she had come to save her.

"Are you all right, duck?" An older woman sitting beside her passed over a handkerchief.

Betty sat up, taking the handkerchief with a sniff and a small smile.

"Thank you. It's nothing really."

The woman reached out a hand and put it on hers. "Don't worry, love. We all need a good cry every so often, and then you'll sort it out. You'll see."

## 24.

The Pendulum was busy, men standing outside smoking cigarettes, shouting and laughing, getting ready for a night of looting. Mrs. Braithwaite glanced over to Baxter's house. It was silent, empty looking.

"Let's go and have a look," she whispered, pausing briefly behind the unruly bush before tottering to the window to peek inside. "The blackout curtains aren't drawn."

The first thing she noticed was that the photograph of the pretty brunette had gone. Another look told her that everything had gone. The place had been cleared.

They both looked at each other.

"He's left."

Mr. Norris frowned. "It's a bit of a coincidence, isn't it?"

"What? That he clears out the day that I get kidnapped?"

"I wonder what this means."

"Let's go and ask if anyone's seen him in the pub."

Mrs. Braithwaite headed into the Pendulum, Mr. Norris following timidly behind.

"They'll know where Baxter is, I'm sure of it," she muttered to herself, gripping her handbag tightly in a thick ball of fist.

The Pendulum was heaving. The war meant good business both for the pub and the crooks who frequented it, especially on nights with a full moon. Heavy air raids gave them a chance to rob and loot while everyone else was too busy to notice.

Eyeing another payday, Bobby Mack recognized Mrs. Braithwaite and came over.

"Back for more information, duchess?" He peered at her handbag.

"I'm still looking for my daughter." Mrs. Braithwaite smiled politely, knowing the man might be of some use. "I don't suppose you know anything about a fascist ring based around here, do you?"

Bobby Mack frowned. "They're around, all right. But we don't know where. They keep out of our way."

"But you must have come across them, in your . . . business?"

"We don't have nothing to do with the likes of

them. Can't trust those nutters, can you? Probably know that we'd do 'em in."

"Surely they're criminals, too, just like you?"

The man looked angry for a moment, and then began laughing. "No, we're **proper** criminals, the decent hardworking ones. We do it for a living, to keep a roof over our heads, food on the table for the little 'uns. The fascists don't know what they're doing, and what's more, they don't know the rules we live by."

"What rules? What on earth do you mean?"

"Last year a few pals got caught by a black-market police raid because the stupid fascists got loose tongues. They're novices, don't know a thing. We wanted to bloody kill 'em." His muscular hands began wringing an invisible neck. "They'll ruin our livelihoods, and then they'll bring in the bloody Nazis to have us all hanged."

"Can't you stop them?"

"They're in hiding, and good at that at least." He tucked his hands under each armpit. "They can be incredibly violent. Ruthless, too. No morals, I'm telling you. Nothing gets in their way." He spat a large globule on the floor next to him, and Mrs. Braithwaite pursed her lips to stop the disgust from showing on her face.

"Have you seen Baxter at all?"

"Baxter? No, but that's not unusual. He comes and goes." He stood watching for a while, then said, "You don't think he's caught up with them fascists, do you?"

"I don't know." She put away her notebook, pulling a pound note out of her handbag.

He waved it away.

"You can have this one on me. In return, you let me know what you find out about this fascist ring. Me and the lads here"—he indicated the thugs waiting behind him—"we'd like words with them."

Unsure whether to thank him or not—a favor for a favor, surely, deserved gratitude, regardless of how unsavory the reasoning behind it—she put the note hastily back in her handbag and said determinedly, "I'll let you know."

He grinned, turning back to his gang of thugs. "You know where to find me, duchess."

## 25.

Outside the Pendulum, Mr. Norris stood in the cool darkness as Mrs. Braithwaite came up beside him and flashed her torch onto the red telephone box on the grassy verge of the common. "Let's have a look, shall we?" she said. "You go inside, and I'll check the outside, where he smeared his hand."

Slipping inside, he began to run his fingers over and under the telephone, the shelf, the inside of the door. Nothing. He felt exhausted, as if he were failing her. Last year at work, the more complicated accounts he handled had been reassigned. It was explained to him that those jobs needed a special kind of training, a special kind of mind. He'd handed them over, and a younger colleague, Jontry, a man who appeared to have neither special training nor a special mind, had taken them away into a special office, wearing the smug smile of a victor.

Mr. Norris hadn't been able to fully trust himself with anything ever since. There had to be a reason why his work had been passed along to someone else. Didn't there?

He shrugged at Mrs. Braithwaite through the glass. **Nothing.**

She yanked the door open.

"I found a smear of chalk on the door. It's a marker. There must be something here."

"Someone might have already come to pick it up?" he suggested. "It might help if we know what we're looking for."

"What would you leave if you were a spy? A note with a secret message? Something useful, like a pistol or a flick-knife." She closed the door on him again, saying, "Use your head, Mr. Norris."

He flashed his torch on the ceiling, putting his arm up and standing on tiptoes to check a dark shadow on one side. It was dirt. He took out his handkerchief to wipe his fingers, and then he spotted something.

It was right at the corner where the door met the floor. He pushed the door open a little and put his fingers down to feel. There was something wedged under the floor mat. He tucked his hand in and brought out a small black booklet, old and tattered, but intact. And as he turned it over in his hand, he realized with a gasp that it was a British passport. He opened it quickly to see the name.

Elizabeth Braithwaite.

He pushed the door open. "Quick, Mrs. Braithwaite. I've found something."

"What is it?" She huffed around from the other side of the telephone box.

"A passport in the name of—Elizabeth Braithwaite?"

She put her hand to her mouth in horror. "That's Betty's name."

Snatching it away from him, she opened the passport to look at the photograph. But it wasn't a picture of Betty at all.

It was the pretty brunette from the frame in Baxter's house.

Mrs. Braithwaite let out a small cry. "What's going on?"

"They must be giving this brunette woman Betty's identity. Sending her to another country, perhaps." Mr. Norris was trying to stay calm, but the sense that everything was flying away from them was overwhelming.

"Who **is** Betty?" Mrs. Braithwaite cried. "What could she possibly be involved in that some brunette is stealing her identity? And why is it Baxter—the man who is supposed to love her—who is giving it away? What did I tell you, Mr. Norris! I knew he wasn't to be trusted."

"What exactly did Betty tell you about what she was doing?"

"She told me she couldn't tell me. She said that it was highly secret government work," she exclaimed hotly. "To be frank, she was more than a little peeved that I was interfering in the first place."

"Well, if that's the case, then she must be a spy, and a good one. Baxter must be working with her after all," Mr. Norris said uneasily.

Mrs. Braithwaite's eyes opened wide with a sudden realization. "Could they be infiltrating the BUF?"

Mr. Norris's forehead crinkled in contemplation. "The thought has crossed my mind, too. That would explain why Baxter looks like a common lout but speaks with an upper-class accent. And why he appears to be giving away Betty's passport. But they must be onto Betty's real identity if they imprisoned her."

"Precisely, Mr. Norris."

"But who are these people? That thug who was holding you—he's not the ringleader, is he?"

"There's only one way to find out. We'll have to stand guard and watch the telephone box until someone comes to pick up the passport." She shoved it at Mr. Norris. "Quickly, put this back where you found it."

Mr. Norris bent down and pushed the passport beneath the flooring, letting the door close as they strode back to the pub.

"If we're going to set up a watch, we need to be well away from Baxter's house." She swerved past the pub to the small row of shops on the left, a newsagent, a grocer, and a tiny curiosity shop. Mr. Norris knew it well from his elephant-hunting days: the cramped interior with its stale smell of must and mildew, the monstrous stuffed creatures guarding the place from the inside, the off-key jangle of the misshapen old bell on the door when a customer walked in. The shopkeeper had been gnarled like a spindly old yew tree, continually amused by some private joke.

They perched on the doorstep of the curiosity shop, where they had a good view of the telephone box, the shape vanishing in and out as clouds of varying density passed innocently in front of the moon. It had begun to rain, on and off, and the step was wet and hard. Mr. Norris began to think about his bed, the things he had to do in the morning.

"Do we really have to stay here all night?" he asked.

She looked aghast. "Most certainly we do. Otherwise how will we know who picks up the passport?"

"But it might be days."

"With Baxter cleared off, it might be our only lead. In any case, if he left it there this morning, then someone ought to come and pick it up soon.

They can't leave it hanging around in a telephone box forever."

Almost as soon as she spoke, a thickset young man came out of the pub, stumbled to the telephone box, digging his hand deep into his trouser pocket to find change. Picking up the receiver, he made a call. And then he left, stumbling out.

But then he turned around, facing the door, looking down.

"He's looking for the chalk," Mrs. Braithwaite whispered furiously. "We've found our man."

But Mr. Norris realized what precisely he was doing.

"He's relieving himself."

**"What?"** Mrs. Braithwaite said in a huff, standing up to get a better view. "How dare he . . . he"— she groped for the right word—"**urinate** on a public telephone box!"

"I hope he didn't dampen the passport," Mr. Norris chortled.

"I've a good mind to have words with him," Mrs. Braithwaite said, making ready to intercept him as he went back to the pub, but Mr. Norris pulled her down.

"We need to stay hidden."

They sat in silence for a few minutes, and then Mrs. Braithwaite said, "My husband used to urinate outside sometimes. When we were in the countryside, up against a tree, like a dog. Men are like animals sometimes."

"We're **all** like animals, **all** of the time."

"How can you say that?"

"We're high-thinking animals, but animals nonetheless. Everything we do in this world is designed to keep us alive longer, and to help our families and communities survive."

"Then tell me, why do you think people do vile things, become fascists and so forth?"

"I suppose they think it will benefit them in the long run, keep them alive," Mr. Norris said meekly. "I've only known a few, although they seemed very abundant several years ago if one believes everything one reads in the newspapers. There was a man at the bank where I work who used to boast that he was a personal friend of Oswald Mosley's, who was the head of the BUF before it was banned. Obviously, I steered clear of him, even then. He was a minor aristocrat, and fascism was all the rage among the lords and dukes during the 1930s."

"How ghastly! Anyone else?"

He heaved a sigh. "There was a vile young man by the name of Glover—I shared quarters with him at Cambridge. Before I arrived, he had already taken the better bed, chair, locker, and wardrobe. He had the desk beside the window, while I had the one beside the door, a door he used every five minutes while I was trying to study. He took it upon himself to unburden me of any of my worldly goods that he, Glover, felt could be put to better use: my pens, books, and a rather nice necktie I had bought in London. He also put me down whenever the opportunity presented itself, which occurred with ever-increasing frequency."

"I hope you gave him a piece of your mind!"

"I didn't. You see, I understood that Glover felt beleaguered by his position in life. He came from a poor family, a wealthy uncle paying for his education. I think that's why he became a fascist. He was always bitter about class. He tried the communists first, and then when they didn't work out, he went for the fascists."

Mrs. Braithwaite was aghast. "How did you deal with him?"

"Well, instead of arguing back at him, which would have caused me a lot of private grief, I decided that I would turn the other cheek. Try to help him." He shrugged. "If Glover felt better about himself by belittling me, perhaps at some point he would reach a state of balance, thank me, and go on to live a normal, even-keeled life."

"Except that didn't happen, did it?"

"No. The more I gave Glover, the more Glover took, and the more Glover took, the less Glover seemed to like or respect me." He sighed. "I wanted to turn him into a happy human being, but instead I created a bully. A man who tormented me."

Mrs. Braithwaite's frown dug down into her chin with vehemence. "How could you have lived like that?"

He looked at his hands. "Every night, I'd turn

my back to him and dream of something else. You see, Mrs. Braithwaite, there is always a different place—a different reality—into which you can slip whenever you choose." A lightness came over him as he remembered Enid Tuffington, his favorite memory playing over and over again as she danced down to the river that bright afternoon. In this other world, he could be happy, alive, and free, as they darted through fresh green pastures, the smell of lush grass mixing with the perfumes of wildflowers: purple foxgloves, red poppies, and buttercups.

When they reached the water, her eyes met his, and for that one fleeting yet somehow everlasting moment, he could see right inside his own soul, and then, as he tried to grasp hold of it—of her— she began to fade out of sight.

It was always the same moment when he was snapped back to reality.

"What utter nonsense, Mr. Norris!" Mrs. Braithwaite's sharp voice brought him back with a jerk, as did his bony behind going numb on the stone step. "Reality is far superior to any dream." Then she softened and said more gently, "Don't you want to see things, experience them? Feel those sensations that well up inside you, the fear, the surprise, the elation of being alive?"

Mr. Norris was about to answer, but someone was coming.

"Shh!" Mrs. Braithwaite nudged him to be quiet.

A woman wearing a black hooded cloak was approaching the telephone box, stealthily, cautiously, glancing around.

"Maybe it's the brunette, come to collect her passport." Mr. Norris tried to make out her hair, but the hood was pulled down too far.

"Look! She's going in," Mrs. Braithwaite said, her voice more excited.

The figure began speaking on the telephone, hunched, her back to them. It was impossible to see her face.

After a few minutes, the woman put the receiver down and slowly came out.

They waited as she dropped something and then stooped to pick it up from the floor.

"She's going to take it!" Mrs. Braithwaite whispered.

And just like that, her slim white hand slipped out and whisked the passport swiftly into the cloak.

Mrs. Braithwaite's hand clasped Mr. Norris's wrist.

"She's our man."

And with that, the woman made her way back down the road toward Wandsworth Common. Keeping a safe distance, the pair of them followed, hiding behind bushes and in people's front gardens, in pursuit of the slim, dark figure hurrying through the rain.

At the bottom of the road, she turned toward Shilling Lane.

"She must live close to us. That's helpful," Mr. Norris whispered.

But then they watched with utter astonishment as the woman turned into the path to Mr. Norris's house, took out some keys, and opened the door.

Within a moment, she'd vanished inside.

## 26.

Betty's heart leaped a little as she got off the
bus and trotted down the dark back street
off Piccadilly. The familiar old movie theater lay
ahead, a TO LET sign propped outside as a form of
camouflage.

The headquarters of MI5, one of the most prestigious spying agencies in the world, had moved
there early in the war after being bombed out of its
existing quarters, and now it nestled safely into its
new disguise.

The back entrance was the usual way in, and
Betty slipped inside quietly, as all operatives were
instructed to do. The place was alive and throng-
ing, even though it was already late. Espionage was

a convoluted game: you had to be on top of it at all times.

The first time she'd been inside MI5 was when she and another girl from her grammar school were offered jobs as filing clerks there in the summer of 1939 when war looked unavoidable. It was a terrific privilege to be asked. Even as clerks, their roles were hush-hush, and they were given false employment records at the sewage works. People learned not to ask too many questions during the war.

In any case, MI5 had bigger plans for Betty. After only a short time as a clerk, her true skills came to light: quick thinking and a knack for deception combined with a tenacity for getting to the heart of the matter. She was reassigned.

"Your clerical work is flawless, Miss Braithwaite," her boss told her. "But we've been told to keep our eyes open for girls who can think on their feet."

He gave her a knowing smile and a letter explaining where she should report, which she took with excitement, fear, and a strange kind of pride that at last her quiet talents had been recognized. After all those years, her brightness hadn't just been a figment of her imagination: she was sharp and much needed by a government at war.

After a few examinations, both intellectual and physical, she passed into basic training, which was a testing ground in itself. Sitting in a classroom, she was taught how to think like a spy: how to disguise herself and her actions, how to lie effectively, how to move around without being followed, and how to follow without being seen. More courses followed: wireless transmission, code making and breaking, and carrying messages, money, and microfilm about her person.

Her training made it clear that romance was off-limits, only to be used in an espionage capacity. One of Betty's classroom lessons involved "techniques for gaining trust," an eyebrow raiser if ever there was one, especially for a naive girl like Betty.

Then they sent her for special training in Scotland. It wasn't a commando course. They didn't want an operative to look like a soldier, but more of a fit civilian who could walk for days in stealth, sleep rough, live off the land, use an array of firearms, and disarm the enemy—or kill if necessary. Lessons in burglary, forgery, and the art of deception taught her how to establish and maintain a cover, as well as to spot someone else's.

The men in charge always liked Betty. Not only did she perform splendidly—she would stop at nothing to root out the enemy—but she looked so terribly normal, with her plain face and light brown hair. No one would ever suspect her.

Back in London, she was given a final interview by the man who was to be her boss. He had sole discretion as to whether or not she was accepted. For Betty, this was the biggest challenge of all. Mr. Cummerbatch was known to be an old hand who could sniff out vulnerability from another room.

A large man who enjoyed his food, Mr. Cummerbatch was sixty years old, with a full head of gray hair. He had a pipe tucked into one hand and a glass of scotch in the other, but Betty knew not to underestimate him.

"Why do you want to be a spy, Braithwaite?" He smiled, leaning back in a familiar way, as if she were a niece or a family friend.

"I know that I can do it. I'm desperate to help keep the Nazis out," she said eagerly. "I know it's a risky job, but I'm happy to give my life for my country."

He looked at her above his glasses. "You're not too emotional, are you? Worried about boyfriends and so forth?"

"No. You see, sir, I don't have a husband or children, anyone who needs me."

Glancing down at her forms, he said, "You don't have a next of kin? What happened to your parents?"

"I'm not close to them, sir. Neither of them cares much about me, so I shouldn't let that worry you."

"But doesn't it worry **you**?" His eyes narrowed questioningly as he watched her.

"I'm fine on my own, sir." She straightened herself in her chair. "And I promise to make the best operative you've ever had."

She watched him for another heart-stopping minute, before he finally said, "All right, let's give you a chance, shall we?"

A thrill of excitement had burst through her. Never before had she wanted anything so much.

They started her immediately.

Her first operation was a soaring success. She was sent to track a mobile wireless operator sending tactical massages to Germany. The transmissions led Betty to some possible addresses in Kensington, and she'd followed a number of individuals before narrowing it down to one, a seemingly innocent woman, Catherine Aldridge, aka Katharina Fischer, who was posing as a Belgian secretary. Katharina's contacts—most of them poisonous Nazi spies passing her messages to transmit to the Reich—met her in cafés, public toilets, and in large department stores. A favorite spot of hers was the Food Hall in Harrods, where a parcel of the best Wiltshire ham might have a coded message tucked between the slices. Every day Betty would wear a different costume, assume a new identity—one day a cleaning lady, the next a librarian—trailing behind to watch and take note.

By the time Katharina was taken into custody, Betty had directed MI5 to fourteen connected spies, all of whom were sent to POW camps or "turned double."

"Good work, Braithwaite," Mr. Cummerbatch told her after the mission. He smiled, but his small eyes scrutinized her in case she had notions of becoming complacent on the back of her success. "I'll have to find something a little more challenging for you next time."

"I'll take that as a compliment," she said rather recklessly, regretting it as soon as she'd said it.

"You're only as good as your last job, Braithwaite."

Her next assignment was to befriend a possible female fifth columnist. There was a room available to rent in the house where she lived in Wandsworth, an ideal situation if ever there was one.

Betty thought she was careful, her disguise and cover flawless.

But then she was caught.

As she stood outside Mr. Cummerbatch's office that evening, she closed her eyes with annoyance. How stupid she'd been to underestimate the enemy.

She knocked on the door.

There was a pause, some small movements, and then a man's voice said, "Come in!"

Utter relief mixed with wary trepidation as she walked into the office.

"Young Braithwaite," he said measuredly. "You live!"

"Well, only just, sir."

"We were a little worried about you for a moment there, Braithwaite. Thinking of sending someone in for you. But evidently you're more than able to get yourself out of these difficulties."

"I have to confess, it was my mother, sir."

"Your mother?" he remarked.

"She came to save me."

He let out a chuckle. "Are you pulling my leg, Braithwaite? I thought you said that she hardly spoke to you."

"Well, yes, sir. It was a little out of character for her. She worked out where I was and came to rescue me. Only then she became trapped with me. But they took me away soon after. I escaped from a delivery van."

"And where, pray tell, is your mother now?"

"That's half the problem, sir. They've moved her to another location."

He looked at her ponderously. "I think you'd better tell me everything from the very beginning."

"It was last Friday evening, at twenty past nine. I was trailing the suspect as she went home. Instead of catching the bus, she descended into the Leicester Square underground station. We took a Northern Line train to Elephant and Castle, and as I followed her up out of the station, a couple of thugs were waiting for me.

"It was a trap. They bundled me into the backseat of a car—I think it was a black Morris, or something like that. The large one—he's called Briggs—held me in the backseat, while the other one drove—he's a vicious shrew of a man, named Marty—so I had no means of escape. Briggs thrust a black balaclava over my head the wrong way around so I couldn't see where I was being taken.

"Once there—I now know that it was the basement beneath that butcher in Clapham—I was dragged from the car, taken down some stairs, and thrown into a dark, empty room, where Briggs tied me tightly to a chair and began to torture me for information."

"What did they want to know?"

She let out a short laugh. "He was such an amateur that he gave it all away. They suspect there's another mole in the group—a more senior one—but have no idea who it is."

Mr. Cummerbatch wrote a few notes in a book in front of him. "What else were they after?"

"They weren't precisely sure who had sent us. I didn't give away a thing."

"Very good. Who did they suspect?"

"Either the police, MI5, or an inside job—a rival fascist group or even the Nazis themselves keeping tabs on how things were progressing. They thought I might have been brought in to investigate Fox, regardless of which organization was behind me."

"That's interesting." He took some more notes.

"Sir, the funny thing is that I can't work out when I was spotted, or by whom. I've started to think it might have been an insider."

"One of us? I don't think so, Braithwaite. Not

many people even know that you're on this operation. Unless it's Baxter."

"No, it can't be him," she said more resolutely than she felt.

"Can't it?" Cummerbatch raised an eyebrow. Nothing escaped him.

But Betty insisted. "Baxter would have to be impossibly cunning to keep that from me. No, it couldn't be him."

He looked back at his notebook. "You realize that you'll have to go underground for a while, until we get this cleared up. You'll be recognized. On their hit list. We don't want to risk operatives on unnecessary rescue missions."

Her heart sank. Going underground meant keeping away from her home—or at least her small room on Shilling Lane—and staying away from any places where the gang might be looking for her. It would also mean coming off the case.

"I should really stay on the case, sir, because now I know all the members, how they act, what they do—"

"You've blown your cover." Mr. Cummerbatch wasn't smiling. "Go to the countryside for a hill-walking break. I'll give you a train pass to the Cotswolds—or would you prefer the Devonshire coast?"

"But what about my mother? She's trapped, sir."

"I'll send someone else in." He sat up straight and wrote something down. "She will be fine. After all, she was only taken this afternoon, and they won't do anything drastic for at least a few days, hoping that you'll come in search of her." He glanced up from his writing. "Perhaps Baxter knows where they'll have taken her."

"I could go to see him," she said, perhaps a little too quickly.

He looked at her severely from beneath his brow. "Braithwaite, I know that you and Baxter are romantically attached, and that, my dear, is a big MI5 no-no."

"I understand," she replied quietly, feeling herself flush from top to bottom.

"I would ask that you stop. Immediately."

"Yes, of course."

"This is a very serious matter, Braithwaite. I won't take it to a higher level. If I did, the pair of you would be thrown out of MI5 and I'd be left without two of my best agents." He sighed heavily, and she suddenly realized how much pressure he must be under. "Don't mess this up, Braithwaite. Not for you, MI5, or the country. We need Baxter, and we can't risk you tarnishing him with your own errors. Your cover is broken; don't break his."

Taking a big gulp, she tried her utmost not to cry, but tears were welling up regardless. "I didn't mean to break my cover—I thought I had been flawless."

Mr. Cummerbatch looked over at her, calmly measured.

"Mistakes happen to us all. But it's how you pull yourself back up that defines you, Braithwaite."

She dried her eyes quickly. "I'll do the best I can, sir."

"Now, I want you to vanish for at least a week, after which report to me back here. I have a potential mission for you in Scotland, which will get you safely away from London for a while."

"Yes, sir," she said, trying not to betray her frustration. Scotland was five hundred miles away. "Although, sir, I would prefer to stay here in London, where the action is."

He shook his head slowly. "You have to realize that it isn't possible for a while."

"I can wear a disguise."

"It's standard procedure to change locations, Braithwaite. You know that. Or have you forgotten all the protocol?" he added ironically.

"No," she stammered. "I'm sorry, sir."

"In any case, you need some sleep. Stay in the Bloomsbury boardinghouse tonight, and then take yourself off for a long rest in Devon. A lack of proper sleep leads to—"

"Poor decisions," she mumbled. That fact had been drummed into them at training.

He drew his lips together in a smile of sorts. "Well, that'll do, Braithwaite. Pick up what you need from Supplies. I'll make sure you get that ticket to Devon, and I will see you back in a week."

He got up and walked to the door with her, opening it.

"Good-bye, Braithwaite."

"Good-bye, sir."

"Be careful out there," he said as she stepped into the corridor. "Remember: they know your face."

## 27

Mr. Norris hadn't known anything about the girls until they'd arrived. The jovial billeting officer, notorious for her ability to persuade people to house war workers, had assured him that they were decent, quiet types who wouldn't put him to any trouble.

**Well, that was wishful thinking**, he reflected as he and Mrs. Braithwaite crept carefully through the front door into the hallway. The three of them **had** put him to trouble, even before this sudden foray into fascism.

Florrie, although friendly, was always coming and going, ruffling Mr. Norris's calm routine in her wake, her countless colored scarves continually knocking over his elephants and throwing pictures off balance. Her bedroom could only be likened to the exploded wardrobe of a circus performer, brightly colored hats and shoes and coats and skirts strewn everywhere. He'd tried to explain to her how he liked the household to run, and she'd nodded enthusiastically, yet seemed completely unable to reform herself.

Mr. Norris had thought of Betty as the serious one. She was always in the sitting room, listening to the news intently, as if absorbing the information would keep her alive. She was far from a child, quite adult in many ways, and even though she went to parties and so forth, he could see there was something more inside of her, as if she were analyzing everything and everyone, in a perpetual search for truth.

He'd enjoyed her company and had wondered what kind of childhood she'd had, whether she'd been ignored, chastised in the way he was. Meeting Mrs. Braithwaite and hearing about Aunt Augusta had begun to answer those questions. One thing was for sure, though. Mrs. Braithwaite, despite her overbearing, scolding nature, would never be cruel. He could see that, at least. Perhaps once Betty was found—once he saw them together—his outstanding queries would fall into place.

Meanwhile, Cassandra was disconcertingly aloof, cold to the point of arctic. Although, one night soon after her arrival, he was certain he'd heard the muffled sound of sobs coming from her room. He couldn't help but wonder what had upset her, but he worried about asking. With all the bad news from the war, people were being encouraged to keep cheery, the notion being that an unstoppable flow of weeping would turn the fighting spirit of the country into a spiral of turmoil and surrender. But that night, as he crept downstairs from his attic room and hovered outside her door, he wondered if it might be better if she talked about it. Pent-up sadness and horrors could, he felt, rapidly turn a person from good to bad. He knew only too well how contagious anger could be: his father's rage had besieged his family, each of them, in turn, converting it into a horror of their own: his mother's despair, his sister's spite, and his own abject fear. And some of that fear had then kept him from intruding on Cassandra's sadness.

In the hallway, right there on the hat stand, was the black hooded cloak, still wet from the rain.

That meant, with Betty missing, the mysterious woman who took the passport from the telephone box was either Florrie or Cassandra.

Mrs. Braithwaite threw Mr. Norris a knowing look and indicated with wide mouthing and profuse hand movements that she would check downstairs while Mr. Norris should go upstairs.

Tiptoeing up, Mr. Norris could definitely hear noises, and a tuneless voice was singing "Kiss Me Goodnight, Sergeant Major."

Naturally, he went to Cassandra's door first. His long-held suspicions that she wasn't all that she seemed were coming to a head: all her late nights out, the thick makeup almost like a disguise, the very insularity of her.

Listening at her door, he heard nothing, and just as he lowered his eye to the keyhole, the door swung open and there she was, frowning at him indignantly.

"I didn't realize that taking a room here would involve being spied upon by the landlord," she sniped tersely.

"Oh, I'm most awfully sorry," Mr. Norris said, standing upright and brushing himself down with nervousness.

**What was he to say?**

"My newspaper is missing, and I wondered if you'd borrowed it," he stammered anxiously.

"No, of course not." She frowned at him as if deliberating about whether he was deranged. "I've only just got in."

"Oh, that must be your cloak beside the door then, the one wet with rain? I wonder if I could ask you to move it to your bedroom as it's making the rest of the coats damp."

Cassandra rolled her eyes and swiftly moved past him, briskly trotting down the stairs in her high heels.

"Well, this isn't mine," she said, picking the cloak up in her hand. "It must belong to Florrie." With that, she turned and stalked back upstairs, shutting the door hard behind her.

Florrie was equally unhelpful.

"It **is** mine, but I wasn't wearing it." She let out a little laugh. "Cassandra must be your culprit. She's always borrowing my things without asking."

"So, where's the coat that **you** were wearing?" Mrs. Braithwaite had been lurking by the sitting room door and came stalking out to challenge her.

"It's under here," she said, briskly lifting the cloak to reveal a smaller dark blue coat that had been tucked underneath.

Mr. Norris felt the material. It, too, was damp.

"Oh well, it must have been Cassandra then," he said, making his way back up the stairs.

He was stalling outside her door when the slow wail of the air-raid siren started up, and he stepped away just in time for Cassandra to swing out of her room and head downstairs.

As she went, she pulled on a tan raincoat, still dark across the shoulders from an earlier excursion. Without a word, she hurried out into the gloom, the front door slamming behind her.

Mr. Norris motioned to Mrs. Braithwaite to go to the kitchen for a conference, carefully closing the door behind him.

"They both have wet coats, neither of which is the cloak," he whispered as they stood beside the table. "Short of searching their rooms to find the passport, I don't know how we can find out."

"And the culprit would either keep the passport on her person or quickly pass it on to someone else." She plumped down onto a chair. "How confounding!"

"We should get underground. If we hurry, we'll get a space in the church crypt—it's a lot more civilized than the public shelter," Mr. Norris suggested. "Maybe one of the girls went there, too; I've seen both of them there from time to time. You get your things, and I'll get some blankets."

And with that, they both went into action, readying themselves for a night in the crypt.

## 28.

After her meeting with Cummerbatch, Betty had gone to Supplies, a maze of a room in the basement. Cupboards and boxes spilled over with used clothes. Shelves housed books, maps, foreign dictionaries. Chests were labeled CAMERAS AND BINOCULARS, HIDDEN WEAPONS—SMALL, or BUGS. There was no one around apart from a young man with spectacles checking inventory against a list at the main desk, so Betty took her time.

Sorting through the array of secondhand clothes, she picked out a raincoat and some dresses and then focused on items that might disguise her well: hats and scarves, a pair of glasses, a dark blue uniform that looked as if it might have belonged to a member of the Women's Royal Navy Service. Then she gathered up maps and torches, as well as a number of other useful items: a brooch with a small compass hidden inside, a slim four-inch dagger that could be concealed in the lapel of a coat, and a handy little device for picking locks.

On her way out, the man at the desk passed her a rail ticket for Devon along with some money "from Cummerbatch." She took it uneasily and slipped it into her bag.

**Was she truly prepared to go to Devon?**

She walked wearily to the boardinghouse. It was the same one she'd stayed in when she'd first arrived in London, an MI5 women's hostel in a large Tavistock Square Georgian terrace. Inside, winding staircases and passages led to small single and double rooms with enough wardrobe and drawer space for girls who packed sparingly.

The room she'd been assigned was a single one, and the memory of her first week in MI5 made her laugh at her utterly naive enthusiasm. How meticulously she'd tidied her belongings as if being watched at all times. How carefully she'd set two alarm clocks so as not to be late. How restlessly she'd lain awake, worrying that she'd make a small mistake and be sent home, humiliation and failure crushing her.

She'd known the clerical job could be the beginning of something else. She'd felt it in her bones. This was her one opportunity. She couldn't blow it.

Two years later, and here she was, a hardened

MI5 agent, half starved and exhausted from being captured and tortured. The unseemly innards of a country at war were far, far worse than she'd ever imagined back then.

And yet she was filled with a wave of pride that she'd made it this far, quickly followed by a surge of conviction that she was capable of anything they put in front of her.

**So why were they sending her to Devon? And then Scotland!**

She hadn't joined MI5 just to sit in a backwater killing time. What about her reputation? Her father had been proud of her when she let on to him that she was doing "something a little bit more special" for the war effort. Hadn't he given her a handshake, as if he finally recognized her as an adult?

"You're a credit to me, Betty," he had said, his eyes glimmering charmingly at her. "I always knew that you would go far."

Yet what about now? She hadn't heard from him in months.

"Maybe Mum was right," she said to herself. "And he just tried to get us to believe he cared when he simply didn't. It doesn't matter how special a job I have, or what I do at all."

He had all the charm, but underneath, despite all of Mrs. Braithwaite's blustering and pomposity, she was the one who had cared.

"It was Mum who came to rescue me, after all."

She thought of her mother, trapped somewhere,

Briggs and Marty harassing her, threatening her, waiting for Mr. Cummerbatch to find an available operative—who knew nothing about the case and would therefore need to be prepared before going out—to send out on a rescue mission.

She glowered at the thought.

"It's no use," she said out loud, with a new determination. "I have to find her."

Betty had been with MI5 long enough to know that the first thing to do in any given situation was to assess the risks, and her big risk at the moment was that she would land herself in trouble with MI5 for disobeying orders and going back out into the field.

The thought made her blood quicken its pace. She got up and covered her hair with a head scarf.

Regardless of the risks, she couldn't just sit back and wait to hear the fate of her mother. She had come to rescue Betty, and Betty had to do likewise.

"If I'm going to find her," she said with determination as she found some clean clothes and began to change, "I need to find the only person who knows where she could be."

Baxter.

Baxter would be aware of the gang's hideouts. He might even know where they'd taken her. She could check each place until she found her.

It would work.

There was, of course, another reason why she wanted to see Baxter. A smile swept briefly across her face as she remembered the way he'd look at her, the musky smell of him, and the softness of his lips, his skin.

Betty had always been a logical, practical sort of girl. "No nonsense" was how they used to describe her at school, and she had liked the sound of that.

So, naturally, it did not sit well with her when she met a man who made her feel somehow **illogi**cal. Right from the first time she met him, she'd experienced a whirl of feelings that sent her completely out of control.

She couldn't wait to see him.

Baxter would have been forced to move house after her mother had followed him. Betty was relieved that they had, many months before, arranged a plan for how to exchange coded messages so that each would always know where the other was.

"The telephone box outside St. Paul's Cathedral," he had said. "It's perfect. Easy to get to, and always open. We can leave a small note in the telephone directory"—he'd paused—"under F for Freud." A smile had played on his lips. He loved these new ideas, different ways of looking at the world. All the books, the ideas, the breaking free of normal thought. Was that why she loved him?

Betty had asked Mr. Norris about Freud when she'd got home that night. He'd given her that gentle smile of his and explained that "Freud believed that our childhood has a big influence on our adult life, making us into the people we are. It's terribly clever, really," he went on, and then proceeded to describe the theory behind it, how the id and the ego lurked behind our every decision. The clock on the mantelpiece had passed midnight before she went up to bed, ideas marauding around her mind, disturbing the dust within the shadowy crevices.

She pulled on her raincoat and ran down the stairs of the boardinghouse. Now that she was set on her course, she could hardly wait to see Baxter.

She was defying Cummerbatch's orders utterly and completely. The train ticket to Devon weighed heavily at the bottom of her bag, and she felt like an errant schoolgirl escaping from detention.

But she didn't care.

It was as if her whole life had come down to this moment.

## 29.

The crypt was packed, and worse, people were singing. Mrs. Braithwaite enjoyed a good sing-song as much as the next person, but their choice of tunes was far from tasteful. "Roll Out the Barrel" was the first one, but because they ran out of words pretty quickly, they moved on to the delights of "It's a Long Way to Tipperary," which would most certainly make one want to bring Tipperary a little closer should it relieve the necessity to sing about it.

Mr. Norris was busy finding a good spot for them to spend the night, an accomplishment he seemed to pride himself on, as he said to her, "Have no fear, Mrs. Braithwaite, I'll have us settled in no time."

"We've missed all the good spaces beside the wall," she said with a huff.

"We would have had to be here hours ago to get one of those." He sighed, adding, "But it'll be nice and cozy, once we have our beds made up. You'll see!"

They began laying the blankets on the floor at the end of a row, Mr. Norris straightening them out. "If everyone keeps their blankets straight, they can fit in more people," he whispered. "The verger comes around to check. It isn't good to have to turn people away."

Mrs. Braithwaite said nothing. She was silently appalled. The place had the dank smell of death. There were tombs and catacombs on each side. Even below them, she realized with a horrified wail, the great stones on the floor were etched with the worn names of the deceased. The lines of blankets reminded her of lines of graves, the different colors in the half-light like the patchwork of flowers and grass covering the plots.

Death was a subject that Mrs. Braithwaite was not used to considering. Aunt Augusta had spoken of it as if it were a disagreeable event afflicting the lower classes, except of course when Queen Victoria herself passed away, which was more of a case of transcendence.

"But I don't want to sleep on a dead person," Mrs. Braithwaite snapped at Mr. Norris, looking around for a spot that might be free from writing.

He stopped smoothing out the blankets. "I know

it's not ideal, but you must believe me when I tell you that it's far preferable to a public shelter. The stench alone is bound to put one off. Come on, help me with this sheet."

She went back to spreading blankets with him, but a thought nagged her, and when they were finished, she sat mulling it over on their so-called beds.

"Do you think it's immoral to lie on someone's tomb?"

"Not really. I think if they knew, they wouldn't think it so bad. After all, there is a war going on. In any case, we're separated from them by a thick stone. I don't think any skeletons are going to come out to murder you, if that's what you're thinking."

He was laughing gently, taking out a flask and pouring hot tea into two cups.

"I don't like thinking about death," she said.

"Death is inevitable, though," he said, thinking of his college friends who had perished in the last war. "To die early, and in a war, is a double tragedy: first, because you've only just begun to live, and second, because it's evidence that human nature has turned on itself. But when I think of my old colleagues, I realize that death isn't the part of life to fear the most. It is the fear of not living up to our true potential."

"What precisely do you mean?"

"Sometimes, when I think about all the things I've been afraid to do, I remember my friends brimming with excitement as they left for the last war." He recoiled at the thought, and Mrs. Braithwaite was rather startled to see his eyes glossing over. "They had more excitement for life than I ever did, even though they didn't live for long." He looked at his hands.

Mrs. Braithwaite frowned with incomprehension. "That's all well and good, but frankly, I'd rather think about being alive. Life is for the living, and all that."

"Haven't you ever had someone close to you die?"

"My parents died," she said quietly, and then added in her usual way, "But I was very young."

"What happened?" He edged a little closer to her.

"There was an accident at sea—we were on a ship bound for France, and it struck rocks just off the south coast. I was rescued, but I nearly died from pneumonia. I was alone in the hospital for a week before Aunt Augusta claimed me."

"I'm so sorry," Mr. Norris said. "What happened to your parents?"

"They were drowned," she said rather matter-of-factly. Then she added, "They weren't good parents, though, according to Aunt Augusta, so it's probably just as well."

"But—" Mr. Norris gasped. "They were your parents! Didn't you care about them? I sometimes wonder if we need to understand where we came from to feel our way forward. How can you expect a plant to grow if you cut off its roots?"

"It's better not to think about it." She briskly began sweeping unseen dust from her blanket.

"Do you think that, possibly, your aunt, with all the best intentions, told you that you were better off with her than with your real parents so that you felt that you belonged with her more?" Mr. Norris said carefully.

"I have to say, Mr. Norris, that I haven't given it a lot of thought," she snapped. "Thinking is a very overrated pastime, and some of us are far too busy putting the world to rights to be wasting our time over such things."

"But sometimes we need to mull everything over, find out what we really feel, or think, or believe. Sometimes, if you don't think about big things that happen in our lives—people close to you dying and so forth—it gets bottled up inside. One day you might just explode."

"I'll do no such thing, thank you very much!" she retorted, tidying the blanket.

But the conversation seemed to have tipped Mr. Norris into a thoughtful mode, and he said rather philosophically, "When people you care for die, something inside changes, and you become a different person. Some say that you take on a part of them yourself, that everything you loved about them is enveloped within you, that you have a responsibility to keep them alive in your heart, whatever it takes."

Mrs. Braithwaite felt a stir inside her, but if she

let the tiniest amount of daylight into that part of her mind, a flood of memories would play back about that dismal night.

"Aunt Augusta instructed me not to think about it," she snapped, wishing he'd change the subject.

"And have you always done what Aunt Augusta wanted?" he said gently.

Mrs. Braithwaite looked at him thoughtfully. "Yes. I mean, I did. Mostly. Betty said today that her rules were cruel." She closed her eyes as she struggled with a thought. "But Aunt Augusta was the one who lived long enough to bring me up. My parents, well, they left me. Aunt Augusta was good enough to take me in, raise me as her own daughter. That alone shows what an upright person she was."

"But it doesn't necessarily mean that. Perhaps she always wanted a child of her own, and your parents' death conveniently provided her with one?"

"Perhaps you should mind your own business. Aunt Augusta was the first to admit that she'd always wanted a daughter, that I was heaven-sent for her to look after as if I were her own. She gave up everything for me."

"How old were you when your parents died?"

"I was six." She looked at the floor, starting to feel cross. "You see, that's what happens when one begins to think about death. It all gets out of hand."

They drank their tea in silence, until a kerfuffle in the corner of the crypt made them turn to see Cassandra, incongruous with her full makeup and tan coat. She was trying to squeeze a blanket into a small space between two middle-aged women, who were clearly suggesting that there wasn't enough room.

Mr. Norris leaned over. "I told you she'd be here. Let's go and see if we can help," he said, getting up. "Then perhaps we can ask her some questions."

Mrs. Braithwaite raised herself from the ground, hoping that Mr. Norris might turn her way and see that she needed a hand to help her up, but he had gone to see the scene unfolding in the corner, and she was left to wriggle up by herself.

Cassandra was becoming vexed with the older ladies beside her. "There's a silly little man at the door who said that I can't stay unless there's room, and this is the only place that's left."

"There's not enough space here," one of the women said. "You'll have to find another spot."

"Cassandra!" Mr. Norris called over. "Why don't you come and squash in beside us?"

Cassandra turned around, her mouth turning from a smirk as she saw Mr. Norris to a scowl as she registered Mrs. Braithwaite.

"That's very kind, isn't it?" one of the women said, scooping up Cassandra's blanket and shoving it into Mr. Norris's arms.

"The verger's very particular," Mr. Norris explained to Cassandra. "We have to work out what's best for everyone. You don't want to be sent away, do you?" He consulted his wristwatch. "You won't have any luck at this time of night. You'll have no choice but to go to the local shelter."

Cassandra snorted a large breath of stale air. "I'd rather face the bombs than go down there." She picked up her expensive-looking handbag and left her other belongings for Mr. Norris to carry. "I suppose I'll come with you," she said rather impolitely, then remembering herself, she tucked her arm through his and gave him a charming smile, adding, "Thank you for coming to my rescue."

**What about me?** Mrs. Braithwaite thought. **And the space that I'm giving up?**

They made their way back to their blankets, and Mr. Norris began repositioning them to fit Cassandra in the middle.

But as far as Mrs. Braithwaite was concerned, one thing was for certain: Cassandra was not going to be beside her.

"Perhaps Cassandra should go on the other side of you, Mr. Norris," she barked, more an instruction than a request.

"Oh, all right then," he muttered, changing them around again, reorganizing their blankets in the narrow space.

Just as Mrs. Braithwaite was about to suggest that it was simply too tight and Cassandra would have to find another spot, Mr. Norris expressed great thanks to her for generously sharing her space.

"You are a very helpful person, aren't you, Mrs. Braithwaite?"

She smiled weakly. She knew Mr. Norris was being generous: she wasn't quite as helpful as she perhaps would like to be. But maybe she could change, **had** changed.

Cassandra leaned over and smirked as she sat down, her legs curled underneath her, looking like a cat that had got a choice position beside the fire. "Yes, thank you, Mrs. Braithwaite. Perhaps you're not so sour after all."

Then she let out a little tinkle of laughter, and Mrs. Braithwaite didn't quite know whether it was a joke or not.

"I must say that I'm surprised to see you here, Cassandra," she said cuttingly. "You seem to be out every night. Heaven knows what you must be doing!"

"You're right! I usually am," Cassandra replied, not at all taken aback; in fact, she grinned knowingly, proud to be a party girl. "But tonight I went to meet a friend"—she said it in that way that denoted something more than a friend—"only he didn't show up, which is most unlike him. He's passionate about me." But furrows appeared on her beautiful forehead. "I hope nothing horrid has happened to him."

"How awful for you," Mr. Norris said.

"He's a navigator in the RAF, so—"

"Perhaps he changed his mind and decided not to meet you after all," Mrs. Braithwaite said crisply, still dwelling on having been called "sour." Yet it struck her that the girl seemed genuinely upset, that this young man could be more than a passing dalliance, so she added, "For good reason, of course."

"You might be right," Cassandra murmured, almost to herself. And it struck Mrs. Braithwaite that she suddenly looked like a little girl, alone and lost, missing her friend. How odd that she made such an effort to be churlish when inside she was just a human being, like everyone else.

Could **she** be involved with the fascists?

"We're still looking for Betty." Mr. Norris plunged in. "And I wonder, did you know Betty's boyfriend well?"

"Not awfully. I only met him that once when I bumped into them outside the Pendulum. They were in a hurry, and he didn't charm me, although I suspect Betty wanted to quell his excitement after meeting me." She gave a small giggle.

"Why's that?" Mr. Norris asked naively.

"Oh, many women don't like their men being around me for too long." She gave Mr. Norris her smoldering look to prove her point, and he in return dropped his glasses with utter terror. "They might have second thoughts."

"But he didn't fall for you, Betty's young man?" Mrs. Braithwaite asked quickly as Mr. Norris began fumbling with the flask, not knowing quite where to look.

Cassandra looked petulant. "I have to admit that he didn't. Although I wouldn't have thought he was

Betty's type. Wonderful looking, of course, but the clothes! And he smelled to high heaven of something awful."

Mrs. Braithwaite grimaced. "What would you say it was?"

"It was like decay. You know, that pungent smell of off meat."

"Off meat," Mr. Norris mused. "I don't suppose he might have been working in a butcher's shop?"

Cassandra shook her head. "All I know is that he most definitely was not the kind of man I'd be hanging around."

"Lights off now," the verger called gruffly.

Mrs. Braithwaite glanced over at Mr. Norris as Cassandra took off her high-heeled shoes and placed them neatly beside her handbag.

"Do you think it's her?" Mr. Norris mouthed, gesticulating with his head.

She shrugged, leaning over to whisper, "She's putting on a good act if she knows Baxter well. That off-meat scent sounds a little too vile to simply make up."

"Perhaps when she's asleep, you can have a look inside her handbag," Mr. Norris said back.

"Can't you do it?"

"No, I'm a man. What if she wakes up and catches me?" he said, outraged that Mrs. Braithwaite should even suggest it. "At least you could say that you wanted to borrow a handkerchief or something."

People were dimming their torches, and the verger was going around telling people to "be more considerate to others" in a rather ruthless fashion for a member of the clergy.

Cassandra stretched herself out under the blanket, a curt pout of annoyance at being there, and then she closed her eyes as if to ignore everyone else. "I haven't slept for days," she said dramatically.

"Lights out now," the verger called as he himself settled down on blankets spread out in one corner.

"He has more space than the rest of us," Mrs. Braithwaite whispered hoarsely at Mr. Norris. They were by now lying down under their blankets, blackness surrounding them save for the weak, flickering light from a small oil lamp by the verger's bed.

"He can have more space if he chooses. After all, it is his crypt," came the reply.

"Surely it's God's crypt."

"He's the one who's letting us come down here, and I dare say his space isn't bigger than ours."

"It looks like it from here. Maybe I'll pop over and take a look. If it **is** bigger, then—"

"What are you going to do about it?" He propped himself up on his elbow, as did Mrs. Braithwaite. "If you cause any hassle, then he'll ask us to leave. And where will we be then?"

She looked over at Mr. Norris. Now that he'd taken off his glasses, his pale eyes reflected the tiny light from the lantern. He was lying right beside her, a narrow trough between them where his blanket ended and hers began. "But he **is** a man of God," she insisted. "If anything, he should take less space."

Mr. Norris smiled gently at her. "I'm quite happy where we are, Mrs. Braithwaite, and if you are, too, I suggest that we both try to get some sleep. If the bombs come tonight, we'll be kept awake again."

"How can I sleep with Betty on my mind?"

"My dear Mrs. Braithwaite, we both need sleep. Today's been too busy already. Tomorrow we'll know what to do next."

"But will we?"

"I will," he said in a very determined manner for Mr. Norris. "Now let's take advantage of the quiet and get some sleep."

**What quiet?** thought Mrs. Braithwaite as she settled back down and closed her eyes. The echoing crypt was alive with snuffling and snoring, a woman singing softly to a small child, people whispering and turning uncomfortably to have their other side numbed by the stone floor, and in so doing ejecting large, unwieldy groans into the cold, dank air.

Exhaustion overtook her, however, and she nodded off for a while, but the next thing she knew, she was awakened by a series of tremendous crashing sounds, the stone beneath her shuddering.

Sitting up with a start, she remembered where she was: trapped in a crypt, death surrounding her, above and below, everywhere.

People began screaming, then shushing to

suppress their fears. A small child began to cry, but someone quickly calmed him or her down. Shouts quickly turned to whispers.

Hysteria was swiftly subdued.

A woman began to gently sing "We'll Meet Again," and others joined in. Soon a soft, lulling chorus washed over them, calming them down, bringing a feeling of warmth and togetherness.

"Sounds like the bombs are coming from the direction of Clapham," Mr. Norris whispered. "The other way from our house." So typical of him to say "**our** house" rather than "**my** house," thought Mrs. Braithwaite. It was his house, after all, not all of theirs.

"How can you tell?" Mrs. Braithwaite hissed back.

"Oh, you get to work it out after a while. A nuanced ear and a little mathematics."

"Are we safe down here?"

"As safe as any underground shelter. It's deep. The ground above us is solid enough to keep the church from collapsing into us." He gave a little laugh. "Do you think I'd come here if I hadn't worked through all the potential dangers?"

She didn't laugh with him. "I suppose not. Still, it's very unnerving—"

Another loud crump of bombs made the place shudder, the verger's lantern swinging with the vibration.

Mrs. Braithwaite couldn't fight off the feeling of claustrophobia, the walls, the ceiling, the floor even, crowding in on her, crushing her to death. She thought about poor Blanche, how it must feel to have a building collapse on you.

Feeling quite nauseated, she lay back down, shivering with fear, trying to think of something else—anything would do. But all she could think of was death. She thought of Aunt Augusta, laid out before the funeral, her pale steely beauty just as it was when she had been alive. Only now she was lifeless, stopped in her tracks, quieted. Mrs. Braithwaite remembered looking down into her coffin—with mixed feelings, if she'd been honest. Part of her wanted to embrace the lovely lady, now that she was so still and quiet, to feel some kind of warmth from her in her silence. After all, she couldn't intimidate or judge anymore. Mrs. Braithwaite had been aware of fighting back a very disloyal feeling, one of freedom, of taking Aunt Augusta's power for herself. But Aunt Augusta had a rule about loyalty: "It is the greatest and most important quality to have." So Mrs. Braithwaite couldn't betray her, even now that she was dead.

Suddenly a terrific explosion thundered around them, blasting the crypt like a volcanic eruption. A tremendous thud splintered through the room, and screams rang out while the lantern swung, wielding wide shadows across the reverberating space. People everywhere got to their feet.

This time the panic could not be quelled.

With horror, Mrs. Braithwaite saw that half the

ceiling had collapsed on the other side of the room, wavering in and out of sight as the lantern pitched wildly from side to side on its hook. People were trapped beneath the weight of debris; splinters and fractured stones coated everything, and dust hung densely in the air, making it difficult to breathe.

A flustered Mrs. Braithwaite picked herself up quickly, shaking with horror. Her brain was crowded with the chaos, and she couldn't think clearly. Grabbing her handbag, she turned and fled toward the door, tripping over people still on the floor. There were too many people down there. It was too small a space.

Stumbling over something, she fell on top of some people still on the floor, moving beneath her like worms in a bucket. Struggling up, she felt her way to the door.

But the ceiling had collapsed around it. Broken stone and brick jammed it stuck, and as scores of other people began heading for it, she started pushing and shoving to make her way through.

"The door's blocked," a man's voice cried, and a rally of shouts and more pushing began, people trying to get to the door.

"The rubble's in the way. We have to make space to clear it," a woman called shrilly.

But no one took any notice. One person would back out of the mayhem for another to enter in the same place. It was useless.

Suddenly, from a side wall, a chaotic gush of water roared out, rising to a tumultuous surge.

People began frantically picking up blankets and possessions, shouting, "There's water coming in!"

"A bomb must have struck the water mains," a woman yelled, picking up chunks of fractured stone and trying to plug a great jagged hole in the wall.

But then another surge of water appeared, and then a third, a spray coming out of the wall, which crumbled as the spray gained strength.

People began panicking, crying, and shrieking, falling over each other to get from one side of the room to the other. The baby was bawling shrilly at the top of its lungs. Mrs. Braithwaite knew that this, surely, was the moment to step forward.

If anyone knew how to gain control, it was Mrs. Braithwaite.

"Listen, everybody!" she bellowed in her best WVS chairman's voice, clapping her hands smartly together. "We will need to work together. Calm co-operation is what's required."

And then, when no one seemed to respond, she opened her mouth and bellowed as loudly as she could, **"STOP!"**

Everyone turned to look at her.

"I know we all want to get out, but we will have to work together. Everyone at the door, take a step back and allow those closest to clear it so that it can be opened." She watched them doing what she said.

"And where the water's coming in? Another team needs to try to plug it to stop the flow."

She went over and organized them, making sure the children and elderly were standing back as the more able carried over larger chunks of stone.

Suddenly, three smaller holes collapsed into one. A huge heaving jet of water gushed in as if a main water pipe were simply emptying its contents. Immediately the water level on the floor began to rise, and quickly. The wall around the gash started to look precarious, as if it might simply crumble away beneath the surge. The water was now more than a few inches deep, and at this rate it would be a foot or two within minutes.

They had to get out.

Heading to the door, she fought through to the front, only to find that after removing the rubble, the door still wouldn't budge.

"I think it's blocked on the other side," a woman said, trying desperately to keep the panic out of her voice.

"We'll have to break the door open." Mrs. Braithwaite stood in the middle of the room, clapped her hands loudly to get everyone's attention. "We need an axe, or something heavy, to break the door down. Can anyone help?"

For a moment everyone looked around, lost.

Then the woman called out, "These chunks of stone are sharp. Maybe I can sharpen it more by smashing it with another piece of stone."

"Yes, try that." Mrs. Braithwaite went over and held it for her so they could knock it into shape. The problem now was that the water was almost two feet deep, and to break the stone, they had to balance it against the wall, which seemed to give way behind it, crumbling into another fracture of tiny water spouts, coming in from all directions.

"We'll just have to try it as it is," Mrs. Braithwaite said.

A middle-aged man took the stone and began plunging it into the door, which little by little began to shred underneath. In a short while, a hole was forming, and a mound of stone and debris could be seen on the other side.

"Faster," a woman was crying. "We need to go faster."

Another woman started to sing, her high soprano voice wavering in out of the shouts and gushing noises, "Abide with Me." Others joined in, haphazardly as they worked, not ready to give up on life yet.

The water was coming in rapidly, swells whooshing around everyone's legs. Mrs. Braithwaite's tweed skirt was becoming heavy with the weight of water. She felt the pull of it tugging her down.

And then, quite suddenly, everything seemed to slow down.

The whirl of the currents, the people's voices, the faltering song, the relentless tug of her clothes, the water as it crept up her body, around her waist, edging up to consume her in one swift gulp, take her under, carry her away. She remembered her mother, trapped in the ship, pushing her six-year-old self up through the tiny porthole to the man in the lifeboat. Her mother's face, her eyes, were dark and anxious, the smell of her breath sweet and wet like dew; the last kiss on her forehead soft and forgiving, as if condensing a lifetime of love into that one, brief moment. Their hands held across the water, then only their fingers, their fingertips, before they were pulled apart.

The verger's light suddenly went out, darkness overwhelming them. The singing stopped midverse. Shrill screams cried out as people splashed around in the pitch black, as if the end of the world had come, the very end of everything.

The pace of the people battering the door down quickened, thrashing away, desperate to get out.

The water was rising over her waistband, seeping cold into her blouse. It was freezing, and yet something inside her seemed calm, as if it were waiting for death, her mother beckoning to her from the other side. How she'd missed her all these years.

A woman came up to her, shaking Mrs. Braithwaite by the shoulders. She was carrying a little girl on her hip.

"You can't stop now! You have to help my daughter. You have to make sure we get out." She was half crying, trying desperately to hold herself together. "You have to save my little one." She kissed her child's forehead with such tenderness, such feeling, that Mrs. Braithwaite felt her heart quicken.

She snapped back into action. Pulling the woman to the door, she barged through the people to create a pathway. Then, taking a large rock from a man, she stormed as hard as she could toward the door, her momentum and body weight driving the stone right through it. On the other side, she fell through the debris, stumbling to the floor in the previously dry corridor as the water gushed relentlessly in from the broken door behind her.

Spluttering and drenched, she stood up. It was dark, and people were beginning to step through the door behind her, the woman with the little girl first.

"Everyone throw or kick the stones to the side to make it easier for the people behind."

Feeling her way with her feet, she finally reached the stone stairs at the end of the corridor, beckoning the woman with the little girl to follow her up, out of the water.

Drenched and exhausted, they hurried up. At the top of the stairs, she opened the door into the sudden silence of the church.

They drew breath as they came out and looked up, up through the gaping roof, at the stars, twinkling with the pale resonance of certainty and calm.

The church had taken a direct hit. The roof had completely caved in. Half of the heavy stone wall had collapsed into the ground, breaking through the thick stone floor, which had plunged the rugged stones down into the crypt. One of them must have struck the water pipe along the way.

Everyone poured out behind her, and she hurried them along to make way for the others, still trapped down there. Mr. Norris had yet to appear, and the water must be high by now.

"God bless you," the woman with the little girl said as she passed Mrs. Braithwaite. "Thank you with all my heart. You saved my daughter."

Mrs. Braithwaite looked at the child, saved, like she was, from drowning. But she still had her mother, and Mrs. Braithwaite felt tears come to her own eyes as she smoothed the girl's hair back from her face. She said to the woman, "Never let her drift away," and then bent down to kiss the small child on her forehead. "And you have to cherish your mother, my dear."

Setting the child down, the mother took her little hand, and they both stumbled over the rubble to get onto the road. Back to their home, regardless of the bombs.

Mrs. Braithwaite watched as bedraggled people filed up through the church, some thanking her, putting a smile on their faces and trying to reclaim normality, a few traumatized, shivering from cold and fear. They made their sorry ways back to their homes, ready to take on the risk of any new bombers that night just to get warm and dry, to sleep in the cozy familiarity of their own beds.

Funny how almost dying puts a different slant on life, making your bed comfier, your moments more treasured, your family more precious.

Yet Mr. Norris didn't appear. And when she came to think about it, she hadn't seen Cassandra either.

The stream of people coming out was dwindling, and then it stopped.

**Where was he?**

Then, suddenly, out he stumbled, dripping wet, his mouth gaping with horror.

"It's Cassandra! She won't come out." He looked at her, aghast with panic. "She's petrified with fear."

"I'll have to see what's happened to her," she said resolutely and headed back down.

"But it's almost completely underwater down there, Mrs. Braithwaite."

But she was already gone.

The bottom six steps down to the crypt were already underwater, and rushing down into the water-filled corridor, she found herself peering above the last six inches of space. Only the very top of the crypt door showed over the water surface.

There was nothing else for it. She held her breath and pushed away from the wall, half walking, half swimming of sorts underwater despite her heavy clothes pulling her down. Mrs. Braithwaite had never been much of a swimmer, but she batted her arms, pushing herself along with her feet on the bottom as she went through the door and into the deadly crypt.

Once inside, she came up for air. The ceiling of the crypt was higher, with enough space to poke her head and neck up. But the water level was rising fast, and there was no light.

"Cassandra, where are you?" she called into the echoing darkness.

"Who is that?" Cassandra's voice was weak and trembling.

Mrs. Braithwaite made her way over to where the voice came from, feeling in front of her until she touched the arm and shoulder of what was without doubt a person. She took her hand. The skin was deathly cold as Cassandra stood rooted to the spot, the water fast rising around them.

"This is Mrs. Braithwaite. Come on, we have to go," she urged her. "Or else we'll drown."

"I can't," she stammered. "Go without me. I'll be fine here."

"No, you won't!" Mrs. Braithwaite exclaimed. "Now come on!"

She grabbed Cassandra's arm and began tugging her to the door.

But she was immovable.

"I want to stay. I'll just die here. It's meant to be."

"Of course it's not meant to be, girl. Now do hurry!" Mrs. Braithwaite huffed, and then, when she realized that Cassandra wasn't going anywhere, "Why is it meant to be?"

"I'm meant to be with Peter." Her voice was dreamlike, as if she were half dead already.

"Who's Peter?" Mrs. Braithwaite said quickly, desperate to get to the bottom of it and get out. She was already standing on tiptoes to keep her mouth out of the water and knew it wouldn't be long until she had to start holding her breath.

"He's my husband," Cassandra murmured. "He's waiting for me. I know it." She took a deep breath. "He was drowned at Dunkirk. Bombed in a rescue boat. You see, that's why I have to drown, too. It's meant to be."

"Don't be ridiculous, dear," Mrs. Braithwaite said, suddenly calmer. She knew what it was like to lose cherished someones, to feel, deep inside, that you can't go on without them.

She tightened her grip on Cassandra's hand. "My parents were drowned, but I had to fight on for another day, and soon one day becomes another, and then another, and your life becomes a different kind of life, but one that's still worth living. And then, maybe one day, you'll meet someone else who means something to you. It may sound impossible, but you have to believe me, dear. You have to give life another chance." And as she was speaking, she realized that she wasn't just trying to convince Cassandra, but she was also speaking to herself.

**How can you expect a plant to grow if you cut off its roots?**

Cassandra began to cry, huge sobs coming out of her. "But I don't want to."

"You have to," Mrs. Braithwaite urged, the water

beginning to come up into her mouth. "Or we'll both be dead."

"No, you have to leave without me," Cassandra cried with determination. "I can't have your death on my head, too."

Mrs. Braithwaite took a firm grip of her arm and said between her teeth, "In that case, my dear, you'll just have to come with me." And very briskly, she scooped a foot around Cassandra's ankle, tripping her up and pulling her through the swirling water to the door.

"Now, dear, you'll have to hold your breath for this part. Can you do that?"

Cassandra said nothing.

"All right, I'll count to three, then take a big breath, and we'll be off." Mrs. Braithwaite knew that the corridor to the stairs would be completely filled with water. It would have to be a very big breath, one that could take them all the way. She'd have to move fast to get Cassandra through it.

"One, two," she made a small prayer, "three!"

Mrs. Braithwaite took the largest breath she could and plunged her head into the water, heading under the doorway into the corridor, dragging Cassandra behind her by the arm, not even checking to see if she'd taken a deep breath.

Either she'd make it, or she wouldn't. It was as simple as that.

The corridor was long, and Mrs. Braithwaite stumbled along the bottom, one hand balancing herself, pushing against the wall, and the other hand firmly holding Cassandra's arm, pulling for all she was worth.

It was imperative that she reach the stairs quickly, and she stumbled forward as fast as she could.

Suddenly something caught her foot. Was it the step?

She put a foot up, trying to find the next one, almost fainting with relief as she felt its solidity underneath her. Choking with relief, she lifted herself onto the step.

**But what about Cassandra?**

She quickly took more steps up, pulling the girl up behind her. Somebody's arms were reaching down from above to help her, grabbing Cassandra's arm and shoulder.

"I've got her," said a familiar voice. "Go up! I can take her from here."

Hearing a cough and splutter from Cassandra as she crawled out of the water, Mrs. Braithwaite made her way with trembling legs up the final steps and into the church, followed by Mr. Norris holding up Cassandra as she staggered to the top.

An air-raid warden had arrived with torches, and suddenly the place was in light as Mrs. Braithwaite plopped down on a church pew, fighting for breath.

Within moments, a dry, warm blanket was laid around her, and a familiar voice was saying, "Well done, Mrs. Braithwaite! You did it!"

"**We** did it, Mr. Norris." She smiled up at him.

"Thank heavens everyone got out! Is Cassandra all right?"

"She's warming up, along with everyone else. You're a bit of a hero."

"Well, my reign as the leader of the Ashcombe WVS had to have some use, didn't it?"

## 30.

Back at the house, after they'd put on some dry clothes, Mr. Norris put the kettle on and pulled the kitchen chairs up to the oven for extra warmth.

"Cassandra, you never told me you'd been married," Mr. Norris said.

"I thought it would be easier if no one knew. I could just build a new life for myself, then I could forget the old me, and Peter. But it doesn't work like that, does it?" She began to cry, and it all came out, how they'd been madly in love, running through the streets of London, hand in hand, delirious with passion and togetherness. They were inseparable, devoted. Nothing could come between them.

Except death.

"If you have true love and lose it," she sobbed,

"you wither, like a petrified tree. You look the same, but you may as well be dead yourself."

"But you can't try to ignore it, pretend that you're all right," Mrs. Braithwaite said. "Someone I know"—she glanced at Mr. Norris—"told me that you need to cherish those that die. Let them stay alive within you. You can't let someone go just because they die. You need to tell his stories, cherish the time you had together, cry because you miss him, because of course you do." She put her arm around the girl's shoulders.

Cassandra, her blond hair drying in soft tendrils down her long, elegant neck, looked fraught, as if she were letting a manic animal out of a cage. "But it's too large. It'll suffocate me."

"Grief feels a lot like fear," Mr. Norris said gently. "We're afraid of it taking us over. But we owe it to ourselves, to those we have lost, to let grief in. Only then can we start to remember them with a cheer in our heart, a cheer for them and all that they were."

Cassandra burst into tears, turning her face into Mrs. Braithwaite's shoulder.

It was a long night. They stayed at the kitchen table talking about the people they had lost until they were all too tired to keep going. Bedtime beckoned, and after Cassandra left for her room, Mrs. Braithwaite gave Mr. Norris a sorry smile. "Well, we misjudged Cassandra, didn't we?"

"What a sad story. Such a lovely girl, and not at all the vixen we thought her."

"Yes," Mrs. Braithwaite said, adding, "And it obviously wasn't Cassandra who took the passport. She couldn't care less about her handbag—I think it's still down in the crypt."

"So if it wasn't Cassandra," Mr. Norris said, "then it must be Florrie. It's a pity that she's still out. We'll have to confront her in the morning."

"Perhaps we could check her room, while she's away. We might even find the passport. She must have left something incriminating somewhere. She's so forgetful."

"Unless—" Mr. Norris glanced over at her.

"Unless what?"

"Unless that's part of her disguise. Did you ever notice how she drops her handbag every time the conversation becomes a bit awkward?" Mr. Norris said evenly, as if everything were falling into place.

"It's happened twice just with me. How devilish of her!" Mrs. Braithwaite blustered. "She **must** hold some answers. Even if she doesn't know where Betty is, she has to know someone who can tell us."

"How are we going to get her to tell us, though? Torture?"

It was a good point.

"We'll have to go through her room," Mrs. Braithwaite said decisively.

As one, they hurried up the stairs, Mr. Norris fumbling to find his spare key to Florrie's room.

He swung the door open and moved to switch

on the light. But even before he did so, they both could see.

The room was empty.

Mr. Norris briefly pictured Florrie sweeping the contents of her dressing table into an empty case, throwing her shoes on top, cramming the spaces in between with her colorful array of scarves and dresses, perhaps even the ominous black cloak from the hat stand in the hall.

He looked for a note, a forwarding address, a little money to cover her as-yet-unpaid rent for the week. But there was nothing.

"Perhaps I should put the kettle back on," Mr. Norris said thoughtfully. It was the only thing to say, really.

Mrs. Braithwaite silently led the way down to the kitchen.

"Florrie's the only link we have to Betty," Mrs. Braithwaite muttered as she plunked herself down on her usual kitchen chair—she liked the one facing the door, whereas Mr. Norris preferred the one by the window. "Where else can we try? Baxter's moved out, and the basement will have been cleared out. I'm sure that Florrie will have warned the others that we might be onto them."

"Don't fret yet, Mrs. Braithwaite. It's past two now. Let's sleep on it. I'm sure we'll come up with something by morning."

But Mrs. Braithwaite had a gleam in her eye. "What's the date again tomorrow?"

"It's the twenty-eighth." Even as he said it, he knew.

"The BUF meeting in Chiltern Church." Mrs. Braithwaite got to her feet and began pacing the room. "We'll go and find out precisely who is running this group. We can stay somewhere nearby. I'm sure there's a hotel or a pub with a few rooms."

"But if we go to the meeting, they'll know that we're spying on them." His voice was becoming panicky. "Why else would we be there?"

"We could pretend we came to the wrong address, the wrong meeting, or something."

"It's too risky. If anyone recognizes us, we'll be left for dead at a bomb site." Mr. Norris had heard rumors about that. Murders happening all over the country, corpses left in bombed-out buildings, meant to be confused for bombing casualties. Hundreds of vendettas being carried out every night, impossible to prove they'd actually been murdered.

"Don't be melodramatic! No one will suspect a thing. We're a middle-aged couple, if anyone asks, looking for a bridge club."

Mr. Norris stopped, blushing heavily. She'd used the term **couple** so idly. He'd only ever been in a couple when he was with Enid Tuffington. He pursed his lips as a vision of her flashed through his mind.

"No one would ever think that **we** were a couple!" he said aloud, then quickly added, "Not that there's anything wrong with the notion, it's just that we're so very different. Opposites really. Don't you think?"

She chuckled. "Yes, I suppose we are. But we're about the same age. No one would know that we are so very unlike, would they?"

**No one would believe that we're together!** Mr. Norris thought to himself: a stout, bossy, square-jawed woman beside a slim, nervous, thick-spectacled man.

But Mrs. Braithwaite leaned over and patted his hand, grinning. "No one will suspect a thing."

## 31

Betty dashed through the Bloomsbury streets, the noise of aircraft and ack-acks fluctuating in and out as the air raid played on, a backdrop to her own crisis. Prolific fire heated the air around her, and she wiped her forehead of sooty sweat. Ambulances—most of them large old motor cars refitted to take bodies on stretchers—screeched around mounds of debris to get to each new emergency, more than one forced to stop and turn around in a narrow street that had been dead-ended by the night's destruction.

People were everywhere. Air-raid patrollers, heavy crews, and fire watchers roamed the streets, followed by an almost invisible shadow of looters waiting for the coast to be clear before sifting through the remains of someone else's life.

Extraordinary how the entire population of a city could do this every night, and then get up every morning and make the best of themselves—a quick comb of the hair—before going to work, carrying on as usually as they could.

Betty strode briskly through the city, her impatience bolstered by exhaustion and a bitter thirst for justice. She hardly ever bothered going to shelters. None of the special agents did. Their jobs were so dangerous that the chance of a bomb killing them before their work got them seemed negligible.

The raid was especially bad tonight. She wondered where her mother was, whether she was panicking, exhausted, locked up in another fascist hideout, or worse.

She could already be dead.

As she turned onto Fleet Street, the fog of smoke and ash became heavier, clouding the view of the City ahead of her. Bright pillars of light from the search beams glowed with brilliant white-gray billows of smoke.

She began to run toward the City. Around her, building after building lay in ruins. Architectural masterpieces, municipal offices, shops, churches, homes, all that had stood majestically for centuries had been flattened in a matter of moments.

Rushing down Ludgate Hill, she could hardly breathe from the fear:

**Had they got St. Paul's Cathedral?**

The eerie light of the moon—transcendental in its silvery hue—struck the colossal dome with a light so mesmerizing that it looked as if it were a sign to her from God himself. The cathedral was there, majestic, surrounded by clouds of dust, like a leftover behemoth from a previous age, unable to understand the world in which it now stood.

Betty felt it, too. That confusion that all of this shouldn't be happening. Not here, not now. This was a metropolis of beauty and culture, a place where people lived and worked, now transmuted into a bloody theater of war.

Mustering a rage that propelled her on, she searched frantically for the preappointed telephone box, finally spotting it in the shadows of the massive edifice.

Betty ran inside and flicked through the telephone directory to the right page. Folded and eased as far as possible toward the spine, a small edge of paper protruded.

She read the tiny coded note and worked out the address: 45 Rathborne Road, Battersea Park. It was close to Clapham. Things must be heating up.

Sliding the note into her raincoat pocket, she put the book back and darted out, keeping her head down.

She couldn't let herself be seen.

If she did, she would be dead.

## 32.

When Mrs. Braithwaite awoke later than usual the next morning, she felt different. Something fundamental had changed within her in that crypt, making her feel crisp and calm.

Cassandra also came down late. She was looking different, too. The hard, brittle attitude had gone, her makeup was less flashy, and she wore a plainer green dress. She seemed younger and, Mrs. Braithwaite thought, prettier, now that she had less armor about her.

"You're looking very nice," Mrs. Braithwaite said, offering her a cup of tea.

Cassandra smiled. "I've decided to turn over a new leaf. Try to go back to being the person I was . . . before." Her eyes shone with a fresh sparkle of tears and determination. "Give it all another chance. The RAF chap, he telephoned. Hadn't been able to meet me because of the raids. Said he was glad to still be alive." She gave a small, sad laugh. "I had to agree with him. I said I'd meet him tonight."

"That's a wonderful idea!" Mr. Norris declared. "I somehow knew that you'll be all right in the end."

After a cup of tea, Cassandra left for work, and Mrs. Braithwaite and Mr. Norris departed for their next exploit: the Chiltern Church meeting.

The trip to Knockholt was lengthier than expected. The train was delayed and then halted for an hour to make way for a military train that had priority.

Mr. Norris, sitting opposite Mrs. Braithwaite, glanced nervously around.

"Have you really thought through all the pitfalls of attending this BUF meeting? If they catch us, they'll murder us."

"If it leads us to Betty, it'll be worthwhile," Mrs. Braithwaite said vehemently.

She gazed out of the window, and it struck her that she truly loved Betty. She'd never really acknowledged a feeling of love before—Aunt Augusta had had very strong notions about the sentiment, which, she now supposed, went some way toward explaining why she'd picked Dickie for a husband.

She looked at Mr. Norris and added, "You'd be surprised what people do for love. Have you ever loved someone?"

He looked as if he might implode at the question; his shoulders caved in and his chin pulled back. "Well," he stammered. "I thought I did, for a while, when I was young. But nothing came of it."

"Oh, who was she?" Mrs. Braithwaite knew that she was prying, but she couldn't help it. She was intrigued. Mr. Norris didn't seem the type to fall in and out of love very often. In any case, she had told him about Dickie, so it was only fair to ask.

He gulped as if he were a cat being strangled. "Her name was Enid Tuffington. She was a very beautiful girl I knew at Cambridge during the last war. One afternoon as we sat by the river, I asked her to marry me, and she said she would, when the war was over." He stopped, a dreamy look in his eyes.

Mrs. Braithwaite had never been to Cambridge. Betty had always wanted to go there to study, but she had always put her off. It would have been an expense and an inconvenience, and she'd felt Betty should be focusing on marriage and children. Of course, now that she knew how Betty excelled as a spy, she couldn't help feeling that, once again, she had been wrong.

"What happened to Enid, then?" she asked.

"Cambridge was desolate then, eerie; most of the young men had gone to war. I was one of the few to remain, which, I suppose, is why Enid even looked at me."

He paused, looking at his hands before continuing.

"But in the end, she decided that I wasn't quite the good catch she'd thought."

Mrs. Braithwaite frowned, feeling rather loyal to the poor man. "Why? What happened?"

"It was because of my brother, Gordon."

"Your brother?"

"He'd lived in a special hospital from the time he was a baby. He grew into a man, a very wonderful man, but he was still living in the same institution. I'd had this notion, a hope, that one day I could bring Gordon home to live with me." He put his head down. "It would have been hard to look after him by myself, but I felt that he was the only real family I had. You see, I'd left home, and never really went back. Only for my parents' funerals: my mother's to lay her poor bones to rest; my father's to make sure he was gone. My sister had grown up to be as angry as my father. But Gordon . . . Gordon was a true brother, the only person who really knew me, and I wanted him to live with me as soon as I had a house of my own."

"And Enid Tuffington didn't agree?"

"Enid got it into her head that she was the one

who was going to have to look after him. She said it wasn't natural—**he** wasn't natural."

"That's dreadful!"

"It broke my heart." He sat wrestling with his thoughts. "I suppose I didn't want to get over her. I didn't want to see the truth."

"What truth?"

"That she was selfish and vain. She couldn't see the good in people—Gordon was a magnificent soul, you see. She was blinded by her desire to better her position in life. I think she thought he'd be a burden on her, on us. She worried that others would judge her. Why do people get so caught up in their own senseless struggle for status that they forget to enjoy the beauty in others?"

Mrs. Braithwaite looked at her hands, feeling a blush come over her face, hoping that he didn't have X-ray eyes to see what had been written in her notebook. Had she, too, wasted her life consumed by a "senseless struggle" for social dominance, missing all the joy around her?

Turning her head away from him, she looked out the window, where the hills suddenly gave way to a view of a large valley, the rolling green fields curving down to a river, winding through trees and beneath bridges, a small crop of houses nestling beside. It looked still, peaceful. The only movement was a small brown delivery van trundling around the lane.

And something inside Mrs. Braithwaite became still, too. As the sunshine sparkled on the winding river and the tiny drops of dew coating the fields, she allowed herself to feel a sense of wonder at the world around her.

## 33

Betty stepped off the bus in Battersea and began looking for Rathborne Road, Baxter's new home. Aware that Clapham was just down the road, she pulled up the collar of her tan raincoat, retied her head scarf, and trotted briskly. Florrie was often in these parts, and she glanced around trying to spot her auburn hair in the crowd, remembering when they'd first met.

At first sight, Florrie was nothing more than a beautiful, flighty girl. A girl who worked the late shift at the telephone exchange. On their first meeting, she'd told Betty that she was "obsessed with finding a rich husband," admitting, to Betty's astonishment, that she wasn't above trapping one by getting conveniently pregnant, should it become necessary.

"Do you have a boyfriend?" Florrie had asked.

Betty had grimaced. It was right at the beginning of the operation and she had yet to meet Baxter.

"Not at the moment," she'd laughed back. Then as she gauged the look of disappointment on Florrie's face, she'd pretended to confide, "My last one couldn't keep his hands to himself, so I had to get rid of him."

They'd both giggled, and Florrie had promised to introduce Betty to "some of her friends," at which Betty professed the precise amount of wary interest a girl employed in the sewage works would.

Of course, within a few weeks of their friendship, Florrie felt comfortable enough to bring Betty along to one of her "meetings" to be introduced to some of her "friends." That was when Betty realized that Florrie, instead of being peripheral, was very much a key figure in the group's success. She was chiefly a courier, but also carried out recruiting and small acts of sabotage: telephone wire cutting, removing beach defenses to enable a Nazi invasion, and a small explosion in a munitions factory, which would have been dismissed as an accident if Betty hadn't sent advance warning.

Betty's pace slowed as she found Baxter's new address. It looked cold and empty.

**Was he out?**

The house was a small semidetached Edwardian, a two-up-two-down built perhaps thirty or so years ago. The blackout curtains were down, even though it was daytime.

She went to the door and gently knocked.

There was no reply, no sound from inside at all.

She decided to break in through the living room sash window. Using a nail file and her fingernails, she had it open in a trice.

Inside, after switching on some lights, she took a look around. Newspapers lay abandoned on the table, along with a few dirty cups and a plate, which showed remnants of toast. She picked up a shirt that had been abandoned on the back of a chair and buried her face in the sweet, earthy smell she knew so well.

In the bedroom, she took in the unmade bed, more discarded clothes, and on the floor, **Brave New World**, lying facedown and open to page sixty-seven, just about where it begins to get good. She lay back on the bed and pulled the sheets up, enveloping herself in Baxter's lingering aroma. After reading a few pages, her restless and curtailed night's sleep in the hospital got the better of her and she fell fast asleep.

## 34.

As the train pulled into Knockholt Station, Mr. Norris heaved a great sigh. As far as he could see, he had three major causes for concern. Firstly, finding Betty was proving incredibly difficult. Secondly, the wisdom in gate-crashing a fascist meeting was highly questionable.

And thirdly, what was he going to tell them at work? He'd promised that he would do some work over the weekend, as usual, and he saw with painful clarity that he was probably not going to be able to do it. They wouldn't be happy. He pictured Jontry, who'd already been promoted over Mr. Norris, drawing a large black cross through the word **dependable** in his performance record.

Mr. Norris liked to think of himself as

dependable, and as they traipsed through the small town to their hotel, he felt a prickling discomfort around his collar. Everything that could be wrong decidedly was.

The Crown was a squat, old Tudor pub advertising "cheerful, comfortable rooms." White with blackened timbers, it listed slightly to the left, as if someone heavy had been sleeping on that side for a number of centuries.

The portly landlord let them in. "You're in luck! We have a double room available upstairs." He seemed to chirp rather than speak, as his smile exposed a row of uneven teeth. His trousers were held up high around his considerable girth with braces that were poorly concealed by an aging green cardigan.

"We can't have a double bed. You see, we're not . . . we aren't together," Mr. Norris said hastily. **Why would the man think such a thing?**

"Oh!" The man's face dropped, then he beamed another smile. "Well, then one of you can sleep in the small room."

"I'll take it," Mr. Norris said resignedly, and they tramped up the stairs behind the landlord.

The double bedroom was large and furnished rather well, with two long maroon curtains hanging down beside a casement window overlooking the fields. Mrs. Braithwaite looked pleased, plumping herself down on what appeared to be a comfortable sofa.

"And yours is down here," the landlord said to Mr. Norris.

He led him through a low-ceilinged corridor, which passed into another, even more low-ceilinged corridor, and finally pushed open one of the doors at the very end.

"Ah," Mr. Norris said.

More of a long cupboard than a room, it enclosed a bare wrought-iron single bed next to a dull, cobwebbed wall. It was the only piece of furniture, probably because nothing else would have fit. A small, square window high on the far wall gave the space the oblique feeling of an abandoned prison cell.

"Sorry, this is all we have," the landlord said. "I'll have the wife give it a quick clean for you, and you can have it at half price." Then he added that well-used adage, "There **is** a war on."

After putting down his small suitcase, Mr. Norris went back to extract Mrs. Braithwaite from her luxury bedroom for an early dinner. They were on a mission, after all.

The landlord showed them into the empty saloon where dinner would be served, and then excused himself to find out what would be on the menu.

The snug interior had white walls covered with cricket memorabilia, including photographs of every village team since the end of the last century. The ceiling was lower on one side than the other, and although the building had been standing for five hundred years, it did cross Mr. Norris's mind that it might choose this evening to collapse under the weight of Mrs. Braithwaite. He decided to keep a tab on everything she ate for dinner, just to be on the safe side.

"I've never eaten in a pub before," she said, looking around. "It's quite different from a restaurant. Do you go to pubs much?"

"When I was at Cambridge, a few of us went on excursions together, climbing mountains around the country." He felt himself smile at the memory. "We went up Snowdon, Ben Nevis, Scafell Pike, Skiddaw. We stayed in bothies or pubs if there was one to be found, though we were in tents sometimes." He took a deep breath of air and relived those heady days, filling his lungs with the fresh mountain air, gaping at the gusty views from the summits. He had felt like lord over everything in sight.

"When we reached the top, we'd laugh, and then we'd just sit and look out over the landscape: the gray mountains, the ocean in the distance, so blue it was disarming."

He felt his eyes close.

"But it was the silence that took your breath away. All the noise gone, so that you hardly dared to breathe. It was as if you were the very first and last person to walk the earth."

There was a pause, and then Mrs. Braithwaite gently asked, "What happened to your friends?"

"Ypres, the Somme, Passchendaele." Mr. Norris clenched his lips together with the thoughts of his friends destroyed so totally. He didn't know precisely how they'd died. Everyone knew that the details the army gave the families were lies. "He died instantly, bravely, a bullet straight through the heart" was a favorite. "Blown up by a grenade, instant death" was another. He knew it hadn't been like that—that death was messier, gorier—and he failed to trick himself into believing otherwise.

"I'm sorry," Mrs. Braithwaite said quietly.

He glanced at her sadly.

"They'd been so excited about going to war, as if it were some kind of ultimate test of their bodies, their spirits. I wonder if they still felt like that at the end."

"And you? Didn't you go to war, too?" Mrs. Braithwaite asked. It was unusual for a man of his age to have avoided it.

"They didn't want me. My health wasn't good enough. I have a weak heart, you see." He let out a small cough, as if to demonstrate. "I was sturdy enough to climb a mountain, but not sturdy enough to die." A lump rose in his throat. "My friends come to me in my dreams some nights. They tell me not to feel bad for them. I can't stop thinking that I should have been there. I could have protected one of them, taken a bullet in his place."

"What were they like?"

He looked at his hands. "Quincey was a top chap, very popular with the girls. Bradshaw was the athlete. He always reached the top first. If any of them was going to survive the war, I'd have thought it would be Bradshaw. Yet he fell the first month he was there. No medals, nothing."

"And the other one?"

"Ludlow."

"What about him?"

"He was just a young man, happy-go-lucky, meaning to get a wife and a good job."

Silence sat between them for a few minutes, then Mrs. Braithwaite reached her hand over and touched his.

"I'm sure they're all happy to hear their names still being spoken."

He said nothing, just opened his hand, turned it over, and held hers.

The landlord reappeared, eyeing them with curiosity. Their hands quickly parted as if the moment had never happened.

"We're all out of proper meat for today, I'm afraid. But we can do something miraculous with Spam."

"Mrs. Braithwaite's favorite," Mr. Norris said, and they both began to chuckle gently as the landlord glanced from one to the other, wondering what on earth had gotten into them.

## 35.

Betty had met Baxter during her first week on the BUF operation. She was given orders to meet her fellow operative at a specified desk in the rotunda library at the British Museum. Dressed as a company clerk in a navy-blue skirt suit and matching pillbox hat, she'd walked purposefully into the library on the allotted day, slowing her pace to marvel at the colossal rounded walls of old books soaring high above her on every side, bolts of sunshine flashing down through several windows in the massive domed ceiling, making the place look like a monumental cathedral of books, a silent religion for questioning minds.

Counting the rows of desks, she turned into the specified row, softening her footsteps so as not to disturb the line of men at the desks, one or two women among them now that the war was allowing them to use their minds, too.

She stopped when she came to a young man seated in the fourth chair, reading one of the books on his desk. Dressed in a plain suit, he looked like an office worker, a civil servant perhaps. Did she have the right man?

"I say, do I see Hemingway's **A Farewell to Arms** there? I wonder if I could have a look at that after you?" She quietly repeated the code, as if it were an everyday conversation. "Will you be long?"

"Only another five or six minutes, if you can wait?" He gave his code response.

**This was her accomplice.**

Then, as he turned his head and his eyes met hers, something inside her stirred: a connection, a longing.

It wasn't because he was handsome, with his tidy dark hair and his deep brown eyes. And it wasn't because he was a proper man, not one of the boys from home.

It was the stupidest thing, really, she told herself later, but when his gentle eyes looked up at her with that mixture of amusement and intensity, she saw a kind of glow in them, an inherent understanding that she'd never seen before.

She stood, rooted to the ground, for a minute, and then recalled what she was doing there. Why she had come.

**Find a desk and sit down. Don't stand around like a lemon drawing attention to yourself.**

The man had kept the desk to his right empty, covering it with a pile of books to prevent anyone else from taking it, as per instructions. She pulled out the chair and sat down, looking nonchalantly at the books as she tidied them to the side.

"Did you ever read it?" the man asked.

"What?" His question hadn't been in the set conversation she'd been given.

"**A Farewell to Arms**."

"Of course I have. Hasn't everybody?" She said it rather abruptly in her uncertainty.

He let out a small, silent laugh. Had she made a joke? Or was it her inexperience?

Soundlessly, he let a slip of paper fall to the floor, leaving her to pick it up.

On it was a row of words, coded, which would be the names of the people in the fascist organization. She put it in her handbag.

"They told me we were to arrange a regular meeting," she whispered.

He hastily wrote something down on another scrap of paper, and although he didn't meet her eyes, he gave a hasty smile before placing it in the book and sliding it across to her.

She opened it, looked at the note.

**Come to my house, Tuesday midnight**
**33 Gainsborough Road, Clapham**

She felt herself blushing. She'd never been to a man's home by herself, especially a man so good-looking and, well, mature. It was all in the name of duty and all that, but what if he—what if she—? What if they—?

**Don't be ridiculous!** she told herself. **It's a work meeting.**

Their eyes met for the briefest of seconds, but even then she could see that within him lurked a quiet type of hunger, not for her body or her mind, but for a deeper kind of connection, as if he were the last of a rare species sensing that she was another, and that they alone could understand their desperate predicament.

She remained seated for a while, and she read the page into which he had slipped the note. It was a love scene, a kiss.

Had he chosen it on purpose?

But when she glanced over at him, he was engrossed in his books, unaware.

There was another small slip of paper in the book, but it was blank, marking only a page where a passage had been underlined in pencil.

**The world breaks everyone and afterward many are strong at the broken places.**

**Did he underline the passage?**

She longed to reach out and touch his arm—only a foot or two away from her, and yet miles away—but he read intently, as if oblivious to her.

After twenty minutes, she got up, returned the slim volume to the main desk, and walked out briskly. The library, the men, and one or two women still at their desks, even her new accomplice, were all exactly as they had been, the sun streaming in around them in a rich, intellectual heaven.

But deep inside her, Betty felt a new light, one that she knew would engulf her if she let it.

That Tuesday night, when she tapped on his door, her nerves attacked her in a way they didn't usually, even with her line of work. Fascists, dangerous Nazis, and possible death evidently didn't unsettle her as much as the idea of being alone with this intense and attractive man.

MI5 operatives were not allowed to be romantically involved with one another. That had been made very clear in her training.

Whatever happened at the man's house, she'd have to remind him of the rules. It was as simple as that.

And yet she felt sweat on her hands as she watched the door open.

"Darling," he said loudly, pulling her in, his head jerking toward the living room as if indicating that someone was in there. "Wonderful to see you. Come in, come in." He made a small laugh, adding in a rather salubrious way, "Let me show you around, make you comfortable."

He tugged her into the living room and pointed to a small device attached to the window frame. It was a bug, one of the types she'd been shown during training. She let out a quick breath, and their eyes met, a quick understanding passing between them. They were being monitored.

"Why, it's gorgeous, darling," she said, entering into the pretense, which was obviously that this was a romantic liaison, not a work meeting. "What wonderful decorating skills you have!"

He looked as if he'd burst out laughing for the briefest of moments. The room was the opposite of tasteful: dirty walls were sparsely covered with brown curtains and old pictures of agricultural machinery. It couldn't have been more depressing.

"Sit down. Let me get you a drink." He made an ironically grandiose gesture to the sofa and went to a drinks cabinet, taking out a bottle of scotch and two glasses, pouring a finger into each and bringing them over.

"Now, where did we leave off last time?" He gave her the glass and loudly clinked his against it, showing her that she should take a drink.

"Chin-chin," she said, adopting the persona.

That was until she took a sip and choked horrifically.

He laughed, slapping her on the back. "Not used to spirits, eh? Here, I think I have some sherry."

After a few slaps on the back, his hand rested there for a moment, in the middle of her spine. His laughter stopped, and with only a second to frantically think, **Oh good heavens, he's going to kiss**

**me!,** the man whom she'd only met once before, a fellow agent and work colleague with whom she was strictly forbidden to have a romantic liaison, leaned over and touched his lips on hers. His mouth tasted of whisky, but warm, sweet, and his lips were soft and gentle as they moved slowly over her mouth, and then down to her neck.

"Now stop that," she said, trying to stay in character. "What about my sherry?"

"I thought you were enjoying it," he said, smiling in a way that made it difficult to work out whether he was still in character or not.

"Sherry, please."

He got up and found a bottle of sherry, asking if she'd like some music as he poured her a glass.

"Oh, do you have a record player?" she said, knowing that music would allow them to have a normal conversation, their speech distorted by the background noise.

"Yes," he said in his smooth seducer's voice. "And I know just the tune to get us in the mood."

She rolled her eyes as he opened a small record player close to where the bug had been placed, and soon big band jazz was filling the room.

"Now, where were we?" he said in a loud voice before returning to the sofa beside her.

"Can we speak now?" she whispered.

"Yes. We'll have to go back to the acting after the record, but we have a few minutes."

They had separate missions, overlapping some

of the same people and fifth-column organizations. Sharing information was critical, as was watching each other's backs. And to do that, they needed to know what the other was doing.

In case anything went wrong.

The record ended, and her new accomplice quickly flipped back to being the seducer.

"Oh, come on, darling. You might find yourself under a bomb tomorrow, and what would be the use of saving yourself then?"

It was a line that was flying around every living room in the country.

Holding back laughter, Betty put on a saucy voice. "Are you sure there aren't any other girls? A man like you must have plenty."

"No one compares to you," he said in a hoarse whisper, his hand under her chin, guiding her mouth to his as he kissed her again.

Betty had kissed a few boys before—Lawrence from the shop in Ashcombe and Jeremy Proctor from the school in town—but she'd always been left wondering: Why? Why did people do this clumsy, claustrophobic exercise with their mouths? It only left one dripping and in need of a handkerchief.

But now she had the answer.

The problem had been with the boy in question.

Not with kissing per se.

In this case, the kissing was rather wonderful.

She felt her body relax into it, and they slid down into the sofa.

After a few minutes, he pulled himself away, saying, "That's the ticket," before getting up to put on another record.

**Did he want to pull away? Was this all part of his character?**

She thought he was kissing her for real, but now she felt unsure, and more than a little cross.

"Let's have something to match our mood, shall we?" he said, putting on a slow number and coming back to sit beside her.

"Do we have to kiss?" she whispered under the cover of the music.

"I thought you liked it," he said, amused. "We don't have to, of course. I wasn't expecting to or anything; it's just that for some reason I—I feel as if it's meant to be. Don't you?"

She paused. Yes, she did think so, or was it just her body convincing her of things she wanted to be true?

"I think we should finish our discussion about the operation, and then we can let our listeners know that I've discovered you're a dreadful cad. Then I'll make a loud exit." She grinned, feeling herself relaxing. "I know we're meant to meet every week, but what should I do if you've had to move locations? Or if you've been chased out? Will you leave me a marker?"

"There's a tawny-colored jacket hanging on a hook over the small window on the back of the front door. You can see it from the outside, even if there's a blackout. If it's gone, you'll know not to come in." He looked at his hands. "Even if I'm being taken out against my will, they'll let me take a coat with me."

"Clever," she said. "And if you leave on assignment, how will I know where you've gone?"

"I'll leave a coded message for you in a telephone book in the red telephone box outside St. Paul's Cathedral."

"Where inside the book?" Training had covered various good public places for hiding messages, and this was one of them.

He pondered. "For you, my darling, it will be Freud, I think." He smirked knowingly and tucked a stray hair behind her ear.

Feeling that it wasn't his place to put her hair behind her ear, she untucked it. "And what if we meet and you're being followed?"

He grinned. "If I am being followed, I shall kiss you."

And then, hardly knowing what she was saying, she looked at his soft, warm mouth and said, "Well, let's hope you're being followed then."

They looked at each other for a few minutes, sizing up the weight of each other's minds as the record approached its end.

Then she leaned forward, whispering, "Perhaps

we should practice." She let her lips gently touch his neck beneath his ear. "We wouldn't want to get it wrong, would we?"

Of course, they didn't need to do that, the next kiss, but it was fun, like playing a game.

But then, over the weeks, it stopped being a game.

Their work, the danger, combined with their passion, the fraught closeness of them, made them shift from sweethearts to lovers, a deeper bond forming every time they met.

## 36.

Darkness had fallen by the time Mrs. Braithwaite and Mr. Norris set out for the meeting. The lane to Chiltern Church was eerie in the light of the waning moon, a narrow passage through woodland on either side. An owl hooted from a nearby tree, making both of them peer around the shadows uneasily. Although it wasn't freezing, Mrs. Braithwaite felt a shiver down her neck.

They hurried their pace until they came across a rundown building nestled into the wood behind. It had a tall, angular roof and a crooked spire, and there were a couple of broken-down walls nearby, as if it had once been surrounded by a small community, long since vanished into myth.

"Do you think this is it?" Mrs. Braithwaite whispered, pulling Mr. Norris into the wood.

"How would we know? Perhaps we should look for a sign or something?"

"We'll listen for voices, then investigate, as planned."

They inched forward through the underbrush until they were only a few yards away. Voices could be heard. Or rather one voice. The booming sound of a man making a bracing speech.

Mrs. Braithwaite turned to look at Mr. Norris and he nodded silently. This must be the place.

At that moment, applause rang out of the building.

Creeping forward, Mrs. Braithwaite hoped to find a window to look through, but they were all painted black. She wondered if it was a cheap method of blackout or the act of people who didn't wish to be seen.

There was nothing else for it, they would have to push the door open and pretend to be looking for the bridge club.

The door was large and strong, a great deal newer than the rest of the building. Perhaps they'd installed it themselves as an extra precaution.

Taking a deep breath, she turned to Mr. Norris. "Are you ready?"

He looked as if he were about to faint, so she didn't wait for him to answer. With a silent "One, two, three," she turned the handle of the door and pushed it slightly ajar. A shaft of dirty yellow light fell onto the tatty grasses around them.

She peered inside, and a very young man— probably too young to sign up even—gave her a grin. "Quick, come in! It's already started."

She pulled Mr. Norris behind her and slid in among the people standing at the back. It was a miracle they hadn't been challenged by the man at the door, and she was moving fast to get lost in the crowd.

There were fewer people there than she'd thought from the applause, at the most fifteen, the sound amplified by the high timbered ceiling. The place was lit by candles, dozens of them dotted around the tall space, giving it a shadowy, shifty mood, not unlike the crowd itself.

The man speaking at the altar was tubby and wearing an old-fashioned tweed suit along with a yellow waistcoat and a pair of round spectacles that did nothing to advantage him. His voice had a loud, tremulous tone, especially when he said something vile.

Which was often.

"We will show them that **we** are the masters!" He made a Nazi salute, making Mrs. Braithwaite and Mr. Norris shudder as a cheer whipped up in the crowd.

Speaking with venomous authority, he addressed the crowd as if they were a group of errant school-children who hadn't done their homework.

"You need to gather more information. So far we have some blueprints for a new type of tank and a map of the beach obstacles at Brighton. But we need more."

Someone at the front yelled, "When's the invasion?"

He barked back aggressively, "Yes, yes! The invasion is imminent. Mr. Fox assures us that the plans are well under way. You all have your orders for the mighty event. We disrupt the home forces, cut communication wires, confuse the civilians. There are no dates yet. It will come at a few days' notice, so make sure we can reach you."

A tall, mustached man near them called out, "Professor, how will they know who helped them?" He was wearing tired and patched knee breeches, like a hunter or gamekeeper. "We've been promised rewards."

"The Gestapo and other authorities are aware of your efforts, Mr. Taplin. There will be no mistake!" The professor raised his finger, pointing emphatically at the ceiling. "Our loyalty to our führer will not go unrewarded. We will take this misguided country and bring back one that is strong and just. We all"—and he put his arms out majestically, raising his head imperiously—"we all will be the victors, and those who have opposed us will realize their foolishness."

A cheer went up, echoing through the roof like the squall of seagulls over split fishing nets.

"What about bombing the rail bridge at Loxton?" Taplin bellowed. "We've got plans to sabotage the whole rail system."

Instead of answering, the professor stepped to the side. "Tonight, as our leader, Mr. Fox, can't be here, we have a visiting leader from Dorset, and he should be able to answer your questions."

As a wiry young man dressed in a suit took to the stage, Mrs. Braithwaite let out a faint gasp.

Of all the people in all the world . . .

It was Anthony Metcalf.

She would have recognized him anywhere, had known him since he was a boy. But today, here, there was something different about him. He had a pompous confidence about him. All those years of being teased as the neighborhood know-it-all had led to this treachery.

Mrs. Braithwaite couldn't help but smirk at the thought of Mrs. Metcalf's face should she ever find out that her precious boy was working for the enemy. How much lower could one get? Mother of a traitor—the village ladies would have no choice but to shun her. Mrs. Braithwaite could return to her rightful position in the WVS.

She whispered under her breath, "That's Anthony Metcalf, Mrs. Metcalf's son."

Without looking, she sensed Mr. Norris shudder. "He'll recognize you. We have to leave."

"But I want to hear what he has to say. I'll hide

behind you." She shuffled behind him, poking her head around his shoulder from time to time.

On the makeshift stage, Anthony looked sour but debonair. His narrow mustache, the same color as his thin brown hair, gave his broad, pasty face the look of a bad-tempered little terrier. Even though he was comically small beside the oafish blackshirted young man onstage behind him, he looked oddly in control, devious even, as though a concentrated dose of conceit had puffed him up inside.

In his polished, upper-class voice, Anthony addressed the man who'd asked about rail sabotage. "It's Taplin, isn't it? Let me explain that Berlin has made it clear that now is not the time for risky infiltrations or operations, at least not until the invasion. We would lose our advantage if we were caught."

"But we won't get caught," Taplin muttered.

Anthony continued, ignoring him. "Our inside sources tell us that the British government doesn't believe there are any fifth columnists left in the country. They've imprisoned the leaders of the BUF and other prominent Nazi sympathizers, and they think that the rest have changed their minds and got behind the country. Now is not the moment to disabuse them of this." He let out a long, slow laugh. "If they're foolish enough to think that the people of Britain are all stupid sheep, let them think that."

Laughter rose through the room, reverberating around the rafters with a sinister echo.

"We will get our chance to act," Anthony said in a low, chiding voice, then he raised his fist into the air. "The time will come when we can show our strength, when we can show them who is master. We have assured Göring of our absolute and unfailing loyalty to the fatherland."

Massive cheers went up. Mrs. Braithwaite cowered, trying to blend in yet not quite able to join the rowdy chorus of approval. The Nazis were brutes, thugs. Their notion of taking over a country was to gather everything for themselves and treat everyone else like slaves or, worse, kill them. She'd heard rumors that after they took Poland, they'd packed half the people off to Siberia and the other half to Germany to work in war factories like prisoners. And what happened to the empty houses, the empty land? They were given to Nazi officers as rewards, prizes.

They looked after only themselves.

She gazed around at these misguided people. Didn't they realize that it wouldn't be long before they'd be Nazi slaves, too? Most of them were men, some younger than conscription age, but most were middle-aged. There were a few women, too. Mrs. Braithwaite somehow expected Nazis to look different: foreign and mean. But they didn't. They were brown haired and dull, the kind who might be a neighbor or a WVS volunteer. One woman was even wearing a head scarf similar to hers: red with ivory roses.

**How dare she!**

A woman stepped up to speak next, forceful and loud. She was in her late twenties, her hair short and practical. A scar ran down one side of her face. Perhaps she'd been caught in a bombed building. Or maybe something more sinister.

"We are close to the invasion! I can feel it in my blood." Her voice was shrill and impassioned. "This week a series of bombs rained down over Sevenoaks, and a thrill passed through me like never before. The tide is turning. We will be the victors, and the useless men and women—whoever is left—will be our slaves."

Mrs. Braithwaite felt the whole of her being fall like a heavy stone. She hadn't realized people, British people, could be swayed by Nazi rhetoric. How could they be so gullible, rallied so easily by false promises, left braying for blood?

She stole a glance at Mr. Norris, who had gone pale and had taken out his handkerchief. Utter apprehension passed between them; they were witnessing the very worst of humankind.

Mr. Norris prodded her in the elbow, then barely perceptibly, nodded to the door. She knew what he meant. She had to get out before Anthony Metcalf saw her. The place was too small to hide.

Fishing in her handbag, she found what she was looking for and prodded Mr. Norris back in the arm, passing it over to him.

It was a small photograph of Betty, taken before she'd left home. Even young, on the cusp of a great adventure, she had that same solemnness about her.

Mrs. Braithwaite gave him a final, meaningful look, which was supposed to convey that he needed to stay, find out more.

She was relying on him to be her eyes and ears.

He gave her a short nod, yes.

Making her way back to the door, she then pretended to the very young man that she was in need of some fresh air. He unlatched the lock for her, and out she slipped into the night.

**How despicable it is,** Mrs. Braithwaite thought as she found a broad oak to hide behind, **that people can be so entranced by these ideas, these speeches, that they believe they're entitled to bully everyone else into submission.**

**They should look inside, see their own souls.**

## 37.

Mr. Norris felt unwell. He watched with incredulity as the vicious woman with the scar—the one who reveled at the thought of Seven-oaks's bombing—finally reached the end of her tirade, to hearty, yet—Mr. Norris was relieved to acknowledge—not so fulsome cheers.

His mind had already begun to search for a good story of why he was there, who he was, and why the lady with him had seemed to have vanished. Getting lost on the way to a bridge club wouldn't explain why he had decided to stay for the meeting. If he could provide a plausible explanation, then he could weave into the crowd and glean more information. But should he not pass muster—a shiver gripped his backbone—he'd be dead by morning.

For a finale, Metcalf once again took to the stage, this time to ask for vigilance. "Every morsel of information we gather will be delivered immediately to the Gestapo, speeding the invasion of Britain."

One final, great cheer went up, and then everyone surged forward, trying to get to Metcalf to find out more about him.

"Here's a little secret message for Göring," an older woman said, pressing a folded letter into Metcalf's hand. "A sketch of the beach fortifications in Worthing. Guard it well."

One younger man boasted that he'd made invisible ink from parsnips.

Metcalf smiled at him, saying in a voice completely devoid of irony, "How terribly clever of you!" At which point the young man became engulfed with others wanting to know the recipe.

Taplin, who was standing beside Mr. Norris, leaned over to say, "Shame Mr. Fox wants us to drop our plan to sabotage the rail bridge."

"Oh yes. Indeed," Mr. Norris stammered.

"We had it all planned out for next week." His voice was throaty and not as upmarket as he looked, in his woolen hunting suit. There was a peculiarly shifty look in his eyes, the type you might see in someone who's not altogether sane, and he was speaking quietly, out of the side of his mouth, as if they were having a little joke together, a conspiracy. "I'm a dab hand with a bomb, and I can shoot, too, being a gamekeeper and all. Destruction is in my blood." He thrust a grimy hand forward to shake.

"I know. It's so frustrating being . . ."—Mr. Norris grappled for the right word—"pinned down by rules when all I want to do is let loose on them." He put on his best angry stance, which made him feel silly.

Taplin gave him a grim I-mean-business smile; then he turned to speak to a man on the other side of him who was small with plump, puffy cheeks, a hamster hoarding nuts.

"Ernie said he's in it with us," he said, turning back to Mr. Norris, who then had to shake Ernie's podgy little hand.

"Taplin says we'd be heroes if we got the rail bridge down," Ernie said, more anxious than heroic.

Taplin was all enthusiasm. "The railways would be in chaos. The Nazis could invade without opposition. Mr. Fox would get word to Berlin, and I'd be certain to get an Iron Cross." He snorted with zealous verve. "Gillian got one last year for stealing the plans for the new Spitfire."

**Iron Cross? Did they have Nazi medals flown over from Germany?** Mr. Norris thought. **And who is Gillian?**

Taplin spotted Metcalf and pulled away to privately press him for an endorsement over the rail bridge sabotage.

Mr. Norris was left beside Ernie, who didn't seem at home here in quite the same way the others did. He lacked the zeal. Mr. Norris mused that Ernie, like himself, would probably much rather be at home with a newspaper, listening to the wireless. There was a confused look about his eyes, as if he couldn't quite comprehend why everyone was so excited.

"Your friend Taplin seems an organized type. Have you known each other for long?"

"Taplin lives next door to me. Known him since we were six years old, when he moved in." Ernie laughed bitterly; it wasn't clear why. "It's only sometimes I wonder—well, I'm not really a violent type, if you get my gist."

"I do, I do. I'm not a fighting type either." Mr. Norris paused and then said quietly, "You know, you don't have to do what Taplin says."

Ernie seemed to stop breathing for a moment, and then he anxiously glanced over at Taplin, who was still in deep conversation with Metcalf. Then suddenly, his fear quickly turned to aggression, and he glared back at Mr. Norris, a snarl on his face. "What are you talking about? Taplin's good to me."

"Oh, I see," Mr. Norris mumbled—how could he have read the situation so wrong, thinking that he could help Ernie out of this? Praying that Ernie wouldn't dwell on it, he said very quickly, "I only meant that some of us aren't the fighting type, are we? The rail bridge sabotage sounds terrific. The sooner this war's over and done with, the better it'll be for everyone. And we're helping things along here, making it easier for the Nazis to win." The words came pouring out of his mouth. He'd heard that argument before: surrender to make the war stop, the Nazis were going to win sooner or later anyway. Mr. Norris didn't agree at all. He'd put up with bombs until the end of time if it kept the Nazis from goose-stepping all over Westminster.

"Yeah, I suppose you're right." Ernie looked mollified. Mr. Norris didn't know what Taplin would do if Ernie told him what he had said. Taplin was a lunatic, that much was clear.

Quickly trying to change the subject, Mr. Norris saw an opportune moment and whipped out the small photograph of Betty. "I've had my eye on this girl. She was caught up in the BUF before the war, and I rather hoped you'd seen her in your meetings?"

Ernie took it in his fingers. "Yes, I have seen her," he said. "Don't know her name. She came in once or twice with Gillian." Red faced, he grinned.

"Gillian?" Mr. Norris said keenly.

"She's the girl I'm going with." Ernie's flush grew.

"I don't think I've had the pleasure. What's she like?"

"Oh, beautiful, she is! Lots of character—loves a bit of chaos, she does. A real looker. Long hair and a smile to die for."

**Could he mean Florrie?**

Thinking fast, Mr. Norris asked, "What color hair does she have?" adding with a smirk, "I'm a blond man, myself." How he loathed this act!

Ernie laughed; evidently girls were a favorite conversation. "She's got glorious auburn hair. Just like Rita Hayworth. Don't get many blondes at the meetings these days. Before the war there were plenty of pretty girls, but now they're all rather plain, and mostly married. Half of them are completely obsessed about Hitler."

They both laughed.

**So Florrie was involved, and Betty had been to meetings with her.**

"Do they know Metcalf at all?"

"Metcalf's new in town." Ernie looked annoyed.

"Wheedling his way in, is he?" Mr. Norris said cautiously, sensing he might have touched a raw nerve.

Ernie frowned. "There's an unwritten rule about pinching another man's girl."

Mr. Norris hid a smile. **So that's it! Both Ernie and Metcalf were after the same girl: Gillian. Or rather, Florrie.**

"I wonder where I could find Gillian's friend," Mr. Norris mused.

"I think they live together, somewhere in South London with an old codger, apparently—"

Blood drained from Mr. Norris's face.

**"An old codger"? Had the girls been referring to him?**

A frown took hold of his forehead as he thought to himself, **But I'm only fifty-two!**

It wasn't precisely young, now that he came to think about it. But what had he done in those years? Dread flooded into his mind: had he wasted his time playing it safe, sticking to his routine?

Well, at least no one could accuse him of playing it safe right now.

Taplin yanked Ernie away as Anthony Metcalf made his way over, obviously wanting to meet Mr. Norris.

"You're new here, I understand?" Anthony Metcalf said, a polite and friendly smile on his face. He had none of the snide hatefulness of the others. His style and manners were those of a gentleman, educated, probably university—Oxford, if Mr. Norris had to guess—and before that one of the better schools. "I'd like to welcome you to our group."

He shook Mr. Norris's hand with the kind of casual shake Mr. Norris would expect from an Oxford man.

"You don't come from these parts, do you?"

Mr. Norris hesitated, trying to adopt the smug air of the others. "No, I've been in Manchester, trying to coordinate efforts up there."

"I've heard we have good support up there."

"Not as good as we'd hoped for, but we keep plugging away." Mr. Norris let out the kind of snorty laugh he'd heard from Taplin. He was getting quite good at this.

"Are you based here now, then?" Metcalf asked, edging closer. Mr. Norris couldn't tell whether he was doubtful or not. His voice was gravelly and a bit threatening.

"No, I'm in London at the moment. Just down here for a few days and thought I'd drop by."

"Who told you about us?"

"One of my colleagues in the London group, Smith." He chose one of the most common names he could think of in the vain hope that there actually was a fascist called Smith somewhere in the area.

There wasn't.

"I don't know any Smith." Metcalf's eyes narrowed with mistrust, his lower jaw jutting out aggressively. "Are you sure you're from the London group?"

Mr. Norris took a step back. Coming to the meeting suddenly appeared to have been a terrifically bad idea. He wasn't made for pretense or, well, downright lying. He should stick to his accounts in the future. If he had one.

He tried a new gambit. "Oh, you must know Smith! He's a middle-aged man, always smoking a pipe. You know, I've often wondered if Smith could be a pseudonym. I've heard other people calling him different names, Williams or Taylor." He gave a knowing nod. "You know what I mean?"

"Taylor?" Metcalf looked bemused. "Yes, I know Taylor. When did you last see him?"

"Oh, last week I think it was."

"Are you sure? The last I heard he'd been sent to an internment camp on the Isle of Man, last year."

"Ah, you must be thinking of the other Taylor." Making up lies on the spot wasn't a skill Mr. Norris had ever had much need for. He added for good measure, "Good friend of Mr. Fox's, smokes a pipe."

"A friend of Mr. Fox's, you say!" Metcalf said, and there was a moment when it could have gone either way, deliberation in Metcalf's eyes, appraising him head to foot. "Where did you meet?" he asked cautiously. "When you were in London."

Mr. Norris made a nervous little cough. What could he say? He was trapped in a ruined church with a bunch of Nazi fanatics.

**I'm done for!**

But then, in a moment of brilliance, it came to him.

"In the basement of a butcher's shop in Clapham," he said evenly, a smile playing around his mouth. He was certain he was on safe ground.

He was.

Metcalf raised his eyebrows, nodding with a new respect. Did that mean the basement under the butcher's was general headquarters, or was it a place only used by senior members for top work, such as torturing female spies?

Metcalf slapped him hard on the shoulder. "Apologies for the questions, old man; we have to be careful. You know how it is. To be honest, there's a rumor that we have a mole in our midst, someone who isn't quite the ticket, if you get my meaning."

Mr. Norris nodded readily. **Interesting**, he thought.

"Nevertheless," continued Metcalf, "welcome to the group."

Mr. Norris took a deep breath and plunged in. "Is there another spot in London where the group meets? It's my understanding that the butcher shop may have been compromised."

"Is that so? Well, I'm only visiting the area myself, actually," Metcalf replied, folding his arms in a forthright stance. "I have yet to meet the London group."

"But you must know Mr. Fox?"

"As I say, we have also yet to meet." He smiled again. "I'm the head of the organization in the South West, you know, although I've been tapped for higher things."

Mr. Norris nodded with the knowing smile he'd adopted. "The organization needs more men like you." Then, thinking on his feet, he added, "They say that Mr. Fox needs a right-hand man."

"Yes, I heard that, too." Metcalf's eyes narrowed petulantly; evidently Fox was foe rather than friend. "It would be most interesting to follow him around." He lowered his voice. "You see, I suspect that he might be the mole."

Mr. Norris gave a gasp. **What an interesting little tidbit of information!** "But how can one be sure?"

"One can't, yet." Metcalf sneered. "Keep it to yourself, though. I can tell you're a little more switched on than the rest of them." He eyed Taplin and Ernie with disparagement.

He then introduced Mr. Norris to several incredibly vile people, including the professor, a younger man who had stolen a map showing the bomb sites in London for the Luftwaffe, and a callous Swedish woman who said that she found the current group "insufficiently extreme" for her tastes.

Mr. Norris felt a desperate urge to escape. But he had yet to find a lead to Betty's whereabouts. Mr. Norris's eyes swept the room for someone who might be able to give him a clue.

That's when he spotted her.

A stunning brunette in a nurse's uniform was standing on her own, watching quietly. It wasn't her beauty or her smile that piqued his interest. No, there was only one very good reason why Mr. Norris wanted to speak to her.

It was because she was the woman from the photograph in Baxter's house. The one in the passport from the telephone box, the recipient of Betty's identity.

"Hello," he said jauntily. "I'm down for the day from London. I can't help thinking I've seen you somewhere before. Do you come to any of the London meetings?" he asked as an opening gambit.

"Sometimes, but I come to the Sevenoaks ones more often," she replied. "I'm Mary Montgomery."

He smiled, eyeing her smart nurse's attire. "I say, do you work in the Sevenoaks Hospital?"

"Yes, that's right."

The girl wasn't much of a talker. Mr. Norris had been hoping that she'd say something about a boyfriend, or Baxter, but no such luck. He had to think fast.

Then it occurred to him. Abhorrent as it was, he would have to pretend to be keen on her.

"You're a very lovely girl, you know," he said, taking a little step closer, hovering his arm around her back, unsure what to do. He was twenty years older than her, for goodness' sake. "I don't suppose you already have a boyfriend, do you?"

He attempted a smile, which probably came across as a leering grin.

She sniffed, looking appalled. "Yes, I'm actually engaged to be married," she said, and then added a little haughtily, "And he's rather high up in the organization if you must know."

A thought occurred to him. "Mr. Fox?" he ventured.

She glanced up at him. "As a matter of fact, yes."

"But of course," Mr. Norris said quietly. "I have yet to meet Fox myself, so I'll be intrigued to go to the next London meeting." Then he added cautiously, "I don't suppose you know where it's being held?"

"Usual place next Tuesday at six," she said curtly before heading away, grimacing.

It took Mr. Norris a few moments to recover from the charade. Lecherous older man was most definitely not a role he relished, and mortification coursed through his body as he regained his composure.

A crowd was forming around the woman with the scar running down her face, who had begun crying with an almost religious fervor about how the führer was coming, "coming to save the people of Britain."

Meanwhile, Taplin and Ernie were in a deep discussion, Taplin's face contorted with fury while Ernie seemed to be explaining something quickly and quietly, trying to calm him down, glancing from time to time in Mr. Norris's direction.

A sudden fear biting at him, Mr. Norris knew he had to escape, so he sidestepped to the entrance and after a hasty good-bye to the young man at the door, he slipped out into the night.

Straight into a heavy downpour.

Looking around, he made out a sodden head poking out from behind a large oak tree. Mrs. Braithwaite's hair was glued to her scalp, and her clothes were drenched. A very cross wet cat.

"What took you so long?"

"It was rather more difficult than I anticipated," he said, taking off his jacket and putting it around her shoulders. "Could I press you to hurry, Mrs. Braithwaite? The faster we get away from here, the better."

## 38.

Betty sat up, alone in the dark in Baxter's bed. There was a scuffling coming from the living room.

Someone else was in the house.

**Had she been followed?**

She got out of bed and riffled through a pair of trousers that had been left on the back of a chair, finding a theater ticket, a small men's comb, and—aha!—a penknife.

Flicking it open, she began to creep to the door of the bedroom, listening intently as the sound seemed to be coming closer, in the hallway, and then nearing the bedroom door.

She deliberated whether to whip open the door and plunge the knife into the intruder before he (or she) could discover she was there. She'd rehearsed this move plenty of times in training, but would she be able to make it work properly when it was a very real, potentially armed, and probably violent enemy?

She'd have to find out.

Counting to three in her head, she swung the door wide, thrusting the penknife up savagely at—

Baxter.

The snarling man in front of her dropped the kitchen knife he was holding at the ready and put his arms around her in a tight embrace.

"Oh, Betty! Thank heavens you're all right!"

## 39.

"Hours, it was," Mrs. Braithwaite huffed as they struggled on through the downpour. The lane back to the village was pitch-black, dense woodland on each side. "I was frantic with worry, not to mention the cold."

"How was I supposed to know it had started to rain? The windows were blacked out. I didn't want to raise suspicion by rushing out."

Mr. Norris gave her a blow-by-blow account of how the evening had played out. Apart from the error of judgment with Ernie, she thought he'd done rather well, especially considering that he was, after all, the most woefully timid man in the world.

"Anthony Metcalf leading a fascist ring!" She beamed at the prospect of holding something over

Mrs. Metcalf. "But does Betty know? I'm sure she would have mentioned it to me. She and Anthony are good friends. He still writes to her."

"By the sounds of it, he's only just come up from the South West. Nobody at the meeting knew him, and he hasn't yet met Fox or any of the main London group," Mr. Norris said. "I wonder if Betty knows about Mary Montgomery, the girl in Baxter's photograph."

"What's she like, this Mary Montgomery?"

"Actually, she seemed quite nice. She's a nurse, and if you ask me, her heart wasn't in this fascism nonsense."

"What do you mean?"

"She lacked the fervor. She told me that she's engaged to Mr. Fox, which could be the real reason she's there."

Mrs. Braithwaite frowned. "But if she's engaged to Mr. Fox, what was her photograph doing in Baxter's house?"

"Unless Baxter and Fox are one and the same?" Mr. Norris gave a knowing smile.

"You think that he goes under two names?"

"What if Fox is Baxter's undercover name? Maybe Baxter works with Betty, and he has infiltrated the gang using the name Fox." He suddenly raised his finger in the air, as if struck by an idea. "In which case, Anthony Metcalf is right: Fox **is** the mole. He's Baxter."

"That would explain why he's sending love letters

to Betty and yet has Mary's photograph displayed. Mary is the fiancée of make-believe Fox, while Betty is the girlfriend of Baxter, the real man."

They fell silent for a moment, thinking it all through, then Mr. Norris suddenly said, "Oh, I found out about someone else, too."

He began to explain that when he'd shown Betty's photograph to Ernie, Ernie had said that he'd seen Betty at some of the meetings. "He said that Betty was with a girl called Gillian, who was courting both Ernie **and** Metcalf."

"The conniving little minx," Mrs. Braithwaite said. "Did he say anything about this Gillian? What she's like?"

"Very glamorous, apparently, with long auburn hair and a love for chaos. Sounds a little like someone we both know."

"A love for chaos." Mrs. Braithwaite gave a laugh of recognition. "Florrie! She said that about herself the first time I met her."

"Ernie must have heard her say it enough times to think that it describes her."

"When it does no such thing."

"In actual fact, it **hides** her; it's a smoke screen of pandemonium behind which lurks a mastermind."

They let the information sink in. Florrie had been playing all of them.

"But it still doesn't answer our question," Mrs. Braithwaite continued. "Where are they holding Betty?"

"Mary Montgomery told me about a meeting in the butcher's basement next Tuesday." He shrugged. "We'll have to go to that."

"But that's not until next week, and who knows if we'll find out anything helpful."

They both walked along deep in thought.

Mr. Norris suddenly clutched her arm more tightly. "I have it! We'll take the train to Sevenoaks and find Mary Montgomery. She told me that she works in the local hospital. It's our only option, and Sevenoaks isn't far from here at all. I bet she'll know where Betty could be, or at the very least she'll be able to tell us where Baxter is."

"What a good idea, Mr. Norris. We'll head off to see her first thing," Mrs. Braithwaite said, hurrying her pace.

The sound of a car came from behind them, its headlights covered so that only slits showed, and Mrs. Braithwaite and Mr. Norris were forced to stop on the side of the road, waiting for it to pass.

Except it stopped beside them.

"Want a ride?" A gruff voice was accompanied by the sound of a car door being thrust open, someone tall getting out.

"No, thank you," Mrs. Braithwaite said briskly. "We're already wet, so it's no bother to continue on."

But as she spoke, she felt a large, muscular hand on her arm, dragging her and Mr. Norris toward the waiting car.

"Unhand us at once," she yelled.

But the man was already shoving them into the back of the car. "Get in."

And as she turned to look, she found herself looking into the face of a very angry man.

Taplin.

## 40.

"Thought we might have a little chat." Taplin pushed his nose up to Mr. Norris's, watching him in the light of a torch as the car swung sharply around the bends of the country lane.

"Oh, er, terrible weather tonight, isn't it?" Mr. Norris tried to make light of it, but he felt a thud of fear inside. Ernie must have told Taplin what he'd said about Ernie not having to listen to him.

Taplin was a dangerous man and a loose cannon—any hint of antagonism toward him or the group and he'd make someone pay.

Mr. Norris could see Ernie in the driver's seat, ever faithful, even though he must have had suspicions that Taplin was unhinged. It was written all over him, from the ranting call for sabotage to the bullying control he wielded over Ernie.

Taplin scowled at them. "Who's your lady friend here, the one you left out in the rain?"

Mrs. Braithwaite was on the other side of Mr. Norris, peering over his shoulder hesitantly.

"She doesn't mind; do you, dear?" Mr. Norris said, turning and smiling at her as if she were a biddable wife.

Mrs. Braithwaite, horrified at first, promptly realized it was an act and put on the meekest smile. "Of course not, dear." Then she added, "I had to wait outside. It was frightfully stuffy in the church."

Mr. Norris cleared his throat. "It's awfully good of you to give us a lift on a rainy night, but may I ask where we might be going?"

"We're taking you to the station, so that you can get a train home." Then he grabbed Mr. Norris by the scruff of the neck, yanking him toward him. "And to make sure you never come back."

Mr. Norris yelped.

"See, I didn't like the looks of you, snooping about, talking to Ernie here about what he should and shouldn't do. So I decided to follow you."

"Ernie must have misunderstood, I only meant—"

But Taplin jerked his collar tighter.

"You keep away from our meetings. We don't like interlopers, do we, Ernie?" His voice lowered to a menacing snarl. "And if I hear you blabbing about the rail sabotage, I'll ruddy well slaughter you."

Mr. Norris yelped as a piercing prick of pain surged across his throat.

Taplin held a knife blade to the light, where it glinted sharply, a drip of blood at the tip.

"No, please—" Mr. Norris gasped.

"Let him go," Mrs. Braithwaite squealed from beside him, flinging herself over to take the man on.

But he was too quick, whisking the blade away, and then lifting it to slash Mr. Norris's neck again.

The car screeched to a halt before he could.

Taplin opened the door and dragged Mr. Norris out after him, slumping him onto the pavement.

"Mr. Norris!" Mrs. Braithwaite stumbled out behind and knelt over him.

"Let that be a lesson to you," Taplin roared, a note of jubilation in his voice as he got back into the car. "Don't come bothering us again!"

The car careered off, leaving the impression that these brutes were everywhere and nowhere, watching, waiting, all the time.

"Are you all right?" Mrs. Braithwaite sobbed.

He looked up at her. "I think I might need some first aid. Where precisely are we?"

She peered around. "By the railway station. They must have assumed we were going back to London." Fumbling in her handbag, she took out a handkerchief. "Let me have a look at that cut."

He winced as she dabbed the wound. "Is it bad?"

"No, it's not deep. There's some blood, but you'll heal up fine." She sniffed, and he wasn't sure whether to believe her. Then, and more like her usual self, she proclaimed, "What a nerve!"

"I can't believe I gave myself away, and with something so stupid. What was I thinking, trying to help Ernie out?" The rain was still coming down, but they were now oblivious to it. "I put you in danger. I'm so sorry."

Suddenly the sound of footsteps came from the corner. The flash of a torch beamed over, and they braced themselves for another onslaught.

A deep voice bellowed, "What's going on here?" and in moments they were surrounded by four men in full uniform.

Four guns were aimed straight at them.

"Stop pointing those things at us!" Mrs. Braithwaite yelped, pulling away. "Who are you?"

"Knockholt Home Guard, night watch patrol." The men brought their heels together with more of a shuffle than a snap.

"The Home Guard! Thank heavens!" Nearly weeping with relief, Mrs. Braithwaite grasped for her torch. From their boots and uniforms, the men appeared to be normal soldiers. From the neck up, however, they were old men, tired from the walk and in need of a hot cocoa and early bed.

"Can you help us?" she stammered. "My friend here is injured."

"Guns down, men," ordered the captain, puffing

out his chest before wheezing slightly. He was the most elderly of them, an alarmingly robust white mustache making him look like a grizzled old sailor. "Where's our medical orderly?"

Two of them had first-aid training, but they all stooped down around Mr. Norris, fussing over bandages.

"Who did this to you?" the captain demanded, his bushy, white eyebrows pulling together into a frown. "We've heard there's a dangerous gang operating around here."

"It was only one man," Mr. Norris said calmly. "He tried to mug us as we came out of the station." It wouldn't do to explain the full story to the Home Guard. If the BUF weren't already aware that they were spying on them, the Home Guard barging in would make that patently clear.

Mrs. Braithwaite shot him a look of surprised admiration at his quick thinking.

"We'll find the rascal," the captain snapped. "Leave everything to us. Come on, men. Let's take these poor devils home and search the area. The blighter can't have got far."

Which explained why, when the landlord of the Crown finally opened the door, he found Mr. Norris and Mrs. Braithwaite joined by a motley battalion of old men.

The landlord helped Mr. Norris in and gave the Home Guard a quick drop of scotch.

"Right, men, no time to waste," the captain

commanded after necking his own scotch and someone else's for good measure. "Let's separate and find the culprit." He looked earnestly at Mr. Norris, then added with a sharp salute, "We'll have him in our custody before you know it."

After waving them off, the landlord helped Mr. Norris upstairs to lie on Mrs. Braithwaite's double bed. The cut, when Mr. Norris inspected it in a hand mirror, was impressive looking but not as deep as he'd feared. There had been a worry that it wouldn't stop bleeding, but it had tapered off.

"What happened to you?" the landlord inquired.

"A man tried to mug us outside the station," Mr. Norris said, and then he met his accomplice's eye with a grin. "Mrs. Braithwaite saw him away with a few hearty swings of her handbag."

## 41.

Swishing the sheet off her naked body, Betty swung her legs out of Baxter's bed. "Wonderful as it is to see you, my dear, I have to go." She scooped up her petticoat and began to put it on. "But before I do, I need some information."

"But you've only just arrived!" Baxter wailed, watching her from the bed. "Don't you understand how much I missed you, darling?"

Picking up her bra, she glanced at him. "I have to find my mother."

"Your **mother**? You're wrapped in my sheets and talking about your **mother**?"

"Yes." Now she came to say it out loud, it seemed extraordinary. "She tried to rescue me, Baxter. The only one who tried, thank you very much indeed."

"You know I couldn't, darling."

She softened slightly. "Of course I do, but nevertheless, it was Mum who came searching for me, with my landlord of all people, and somehow they managed to find me. The problem is now **she's** been taken." She paused, hands on hips. "I have to help her."

"You can't possibly be serious. They'll recognize you instantly, even in disguise," Baxter said, frowning. "It's absurdly dangerous. Tell Cummerbatch to send out someone else."

She stopped, halfway through pulling on her blouse. "There's no one else to send out, and by the time your someone else has been found and briefed, my mother will be floating down the Thames."

"I thought you didn't get on with your mother."

"Well, perhaps we will a little better now. When she rescued me, she seemed different. She looked the same, obviously, and still wore an appalling tweed suit, but this time she was, well, nice . . ." She paused, thinking of the right word. "Plucky. Less selfish. She'd been searching for me for days, thinking of nothing but how to get me out of there."

"What's she normally like?"

"Permanently cross, controlling, and rather cold. Full of strict notions on how to live, most of them gleaned from my overbearing aunt who brought her up as if she were in Queen Victoria's court. Did

I never mention my Aunt Augusta? She lived with us until she died a couple years ago. I'm sure she was part of the reason why my father left."

Baxter lay on his side, watching as she pulled on a stocking. The sheet had come off most of him, and his body looked utterly soft and inviting. He leaned over and stroked her thigh. "Poor darling. Your childhood sounds horrific."

She shrugged. "Oh, it wasn't that bad. I started at the grammar school in town when I was eleven, and we could avoid each other for the most part." She looked for her skirt and found it behind a chair. "What are your parents like?"

"Oh, you know, lovable in their way. My mother is rather a wit and writes poetry, and my father grumps around the garden a lot, talking about the last war and the medals he won."

"They sound uncomplicated."

"Sometimes I think my parents understand each other better than they understand themselves."

"That's a very tender thing to say."

He smiled, getting up and coming toward her, cupping his hands beneath her chin. "Perhaps one day, you and I might know more about each other . . ."

"I think I'm a relatively easy person to know, actually," she said matter-of-factly. "You, my darling"— she leaned forward and kissed him—"are far less so. It's lucky that I'm clever enough to get to the bottom of you."

He grinned. "Please do. I'll submit to a thorough investigation."

But after a few kisses, Betty stepped away.

"Except not right now. I need to get back out there and find her." She leaned over and scooped up one of her shoes from under the bed. "Do you have any thoughts as to where Briggs might be holding her? They won't use the butcher's again; they'd know that's where I'd look."

"Well, there's that church in Knockholt, but I doubt they'd hold someone there, or the garage behind Clapham Junction Station—it's behind a bombed nightdress factory beside the park. It's mostly used as a drop, but they might hold someone there if the butcher's basement wasn't safe. It's also possible that they took her to one of their homes. The professor has a few spare rooms he's always giving up for the cause."

"What about Mary Montgomery?" Betty had never felt quite comfortable with the idea that her boyfriend had a pretend girlfriend, especially one as beautiful as Mary. "Could you ask her?"

"She isn't speaking to me at the moment," he said flatly. "Suspects that I'm having a fling with Florrie, for some reason. Utterly absurd, of course. Florrie isn't my type at all."

"And who is your type?" She couldn't help but ask.

He took her wrist and pulled her toward him. "You are, of course."

Betty smiled, but then stalked off to find her other shoe. "I'll try the garage. Let's hope she's there." Her shoe was wedged between the bed and the cupboard. "It's just so unbelievable that Mum came."

"I would have been in there myself if Cummerbatch let me, but he was determined that I shouldn't break my cover."

She came up from the other side of the bed, shoe in hand. "I'm quite able to look after myself."

But deep inside she knew that she'd been scared. Briggs and Marty were novices, yes, but they were also violent and clumsy. She could have ended up dead by the slip of a knife or a spot of remiss torture. She hadn't been at this game long enough to have that cocksure confidence that she could get out of anything.

After an abrupt sniff, she pulled herself together, gave him a quick peck on the cheek, and said, "I'll be back later."

At the door she paused, turning back to him. "You know, I simply can't work out how I could have been exposed. You don't suppose it was an insider?"

He yawned loudly. "You mean someone in MI5? I can't think who could do that, darling. Not many people know who's on this operation."

Her forehead creased in thought. "But it doesn't make sense. I was frightfully careful, you know."

He shrugged. "Sometimes it's just bad luck.

A civilian in the wrong place at the wrong time, watching from a different angle, unthinkingly passing on what he saw."

"But—"

He walked over, half naked, and planted a kiss on her lips. "You can't analyze everything, Betty. Sometimes we simply don't know why something happens. We just have to carry on."

"I suppose we do." She felt for the doorknob behind her.

Worry lurked in the back of his eyes, even though he smiled and joked, "I'll come and rescue you if you're not back by midnight."

But as she went off into the chilly morning air, turning and turning to get to Clapham Junction, she couldn't help wondering if he had a point: going back in, without the support of MI5—without even a disguise!—was complete and utter madness.

## 42.

As soon as the landlord left them alone, Mrs. Braithwaite sat down on the bed beside Mr. Norris, leaning against the headboard. The immediate panic over, she felt a lingering dread.

"These people are ruthless," she muttered. "You don't think they could have followed us back to the pub?"

"Don't worry, Mrs. Braithwaite. The Home Guard would have put them off. And even if they do come, what can they do to us?"

"Kill us."

The words hung in the air.

She thought about their whirlwind quest so far. Everything had been about protecting Betty rather than themselves.

**Especially poor Mr. Norris.**

"What have I put you through? All this—" She indicated his nasty neck wound, which frankly could have been so very much worse. "All you wanted to do was keep safe, stay at home." She made a small sob. "It's completely my fault."

"Nonsense, Mrs. Braithwaite." He sounded rather cheerful for a man of little bravery who'd lost a fair amount of blood. "It's been a bit of an ordeal, but you were quite right all along. We simply have to find Betty. I can't imagine how she's managing with those louts."

Mrs. Braithwaite sniffed loudly. "I think we should go home tomorrow and tell P.C. Watts all about it. I've put you through enough, and now it's time to leave it to the police." A tear coursed crookedly down her cheek. "You might have been killed."

"Now, look here, Mrs. Braithwaite. This isn't like you." He rubbed her hand warmly and gave a little chuckle. "Where's your oomph?"

She didn't laugh. "I'm not sure I want oomph anymore, Mr. Norris. Life isn't all about bluster. It's about looking after other people."

"You're looking after my wounds very well," he said gently.

"But I've hardly considered your well-being at all," she said. "Or Betty's, for that matter." She looked tiredly at him. "I should have spent more time in the basement asking her about the fascists. Instead, we spent the time bickering about how distant I'd been to her . . ." She paused. "The truth of it is that I wasn't always as understanding of her as I should have been." She glanced at him. "She always loved science, wanted to go to university, but I couldn't find the money. I didn't really try, I suppose. In any case, science is dreadfully . . . unfeminine."

"Some girls are made for it, you know," Mr. Norris said. "Pity they only get to have boring clerical jobs, and only before they marry. The war is giving them new opportunities, though. Perhaps things will change in time."

Mrs. Braithwaite sniffed. "Marriage is good enough for most girls. What's wrong with hoping that Betty gets married?"

"All I'm saying is that it's a pity these clever girls have to choose. Men can follow their passion **and** get married. Girls have to choose between marriage and a job, and often the jobs on offer aren't as good as those given to men. It's a shame. Someone like Betty has much more sense than some of the nincompoops I know at work."

"I tried to do my best," she said quietly.

Mr. Norris shuffled closer. "I'm sorry. I didn't mean to upset you."

She lay down beside him on the floral counterpane.

He looked at her wistfully. His eyes, without his glasses, were as blue as Wedgwood china.

"You look tired," he said. "I should really let you go to sleep."

She helped him up and through the corridor that became smaller and smaller to his little room.

"Are you sure you'll be all right?" she asked.

He gave her a small smile. "Please don't worry about me, Mrs. Braithwaite. The cut is healing nicely. I'll be fine by the morning." He quietly closed the door, and she was left to her own thoughts.

Inside her room, Mrs. Braithwaite put on her long floral nightdress and matching robe—one never knew when one would have to go into an air-raid shelter these days. The evening had been a dismal one: a meeting full of fascists followed by a gruesome attack, poor Mr. Norris horrifically injured. What did Betty have to do with this gang? Where could she be? And then there was Anthony Metcalf. How had he grown into such a hateful monster?

There are certain moments when one realizes that perhaps the world isn't the way it has always seemed to be. That it is, in fact, bigger, more complicated, nastier than you'd ever imagined.

And from that thought springs another, more cumbersome one: that perhaps one hasn't been completely correct in one's interpretations of things.

Mrs. Braithwaite's mind flashed back to her now outdated beliefs that humans have a natural moral dignity, that the British would always defend their country against its enemies, that people weren't hateful enough to enjoy the news of their neighbors' being bombed. Was she pathetic to have believed as she did?

She thought of Betty, trapped by these terrifying people.

She pulled out her notebook and flipped through the pages. There it was, the question she'd posed at the start of her trip:

**How do you measure the success of your life?**

Beneath it, she'd written,

**Social standing: how everyone around you judges you.**

Since then, she'd had other thoughts, that it was about family and kindness, or that it was about uncovering the bad influences in your life and finding your own truth. But now, she added a new answer:

**The things you have done—your actions— were they helpful or harmful?**

Restlessly she began pacing the room, and then, unable to help herself, she went to knock quietly on Mr. Norris's door.

"Are you in there, Mr. Norris?"

There was a kerfuffle, and then he opened the door. He was wearing ironed blue-striped pajamas and was looking less than happy.

"Are you all right?" she said.

"Not especially," he said bitterly. "I'm trying to get to sleep, but there's a drip in the roof. And people keep disturbing me."

"Who's been disturbing you? I'll speak with them!"

"**You**, my dear Mrs. Braithwaite, are disturbing me. The landlord came in ten minutes ago to see how I was, and then his wife came in to give me a bucket for the leak." He looked pained for a moment. "It's not ideal."

Mrs. Braithwaite peeked into the tiny room. The bucket, now placed at the end of the bed, was collecting a stream of water coming from the ceiling, the rain still coming down in torrents outside. Another leak at the pillow end was also going strong, and a few drips were also making inroads around the rest of the room.

"This will never do," Mrs. Braithwaite declared loudly, as the landlord reappeared to find out what the noise was about.

"I told him about the leaks, but he still wanted the room," he explained. "Although I think it's getting worse. The roof needs mending, but there are no builders around, what with the war and all."

"Well," Mrs. Braithwaite said impatiently, "he'll

have to come and sleep in my room. There's plenty of room on the sofa."

Mr. Norris grimaced. "But, my neck—"

"Now, don't be silly, Mr. Norris. You take the bed. I'll sleep on the sofa."

"I couldn't possibly expect you to—"

"Well, that's settled then," she said, reclaiming her usual oomph.

Mrs. Braithwaite led the way back to her room, and they made up a bed on the sofa, which, fortunately, was of the large variety.

"Perfect," Mrs. Braithwaite said contentedly, fueled by the notion that she was truly helping someone. She wasn't just ordering people around, as she had in the WVS, but giving up something herself. It was a new sensation, and one she rather liked.

Mr. Norris kept saying, "Are you sure, Mrs. Braithwaite?" and "That's so terribly kind" and "What a good friend you are!"

Mrs. Braithwaite ushered Mr. Norris into the double bed, and he slipped between the covers with a hasty and embarrassed "Good night, and thank you again!"

Far from being ready for sleep, Mrs. Braithwaite pottered around with her own things for a while, refolding her clothes into a neat pile so as not to be outdone by Mr. Norris and looking over to make sure that he was quite comfortable.

"Are you all right over there, Mr. Norris?"

"Yes, very good, thank you."

"It must be a little like being in university dorms." She made a little titter.

"Not really," he said, yawning.

"Let's turn the light out, and I can tell you what I was thinking."

She tottered out to the bathroom down the hall, then tottered back in, climbing into her made-up bed on the sofa and switching off the bedside lamp, thinking how cozy it all was, and how funny people could be about sleeping in the same room, when it was quite fun once in a while.

"Mr. Norris, are you still awake?"

"Yes, Mrs. Braithwaite."

"Good. Now let me tell you what I was thinking about those despicable people." And she proceeded to tell him how she'd decided that she'd been so wrong about human nature.

"Maybe you're right, Mr. Norris. Maybe we **are** all animals, trying to outlive the other animals."

But Mr. Norris didn't reply.

He had already fallen fast asleep.

## 43.

Betty stood in front of the old garage behind Clapham Junction Station. The factory adjacent to it was a husk, half obliterated by bombs, with bricks and fragments of roof littering the forecourt.

The place was deserted.

With the help of the lock-picking device, she quickly had the padlocked door open, and hastily slipped inside. Her torch beam swooped around the small brick room, half full of vegetable crates stacked one on top of the other. Some of them were printed with the name of a company. C. S. Berry Ltd., presumably a greengrocer. But as she ventured closer, she realized that they didn't hold vegetables at all.

They held guns.

Handguns, assault rifles, some of those old pistols left over from the last war, they were all there. Piles of them. Bullets, too; rounds and rounds of ammunition, plus a crate full of grenades.

"They really are preparing for an invasion!" she said quietly to herself.

Her mother wasn't here, and she had to leave, fast. If they found her, they'd take out one of these guns and shoot her on the spot.

Opening the door, she checked that the forecourt was empty, and then stole out, relocking the padlock behind her and darting back to the street.

It was late, but there were people about, mostly men coming home from pubs, and some gangs of older children—the war meant that a lot of youngsters, especially city ones, were growing up rather recklessly. She kept her head down, tying her head scarf tighter, and briskly made for the station.

"Is that you, Betty?" A voice came from behind her, and she looked up. Of all the people in the world! Her face lit up to see her old friend.

Anthony Metcalf.

"Fancy meeting you here!" he said, smiling broadly. "I say, what are you doing in a place like this?"

She laughed, taking a step back with surprise and delight. "Anthony! What are **you** doing here, more like?"

He fell into step beside her. "Oh, you know, war work of sorts. Are you heading to the station? I'm walking that way myself. I'll come along with you. Keep you safe from marauders!" He chuckled, and she felt a surge of warmth, a nice relief from the past few days.

"I thought you were doing something terribly hush-hush in Hertfordshire," she said, but then she remembered his letter, in which he told her that the government job he'd bragged about hadn't come into effect for some reason. Had they tested him and found him wanting? For all his claims to intellect, Betty had the better brain; she knew that, even though her mother hadn't let her go to university. Aware that Anthony wouldn't want to be reminded of his failures, she quickly added, "Or were you evacuated with your college?"

"Let's just say I'm on a special mission." He sneered as if he were doing something far more important than anything she could imagine, reminding her of how frustrating he could be. Anthony was nice enough, but he always wanted to be on top.

"The raids have been something rotten, haven't they," she said, changing the conversation.

"I'd have thought you'd be back in Ashcombe, although I expect you're better off, with your mother and the divorce and all."

Betty stopped, containing herself. She couldn't tell him about her mother's attempt to rescue her. "My mother isn't that bad, Anthony. She's put her life and soul into that village." She looked forward at the ground between them. "I don't see why everyone should be horrid to her just because Dad divorced her."

"I would have thought **you** would be the most upset with her, under the circumstances."

"Under what circumstances?"

"You mean, you don't know?"

"Don't know what?"

"Her secret, of course." He smirked at her. "Well, it's not really **her** secret, is it? It's your family's secret really. Probably **your** secret most of all."

"What are you talking about?"

"**My** mother told me all about it when I was at home last month." He had a curious look in his eyes, as if he meant trouble. "Come and have a drink with me, and I'll tell you."

She stopped, hands on hips. "Come on now, Anthony. This is just another of your silly pranks."

"If you're not interested, then we can leave it." His face was so smug that she felt like hitting him, and not for the first time.

"I jolly well will leave it." She glared at him, annoyed. "Now if you'll excuse me, I have to get home." She began striding purposefully down the road.

"But don't you want to know what it is?"

"What I'd really like to know is how, if it's such a big secret, you know about it and I don't, when whatever it is has absolutely nothing to do with you."

"I'm only too eager to explain."

She rolled her eyes, expelling a large sigh. The

man was infuriating. "Oh, all right. I'm in a hurry though, so I can't stay for long."

"Excellent!" He linked her arm through his and began walking with enthusiasm down the road toward Clapham Common. They drew to a halt outside the Pendulum.

"I do hope you're not taking me to that dodgy pub," she said, exasperated.

"No, of course not, my dear!" He glanced around and then crossed the road, taking her arm in his. "There's a little place just over here. Terribly quaint. It used to be a curiosity shop."

## 44.

We're going in here?" Betty stood, hands on hips, glowering at Anthony Metcalf.

Even in the darkness, she could see that the purple-painted front of the old curiosity shop was ancient, almost sliding into the ground with deterioration. An assortment of moth-eaten oddities sat in the window: an old wooden rocking horse that looked scrawny and bald, a teddy bear with one eye missing, a barometer predicting storms.

"It's a private club." Anthony smiled. His hand behind her back, he gently guided her to the door. "A friend told me about it." He knocked three times on the door, and then waited, grinning at her.

"Anthony, what kind of place is this?" She was getting cross. "I simply haven't got time for—"

Her words stopped.

The monstrous form of Briggs opened the door before her, a sneer curling his lips. Marty lurked behind in the murky shadows.

Anthony pushed her forward from behind. "In you go, Betty."

Briggs pulled her in, shoving her through the musty shop, the sound of the door clunking shut behind her.

It was a trap.

And Anthony Metcalf had been behind it.

She screamed for help as Briggs dragged her into a cold, grimy back room lit by a few gas lamps. He threw her onto a chair and began tying her wrists and ankles. Kicking as hard and furiously as she could, she felt Briggs's massive, grubby hands securing the ropes. She had no chance.

Betty was left once again tied to a chair, but this time she was glaring, unbelievably, into the face of Anthony Metcalf.

He smiled. It was not a happy smile or a grin, but rather the solemn little smile of someone who knows he's finally scored the winning point.

At that moment, the enormity of her situation crashed down on her: he knew she was a spy, he knew about her mother's rescuing her, and most disturbingly, he probably knew where she had just been coming from and what she had most likely seen there.

She was as good as dead.

"Alone at last, Betty." He switched on a torch, beamed it into her face.

She blinked sharply and pulled back.

"Stop it, Anthony!" she shouted angrily. Even if he was her captor, she couldn't help speaking to him as if he were still the boy she'd known since school. "Stop acting like you're a big man. You're only using this ridiculous organization to get yourself a bit of power. You're not a fascist."

"My dear girl," he replied suavely. "All that matters to me is that I'm on the winning side." He picked up another wooden chair and brought it to the middle of the room, where he sat down, facing her, only a few feet away. "After the invasion happens, I'll be given a title, while you, my dear, will be put on trial and hanged. Unless they decide to put you in a work camp." He looked almost pleased at the thought, reaching forward to draw a pale fingertip down her cheek. "What a shame it will be to see your pretty face getting thinner and thinner." He made a low chuckle. "I wonder, would you still be so alluring?"

She jerked her face back. "Don't be melodramatic, Anthony. What happened to you? I thought you wanted to work as a code breaker. How could you change sides so completely?"

Fury flashed across his face. He got up and began storming around the room. "The code breakers are all snobs! Wouldn't take me because I wasn't the right pedigree. The place was full of upper-class idiots who looked down their noses at everyone." He was raging, his hand caught into a fist. "Who do they think they are?"

She watched him for a moment, torn between trying to appease him and wanting to show him that he was wrong. The Nazis were feeding on his wounded pride.

"Is it possible the code breakers turned you down because you weren't as capable as the others?" she said gently, waiting for him to explode.

He strode over to her, whipping his hand across her face.

"Of course I was **capable** enough, you stupid girl. Aren't you listening to a word I say? They rejected me because I wasn't one of them. It was as simple as that."

She winced, taking a deep breath as the sting of pain subsided. "But how did you get dragged into working with these hooligans?"

Now that she thought about it, the fascists were right down Anthony's street, with their gift for helping weak-minded people feel strong. It didn't surprise her for a moment that he was siding with the Nazis. She knew that he couldn't fight because of his litany of physical ailments, most of which had been indulged by his mother from a young age: headaches, a proneness to colds and influenza, chesty coughs. According to Mrs. Metcalf, Anthony was too fragile for "common" life.

He narrowed his eyes, his lips pursed together

beneath his mousy mustache. "My university was evacuated to Somerset. That's where I met Gillian."

Saying her name seemed to calm him down, and he sat back down on the chair opposite her, a smile coming over his face.

"Gillian?" Betty's insides turned over. **Florrie. Was there anyone who'd escaped her?**

Anthony had never had a proper girlfriend. He wasn't precisely ugly, but no one in her right mind would want to run her fingers over his pale, damp skin or through his thin brown hair. "Let's just say that she fell for me, utterly and completely."

It was all that Betty could do to stop herself from rolling her eyes. Had Anthony fallen for the oldest trick in the book? "You met a woman—"

"A gorgeous woman," he corrected her.

"You met a gorgeous woman who no doubt made you feel good"—she'd learned all about that kind of coercion at spy training—"and she persuaded you to join the enemy? How could you be such an idiot?"

He stood up swiftly, the chair making a loud grind against the floor. "It was nothing of the sort. **I** had to convince **her** to join in the end." He said it simply, quickly, yet Betty couldn't help wondering if he wasn't half doubting it himself. His brow was creased, and his eyes shifted to the left, as if struggling to recall the details—things she'd learned to look out for in training.

"You don't seem completely sure of that."

"I'm not a fool, Betty. Just because you don't understand the ways of the world, please do not assume that I'm equally as naive."

As teenagers, Anthony had always had an air of being in charge, the one who knew everything. Betty, he'd assumed, being younger and a girl, knew nothing. But she knew he'd never had so much as a kiss. Again and again he'd tried to convince her that they both needed "practice in the art of romance." She was quickly made to understand that this involved him pressing her up against a tree, pushing his thin lips against hers. She'd been adept at slipping from his grasp before anything unseemly could happen. She didn't tell anyone—least of all her mother—because she'd have thought that Betty had encouraged it. Some things were better buried quickly. There was nothing to be gained except recrimination.

Looking at him now, she had no doubt that he'd lost his head, his heart, and possibly his virginity to a woman who had no other ambition than to drag him into her fascist den.

"Sex can be a powerful tool, especially in war," she said. "What is she like, this Gillian?"

"She should be in the movies. Her hair, her magnificent auburn hair, like—"

"Rita Hayworth."

"Yes," he said, frowning. "Just like Rita Hayworth."

"And does she have a mole on her right cheek, just below her cheekbone?"

His face had fallen, his spirits slowed. "She has a mole, but I can't remember which cheek."

"And is she also known as Florrie?"

Betty must have struck a raw note, as his confusion flipped quickly to anger, and he shot her a look of rage before kicking her chair over sideways, sending her crashing onto the floor. Pain shot through her head, stunning her for a moment, before she registered the sting in her shoulder where she'd fallen.

"I know your game, Betty. Don't try to make Gillian into a witch to turn me against her."

From her position, lying on the floor, her lips against the floorboards, she muttered, "Gillian's a fascist courier, Anthony. I live with her."

"Since I became a leader, she's been working on sourcing war secrets, so she may well have adopted a cover name, if indeed she is also known as Florrie."

"And does she also have a cover boyfriend?"

"What are you talking about?"

"Have you ever met Ernie Flagg? She was all over him last month. It was very apparent what their relationship entailed; let's just say that it was more than kissing and cuddling. Actually, now that I come to think of it, I recall that she didn't introduce him as her boyfriend. She said he was her fiancé."

He kicked her chair, and her, across the room.

The door burst open. Briggs took Anthony's arm and dragged him out. "We're supposed to get information, not kill her."

"She'll be fine," Metcalf snapped. "It'll be a lesson to her. Let's leave her to dwell on it for a while. I'm sure she'll see sense now that she knows what's coming her way."

With that, the men left, and Betty, tied to the knocked-over chair and lying on the cold, hard floor, wondered whether—by some remote chance—there was anyone out there who could help her. MI5 thought she was in Devon; why hadn't she listened to Baxter?

"How could I have been so stupid as to not leave a message for Cummerbatch?" she muttered under her breath, pulling the ropes to see if they had any give. There didn't seem to be any possibility of escape.

As Betty lay on the ground, unable to move, she thought of her mother. Where was she being held? Was she tied up, tortured, or something far worse? Tears came to her eyes, and a feeling of utter grief crept over her, that she hadn't tried harder to connect with her mother in the past, that she hadn't at least used the time they were locked up together to tell her how much she loved her.

Every fond memory of her mother came back to her. Most of them were from her young childhood, her mother rubbing her hands to warm them up when she'd been outside building a snowman.

The way she'd taught her how to play cards, letting Betty win. Those times she lifted her onto her lap to tell her stories, most of which were about industrious rabbits whose hard work and ruthless determination always saved the day.

"She's a wonderful woman," she whispered.

And Betty had led her to her probable death.

The thought stuck in her head, turning around and around. How unthinkably horrific that she only realized how much her mother meant to her at the moment they were both in such peril!

"Please, Mum," she whispered out loud, as if it were a prayer. "Please forgive me. You went through so very much just to save me, and this is how you are repaid—" She began to cry. "I never dreamed that you'd come to find me and I, well, I just let you die, as I surely shall."

At these words, she began to sob again, both for her mother and herself, the two of them now at the mercy of the same, ruthless enemy.

## 45.

The next morning, Mrs. Braithwaite insisted on cleaning and rebandaging Mr. Norris's wounds before they set off for the station. He assured her that he felt well enough for the day ahead. The previous night's violence had served to heighten her fears for Betty, and she found that she could hardly wait to find Mary Montgomery. Mary would be certain to know the whereabouts of Baxter, and surely Baxter would lead them to Betty.

Unfortunately, the train they took was delayed for war transport, and Mrs. Braithwaite's patience began to wear thin. But it wasn't until the train had been standing in a tiny station in the middle of nowhere for twenty-five minutes that she began to pace the carriage.

"The train won't get there any faster by your willing it to," Mr. Norris said gently. "Sometimes it's better to relax and take stock while you can."

She looked at him and snapped back, "Anyone who waits patiently while situations grow beyond their control is completely idiotic. It's tantamount to letting the world trample all over you."

"Sometimes we need to take these moments—"

But Mrs. Braithwaite had stuck her head out of the window and was yelling down the platform at a hapless stationmaster. "Why have we stopped?"

After the second time she called, he came over to speak to her.

"We're waiting for a special train coming through." He looked at his wristwatch. "It's due in a few minutes. They can't change the points until it's past."

"Well, it had better hurry up!"

A minute later, a long train drew onto the opposite platform.

A voice came from behind her in the carriage. "It's the ambulance train."

"I beg your pardon?" Mrs. Braithwaite said to the somewhat unkempt older woman who'd spoken. Beside her, a boy of around eleven was engrossed in a tatty comic.

"They come through here every day, taking wounded soldiers to the military hospital just up the road." The woman leaned forward. "It's supposed to be secret. They don't want civilians knowing there are so many casualties coming in." A look of gloom came over her face. "I suppose we have enough casualties of our own, from the bombs, without having to worry about those coming in from abroad."

Mrs. Braithwaite poked her head back out of the window, and sure enough, a few faces of young men peered out of the train opposite, some bloodied and bandaged, others gaunt and grubby—or was their skin browned from the sun? They looked so terribly young. Eighteen or nineteen, some seemed hardly older than the boy reading the comic.

"Where have they been fighting?" she asked the older woman.

"North Africa, most of them. Some have been in Greece. They're not allowed to say, but sometimes they give us clues, don't they, George?"

She nudged the boy, and he looked up, glumly nodding.

"You've spoken to them?" Mr. Norris asked, intrigued.

"We go to the hospital to cheer them up. Sometimes we have some cake, but not so often these days with the rations going up."

"That's jolly good of you," Mrs. Braithwaite said, trying not to feel competitive. It could have been so very easy to point out that she herself had recently been involved in cheering up dear Blanche. Instead, she gave the woman a benevolent smile. "How frightfully kind."

"I do it with the WVS. Doing my bit." She clenched her lips together with stoicism. "Best thing I can do since my daughter was killed."

A pained look came over her face, her mouth puckering. She leaned her head toward the boy, wordlessly, indicating that it was his mother who had died.

"I'm so sorry. How incredibly sad for you." Mrs. Braithwaite's face fell.

"We do what we can." The older woman drew in a deep breath. "Helping others, that's our way of getting through it, isn't it, George?"

"Yes, Gran," he said in a mechanical way.

They sat in silence for a moment, until the train began to chug away from the station.

"I hear that some of the WVS groups are extremely helpful," Mrs. Braithwaite said, trying to loosen the conversation.

"Most of them are very helpful indeed, although you do hear stories."

"What stories?"

"Sometimes they're badly run, too much internal strife and not enough generosity." She nodded, as did Mrs. Braithwaite.

"Too bound up with village politics, squabbles, and gossip, who's in charge and so forth, I imagine," Mrs. Braithwaite muttered, as if she didn't know. "I suppose those women simply don't realize what the real war is like. There they are, sitting in their cozy homes, listening to the news about the bombs on the wireless, the men fighting the war in North Africa, and yet somehow it doesn't seem to sink in."

The older woman frowned. "People can be selfish."

Mrs. Braithwaite felt a lump in her throat. "You must miss your daughter."

"I still can't believe that she's gone. It's as if she's just popped out for milk and will be back later." She smiled suddenly. "Sometimes I think it's best not to believe it. She can just live alongside us, in the next room, where we can think we'll see her again soon." She slowly let out a deep breath. "If I call her, she'll call me back, the way I'd call her down for dinner when she was young. 'Maggie,' I'd shout up the stairs, and she would answer, 'I'll be down in a minute, Mum.' "

Mrs. Braithwaite felt tears come to her eyes. "My daughter's missing," she said. "I miss her so much. I don't know how I'll cope if she hasn't made it."

The older woman smiled sadly. "Cherish your love, for those who are with us **and** those who are gone. Just because they're not here, it doesn't mean that we love them any the less."

The train had pulled into the next station, and the older woman and boy stood up.

Mrs. Braithwaite opened the door for them. "Keep up the good work," she said.

The woman nodded as she stepped off. "We will,

won't we, George?" Then her eyes met Mrs. Braith-waite's. "It's all we can do."

With that, she slowly trundled down the plat-form, muttering to the boy.

As the train began to draw away, Mrs. Braith-waite sat down, a frown crumpling her forehead.

"It isn't the way life is supposed to be. A mother is the one who should die first."

"Well, there is a war on." Mr. Norris patted her hand.

"But how do you ever get over the loss of your own child? A whole part of your life, your soul is simply missing, gone." She took a great gulp of air. "That part of Betty that makes her hold her chin up the way she does, and how she bites her lip when she's thinking or about to say something that isn't completely true. That lilting way that she runs, that sparkle in her eyes when she knows she's right. How can I even begin to live without her?"

Mr. Norris took out another fresh ironed hand-kerchief—he had taken to carrying a spare.

"That poor woman was right." Mrs. Braithwaite sighed, wiping her eyes. "Love is the most crucial thing we have. Above reputation, above beauty, above our kindest actions." She gasped, struggling to get out her notebook. "That's it! That's the mea-sure of success, isn't it?"

"What is?"

"The amount that you love and are loved. It's love—don't you see?"

They sat there together in the jolting carriage, the word floating in the air.

The whole of Mrs. Braithwaite's life seemed to pass through her mind, a drab play where the lead character was so intent on power that she'd become despised by the people around her.

She'd always firmly believed that the way she'd lived her life was correct. Aunt Augusta had told her to conduct herself "as if a lady were watching." It wasn't so much living a life as passing a test. In any case, who was this "lady" looking over her shoulder? Was it Lady Worthing, whose visits to the Ashcombe WVS were so important that she'd berate the other ladies? Was it Aunt Augusta herself, following her around like a ghost, ensuring that her loyalty was never lost? Or was it society, the small-minded culture of one-upmanship that taught her that the Mrs. Metcalfs of this world would get the better of her if she let her guard slip?

She thought of the other Mrs. Braithwaite, Blanche's mother, the kind, loving mother whom she'd never met. When she died, was she content with the way she'd lived her life? Did she have any regrets? Did she care that her nasty neighbor loathed her?

Mrs. Braithwaite felt sure of only one thing. Anyone with love in her heart didn't spend her life looking over her shoulder.

## 46.

The train pulled into Sevenoaks Station. After a quick inquiry at the ticket desk as to the whereabouts of the hospital, they marched down the road in its direction, Mrs. Braithwaite leading the way at a brisk trot.

"Not a moment to lose!"

The hospital was a ramshackle collection of buildings, all constructed in different eras; the main building was Victorian with a large Edwardian wing, some ugly outbuildings added since the last war connected by brick corridors.

"We need to speak to one of your nurses," Mrs. Braithwaite told a weary receptionist at the front desk. "Her name is Mary Montgomery. It's terrifically urgent!"

The woman looked them over. "You've just missed her, I'm afraid. Her shift ended at three."

Mr. Norris stepped forward, knowing that he was the best person to handle this particular situation. "I don't suppose you know where she lives, do you? We have a message for her, you see. It's of the utmost importance."

"I can't give you her address," the woman snapped. "Unless you're family."

"Well, we're her aunt and uncle, actually," Mr. Norris said quickly, turning to Mrs. Braithwaite with a sad smile. "We've come with news about her parents."

"I'm not sure—"

Mr. Norris took out his handkerchief and, although he loathed to do it, allowed the very corner of his mouth to wobble.

"Oh well," the woman said, looking positively petrified that the man in front of her might begin to weep in public. "In that case, she lives in Hartley Street, number four. It's up the road and second on the left."

"Thank you for your kindness," Mr. Norris stammered, before grabbing Mrs. Braithwaite's arm and tugging her toward the door.

They managed to find the right road, despite the lack of signage.

"It might be good for national security to take away all the street names," said Mrs. Braithwaite, "but it's not especially helpful for people on an important mission."

Mrs. Braithwaite gave the door one of her bracing knocks.

Relief spread through them as it was opened by Mary herself, looking tired but pretty in her nurse's uniform. She'd been unpinning her nurse's cap, and a large curl of beautiful brown hair cascaded down the side of her face.

"Oh, hello," she said prettily. "What can I do for you?" Then she saw Mr. Norris, whom she evidently remembered from the Chiltern Church meeting, and she sucked in her cheeks and scowled. The memory of how he'd flirted with her to get information filled him with revulsion. Of all the unpleasant things he'd had to do, that surely was the absolute worst.

"Hallo there," Mrs. Braithwaite began. "We were just in the neighborhood and heard that Mr. Fox had moved down here, and we have a few items that belong to him, so we thought we'd return them." She was using her polite WVS voice, the same one she'd use if she were asking Mary to come for Sunday lunch.

Mary blushed. "I'm afraid he's not here at all," she said. "I don't know where you heard that. He's still in London, although he did move house. Why don't you give the things to me? I can pass them on."

"No, I'm afraid I have to give them to him in person." Mrs. Braithwaite gave her a no-nonsense smile. "Do you happen to know his new address? I think he may need his things."

"I'm sorry, Mrs. er—"

"Mrs. Br—" Mr. Norris nudged her. If Mary had Betty's passport, then she knew Betty's last name. Mrs. Braithwaite eyed him, and then smiled, saying, "Mrs. Brail."

"Well, Mrs. Brail," Mary said, covering a yawn. "I don't know his new address, but you could take it to the curiosity shop up by Clapham Common." She smiled, polite yet trying to get rid of them. "He's there quite often these days, and—"

"What's going on?" A woman with short brown hair came up behind Mary, a hand on her shoulder protectively. When she turned to the side, Mr. Norris saw a long scar down the left side of her face.

**It's the woman who spoke at the church meeting,** Mr. Norris thought to himself. **What had she been talking about again? Oh yes, her joy at the bombing in . . . Sevenoaks.**

Mr. Norris's heart shuddered.

"Have you met my sister, Kathleen?" Mary said innocently, looking around to her with a smile.

But the woman didn't look back at her sister. She was looking at the newcomers, her eyes engaging for a moment too long with Mr. Norris's, and then, horrifically, she smiled. "Won't you come in?"

"I'm afraid we're in a bit of a hurry," Mr. Norris said nervously, shuffling back.

"We can stop for a while, can't we?" Mrs. Braith-waite said sternly, grabbing his arm and trying to drag him over the threshold. She obviously hadn't recognized the woman and was desperate to get more information out of Mary.

"Come in for tea," the ghastly woman said, grinning as if her life depended on it. "We have toasted tea cakes today."

"No, we can't, my dear." Mr. Norris gave Mrs. Braithwaite a very wide-eyed look. "I have to get back to work."

"Oh, come on! You're always working too hard." She yanked him back, smiling at the women. "A cup of tea would be lovely, thank you!"

Short of any other solution, Mr. Norris took a firm hold of Mrs. Braithwaite's wrist and began striding quickly down the road, calling, "Not today. Thank you, though. Such a lovely offer."

"What's going on?" yelled Mrs. Braithwaite, as she plunged down the road behind him. "What in heaven's name has got into you?"

"Didn't you realize? Mary's sister is the vile woman from the Chiltern Church meeting," he whispered hoarsely through the side of his mouth as he dragged her up the main road back to the station. "If they weren't onto us already, they certainly will be now. That's why she was trying to get us to go in, so that they could trap us."

"Good gracious!" Mrs. Braithwaite declared, gathering her handbag and upping her speed toward the station. "We have to get to that curiosity shop."

"My thoughts precisely," Mr. Norris said. "It must be the one beside the Pendulum—we sat on its step to watch the telephone box. It was under our noses all this time."

They trotted at pace into the station, only to find that the next train to London wasn't for another twenty minutes.

"We'll just have to stay hidden until it leaves," Mrs. Braithwaite said, as they dashed out onto the forecourt.

Heading into a newsagent's, they took cover behind two early editions of the **Evening Mail,** peering around every few minutes to check that they hadn't been followed.

But they had.

They watched with dread as Mary and her sister ran into the station, along with the blackshirted thug from the meeting.

"What are we going to do?" Mr. Norris gasped. "They'll see us getting onto the train."

Mrs. Braithwaite gave him a furtive smile. "We'll simply have to find another way to get back to London."

## 47.

In the dark, windowless room, Betty couldn't tell how much time had passed. Anthony and the men were still there. She could hear their voices in the next room, arguing about what to do with her.

Briggs wanted to resume the questioning that had been suspended after Mrs. Braithwaite had barged in to rescue her. Marty, who suddenly seemed like the brains of the bunch, leaned toward contacting Mr. Fox to find someone more competent to carry out the interrogation. Anthony was adamant that he should interrogate her, alone.

Betty lay on the floor, tied to the chair, assessing her options. If Briggs left, there was a chance that she could talk Marty into loosening her ropes, which could give her leeway to use her combat training against the remaining two. Anthony was hopeless at fighting—when they were younger, he'd relied on height and strength to overpower her, but she knew that now, with her training, she could floor him easily. Marty was short but had the potential to be a vicious, street-fighting type, and he almost definitely would have at least one knife about his person, if not a gun.

Her thoughts kept turning to the possibility of rescue. She had been trained not to expect anyone to come for her; it might be dangerous and could uncover another agent. But she kept thinking of Baxter's last words as she left, that he'd come to find her if she wasn't back by midnight.

**But how would he know where they'd taken her?**

She sighed. It seemed so unfair, so unreasonable, that his old house was so close, yet she felt a million miles away.

Suddenly there was a kerfuffle coming from the other room. New people had entered, the gruff voices of more men. It sounded as if they had another prisoner.

She strained her ears to hear.

"Are you sure?" Marty was saying nervously.

"I always knew he was a traitor," Anthony said savagely.

"What shall we do with him?" one of the heavies grumbled.

"I'm not a mole, you idiots. You need to let me go." A familiar voice cut through the others.

A hard lump formed in her throat.

It was Baxter.

"Kathleen Montgomery told us to get him, said she'd suspected Fox was a traitor for a while—and now she has proof." The man spat loudly, probably at Baxter.

"Don't be a fool, Briggs." Baxter's voice was calm, dignified. "Do you have any idea how much trouble this will cause in Berlin? Göring will be furious! We'll all be in for it." Baxter was still in character, using all his skill and experience to convince them that he wasn't the mole.

"What are we going to do with him?" Marty said, obviously worried in case they had the wrong man. "We'll have to question him. Find out the truth."

"**What?** As if he'll just blurt out that he's a blooming mole, you dunce?" Briggs said.

"This is nonsense, I tell you!" Baxter exclaimed. "Kathleen Montgomery is lying to score points in Berlin."

"Let's tie him up in there with the girl and then decide what to do," Anthony said confidently. "I'm the most senior member here now that Mr. Fox has been demoted"—he let out a small laugh—"so I will take charge."

**Typical!** Betty thought. **Their leader is accused**

**of being a mole, and Anthony's trying to use it to better himself.**

The door opened, and the two thugs who had brought Baxter in pushed him into the room, holding on to him from behind. Grabbing the other chair, they tied him down in the same way they had her, this time gagging his mouth with a strip of cloth.

Baxter glanced at her, their eyes meeting for a glimmer of a second, before he looked away. The men, instead of leaving, had pulled up chairs and had settled into watching them. They couldn't give away a thing.

Betty felt her heart implode. He had come to find her after all, true to his word. He must have gone to see Mary Montgomery to find out where they might have imprisoned her, and that obnoxious sister of hers suspected something and brought the heavies around.

Suddenly a pang of horror struck her. She, Betty, was the orchestrator of Baxter's imprisonment—maybe death—as well as her own and possibly her mother's, too. Her reckless determination to continue on the mission—instead of taking Cummerbatch's ticket to Devon—would be the downfall of them all.

It was one thing to put oneself in danger, but to put another agent at risk was bad espionage at its worst.

She made a small cough, and he looked up, and for the briefest moment their eyes met. A look of intense love told her that all he had wanted was for her to be free. And now he had failed.

They had both failed.

## 48.

"Excuse me, please," Mrs. Braithwaite said to the station newsagent, who was starting to get annoyed at their taking up residence behind newspapers in his shop.

"What is it?"

"Is there another entrance to the station? We're trying to avoid someone."

"I would never have guessed," he muttered sarcastically. "Take a sharp right outside. There's a side door at the back of the station."

"Thank you," she said, glaring at Mr. Norris and indicating that they should slowly walk out of the shop with their newspapers in front of their faces.

Taking side steps, like a crab, she headed out, then right, and once she was behind one of the broad iron pillars, she took the newspaper down and darted for the side entrance, which brought them out onto a side street.

Mr. Norris appeared beside her, and they both looked around.

"We need to find someone driving to London." She glanced around and spotted a van on the other side of the road. "Let's start with that deliveryman over there."

She stalked across the road to a fellow in overalls unloading groceries.

"I say, would you happen to be driving to London this afternoon? We've missed our train back and need a lift."

"'Fraid not," he said, turning to her. He seemed a friendly sort of chap. "We're off to Westerham after this." He scooped off his cloth cap and scratched his head. "But I think Bill might be going that way. He'll be at the canteen by the station, if he is."

Thanking him, the duo turned back to the station and cautiously headed for the canteen. It was a makeshift affair, a small hut with a lady making tea and handing out biscuits and scones.

"We're looking for someone called Bill," Mrs. Braithwaite announced to the few men standing around. They were varying degrees of dirty, and when the dirtiest of them stepped forward and told her that he was Bill, she resisted the urge to hold her nose.

"Would you be able to give us a lift to London?"

she asked in as cheerful a way as she could while breathing through her mouth.

Bill looked them up and down and grinned.

"If you make it worth my while. Ten shillings?"

Mr. Norris stepped forward politely. "That's fine, but we need to get there fast. When are you leaving?"

The man chuckled chaotically. "Right now, if you make it twenty."

"Oh, all right then," Mrs. Braithwaite said less politely. "Where's the van then?"

"I need the money up front," he said, grinning again. Mrs. Braithwaite wished he would stop doing that. Someone should give him the much-needed advice that his yellowing teeth were not his strong point.

Neither was his breath, she discovered as they settled snugly into the cab of the battered old delivery van. Mrs. Braithwaite was sandwiched between him and Mr. Norris, and she pushed up to Mr. Norris, who was already squashed against the door.

"Just have to make a quick pickup," Bill said, throwing the steering wheel around and flinging them into the door on Mr. Norris's side.

"Not too far, I hope," she said. Her voice wobbled as she took in the style of his driving: fast and furious, taking corners tightly, precariously on two wheels, occasionally accompanied by a loud screech.

The van careered down to a row of shops in the town.

"Wait here," Bill instructed, nipping out and into a shop, coming out with a stack of large boxes and putting them into the back of the van. As he went back for more, Mrs. Braithwaite glanced at Mr. Norris. "I do hope this isn't black market or anything. What do you suppose it is?"

"Well, it could be—" Mr. Norris began, and then the smell issuing from the back of the van snaked its way into the cab.

It was unmistakable.

"Fish."

They both looked at each other in horror.

"How long will it take to get to London?"

"An hour."

She looked at Mr. Norris and heaved a great sigh.

"Let's get going, shall we?" Bill stepped back into the driver's seat and revved up the engine.

The journey went in stops and starts, the van shuddering to a halt every time they saw a canteen so that Bill could get a strong cup of tea to "improve the concentration."

Mr. Norris talked to him most of the way, about the war and how Bill was doing rather well with a side business of his, which Mrs. Braithwaite felt must refer to something both illegal and smelly.

There was an awkward moment when Bill asked Mr. Norris, "Do you live in London, you and the wife?" and Mr. Norris flushed, replying, "Well, actually we're not married."

"Oh, it's like that, is it?" Bill chortled salaciously with a wink.

"I'll have you know that we're friends traveling together," Mrs. Braithwaite snapped. "There's nothing untoward about us at all."

And just at that moment, Bill threw the van into a large swerve, throwing her against Mr. Norris.

"Oh, do excuse me," Bill said with a smirk.

"He did that on purpose," Mrs. Braithwaite muttered to Mr. Norris.

It was gone seven o'clock before they reached the outskirts of London. Daylight was dimming to a navy-blue dusk as Bill dropped them at a corner of Clapham Common. They exited hastily, glad to be breathing fresh air once again.

With a wave and a cheeky laugh, Bill was gone and Mrs. Braithwaite and Mr. Norris strode quickly down the road, past the crowd of criminals standing outside the Pendulum.

"All set for another good night?" Bobby Mack called over, recognizing them.

"No time to talk," Mrs. Braithwaite said, hurrying past. "We have a daughter to rescue."

"Good luck with that!" he called after her as she trotted across the road.

The curiosity shop looked as old and unkempt as it had a few nights earlier. They drew to a halt outside, and then Mr. Norris beckoned her to hide with him behind a bush on the opposite pavement.

"Are you sure Baxter will be in there?" Mr. Norris said nervously.

"We'll find out soon enough," she said, as she started creeping toward the building. "I'll go in. You stay there," she whispered to Mr. Norris. "You never know, Mary Montgomery might have already warned them. We might walk straight into a trap."

Edging up to the door, she began peering in through the dusty front window. Inside, there were all kinds of oddments. An old globe, a broken gilded picture frame, a battered copper birdcage housing a stuffed parakeet, green and gold beneath the dust.

**It looks like the kind of place where someone would hide a dead body**, she thought with a shiver.

She tried the door.

The handle turned easily.

"Why wouldn't they lock it?" she muttered to herself.

**Unless they were already inside.**

Shuddering at the thought, she took a deep breath and pushed the door open. A little bell jangled annoyingly as she poked her head inside.

Although she expected the air to be musty, it was surprisingly fresh.

**Someone must have been here recently.**

Making haste to the back, careful not to upset the

shelves lined with an array of antiques, she began to search for a door. Mary Montgomery seemed sure that Fox—or Baxter—spent a lot of time here. There must be a back room.

She began pushing things aside, a full-size broken mirror that was leaning against the wall, a small bookcase packed with dusty clothbound books that had long since lost their jackets, a deep green curtain full of cobwebs. And it was behind this last item that she found a small, narrow door.

It creaked as she opened it.

There were voices.

"The girl's not talking," a man said gruffly. "Don't know what to try next."

"We need to get her mother back."

**Was that the voice of the thug who'd held her captive? Briggs?**

"Then we could make her talk."

Suddenly Mrs. Braithwaite felt a movement behind her and turned quickly to see the curtain swish to the side.

And there, out of the shadows, a man folded his arms and chuckled as he registered precisely who was in front of him.

It was Anthony Metcalf.

"Look who it is! Did you come to save the day?"

He grabbed her arm.

She snatched it away.

"How dare you, Anthony! Just you wait until I tell your mother!"

He laughed, the kind of slow, rhythmic laugh of someone who knows he's in charge.

"Come on, Mrs. Braithwaite. You may think you're still queen of the village, but right here you have no power at all." He put a condescending hand on her shoulder. "Come with me. I've got some people in here who are longing to meet you."

Inside the long, darkened room, Briggs and Marty sat around a small, old dining table, quickly standing to take charge of Mrs. Braithwaite.

"Well, well, ask and you shall receive!" Briggs laughed, taking her wrists. "There's no getting away from us this time."

She kicked him hard in the shin, and he worked hard at not showing any pain.

"I'll never tell you anything," she spat.

"But, Mrs. Braithwaite, you don't have to," Anthony brayed, walking across the room to another door on the opposite side. "All we want from you is a few screams of pain."

He opened the door. Inside was another room in darkness. Although she couldn't see inside, she knew that Betty was in there.

They were going to use her to make Betty talk.

"Don't tell them a thing, Betty!" she called over vehemently.

"Shut it!" Briggs slapped her hard around the face.

After rummaging around in a bag on the floor, Briggs stood up and came toward her. In his hand, he brandished a small pocketknife, the blade glinting in the dim light of a bare lightbulb.

He was going to cut her.

And she had to do her utmost not to make a sound.

Self-control was something Mrs. Braithwaite prided herself on. She believed emotions of all types could be reined in if one had the will. But it wasn't until that blade flashed in the light that she was forced to concede that perhaps the control of physical pain had never been a strong point.

"Let's have a little go, shall we!" Briggs snarled.

A whimper broke out of her.

How had things become so shockingly out of control? All the terrible pieces of this adventure so far—Betty in danger, the flood in the crypt, the horrific sadness of Cassandra, Mr. Norris's wound—withered in the face of this actual torture.

She winced, gritting her teeth and clenching her mouth closed.

Briggs laughed, a cackle usually reserved for having a go at someone in a pub, not slicing into a respectable housewife.

"You won't get anything out of me," she said determinedly, in the most upright voice she could muster. Then she called out, "Don't worry, Betty dear. They can't hurt me!"

This seemed to enrage Briggs. "Shall we try then?" And he lunged forward with the knife, pulling the soft fabric of her blouse sleeve up, turning her wrist to expose her veins. The blade came down, the cold of the metal touching her skin, and Mrs. Braithwaite closed her eyes with trepidation.

A million thoughts surged through her head: Betty as a little girl, her long hair swinging around as she danced; then herself as a child, skipping, her parents beside her, the warmth of her mother's hand, her father's. Like a flurry of soft white snow descending onto her, around her, beaming with brightness, she felt almost heady with the sure knowledge that the true value of life was not how you lived, but how you loved. Giving love—and receiving it, if one was lucky enough—was the very best legacy that she could leave.

"I love you, Betty," she called into the darkness.

Suddenly there was a massive crash, and a man was shouting from across the room, "Stop! Leave her alone!"

Her heart stopped. She looked over, recognizing the voice.

Mr. Norris stood at the door.

His feet were apart, and he held up one hand. "Stop!" he ordered in an uncharacteristically stern shout.

**He had come to save her!**

Briggs growled. "Not you again."

"Release her immediately," Mr. Norris bellowed, ignoring him.

"Or what?" Marty had started to laugh, the others joining in. "What are you going to do about it?"

Briggs pulled the knife back from Mrs. Braithwaite and went toward Mr. Norris, brandishing it.

"I wouldn't do that if I were you," Mr. Norris said forthrightly.

"Why not? You got a bigger knife?" They began laughing.

But then, Mr. Norris, as calm as a parson, took down his hand and said, "Because you might upset my friends."

Behind him at the door, one by one, a horde of ruffians started entering the room. They were shoving each other to get in, some wearing misshapen suits, others grubby shirts, all looking as if they'd been dragged through a hedge backward. At the head of the group was a large man with a bald head, a thick blade in one hand.

He grinned at Mrs. Braithwaite and gave her a wink.

"Bobby Mack," she gasped.

Briggs and Marty started to back away.

But Bobby Mack yelled, "Charge!," and the motley gang of criminals stormed forward, jumping on Briggs and taking him down with a mighty thud.

A particularly rough-looking man took Marty from behind in a viselike grip, strangling him.

Marty kicked him hard in the shins, sending him reeling backward, and made a dash for the door, but was stopped by another ruffian, who scooped up a large Chinese vase and smashed it onto his head, bringing him down in a heap.

Mr. Norris spotted Anthony Metcalf creeping around the edge of the room toward the door and leaped over to stop him in his tracks.

"Where do you think you're going, Metcalf?"

"Get out of my way," Anthony growled, pointing a pistol at him.

Mr. Norris put his hands up and tried to back off, but Anthony pulled Mr. Norris in front of him, put the gun against his head, and shouted to the marauding crowd, "Let me go, or this buffoon gets it!"

The men all turned.

"I'm warning you," Anthony yelled, his voice wavering with fear that he was losing control of the situation. "I'll shoot him!"

"And you think we'll let you get away with that?" Bobby Mack said, walking forward.

Anthony was panicking, the pistol in his hand shaking.

"You're not up to this, are you, you sad little fascist?" Bobby Mack said, taking another step forward.

One of the other criminals gave a laugh. "I don't think we should kill him straightaway, Bobby. You've got to let us have some fun and games with him first."

"Help me, Briggs!" Anthony hollered, fear gripping him.

But Briggs was watching him sternly. "A minute ago, you were going to leave without me, and now you're begging for my help?"

"Help me, or else!" Anthony demanded.

Briggs strode forward, but as he did so, Bobby Mack tripped him from behind, sending him flying across the room.

Anthony dropped the gun in panic and ran for the door.

But they were on him, pushing him to the ground, pinning him down, and tying him up.

Two of them grabbed Briggs, who was still on the floor, tying him up, too.

"You lot ain't going nowhere!" Bobby Mack said, a grin on his face. "We've been trying to get you traitors for a long time. Looks like we found you right under our noses."

A rowdy cheer went up as they pushed the men outside.

Mr. Norris untied Mrs. Braithwaite, and she clung to him, tears in her eyes, muttering, "I knew you would come."

She hurried into the back room, where they found Betty.

"Betty! Are you all right?" Mrs. Braithwaite cried, untying her. "Talk to me!"

"I'm fine, Mum," Betty said, crying as she hugged her mother. "I really am incredibly, surprisingly, and wonderfully fine."

In the same room, a man was also tied to a chair.

Baxter.

"And he's here, too?"

"It's a long story, Mum." Betty raced over to untie him and take off the gag they'd put over his mouth.

"Oh, darling, thank goodness," he breathed, stroking her face once his hands were free. Then he looked over at Mrs. Braithwaite and smiled. "And thank you, too. I'm very much obliged." With a few large strides, he hurried out to help Bobby Mack and the others with the new prisoners.

"So, is he your young man?" Mrs. Braithwaite asked, trying not to show skepticism.

"As a matter of fact, he is, Mum," Betty laughed. "I know he might seem like the villain in all this, but he really is the best kind of man. Truly."

"But what about his affair with Mary Montgomery?"

She laughed. "He was courting her to infiltrate the fifth columnists. Her sister, Kathleen, is a prominent member, and we used Mary so that we could keep tabs on her."

"So he was pretending with her, not with you?"

"Well, he had to do what was necessary. But you have to believe that he really is devoted to me."

Outside, activity on the pavement was lively. The police were packing the suspects into the back of a police van, and the criminals from the pub were milling about congratulating themselves.

"You'll remember this in the future, won't you,

gov?" Bobby Mack was saying to the chief inspector. "How we helped and all. You know, give the lads here a bit of a break?"

The chief inspector seemed much more serious about his law enforcement responsibilities than P.C. Watts. He gave Bobby Mack a pat on the shoulder. "Let's just wait and see, shall we? In the meantime, contact us if you come across any more of these groups." He handed Bobby Mack a small, folded slip of paper, giving another, with the same information, to Betty, who was standing aside as Anthony was being hauled toward a police van.

"I can't believe you'd have let them torture me," she said to him. "What cause could have been so big that you'd stoop to that?"

Anthony's eyes were teary with pure anger as he shot her a look of disgust. "We're on the winning side, Betty. You just can't see that, can you? Just you wait and see." A policeman shoved him forward, and he turned ferociously toward Betty. "You ruined everything."

"No, not just me," she retorted, taking Mrs. Braithwaite's arm in hers. "My mother and my landlord helped, too!" She laughed and threw a grateful glance toward Mr. Norris, who was looking rather pleased with himself.

The door of the police van slammed shut behind Anthony and the others, and Betty watched with revulsion as the van drew away to the shouts and cheers of the men.

Mrs. Braithwaite found Bobby Mack, who was gleefully cheering with the others.

"I'd like to thank you for coming to my rescue," she said, beaming a jolly smile at him. "I thought I was 'a goner,' as you would put it!"

"Lucky we were there to help out. Your friend here begged us to come, duchess. Said he'd hand us in for looting if we didn't, so we thought we might as well." He grinned, giving Mr. Norris a hearty slap on the back. "Seeing it was you and all."

"And in the light of a few pound notes I passed around," Mr. Norris added with a knowing smile.

Mrs. Braithwaite beamed at him. "So I have you to thank."

Mr. Norris smiled back at her and said modestly, "Well, what's a man to do when a friend's in trouble?"

She took his hand in both of hers and squeezed it. "Thank you from the very bottom of my very alive heart."

And they stood there, together, with Betty and Baxter, for many minutes while the crowd of criminals dispersed.

Baxter had to hurry to HQ to send out some alerts. "I need to ensure that everyone knows what happened." He turned to Mrs. Braithwaite and Mr. Norris. "Thank you again, Mr. Norris. I don't know how we'd have got out so quickly if it hadn't been for you. And Mrs. Braithwaite, it was nice to meet you, as my own self this time. I hope Betty and I will see more of you soon." He kissed Betty and hurried away.

"Well, Mr. Norris," Mrs. Braithwaite said, "you deserve a good cup of tea after saving the day."

Mr. Norris blushed. "I'm not sure I should take all the credit. But let's just say that when I saw Anthony Metcalf let himself into the shop, I knew that I was going to have to do something."

"But how did you two know Anthony was involved with the fascists?" Betty stammered.

Mrs. Braithwaite tucked a hand through Betty's arm. "Ah, that's rather a long story, my dear."

And as they slowly made their way back to Shilling Lane, they explained the series of long, complicated, and often daring events that had led them to her.

## 49.

As soon as they got back to the house, Mrs. Braithwaite helped Betty to bed for a much-needed rest while Mr. Norris did the sensible thing and put the kettle on.

"It's hard to take it all in." Mrs. Braithwaite settled herself into her usual kitchen chair. She'd had time to chat with Betty and could hardly wait to discuss it all with Mr. Norris. "Betty doesn't seem at all surprised that Anthony Metcalf was at the center of it. She said he's always been repugnant, even when they were young. When it started looking like Britain would be invaded, Anthony decided it might be better to be on the other side."

"How disturbing." Mr. Norris sat down beside

her. "But on the good side, it looks like we had it right about Baxter being the elusive Mr. Fox."

"Betty said that at the beginning of the war Baxter cemented himself as the main Nazi contact for the fifth columnists in Britain. Quite an impressive job he did, too. He's been pretending to be in direct contact with Göring, and even had some replica Iron Crosses made to ceremonially hand out at meetings. He was the linchpin of the entire thing, collecting information to pass to Berlin—which of course didn't get there—and organizing secret meetings in cellars and disused buildings. Apparently, clandestine meetings in strange places gratifies the fascists' notions of top-secret espionage. But although he keeps instructing the members not to carry out sabotage, kidnappings, or assassinations, they still do."

"Probably eager to get an Iron Cross," Mr. Norris said. "Perhaps his medals are too enticing."

"Anthony was especially keen to get recognition. He wanted to ensure his position at the top of the new order in Britain, which was why he wanted to hear all about Taplin's plans for the rail bridge."

"What about Betty's kidnapping?"

"Anthony must have heard through the grapevine that Betty was a possible mole. He made it his very own mission to capture her, although I can't think how he knew she would be at the garage. Perhaps it was a lucky guess: he knew she'd go to check it sooner or later."

"How did the fascists get wind that Fox wasn't on their side, then?"

"They'd suspected there was a mole still infiltrating the group, but they didn't know who it was."

Mr. Norris frowned. "But how did they find out it was him? They seemed jolly certain."

"Baxter told Betty that he went to see Mary Montgomery to find out where Betty was being held so that he could rescue her. Her nasty sister, Kathleen, overheard and smelled a rat."

The kitchen door opened, and they turned to see Cassandra coming in, smiling a little. "I just saw Betty," she said, her blue eyes alight with intrigue, then she sat down, leaning forward and lowering her voice. "You found her?"

Mr. Norris exchanged knowing glances with Mrs. Braithwaite, who said, "It's all a bit hush-hush, I'm afraid."

What with so many people doing wartime jobs, everyone had become used to not asking questions and certainly not expecting answers about missing people suddenly turning up looking tired and a bit shabby.

But Cassandra wasn't giving up.

"I've been thinking it all through," she whispered hurriedly. "And it all fits into place, how it was that Betty went missing, how you two both have been so frightfully busy, dashing around the countryside, and so forth."

Mr. Norris sighed and muttered, "Well, perhaps

you should stop thinking about it so much." Then he added, "Knowing too much can be dangerous."

"I just wanted to say a hush-hush 'well done.'" She grinned. "You two are quite the cavaliers, saving first me and now Betty."

## 50.

When Betty woke up the next morning, Mrs. Braithwaite was sitting on her bed.

"I still can't quite believe that you came to my rescue, Mum," she said, putting her hand out. "I'm so grateful, but it still seems so, well, unlikely." She looked at their hands, linked together.

Mrs. Braithwaite smiled. "After Mrs. Metcalf ousted me from the WVS, I realized that I'd been missing something. It was suddenly as clear as the light of day that **you** are the most important thing in the world to me." She took a deep breath, and then in a different kind of voice, lower and sadder, she said, "Regardless of whether I gave birth to you or not."

Betty shook herself. "What? What do you mean, Mum?"

"That is what I needed to tell you, dear. What I came to London to tell you. You're not actually my daughter by birth. Although you are your father's child."

"But how?" Betty struggled to understand what her mother was saying, what it meant.

"Your father had an affair with a young, unmarried woman—he had affairs with relative frequency, to be frank. Well, with this one, she became pregnant, and was sent away to relatives to have the baby." She paused, unsure how to say it. "That baby was you, my dear."

"What happened to my mother?" She shook her head—she was **speaking** to her mother. "Well, the woman who gave birth to me."

"She died a few days after you were born, internal bleeding."

Silence hung in the air for a moment, then Betty said, "But how did I get to you?"

"Her relatives were too old to keep the baby. They were pressing us to take it, threatening that they would expose your father." Mrs. Braithwaite leaned forward and gripped Betty's hand. "It was decided by Aunt Augusta and your father that because I had failed to produce a baby in our five years of marriage, I should take the child and raise it as my own."

"And that was me?" Betty felt as if the world were standing still.

"It was. They brought you to me when you were only a few weeks old, and Aunt Augusta rented a cottage for us by the sea for a few months so that no one would suspect that you weren't mine. We fought to keep it quiet, and only a few people ever knew."

"Mrs. Metcalf," Betty said slowly, all the pieces coming together.

"You know?"

"She must have told Anthony," she said drily. "He used it as bait to get me to the curiosity shop."

Mrs. Braithwaite's face creased with revulsion. "I can't believe that she told him."

"But how does she know in the first place?"

"We used to be good friends, both young wives, new to the village. She was more quiet back then, while I usually took charge. Then she started to have children, first Patience and then Anthony, while I seemed unable to produce anything.

"When I arrived back in Ashcombe with you, I didn't know what to do, how to act. I confided in her. I thought we were true friends."

"I don't understand," Betty said. "You hardly speak to her now."

"We've been growing apart from each other for years. She quickly found a way to lord my secret over me, undermining me in the village. I had to be on my guard continually, watching out for her, protecting myself. That's why I always felt that I had to be up to snuff with the village women. I was busy protecting my name. Protecting you."

Betty felt the blood flowing into her face. She'd always found it easy to blame her mother for everything, and yet the truth was far more complicated. "I'm so sorry, Mum. I never knew any of this."

"After the divorce, Mrs. Metcalf used my downfall to turn me into a pariah, to propel herself to the top spot. She—and then most of the other women in the village—avoided me. No one wants to be friends with a divorced woman, you see, just in case his immorality was catching. I ask you, why would I suddenly lose all sense of propriety just because your father did?" Mrs. Braithwaite sniffed with annoyance. "Mrs. Metcalf made it clear that her mission was to hound me out of the village." She let out a big sigh. "Although I have to take some of the blame, I don't think I was as kind as I should have been, especially when I ran the WVS. But to threaten to expose my secret—"

"Is that what she was using against you? The story of my birth?"

"Yes, and that's part of the reason I decided to finally explain it to you, my dear. I began to see that it had been wrong to keep it from you—it would be appalling for you to hear about it through village gossip. After all, it's you that it's about. Not me, or even your father for that matter."

"But it's **your** reputation that suffers." Betty sighed.

"I have to admit that I didn't relish her ruining me with it. But the funny thing is, now I don't really care what people say." She leaned forward and put her arms around Betty. "You and I have each other, and even though you're not my daughter by birth, you're still my precious child." Mrs. Braithwaite smiled at her, wiping a tear from her soft cheek.

Betty pulled away. "But it's so terribly unfair that you should be punished for doing something as wonderful as taking in another woman's child! You didn't do anything wrong—what you did was generous and kind. It was Dad. He should be the one who suffers, and yet he's completely fine, off married to another woman and living the good life. Everything's wrong. People should have been kind to you, when they simply cast you out." Betty felt a lump form in her throat. "And I could have been kinder, too, Mum. When I heard about your divorce, I decided that it was easier to stay out of it, when I knew, deep down, that Dad wasn't playing fair. How could I have done that? When you were the one with a heart big enough to take me in."

Mrs. Braithwaite grasped Betty's hand in her lap. "I confess that I didn't take you in because of the kindness of my heart, my dear. It was because I had no children of my own. Aunt Augusta pressed me into it to save the family name." She sighed. "She came from a different generation.

People had to look after themselves, guard their position in life."

"Aunt Augusta was a terrible woman."

"I've been thinking about Aunt Augusta, how she manipulated me." Mrs. Braithwaite frowned. "She and my mother grew up in a great mansion; their father was an earl, you know, and they were brought up with governesses and strict upper-class manners. My mother married, and I think that Aunt Augusta was jealous. I even wonder if she had her eye on my father herself; she always spoke about him with great respect—far more than she had for my mother. She told me that no one was ever good enough for her to marry, and then I arrived in her life, my parents conveniently drowned. They left her their child and their fortune, which was quickly whittled down on bad investments and keeping up appearances. In a way, it was her own insistence on proving her superiority to everyone that made her spiteful and cold. As far as she was concerned, I was a convenient child, and you, my dear, were little more than an embarrassment that we could use to fill the gap in the image she was creating. She never wanted either of us." She made a big sigh, holding Betty's hand tighter. "There was never any space for love in her heart."

Betty felt tears appearing in the corners of her eyes. "Why didn't you tell me that you adopted me?"

"Aunt Augusta told me that I should never tell anyone. She made me feel ashamed for not being able to have my own child. She said that I was a disappointment to our family, not a complete woman." She tried to stop herself from crying. "She convinced me that if I told you, my whole world would collapse around me."

Betty had never seen her mother upset, but as the tears were hastily wiped away by a clean handkerchief, she realized that being a mother was far, far more than giving birth to someone. And it wasn't just about being strong and resilient, although that was certainly part of it.

It was about being human.

"But what happened between us, you and me?" Betty said. "You were warmer when I was young, and then you changed."

"I can't blame Aunt Augusta entirely, but I think when she moved in with us she began to poison me against you. She kept pointing out how different we were, how you clearly weren't one of 'us.' She wanted me to herself—I see that now—not squandering any energy on you, the cuckoo in the nest, as she put it."

"Cuckoo," Betty said quietly. "That's why you became cold and distant."

Mrs. Braithwaite looked crestfallen. "I made a very big mistake, Betty, shutting you out like I did. But now I mean to make it up to you." She put her arm around her daughter. "I've spent a lot of time thinking over the last few days, and I realized that you **are** my daughter, and I am your mother. And why should we miss out on the greatest bond—the love between a mother and daughter—because some old bat bullied me into thinking of it as a humiliation and not a joy?" She pulled her in close. "That's going to change."

Betty began to cry. "I never knew why you had become so distant from me."

"I'm so sorry, my dear, lovely child." Mrs. Braithwaite smoothed Betty's hair back from her forehead. "I can't turn back time—believe me, I wish I could. But I'm determined to make up for it now. We can try to find the relatives of the woman who gave birth to you, uncover more about your origins, if you'd like. I've become quite good at investigating. Aunt Augusta did me a great disservice by forcing me to forget about my own parents, and I most definitely don't want that for you, dear Betty." She held her daughter's hands tightly in hers. "But I want you to know one thing: From now on I will do my utmost to be the very best mother I can be."

Betty looked up, and through her tears, she gave her a weak smile. "Well, I have to say, Mum, you've made a jolly good start!"

## 51.

After lunch Mrs. Braithwaite took the train to Waterloo Station, stepping off into the crowd and striding out toward the river. But her pace slowed as she approached St. Thomas's Hospital, and then she ground to a halt.

It had been bombed.

A ragged chunk was missing from the left side of the imposing structure. Masses of broken planks and bricks were piled around the forecourt.

But hospital life went on as usual: nurses, people in uniforms, and local civilians were stepping over or around the debris, bustling in and out of the massive doors.

"What happened to the building?" Mrs. Braithwaite asked the girl at the reception desk. "Shouldn't the hospital close down for repairs?"

"We need all the beds we can get," the girl replied. "We can't stop just because we get bombed ourselves."

"Were many people hurt?"

"It was the nurses' block that was hit. A couple of nights ago—sounded like the whole world was exploding."

"Oh goodness!" The poor girl. She looked hardly more than sixteen.

"It was terrifying. We all rushed through the building to see what had happened. I was running through a corridor that was completely normal one minute, and then, suddenly, it just collapsed in front of me. Bricks and planks and bits of things from the nurses' rooms above, iron bedposts, white towels, the arms of a brown coat, all higgledy-piggledy in the mess."

"Was anyone caught in it?"

"Yes, we could hear some nurses calling from under the rubble. Most were very calm—they didn't want to set the others off panicking. One of them was even making jokes, trying to cheer the others up. I remember she said, 'That's my last pair of stockings quite ruined!' And the other trapped girls laughed along. So brave!"

"There couldn't be anything worse than being buried under a collapsed building." Mrs. Braithwaite looked up at the heavy ceiling grimly. "Did they get out?"

"Some of them did." The girl bit her lip. "A few of them were stuck in there all night. Everyone in the hospital came to help get them out, even though the bombs were still coming down around us. We were carrying away the rubble piece by piece, then some men—doctors mostly—came and helped lift the heavy beams out of the way. But there were some women we just couldn't get to." Her voice became broken at the memory. "We couldn't even see them, we could just hear their voices, telling us they were all right."

She wiped a tear from beneath her eye.

"Ten of them didn't make it. The last one to go, Sheila Young, took hours." She took the handkerchief that Mrs. Braithwaite offered and blew her nose loudly. "They simply couldn't get her out. I went off and back on duty, and she was still there, telling us she was still fine, but weak. Trucks and men came, trying to get her out, but she was too deep. Just after daybreak, we stopped hearing her voice."

Mrs. Braithwaite gasped.

"They got to her body the next day." The girl pointed to a series of pictures on the far wall. "There are some photographs of the nurses over there. They're going to put up a plaque after the war." Then she added in a quieter voice, "Unless we get bombed again."

Mrs. Braithwaite found herself wanting to see

them, to see their faces, although afterward she wondered whether she should have, as she'd given her handkerchief to the girl at the desk.

Each picture showed the face of a clean and tidy young woman, complete with nurse's cap and uniform, a busy machine of efficiency and caring and brisk common sense. People spoke a lot about common sense in this war, as if it were the glue that would hold everyone together, keeping emotions in check, delivering a million small but significant positive reactions that together would win the day—win the war. Nurses were at the very peak of this "thinking before doing."

The bravest of them all.

The last photograph, Sheila Young, the poor girl who had spent hours trapped and dying, seemed to sit apart from the others. She had a friendly face, a vague squint in one eye and a cheery smile. She might have had a young man, and a mother, somewhere. A mother who was now mourning the death of her beautiful, vibrant daughter.

Reaching the top of the stairs, Mrs. Braithwaite walked slowly to Ward 10. The nurse was nowhere to be found, probably attending to another patient, so Mrs. Braithwaite trod quietly down to the silent room.

The place was in half darkness, as usual, the same women in the same beds, bandages and plastered limbs gleaming out in the darkness. As she neared Blanche's bed, Mrs. Braithwaite looked for her familiar shape beneath the covers.

But it wasn't there.

She quickened her pace, making sure she had the right bed.

She did.

And as she stood at the foot of the bed, she knew for certain.

Tears came fast to her eyes. Blanche had slipped away.

Mrs. Braithwaite's heart fell, as if the bottom of the world had opened up.

She went slowly up to the pillow, now neatly cleaned and tucked in, waiting for a new patient—another bomb victim whose life would be ruined forever. She pulled up a chair.

"What happened to you, my dear Blanche?" she said, distraught, touching the empty pillow. "I never got to say good-bye. I'm so sorry I couldn't help you." She heaved a long, sad sigh. "I suppose I was never going to make a real difference, was I? It was just this foolish fancy of mine that you needed a mother, someone to care if you lived or . . ." She paused at the onset of tears, unable to say the word. "Someone who made you want to stay alive."

She smoothed down the blankets.

"I suppose it was meant to be this way. I got Betty back, and so you've gone." She sat back, wondering how it had happened, whether it was short, fast, painless, or if it was long, messy, agonizing.

"I want you to know that I'll always remember you, Blanche."

"Mrs. Braithwaite?"

The voice came from behind her. She turned to see the nurse.

"What happened to her?" Mrs. Braithwaite asked sadly.

The nurse put a hand on her shoulder. "She's left us."

"Was she conscious when it happened?" Mrs. Braithwaite felt a horror pass through her. "Aware of her own departure?"

The nurse looked confused. "They took her out on a stretcher. I'm sure she was quite pleased to be out of here."

"How can you say that? I know she was in a bad way, but there's no reason to think that she would have wanted to die."

The nurse looked at her, baffled and speechless for a moment, and then she began to gently laugh. "Oh, I see what you mean now."

"Well, it certainly isn't funny, and I'm not sure that I—"

"She left us and moved to Ward B2 on the third floor." She smiled at her, patting her shoulder. "She came out of the coma. She's getting better!"

Mrs. Braithwaite looked from her delighted face to the bare, clean pillow she had been talking to, then stood up hastily. "Well, why didn't you say so in the first place?"

Ward B2 was a small room with fewer beds. Because there was no nurses' desk, Mrs. Braithwaite walked straight in and began searching the patients to find Blanche.

She recognized her straightaway.

Propped up in bed, a bandage still over half of her short brown curls, Blanche gazed wistfully out of the window, completely ignoring the book on her lap. There were still a lot of bandages on her face and body, but otherwise she looked—well, she looked like a very alive young woman.

"Blanche Braithwaite?" Mrs. Braithwaite boomed, marching up and putting forward a hand.

The girl beamed. "You're Mrs. Braithwaite, aren't you?"

"Yes," she replied heartily. "Do you remember me?"

"I can vaguely recall you talking to me, and after I woke up, the nurse told me about you."

"I'm simply thrilled that you're all right. How do you feel?"

"Rather good, in light of what happened." She motioned her to pull over a chair. "Did you find your daughter?"

"Yes, I found her, and then I rescued her, and then Mr. Norris—he's a good friend—" She was talking incredibly quickly, trying to get everything out. But then suddenly she stopped, seeing the girl's bewildered expression. "Did they tell you about your mother?"

"Yes, they said that I had you to thank for going to my home to find out." Her brow creased. "I have to say that half of me wanted to go back into the coma when I heard. She was such a wonderful person. She was all that I had."

Mrs. Braithwaite put a warm hand on hers. "Well, I have already suggested a solution for that, and you didn't object, so I think it was a good one. You'll be like a daughter to me from now on. You see, when my daughter was missing, you stood in for her. It doesn't matter whether you're my real daughter or not. It's having someone who cares that's important."

Blanche's eyes began to moisten. "I'm glad you found your daughter."

"You'll have to meet her. Her name's Betty. She's clever, an intellectual type." Mrs. Braithwaite smiled as she remembered always referring to Betty as being "bookish," but those days were gone. Now she was proud to be able to say that her daughter was clever—clever enough to be doing special work for the War Office, although, annoyingly, she couldn't tell anyone about that.

"She sounds very nice. What about the rest of your family?" Blanche said, lying back on the pillow ready for a long chat.

"But I've already told you about them!" Mrs. Braithwaite chuckled. "We'll have plenty of time for going back over things. First things first: You tell me all about your mother. I very much know how it feels to lose your parents."

And so, with tears on both sides, Blanche began telling Mrs. Braithwaite about her mother, how she'd wake up to her beautiful voice singing "Tea for Two" as she moved around the house, opening curtains and letting the sun in. "She was like sunshine herself," Blanche said. "She made the world seem full of love, with so much fun to be had."

"She sounds like a wonderful woman," Mrs. Braithwaite said sadly. "Perhaps you'll start singing around the house when you get out of the hospital." She smiled at her, squeezing her hand. "Try to keep her alive through you."

"I never thought of that," Blanche sniffed. Her eyes glazed over.

"At least you had her for as long as you did," Mrs. Braithwaite said. "My parents died when I was six. I hardly knew them. I was brought up by an aunt." She heaved a great sigh. "Sometimes you have to feel grateful for what you have, see the good, and only the good. We only have one life. One chance for happiness. And sometimes we forget that we can actually choose whether we want joy or cynicism. Let's pick joy."

"You're so very right, Mrs. Braithwaite." Their eyes met. "It has to be joy, every time."

## 52.

Mr. Norris had spent much of his life worrying. Part of him knew that it was pointless, but he couldn't seem to help himself. He would worry in the middle of the night, and then on his way to work, and especially when he was on the tricky business of buying food with wartime rations: one could never tell what distasteful dishes one was going to have to try next. Most of all, though, he worried in the evening. With time to himself, especially as he did his chores—cooking, washing up, ironing his clothes for the morning—his mind was free to ramble unrestrained among all manner of anxieties.

But tonight, as he walked home from work, he

felt satisfied to have found an answer to one of his most persistent worries. Jontry, the young man who had been given his accounts, his office, and his promotion, had been seen lunching with Mr. Brunswick, the head of accounts. A familiar look about them, the way they smirked smugly while ordering another scotch, clarified something.

Jontry was related to the boss.

Mr. Norris hadn't been demoted for any of the reasons stated: that he was lacking in skills, that his head wasn't quite right for figures, that he didn't have what it took to go higher in the company. No, Mr. Norris had been ousted by nepotism.

The notion had put a small skip in his step. He could have complained, gone above Mr. Brunswick and demanded answers, but Mr. Norris found that he didn't care.

"At least now I won't feel guilty if I miss work," he said to himself as he strode into the house. Missing work was a situation that he felt might happen sooner rather than later.

For although Betty had been found, there was now another element of the matter on his mind.

He wanted to know what was going to happen to the rest of the BUF group.

Not the thugs and Anthony Metcalf, who had been captured by the police. The other ones, the ones from the meeting in the church: Taplin and Ernie, Mary Montgomery and her ruthless sister, the professor, and of course Florrie. He still bristled at the thought that he had been harboring the enemy beneath his roof.

Mrs. Braithwaite was already in the kitchen. There was an eagerness about her. Something had happened and she couldn't wait to tell him.

"Sit down, Mr. Norris, and let me put the kettle on."

"But I was going to start making dinner—"

"Never mind that. In any case, it's already done. We have a visitor coming for dinner: Betty is bringing Baxter over. We'll be able to meet him properly, get to know him outside of a major espionage operation." She gave a little chortle of laughter. "But before they come, there's something that we urgently need to discuss."

"Well, in actual fact, there was something that **I** very much wanted to discuss, too—"

"The fact of the matter," she said, interrupting him—Mrs. Braithwaite might have changed in many ways, but some habits were imprinted in her character. "The fact of the matter is that Florrie is still at large. We need to track her down."

Mr. Norris laughed. "That's precisely what I wanted to discuss with you! My feeling is that I should join them at their next meeting. Mary Montgomery told me at Chiltern Church that they were meeting in the basement of the butcher's tomorrow evening—"

"And perhaps we can get the police to join them all as well."

"Exactly so." Mr. Norris nodded. "Provided they haven't seen fit to change the plan."

Mrs. Braithwaite stopped in the middle of pouring the tea. "They may have canceled it after they heard about the arrests at the curiosity shop."

"I shouldn't think that they would. There's not enough time to spread the word," Mr. Norris said. "And because their leader, Mr. Fox—Baxter to us— has been implicated as a mole, surely they'll need to meet to keep everyone up to date. I'm certain there are a number of people ready to step into the leadership role now that it's become available."

The sound of the front door opening stopped them in their tracks. Voices flowed through from the hallway, male and female, as well as the sound of people hanging their coats on the hat stand.

Mrs. Braithwaite quickly put her finger to her lips, indicating that they should stop talking, whisking it away just in time for Betty to come in, followed by Baxter.

"Hallo, Mrs. Braithwaite," he said in a jovial, rather upper-class way. He put his hand forward to shake first her hand and then Mr. Norris's. "So lovely of you to invite me over in a more, shall we say, relaxed setting." He smiled in a cumbersome way, as if he were an overgrown schoolboy.

"Oh, it's our pleasure." Mrs. Braithwaite sat him

down on the closest chair. "It's nice to finally meet the real you, Mr. Baxter. Tell me, is that your real name?"

Baxter coughed slightly. "Yes, as a matter of fact, it is."

"And if you're not a scruffy black marketeer or a fascist," she snapped in a more pointed manner, "then would you mind telling us who you actually are and where you come from?"

Betty laughed, saying to Baxter, "I told you my mother would make no bones about questioning you."

"Don't worry, darling." Baxter laughed. "I'm happy to tell all."

And so he did, quite charmingly, too, his story nuanced with amusing details, such as the time his dog, Iago, chewed his favorite riding boots, and the fact that his father sent him to boarding school in Dorset "because he'd been there himself, as though **he** was something that **I** should be aiming for." He grinned.

"How did you come to be in MI5?" Mrs. Braithwaite asked.

"Uncle Henry had words with people, and then I was approached. That's how it used to be, before the war. Everyone was on the lookout for people they knew. I hadn't even known that Uncle Henry was in it himself until I bumped into him at a meeting. Funny old world, MI5. It's changed a lot since the war began."

"How?" Mr. Norris asked.

"It's become bigger, and better perhaps, too. They've needed a lot more personnel, especially once all the Germans and Italians in the country had to be vetted. We couldn't advertise, so it had to be quiet recruitment through universities and some of the top schools." He looked at Betty. "They did rather well at finding some good operatives, don't you think, darling?"

"The best they have!" She smirked back at him.

"I sincerely hope that you mean to treat my daughter well, young man," Mrs. Braithwaite said haughtily, making everyone laugh, and even she joined in, adding to Baxter, "Well, do you?"

"Mum, of course he does," Betty said, but Baxter cut in.

"No, let me answer, darling." He gave a little cough, as if about to make an important speech. "Mrs. Braithwaite, I have never met anyone quite like Betty. She's fearless, clever, and devilishly beautiful, and I plan to keep her as happy as I can so that she stays with me forever."

He stretched his hand over the table, and she put hers on top of his.

"We make a terrific team, don't we?"

Mrs. Braithwaite's eyes met Mr. Norris's, and she gave him a smile.

Dinner was a measured success. Mrs. Braithwaite had prepared a Spam and vegetable pie, which turned into more of a soup in the cooking, but the company was too busy dissecting the fascist underground movement to concern themselves with food.

"Mr. Norris and I have been wondering what happened to Florrie," Mrs. Braithwaite began.

"You see," Mr. Norris said quickly. "She's still out there, with the rest of the fascist gang. It seems rather dangerous to leave her at large."

Betty looked at Baxter, who nodded, and then she said, "We've been talking this through, and we think that Florrie is somehow tied up with an MI5 insider, someone who's telling the fascists about the MI5 infiltration operation."

"What do you mean?" Mrs. Braithwaite sat up straight, all ears.

Baxter spoke first. "Neither Betty nor I can pinpoint when we slipped up, how we let our cover drop."

"I was caught not once but twice," Betty said. "First when I was following Florrie into the Elephant and Castle underground station, and the second time when Anthony Metcalf trapped me."

"And what happened to you?" Mrs. Braithwaite asked Baxter.

"I went to Mary Montgomery's house to get information about Betty's whereabouts. Her sister, Kathleen, overheard. She must have heard warnings about me beforehand as she had the blackshirts onto me straightaway."

"You see," Betty said. "It's as if there's someone

who knows what we're doing—and that person is telling the rest of them."

"But how many people know?" Mr. Norris asked.

"That's just it," Baxter said. "There's only one person who is aware of Betty's and my movements."

Betty leaned forward and whispered, "Cummerbatch."

"He's our boss at HQ," Baxter elaborated. "One of the older set, established. Not a whisker out of place."

They were all leaning into the middle of the table, speaking softly in case anyone could hear.

"Why don't we go after him?" Mrs. Braithwaite suggested, sitting back.

"No," the rest of them said together, forcing her to lean back in with them.

"He'll just deny it. It'll be his word against ours." Betty looked from one to another. "No, we need to make sure we get him properly. We'll only get one chance."

"We need a trap that will pull him in completely," Baxter concluded.

They sat for a few minutes, each thinking hard. Mrs. Braithwaite took her notebook and ballpoint pen out of her handbag.

"All right, I have a plan, but it's complicated," Betty said.

"Go on," Mrs. Braithwaite responded, pen at the ready.

"I need to tell him a lie—for instance, that I

suspect Baxter is a double agent. Then I'll explain to him how I plan to deal with this in a highly dangerous way very quickly, maybe by setting off a bomb in one of their meetings or something like that. His reaction will be to go there himself to warn them, and we'll be waiting for him."

"Surely Cummerbatch will simply order you to get off the operation," Mr. Norris said. "Just as he did last time."

"Ah yes," Betty said. "But I disobeyed him last time, so he'll expect me to disobey again, take the law into my own hands. He would have to do something fast to prevent it."

Baxter put a hand on her arm. "Darling, you're a genius!"

Betty went on. "The pattern seems to indicate that Florrie is his main contact—and perhaps Anthony, too, but because he's currently in Pentonville Prison, I don't think we need to worry about him. We should be watching Florrie. She will be the one who reacts when he tells her."

Mr. Norris was ahead of her. "And she would tell her thugs to stop Betty, or at worst, she'd cancel the meeting."

Betty leaned forward again. "Not if there isn't enough time. They'll have to go ahead with it, everyone present, and then we'll get them all."

Mr. Norris blushed slightly as he said, "There's a meeting tomorrow evening, in the basement of the butcher's at six."

Betty looked around at everyone, an expectant gleam in her eyes. "What do you think?"

"Let's do it," they all said at once.

Because Betty had been following Florrie for a number of months, she left immediately to track down her current whereabouts. When she returned at around eleven o'clock, Mr. Norris and Mrs. Braithwaite were still sitting at the kitchen table, only now they were surrounded by a large quantity of papers, all covered with Mrs. Braithwaite's meticulous hand, accompanied with diagrams and arrows. Baxter had gone to buy a bomb from one of the crooks in the Pendulum.

"Did you find Florrie, dear?" Mrs. Braithwaite asked.

"Just as I thought, she's staying in the professor's house by Clapham Junction. She was the one who recruited him into the group in the first place. They're awfully friendly." Then Betty added with a grimace, "I don't know how she came to choose these people!"

Mrs. Braithwaite, writing in the notebook, asked, "What's the address?"

"Venn Street, number thirty-nine. She probably won't be up early in the morning, but if you're the one following her, you should be there before seven in the morning to be on the safe side."

Baxter returned with a black bag. He showed them the bomb, which to Mr. Norris looked rather too homemade for comfort.

Then they went over the plan for the next day.

At precisely three o'clock the following afternoon, Betty would enter Cummerbatch's office,
and furious and devastated, she would tell him that
Baxter was a traitor and that she intended to bomb
the meeting, blow them all to smithereens. As
Cummerbatch knew that Betty was romantically
attached to Baxter, he would guess that Baxter's
treachery had pushed her over the edge. He would
order Betty not to do it, and she would agree to
hold off, although he would know that she would
disobey him and go ahead with the bombing plan
regardless.

What Betty wouldn't tell Cummerbatch, of
course, was that he was the real target, that it was a
trap. After she told him what she was about to do,
with or without his blessing, he would have three
hours in which to warn Florrie and stop the bomb,
which he would undoubtedly do if indeed Cummerbatch was the real mole.

It was his involvement and capture they were
after. They were hoping that he himself would go
to the meeting, which would make it all the easier
to nail him. Betty and Baxter needed solid evidence
because Cummerbatch was certain to deny everything. He was a highly respected member of MI5,
which made him devious in the extreme.

Mrs. Braithwaite was to follow Florrie for the
entire day, camouflaged with a hat and a fur stole
borrowed from Cassandra. Mrs. Braithwaite's role

was to see if she could actually verify if, where, and when Florrie received Cummerbatch's message, and then what she would do with that information.

Baxter, meanwhile, was to follow Cummerbatch within MI5 headquarters, then as soon as he left the building, he would go to his seniors and gather a group to go to the butcher's basement to witness Cummerbatch's duplicity.

Mr. Norris would be waiting outside MI5, ready to follow Cummerbatch once he left the building, which he probably would do very promptly after the meeting with Betty, especially if he needed to get hold of Florrie urgently. Cummerbatch wouldn't recognize Mr. Norris, so he would be able to follow him closely.

They would stay in contact with one another via public telephones. Baxter knew the phone numbers of several red telephone boxes in Clapham, Wandsworth, and Piccadilly, and these were distributed on small slips of paper.

At one o'clock in the morning, feeling comfortable that the plan was right and tight, they went off to bed, Mrs. Braithwaite sleeping in Florrie's old room, Baxter on the sofa in the living room.

Yet as he lay in bed, Mr. Norris couldn't help going over and over the plan. The more he thought, the more he worried. He felt as if some small, hardly significant thing they'd missed were hovering in the air above him.

He just couldn't put his finger on it.

## 53.

Betty awoke early. This wasn't the most urgent operation she had ever performed—that would be the time she'd had to take out a knife to threaten a fifth columnist in the charcuterie department of Harrods Food Hall. In that instance, however, the man involved was too pleased with his purchase of sliced Wiltshire ham to be on the lookout for MI5 agents, and he proved easy to capture.

Nor was it as complex as the time she'd been involved in the convoluted rescue of a fellow operative at a West End nightclub, requiring her to simulate a brawl without letting any of the revelers realize what was going on.

But getting Cummerbatch was without doubt the most dangerous.

The fascists wouldn't hesitate to kill her, quick as a flash. There were plenty of thugs waiting for a bit of blood, desperate to get their hands on a fake medal. More crucially, they couldn't have a more cunning and powerful adversary than Cummerbatch. Although large, old, and almost perpetually a little intoxicated, he was made of steel underneath. Under the belly and the charisma lay a deadly, ruthless man, and a handgun, no doubt, lay hidden about his person, ready to use at any opportunity.

Betty had been taught to assess the risks at the beginning of every operation, and she trembled as she thought of what he could do to her. Not only could he kill her, but he could bring her down, twist the truth to show the world how **she** had been the collaborator, that **she** was the real traitor.

And more than anything—more than death itself—Betty couldn't bear that anyone might think that she was in league with the enemy.

She dressed. Today she was going to get everything right.

**They** were going to get everything right.

She worried because her mother and Mr. Norris were untrained novices, which meant that she had to be prepared for any eventuality. There were a lot of variables, factors that couldn't be counted upon completely.

Which is why she tucked a small piece of paper into the cuff of her blouse before leaving her room.

After waking Mrs. Braithwaite and seeing her off

with a long hug, just in case, she woke up Baxter, smelling the sweetness of his skin as he pulled her on top of him, kissed her, and begged her to stay for a while.

"Business today, I'm afraid," she said, pulling herself off.

Mr. Norris was busy making breakfast, as usual. He was wearing his office suit.

"I thought I would blend in," he said, putting the kettle on for more tea. "Like any other office worker."

Agreeing with him, she sat and had some breakfast, talking it through before heading out of the door into the morning sunshine.

She spent the morning pretending to carry on with her work, as usual, and then, after lunch, she made her way to Cummerbatch's office.

All the way there, she'd gone through what she'd say in her head, how exactly she would say it. It wasn't until she was standing outside his door, that she suddenly felt awash with panic.

**What if he saw through their plan?**

She knocked.

"Come in," the familiar bellow came.

Sitting at his desk, pipe in hand, a small smile on his face, Cummerbatch looked so convincingly part of the establishment that she couldn't help wondering if they'd got it all horribly wrong.

**Could this cozy MI5 professional really be a fascist?**

"I thought I'd sent you to Devon, Braithwaite."

She sat down on the chair opposite him, carefully taking on her new persona.

"I was worried about my mother, sir. I had to rescue her." She already looked angry, upset, sniffing loudly. "Of course, it wasn't easy, and I ended up being caught," this referred to Anthony Metcalf's trap, which Cummerbatch—if he was a defector—would have known about, "but in the end we were saved."

"Do you require yet another ticket to Devon?" he asked, pulling out his pad to write a travel order.

A ferocious look on her face, she came out with it. "I've found out who the double agent is." She watched closely, waiting for a flicker in his eyes, his hand moving to his face—all things she'd learned in lie-detecting classes. But he looked rather unhappy. He picked up a pen.

"Who is it then?" He sighed in a resigned way.

"Baxter," she spat venomously.

He looked at her, and then raised an eyebrow. "The Baxter with whom you've been sleeping for the past three and a half months?"

**Had they been tracking her to that extent?**

"Yes," she fumed. "It was all a lie."

"Well, **that,** my girl, will teach you a good lesson." He met her eyes without an ounce of humor. "I take it you've now learned why we advise operatives not to become romantically attached?"

She didn't reply, staring moodily at the wall.

"I admire your work, Braithwaite," Cummer-batch went on, while writing something down. "But we can't have operatives defying orders to go to Devon, taking it upon themselves to rescue their mothers. I know that it flies against one's instincts, to leave one's mother in peril, but orders, I'm afraid, are orders." He paused, writing something down. "I have to ask you this time to **go to** Devon, Braith-waite. The ministry simply won't put up with any more insubordination. We will look into your sus-picions about Baxter."

"But I have a plan," she said with fervor. "We should bomb them—him—all of them."

Not reacting, he looked at her in a measured way. "You can't be serious."

"I **am** serious. Baxter will be at a BUF meeting tonight at six. We can get all of them, cleanly. It's perfect."

"How will you get the explosives?"

"I already have them. A bomb. It's homemade, but it's big, powerful enough to blow up that dingy basement of theirs."

"So you know where the meeting is being held?"

**Was it a question, or did he already know?**

"I do, and I know that you'll say that we should monitor these people, keep them under our con-trol, but I think you're wrong. The agency's wrong. These people are already out of our control. They're getting more committed to sabotage, trying to se-cure their positions for when the Nazis invade. It's too dangerous to keep letting them operate. We have to close them down." Her voice rose. "Including Baxter."

"What proof do you have that it's him?"

"He's made too many slips. The trouble is none of them can be proved." She gritted her teeth, irate. "I know it's him, and I'm pretty certain that he knows that I know, too."

Cummerbatch thought for a moment, then pushed his notepad to one side. "I'm going to let you in on a secret, Braithwaite, and you're not to tell a soul. We've had our eye on Baxter for a while now. He's a top operative, but there are just one too many coincidences."

"That's exactly what I mean, sir. Too many operatives being captured, when no one else would know."

**Except for you**, she thought.

"Precisely." Cummerbatch coughed hoarsely, then adjusted his large form upright. "But we can't go around bombing basements, Braithwaite. We don't kill people. We take them in. We question them. We find out what they know. We try to turn them double. Only then do we begin to think about how to dispose of them." He stood up, walking to the window. "I don't think I realized until now quite how much of a break you need. The captivity must have unsettled you." He turned around, giving her a penetrating look. "I'm going to ask you, Braithwaite, to leave town immediately."

"But Baxter—"

"I'll get a special team onto Baxter. We can't risk anything. He's highly dangerous, and we don't want precious operatives, such as you, drawn into it."

Betty looked at her feet. "No, sir."

He took a new sheet of paper and drew out his pen. "Now tell me, where would you like to go? I've heard that the Lake District is wonderful at this time of year."

"Oh, all right," she said rather flippantly, getting up. "Make it the Lake District, then." She turned and gave him a quick false smile.

He smiled meekly back, watchfully.

**He knows I'm not going anywhere near the Lake District**, she thought. **My first task is done.**

"Pick up the ticket from Supplies," he said, as she left the room.

After an obligatory look into Supplies, where she absentmindedly left the ticket to the Lake District on a desk for good measure, she headed outside.

The plan was afoot.

But there was a small matter to which she still needed to attend.

As she walked briskly through Trafalgar Square, she stopped at a telephone box.

There was one call she had to make.

Digging into the cuff of her blouse, she pulled out the small strip of paper.

Mr. Norris watched as the unmistakable figure of Cummerbatch came out of HQ. Positioned behind a letterbox on the corner and armed with a good description of the man, Mr. Norris affixed his bowler hat on his head and moved quietly and confidently behind Cummerbatch as he walked with haste up St. James's to Piccadilly.

The pedestrians were thicker there, and it was easier for Mr. Norris to go unnoticed. He knew that when Cummerbatch came out of HQ, he would have to act fast. There were only three hours until the meeting.

Therefore, it surprised Mr. Norris to see the man disappear through the grand, gray arches and into the golden interior of the most prestigious of London hotels, the Ritz.

"Typical!" Mr. Norris said under his breath.

Although he had been to a top university, Mr. Norris knew that his station in life was solidly middle class. The Ritz, on the other hand, was a hotel catering exclusively to the needs of the upper crust. He had never set foot—nor had he especially wanted to set foot—in such a place, knowing that his appearance, his accent, his very nature would mark him instantly as being entirely out of place.

As he approached, the door was opened smoothly before him by a silent, immaculate doorman, and he felt a shudder of self-consciousness: should he thank him or not? In the end, he mumbled a thanks because not doing so caused him more worry than the possibility of getting it wrong.

In the grand entrance hall, men in expensive suits shook hands jubilantly, and a group of women were braying like young fillies, talking excitedly about meeting the royal princesses for tea the following day. He felt a flush of embarrassment wash over him. He didn't belong here.

**Pull yourself together**, a small voice inside him said. **You're on a mission. Pretend you come to places like this every day. Look around for Cummerbatch.**

He scanned the hall, spying the large man vanishing down a lavishly decorated side corridor. He then looked at a small sign on the wall, and his face fell.

Was Cummerbatch going to the gentlemen's lavatory? How could he follow him into such an enclosed, personal space?

But as he nipped smartly down the corridor behind Cummerbatch, he let out a puff of relief as he realized that it wasn't the lavatory he was heading toward at all.

Attached to the wall, about halfway down the corridor, was a public telephone. Without even pausing to look around, Cummerbatch went straight up to it, picked up the receiver, and began dialing a number.

Mr. Norris walked past him, as if heading for the lavatory himself, and listened carefully to the clicks of the telephone dial so that he could try to guess the number, memorize it.

Walking casually into the gentlemen's room, he quickly pressed his ear to the door, hoping to be able to hear some of the telephone conversation.

"I believe you have someone there by the name of Andrews," he said in his lavish, upper-class way. "This is important war business."

**Was he calling Florrie?**

"I hope they have a good selection of scones in Clapham," Cummerbatch said clearly. "The place in which I took breakfast in Piccadilly was completely out. We need to make better plans for the very near future."

Mr. Norris only had seconds to leap away from the door and pretend to be washing his hands as Cummerbatch came into the lavatory, relieving himself lengthily in a urinal with a large sigh, and then standing beside him at the row of sinks as he washed his hands.

"Rather warm for this time of year, don't you think?" he said, not meeting Mr. Norris's eyes.

**Was it a code? Did he** know **that Mr. Norris was following him?**

Frightened to his core, Mr. Norris fought to pull himself together. Putting on his best upper-class accent, so as to fit in with his surroundings, he replied, "Lovely weather for the bombers, too, unfortunately for us."

His eyes met Cummerbatch's for the briefest of moments, and Mr. Norris smiled, a genuine, polite little smile, the type of smile a gentleman in the gentlemen's lavatory in the Ritz might give another gentleman.

Cummerbatch smiled back, wiping his hands carefully on a hand towel before going through the door, wishing Mr. Norris a cheerful "Good day!"

Mrs. Braithwaite, meanwhile, had spent the morning in Clapham market following Florrie. There was a fruit and vegetable stall there—C. S. Berry, of all the apt names for a fruit seller—to which Florrie was somehow attached. She was possibly an employee, although it was difficult to say precisely what was Florrie's connection with the place, given that she seemed to be arguing continually with the man there, accusing him of stealing something.

Hiding behind a bookstall, where she deliberated between an old Dickens and an interesting little book by someone called Nancy Mitford, Mrs. Braithwaite watched it all. They didn't seem to be in a romantic alliance or anything of that type. No, it was something more businesslike.

Around lunchtime, Florrie left to buy a meat pie from a café around the corner, then she returned briefly before heading back toward Clapham Junction, where the professor lived.

Mrs. Braithwaite scooted after her, plunging into bushes wherever necessary to avoid being seen.

By three o'clock, when Betty was supposed to be walking into Cummerbatch's office, Florrie was sitting at a table in a café beside Clapham Junction Station, reading a magazine.

This was the moment when things should start happening—she'd been waiting all day!—and yet Florrie was just sitting.

The telephone rang in the café.

After answering, the old woman behind the counter yelled, "Anyone 'ere called Andrews?"

Florrie stood up quickly, as if she'd been expecting the call, and dashed over, picking up the receiver.

Mrs. Braithwaite moved to the counter so that she could hear the conversation, repositioning the fur stole up over her chin and pulling down the wide-brimmed purple felt hat that she'd borrowed from Cassandra. At first she had been worried at the oddity of her new look, but that passed after a few minutes in Clapham, with its own peculiarities.

Behind the counter was a selection of cakes, and Mrs. Braithwaite, who already had a half-eaten slice of apple pie on the plate at her table, deliberated whether to try something else, too. Spying was arduous work, after all. There was an empty display plate where the fruitcake should have been, so she had to make do with a scrawny-looking scone.

Florrie spoke clearly into the receiver. "The fruitcake is lovely here."

**It must be a code**, Mrs. Braithwaite thought, eyeing the bare fruitcake plate. **Unless Florrie had the last slice**, she added crossly to herself.

Mrs. Braithwaite could hear a man's voice on the other end of the line, and then Florrie, a look of vague alarm coming over her face, said, "I'll bring a slice for you, good-bye," and hung up.

Instead of sitting back down, finishing her tea, or even looking to see if there was another slice of fruitcake, as she'd promised for the man on the telephone, Florrie simply slipped on her coat, left a few coins on the table, and strode out.

Mrs. Braithwaite, who'd only had a few bites of scone, was forced to abandon it, taking one large final mouthful before she nipped out into the street.

Florrie was heading down the high street and then beyond, past the shops and up toward the common. Mrs. Braithwaite followed at a discreet distance until Florrie stopped, looked around, and went inside somewhere Mrs. Braithwaite would never have imagined.

The Pendulum.

Mrs. Braithwaite stood outside deliberating

whether to follow her inside. After all, she could hardly keep her cover in a pub where everybody knew her name.

But what really bothered her was why Florrie was in there. Did the criminals know her? Did she have friends there? Was she connected in some way to the black market?

**Did the criminals know that Florrie was a fascist?**

She hurried over to the telephone box opposite and quickly dialed a number.

A man's voice came on the end of the line. Baxter. "Hello, why are you so terribly late? The play starts at six."

That was the code.

Mrs. Braithwaite replied, "I was caught up in a queue for lamb chops."

"Where are you?" he said hurriedly.

"Florrie knows, and now she's gone into the Pendulum," she whispered. "I can't follow her in there. They know me too well."

"I'll be there in half an hour."

She put the receiver down and began snooping around the pub, trying to look into the windows, listening to any conversations she could hear.

This wasn't how the plan should have worked at all.

## 56.

After the torturous episode in the gentlemen's lavatory, Mr. Norris watched as Cummerbatch walked out of the Ritz and asked the doorman to hail him a taxi. Mr. Norris had no choice but to follow suit.

"Could you hail me a taxi, please?" he asked the doorman, hoping he'd used the correct terminology. He'd never spoken to a doorman before, let alone requested that one hail him a taxi.

As soon as the doorman stepped toward the road, a taxi halted beside him.

"Thank you," Mr. Norris muttered, nipping inside and telling the driver, "Would you be so kind as to, er, follow that taxi?"

After a little confusion about which taxi they

were to follow—Piccadilly was awash with black cabs—Mr. Norris felt sure that they were heading toward Clapham.

But as Cummerbatch's taxi sped through Clapham High Street, past the butcher's shop, and toward Clapham Common, Mr. Norris realized with a thud precisely where he was being taken.

The Pendulum.

## 57

Betty, having made her telephone call, walked hastily to the cloakrooms in Charing Cross Station, where she passed across a cloakroom ticket and received, in exchange, a large black bag.

Taking the bag, she jumped onto a bus for Clapham, alighting at the high street, bag in hand, and made for the black door beside the butcher's shop.

The place looked deserted. Caution was paramount, so she hid in the alleyway opposite for a few minutes, checking for a sign of life. Nothing.

Then, the lock-picking device in her hand, she walked swiftly and casually over to the black door and had it open in a matter of seconds. As it pushed ajar, she listened for voices, any sort of noise, but it was silent. In she crept, pulling the door closed behind her.

The musty smell made her recall all too vividly her imprisonment in the place. Whether she made light of it or not, she'd been terrified.

"Hello?" she called, just in case. Better to know she wasn't alone while she was on the stairs beside the door.

But there was nothing.

Gingerly creeping down, she went into the main room, looking for a good place to plant the bomb. Inside the meeting room were a number of tall cupboards, underneath which she was hoping to find a loose floorboard.

She didn't intend for the bomb to go off. It only needed to be found, eventually. It was her means of getting Cummerbatch to the venue, and he'd smell a fish if it wasn't unearthed somewhere. Yet it had to be well enough hidden to flummox them until the meeting began. If they found it too soon, they'd let Cummerbatch know, and he would simply go back to work. Their plot would have failed.

No, it had to keep them on their toes until the meeting itself.

Pulling a cupboard away from the wall, she tugged at a floorboard, using a screwdriver she'd brought along to wriggle it loose. Then she lowered the hefty bomb into the narrow space beneath, where it fit snugly. Checking that the timer was set for half past eight—if necessary she would evacuate before then—she replaced the floorboard and the cupboard. Then she swiftly retreated to her hiding place, which was in the cupboard under the stairs, behind some old boxes and building planks.

Now all she had to do was wait.

## 58.

Mrs. Braithwaite watched from behind a tree as a taxi pulled up outside the Pendulum. A portly man clambered out, whom she instantly recognized from his description: Cummerbatch.

"Wait here!" he ordered the taxi driver, before striding in.

**Was he going in to meet Florrie?**

Mrs. Braithwaite now knew that, whatever else she did and didn't do, she had to get inside the pub. Without Betty and the others there, it was up to her to be their eyes and ears.

**She had to find out what was going on.**

There had to be a back door to the pub. She darted from behind a tree to the corner of the building, running up the back until she came upon a door. Creeping up, she turned the handle. It was unlocked. She pushed it ajar.

"I saw you take the money," an angry-sounding voice came from behind the bar.

"You saw nothing, mate!" a harder, threatening voice said.

She pushed her nose through the crack to see two barmen arguing, one of them raising a fist.

Seizing her chance, Mrs. Braithwaite slid in, keeping herself low and worming her way through the back room into the area behind the long bar that ran across the rear of the pub.

Popping her head up and down so that she could see over the bar, she instantly spotted them not five yards away from her. Cummerbatch was standing beside Florrie, his hand on her waist.

**Had Florrie seduced Cummerbatch, too?**

They were talking to two ruffians and seemed to be negotiating a price for the contents of a large box.

The name on the box was C. S. Berry.

**Wasn't that the name of the fruit and vegetable stall in Clapham market?**

She frowned. They wouldn't come all the way to the Pendulum to buy fruit. Food rationing had become ridiculously severe recently, but still.

As she watched, one of the ruffians opened the box and pulled something out. It wasn't fruit at all.

It was a gun.

Sensing something, Cummerbatch suddenly turned in Mrs. Braithwaite's direction.

Just in time to see her head bobbing back down behind the bar.

"Come out, my good woman," he said jovially. "Don't I know you from somewhere?"

Mrs. Braithwaite stood up, though deciding not to move to the other side of the bar. "I just work here," she muttered, even though it was patently obvious that she didn't. "I don't believe we've met," she added, for lack of anything else to say.

Florrie spun around, furious. "She's the Braithwaite girl's mother." Taking in Mrs. Braithwaite's counterfeit apparel—Cassandra's fur stole and the wretched hat—she said, "What are **you** doing here?"

"I'm meeting some friends, actually," Mrs. Braithwaite replied in the most even voice that she could. "Ah, there they are. Over there!" She looked around for Bobby Mack in his usual corner, but he wasn't there.

**Typical of him to be elsewhere when she needed him!**

"I think you should come with us, Mrs. Braithwaite," Cummerbatch said evenly, holding one of the guns loosely yet threateningly beside his hip, and beckoning her over with his other hand. "We have a meeting to get to."

Which is why Mrs. Braithwaite found herself being forced into a taxi ahead of Florrie and Cummerbatch and heading at speed toward the butcher's basement.

## 59.

Having witnessed Mrs. Braithwaite's capture in the Pendulum from a position behind the pool table, Mr. Norris watched with horror as they took her off in the waiting taxi. Naturally, he had let his own taxi go—it had been pricey enough as it was, frankly. Mr. Norris was not in the habit of taking taxis.

Yet now, watching them go and uttering a small "Blast!" from under his breath, he came to terms with the fact that he might have lost them.

He thought about trying to telephone Baxter, but Baxter would be in the midst of his own part in the operation: collecting MI5's senior management, explaining it all so that they could come to witness Cummerbatch's duplicity.

After pondering for a few minutes, he decided to make his way, quickly, to the butcher's basement.

"They would, in all probability, go there next," he muttered to himself as he began walking fast, then running, to the high street.

The pavements were busy again. People coming home from work, collecting children, going to shelters just in case.

As the black basement door came into view, Mr. Norris shuddered with the recollection of his last dealings in the place.

Two blackshirted youths arrived at the door and went in, probably for the meeting, which, according to Mr. Norris's wristwatch, would begin in around twenty minutes.

If Cummerbatch and Florrie were in there already—which was probable—he would be heading straight into them. Florrie would recognize him, then he, too, would be taken prisoner.

"And what would be the use of that?" he said under his breath.

Taking a deep breath, he knew what he had to do.

He had to go through the back again.

Trotting down and around to the houses at the back, he easily recalled the house behind the butcher's shop and clambered over the fence, through the garden, and into the backyard.

The window had yet to be mended, so he slipped through quickly. The axe was there in front of him, but he quickly decided it was a bit unwieldy. He'd be better with a smaller, yet very sharp knife that he found beside the butcher's block. The door to the basement had yet to be mended, too, and he crept through it down the back stairs, voices coming up from a room at the end of the corridor.

"It must be here somewhere." Florrie's voice rang out over the others, accompanied by the sound of things being moved around. "Come on. Help me find it, will you."

Mr. Norris tucked himself inside one of the other doorways, listening hard. He recognized the voice of the professor as well as Mary Montgomery and her vile sister, and a few of the other characters from Chiltern Church.

"What's **she** doing here?" one of them said.

"We're keeping her hostage for tonight," a booming upper-class voice said. Was that Cummerbatch? "I'll explain it to you all when the meeting begins."

**Were they referring to Mrs. Braithwaite?**

As more people came in, the search for the bomb seemed to become more subdued, although he could still hear the scuffle of moving furniture.

Florrie and Cummerbatch must have come into the corridor for a private word, as suddenly Mr. Norris could hear them much louder and clearer.

"Maybe she didn't have time to plant it," Florrie said. "In any case, I don't know where she would get a bomb at such short notice."

"I would have thought she'd be here herself," the deep voice said quietly.

"We've looked everywhere. Are you sure she really meant to do it?"

He let out a sigh. "Let's start the meeting quickly, get them out before anything happens, just to be on the safe side."

Reentering the room, he clapped his hands together, calling for silence, and there was a scuffle as people found chairs and rearranged themselves for the meeting.

But Mr. Norris wasn't paying attention.

A noise was coming from behind him. Someone was descending the back staircase, the one he had used to come down from the butcher's shop.

Petrified, he stayed as still as he could, until, as the figure came closer, he realized with utter relief that it was Baxter.

"Mr. Norris, I thought I'd find you here," he whispered, coming up beside him. "How is everything going?"

"Not at all good. They've got Mrs. Braithwaite. They haven't found the bomb, though." He glanced around at him. "I thought you were supposed to be bringing the chaps from MI5."

"Oh, they're waiting outside. We have to wait until things get going first. They have to catch Cummerbatch in full swing, you see."

"Oh, of course," Mr. Norris said.

"Come on, let's go closer down the corridor so that we can hear."

Baxter went first, followed by Mr. Norris, nervously listening as Cummerbatch took to the stage in the meeting room.

"Things are about to change, for us, for the Nazis, and for Britain," he was saying in booming, celebratory tones.

Within minutes, Baxter had found Betty and pulled her out from beneath the stairs to join them.

"There you are, darling," he whispered, although something seemed to have changed in his tone.

"Where are the MI5 chiefs?" Betty whispered back. "We need them here now."

Baxter gave a whistle toward the staircase, and the door crashed open, followed by heavy footsteps coming fast down the stairs.

Mr. Norris looked around in time to see four burly men who didn't look at all like MI5 chiefs, storming toward them.

"Baxter!" Betty gasped, as one of the thugs grabbed her, plunging her into the meeting room— the door kindly opened by Baxter.

Another thug brought Mr. Norris in, forcing his arms behind his back, his butcher's knife falling with a clank to the floor.

"I see that Mr. Fox has joined us," Cummerbatch said smoothly from the front, "with a few more hostages." He gave a low chuckle.

Mr. Norris could see Mrs. Braithwaite, tied to a chair at the front, her mouth gagged.

"Bring them up here so that we can see them."

The thugs dragged them up, tying them onto chairs beside Mrs. Braithwaite.

Baxter walked up to Cummerbatch, and they had a short conference in low voices. Baxter then dropped back to position himself beside Betty.

"How could you?" she spat at him.

"Oh, darling. You were never **that** good a spy, were you?" he said, smiling sadly at her. "That's why Cummerbatch chose you for this job. He knew you weren't good enough to catch up with us. Now be a good girl and tell me where you put the bomb."

"I'll never tell you."

"Well, in that case, we'll all be blown to pieces, you and your dear mother included." He looked at her coldly, then said, "It's of no consequence anyway. I severed the detonation cord before giving it to you last night." He gave her a steely smile. "It won't go off."

"How do you know that I didn't fix it?"

"Because, my dear Betty, you simply aren't that thorough."

Cummerbatch was standing in front of the group, which now comprised more than twenty widely assorted individuals. "We might have had a setback in recent days, losing a few of our men, but let it be known that from now onward, this organization will be run like clockwork. There'll be no more mistakes, no more poorly thought-out schemes." He looked pointedly at Betty, his voice lowering to a threatening rasp. "No more spies."

A ripple of applause went through the audience, but he quickly quieted them down.

"Today we will start anew. The führer is beginning the—"

A terrific chorus of gunshots came from the stairs, followed by shouting, men's voices, and loud footsteps.

Then they broke into the room.

There must have been more than a dozen of them, quickly filtering through to dominate the motley crowd.

It was the police.

Astonished, Mr. Norris watched as they grabbed and handcuffed every member.

"We are arresting you all on suspicion of treason," the chief inspector called out to the fascists.

**Funny, he looks familiar,** thought Mr. Norris.

And then he remembered. It was the chief inspector who had come to arrest Anthony Metcalf outside the curiosity shop.

His head shot around to look at Betty.

"Did you . . . ?"

She grinned. "Well, if someone gives you his telephone number, it's rather rude not to use it."

## 60.

It was after ten o'clock that evening by the time they'd finished the initial questions from the police. Betty stood outside Scotland Yard with her mother, who was retying her head scarf, waiting for Mr. Norris before heading back to Shilling Lane. They would have to go back to Scotland Yard in the morning to make an official statement. The police had to have enough evidence to imprison the BUF members for a very long time.

"Betty dear, I'm sorry about Baxter. I know you were very fond of him." Mrs. Braithwaite put an arm around her. "How did you know?"

"Well, it was more of a calculated guess, to be honest. Baxter mentioned that Mary Montgomery suspected him of having a fling with Florrie, which was a ludicrous suggestion—so ludicrous, in fact, that it almost had to have a grain of truth in it." She gave her mother a tight-lipped smile. "Mary isn't a daft girl, so the only reason I could see for her suspecting that Baxter was having a fling was that she had seen them together. After that, it was an obvious next step. Why wouldn't he have come clean about seeing Florrie if it was innocent? No, there had to be a bigger story."

"Had they been together for long?"

"From what I gather, Florrie was shared between Baxter and Cummerbatch, sent out to recruit when she could. She didn't belong to anyone as such, rather she belonged to the group, ran the group in her own way. She was the link that held them all together, the mastermind."

"The police are saying that even Cummerbatch was her pawn."

"Yes, she was the one who controlled the trafficking of the illegal guns to the garage in Clapham. She was their contact with Berlin." Betty grimaced. "It's rather sordid, don't you think?"

"Indeed, I hardly know how she kept up with it all."

"She's a very cunning young woman."

Mrs. Braithwaite shrugged. "Not as cunning as you are, my dear. What will happen to them?"

"Cummerbatch and Baxter will be imprisoned, and the Montgomery sisters and the others will probably be interned on the Isle of Man. That's where problematic civilians and German and Italian nationals are being held to keep them out of harm's way. The chiefs at MI5 are bound to try to turn Florrie double—she'd make an extremely valuable double agent now that she has proved her worth to the BUF and the Nazi establishment."

Mr. Norris joined them. "Right, I think it's time for us to go home for a nice celebratory pot of tea."

"I have to report to MI5 headquarters first," Betty said, heaving a large sigh. "I know they'll be livid with me for breaking rank."

"Of course they won't," Mr. Norris said. "They'll congratulate you on a job well done!"

However, as she walked into HQ twenty minutes later, she had the feeling that word was already out. People in the corridor looked sideways at her. The receptionist informed her brusquely that Mr. Ratchington was waiting for her. Even the lift operator knew which floor she was going to without her having to tell him.

"Come in, Braithwaite," Mr. Ratchington said when she knocked, and taking a deep breath, she walked into his office.

As one of the most senior MI5 chiefs, he had an office at the top of the building, lavish by war standards. He sat behind a large mahogany desk, his elbows placed neatly on either side, his fingers touching. His stern, slim face showed the deep frown lines of a man who had lived to middle age and had seldom smiled for the duration.

"Sit down, Braithwaite."

She sat.

"I heard a curious story this evening, and you appear to be at the center of it." He cleared his throat and leaned back in his chair. "Do, pray, enlighten me."

Starting at the very beginning, Betty told the story. All about how she'd been captured, twice, how her mother had become involved, along with her landlord. How she suspected first Cummerbatch and then Baxter, and then finally, how she decided to stop them in their tracks.

"I suspected it was a trap, sir. I just wanted to cover myself, which is why I called the police beforehand."

He looked at her severely, and then leaned forward in his chair, his fingers forming the spire of a church. His eyes narrowed as he took out a notepad and wrote something down.

"Perhaps you could have dealt with the situation earlier? You could have done it far more cleanly if you had, you know."

"Well, I'm not sure if I would have—"

"Why did you allow them to capture you a second time? Why didn't you see it after the first?"

"Yes, sir." She blushed.

"After the police have finished gathering evidence, you're to take forty-eight hours' leave and then report to Ingham on the seventh floor."

"Is he—can I be sure that he's not—"

"He's not a defector. Is that what you're blubbering about, Braithwaite? Ingham is head of the team that turns Nazi spies into our own spies."

"How exciting!" Betty said, trying to contain her elation.

Mr. Ratchington scowled. "No, Braithwaite," he said very seriously. "Our work is anything but exciting. It's methodical, carefully considered, and thorough." His eyes penetrated her. "Now, take your forty-eight hours to absorb all of this and come back ready to work."

She stood up. "Yes, sir. Thank you, sir," she said, and headed for the door.

"One more thing, Braithwaite."

She turned her head.

"Well done." At last, a flicker of a smile.

## 61.

Mr. Norris arrived home at five o'clock. But today he was not coming home from work. He hadn't been to work for a few days. Today, after lengthy interviews with first the police and then MI5, he and Mrs. Braithwaite had finally been dismissed.

Mrs. Braithwaite was to leave for Ashcombe in the morning, and his routine, which had been turned upside down in the last few weeks, would finally be restored.

He made a great sigh as he bustled into the kitchen. If he was honest, he couldn't remember a more exhilarating time. The past week had made him feel alive. He'd forgotten about the accounts, about the ironing, and about getting a good night's sleep. He'd even been unbothered when Mrs. Braithwaite insisted on cooking Spam, messing up his tidy kitchen.

Today he'd stopped on the way home to procure some lamb chops for dinner, taking advantage of some of the new contacts he'd acquired inside a certain pub beside Clapham Common.

"It's only because it's a special occasion," he said as he pulled a chair out for Mrs. Braithwaite.

For once they were eating in the dining room, a usually miserable room that he'd spruced up with a candle and a vase full of daffodils from the garden. He'd even brought in Cassandra's record player, which was currently playing a lilting jazz song, "All of Me."

"Well, all this is rather splendid, especially after the week we've had." Mrs. Braithwaite made herself comfortable, and they once again dissected the case—how thrilling it had all been, especially now that they knew everything was going to end up all right.

After dinner they cleared the plates to the kitchen, where Mr. Norris began to wash, Mrs. Braithwaite to dry, as usual.

Mr. Norris wasn't entirely sure how he felt about Mrs. Braithwaite going back to Ashcombe. When he'd gone to bed the previous night, he'd stayed awake thinking about her, what she'd come to mean to him. Who'd have thought the brash harridan who had bombarded his home a few weeks ago would become someone he'd come to, well, now that he thought about it, to like quite immensely?

He'd chuckled to himself when he remembered how she'd demanded answers from them—rightly so with Florrie, as it turned out. He liked to think, over the course of their adventures, that he'd been a good influence on her, that she'd learned to be more careful, to get information out of people through more subtle means.

"And she seems to have found her heart," he'd said softly into the darkness of his attic room.

It was as if she'd shed her hostility, become quite caring. He could hardly believe how much he looked forward to discussing his day with her, to do the washing up with her. How he was going to miss her.

She took another plate to wipe.

"I'll be back to visit, of course. After all, Betty's here now, as well as Cassandra, and Blanche isn't far away either." There was a pause. "And, of course, there's our own friendship, too."

"Friendship," he repeated softly after she'd said it. "Is that what it is?"

"Well, I think we can call it a friendship, after all the times we've helped each other out, saved each other's lives, that sort of thing."

He didn't say anything, but he did think that it was **he** who did the saving of **her** rather than the other way around. But he let it drop. After all, it made a nice change to be the hero instead of the one who sits on the sidelines.

She looked at the sink, avoiding his gaze. "Don't **you** think that we're friends?"

"I suppose we are," he said, laughing, slightly embarrassed. "Although I dare say that **partners in crime** might be a better term."

She laughed. "We did make a good team, didn't we? Well, when you weren't being too much of a coward to come along."

"I don't think you can call the man who saved you—no less than twice, I might add—a coward, my dear Mrs. Braithwaite. I may be cautious, perhaps a little anxious, but I most certainly am not a coward."

"Of course you're not," she said, a half smile on her face.

Mr. Norris shook his head, laughing. "Would you care for me to show you how I took Briggs down in the basement?" He grabbed her dishcloth, trying to wrestle it away from her. "Then you won't be able to go back to Ashcombe. You'll have to stay here."

She let her hands fall from the dishcloth, suddenly becoming more serious.

"But I have to go back. It's my home, my house, my life. I came up here to find Betty, and I promised you that I'd leave once she was found. So leave I must."

"Don't be ridiculous," he said, putting down the cloth and taking her hand in his. "You know you don't have to go. And I'm certain that you have no intention whatsoever of handing your front door key back to me, do you?"

"Of course I do," she said with great haughtiness, as if the thought would ever have crossed her mind. "And I know that you'll give away all my tins of Spam as soon as my back is turned, won't you?"

He smiled. "How perceptive you are, Mrs. Braithwaite."

She looked at him slightly coyly. "Because we have agreed to be friends, I think you should call me by my first name."

Mr. Norris's forehead furrowed. He wasn't sure he wanted to start addressing Mrs. Braithwaite in any other way. Although, it depended upon the name itself. Some names, after all, are easier than others. They flow better, trip off the tongue. "Might I ask what your name is?"

"Phyllis," she said simply. "And what is yours?"

He hesitated. "Well, all of my friends call me Norman."

She looked at him quizzically. "Are you saying that even though your friends call you Norman, your real name is actually something else?"

He paused. "I'd rather not say, if it's all the same."

She eyed him. "You have to tell me."

"Promise not to laugh."

She nodded.

"It's Lancelot."

Mrs. Braithwaite muffled a giggle. "Well, you certainly came to my rescue!"

"My mother liked Tennyson. But no one ever called me that, except for Gordon, of course."

"Your brother?"

"Yes, my brother." Mr. Norris—Lancelot— began explaining about Gordon's contagious laugh, his pleasure at the world around him, the walks they'd take to the park, spotting birds and playing car number-plate games along the way, and they remained at the kitchen table until the early hours of the morning, talking about their lives.

**Isn't it strange**, Mr. Norris thought as he went up to bed, **that you hold all of your stories to yourself, and then someone comes along, and suddenly you can't wait to tell them.**

It was as if his heart had been cracked open and an array of experiences and sensations had come tumbling out, as if they'd been carefully concertinaed inside, waiting for the right setting, the right evening, the right company.

## 62.

It was the middle of the following afternoon when Mrs. Braithwaite opened her front door in Ashcombe. The walk from the station had been a long, arduous one, the stationmaster having firmly professed himself too busy to give her a hand with her suitcase.

Her house was exactly as she left it, and yet it felt strange, as if it belonged to a different person, a different Mrs. Braithwaite. She went into the kitchen to make herself a cup of tea, and as the kettle was coming to a boil, her eyes rested on the Royal Doulton tea set, immaculate and ready for service at a moment's notice. Aunt Augusta had given it to her as a wedding present "for when special people visit."

Mrs. Braithwaite gave a dry little laugh. "I haven't used it in years," she muttered, moving it onto the kitchen table to box up later. "I've been clinging to these things far too long, when they only serve to remind me of what's gone wrong in my life."

Perhaps she could sell it. Give the money to Betty. One thing was for sure: She wasn't going to give Betty a tea service for her wedding present. What on earth would a spy do with a thing like that?

She walked into the sitting room, plumping herself down on the floral sofa and remembering the last time she'd sat there, only a few weeks ago now, raging about Mrs. Metcalf, and deciding to find Betty.

"And thank goodness I did," she said out loud. "Otherwise I'd still be here, trapped by it all."

Realizing the time, she got up, retied her head scarf, and headed out. She had to find Mrs. Metcalf, thank her for what she had done. If Mrs. Metcalf hadn't pushed her out, she'd never have gone in search of Betty, never realized there was so much more to life than her village standing.

The weather was blustery, bright sunshine interspersing with shadowy clouds, the odd bout of rain hurrying past, making the pavement glisten in the late afternoon sunshine.

Mrs. Braithwaite walked swiftly down to the village. If Mrs. Metcalf was taking her new office seriously, she would be in the village hall, or the office behind, seated at Mrs. Braithwaite's old desk, meticulously running through the progress of the sewing bees, the mobile canteen, the metal-for-armament collections, and the jumble sales. The memories of the job flooded into her mind: how important it had seemed then. How she'd taken it far too seriously, let her bossy tendencies take over, forgotten, frankly, that it was a voluntary organization for housewives and not a major military operation.

The village hall was bustling. The women were preparing for a jumble sale. Folding tables were set up with ladies rummaging through great piles of old clothes, sorting them into sizes and types.

Someone—Patience perhaps—had brought in a gramophone, and they all swayed their hips and hummed along to "In the Mood," the saxophones of the big band enlivening the space with jazzy beats.

One of the ladies spotted Mrs. Braithwaite and quickly put her head down and got on with her work, trying not to meet her eyes. But Mrs. Braithwaite walked up and gave her a big smile. They were rather surprised to see her. The hectoring, authoritarian attitude she'd had toward them made the smile seem incongruous.

Had they ever seen Mrs. Braithwaite smile before?

"Hello, everyone! Can I join in and help you today?"

Patience appeared beside her. "Are you back already? I hope you enjoyed your time in London."

Mrs. Braithwaite beamed. "Well, it was quite an adventure, if you must know."

"I'm sure that it was, if **you** were involved," she brayed meanly, her high-pitched voice echoing condescendingly through the room.

The old Mrs. Braithwaite could have put her in her place with a few choice words, but the new Mrs. Braithwaite sought to make amends.

"Betty was in trouble, and I shan't go into the details now, suffice to say that I made some new friends and we found ourselves very much up to the task of finding her and bringing her home." The ladies looked at each other nervously.

Others began to gather around, and Mrs. Braithwaite started to regret saying as much as she had. After all, Betty's superiors from MI5 had made her sign the Official Secrets Act, and Betty had warned about saying anything, especially anything about Anthony Metcalf.

Mrs. Braithwaite gazed at the familiar faces. "Well, it wasn't that much really—"

"What wasn't much?" A haughty voice bellowed over, and the crowd of ladies peeled apart to let Mrs. Metcalf in. She must have been in the back office and heard the commotion. "Oh, Mrs. Braithwaite, good to see you back," she said in a way that implied precisely the opposite.

She took a few steps toward them.

"I was just telling the ladies about my time in London," she said, momentarily surprised by Mrs. Metcalf's supercilious attitude. Of course Mrs. Metcalf didn't know about her precious Anthony yet. He was still being questioned, and his family wouldn't know that he'd been taken into custody.

She could say something, use Anthony's dishonor as a bat to thwack the arrogant smile off Mrs. Metcalf's face.

But that would be the old Mrs. Braithwaite.

Instead, she felt an overwhelming sorrow for Mrs. Metcalf. The horror of what was coming in her direction she wouldn't wish on anyone.

"Let's just say that it was an adventure," she said by way of an explanation.

"Oh, was it?" Mrs. Metcalf replied coldly, then added, looking around at the ladies, "Well, we here have more important things on our plate than 'adventures.' We have our largest ever jumble sale on Saturday, and you of all people must know that the success of a jumble sale is in its organization. Who will come and buy if our offerings are muddled?"

Patience added, "We want this jumble sale to raise enough money to pay for a new Spitfire. They say that they'll name it 'The Ashcombe Lady' in our honor."

"Oh, that sounds wonderful!" Mrs. Braithwaite said heartily, the ladies looking on with curiosity at this utterly confounding change in character.

"I say," one of them said. "Do you feel quite well, Mrs. Braithwaite?"

Another one whispered audibly, "I think she's been drinking."

"I feel perfectly well, thank you!" Mrs. Braithwaite chirped. "In fact, I feel quite marvelous." She took a large breath, as if enjoying the country air, and announced, "Let's get back to work, shall we? Saturday's only a few days away, and I'm sure we can get that Spitfire if we put our minds to it!"

She went to follow the ladies back to the tables of jumble but was stopped in her tracks by Mrs. Metcalf.

"I hope you haven't returned with a plan to take back the role of leader. We've been having a very productive time since you've been gone."

"Yes," Patience sneered. "We're running like clockwork with my mother at the helm."

Another smaller, anxious woman piped up as if she couldn't stop herself, the words flooding out in a torrent. "You're not wanted here anymore, Mrs. Braithwaite. You come in here acting all nice and cheerful, but you'll go back to your old ways, bossing us all about, acting like you're high and mighty above us all, when you're just the same as everyone else. Worse even. At least **we** didn't scare our husbands away."

Mrs. Braithwaite's face fell. "Is that really what you think of me?" Everyone was watching, pretending not to, as she looked from face to face. "That I bullied everyone and drove him away?"

Her shoulders sagged, unhappiness seeping out

of her, and she took a firm grasp of her handbag and slowly turned to the door.

"I didn't drive him away," she murmured, half to herself. "He left me, and I couldn't stop him. He broke our marriage and destroyed my life, in one fell swoop." Then she raised her head and looked at them. "Don't blame me because my rotten husband left. If anything, pity me. But most of all, we women shouldn't be condemning each other because of something bad a man chooses to do to us."

Everyone had stopped work, looking up at her.

"We shouldn't be blaming each other. We should be supporting each other. This isn't a race whereby one of us wins and the others all lose. Do we want a world where men can isolate us from society for no fault of our own? Or do we want a world where women stand up for ourselves together?"

She looked around to see the crowd of women, all slowly coming forward toward her.

"I know I was a bit bossy in the past, and I'm sorry for that."

"More than a bit bossy!" someone called out from the back.

"I **was** bossy, but that's over now. Giving my time, my energy, my heart is how I'd like to be remembered. When all is said and done, I'd like people to talk about how I helped them, how I solved their problems, how I lifted their spirits when they were flagging. Life isn't about class or money. It's not about putting people down. And it most certainly isn't about judging people based on their family members."

She glanced at Mrs. Metcalf, yet to feel the shame her adored son would bring on her. The sad irony was that Mrs. Braithwaite's speech was paving the way for the group to support Mrs. Metcalf. Once the truth about Anthony was out, she didn't want the village ladies to turn their backs on her, too. No, Mrs. Metcalf would need them like never before.

The thought made her nod slowly as she looked around the crowd. "I shouldn't be blamed for my husband deserting me, and in the same way, we need to stand by any member who is let down by a man. Envelop them with our kindness, not our reproach or resentment. We have to stand together and stand strong."

A few of the ladies began a small swell of a cheer, a few voices piping up with "She's jolly right" and "Well said."

Mrs. Metcalf moved to the front and put on a smile that didn't quite reach her eyes. "Thank you, Mrs. Braithwaite," she said, herding her toward the door. "I think you've helped enough for the day."

"But I wanted to give you a hand with the jumble sale," she stammered, trying to move around Mrs. Metcalf, back toward the ladies. "I know I never used to help sort the jumble, but I'm sure I'll be competent."

Mrs. Metcalf leaned forward to take hold of the

door and swung it open. "I'll thank you to leave us to get on with our hard work. Such a lot to be done."

And then something extraordinary happened.

"Why shouldn't she stay and help?" It was Patience, stepping forward from the crowd. "She's right. We should stick together. A lot of us here have been through hard times, and most of it hasn't been our fault in the least. If we only stuck together, we all would do much better."

Another lady stepped forward, older and hunched. "I agree with Mrs. Braithwaite. Wouldn't our village be a lovelier place if we supported each other?"

"Hear, hear!" a few more ladies cried, more of them stepping forward.

"Mrs. Braithwaite," Patience said, almost smiling, "I think we're onto something."

Huge cheers went up through the room.

Mrs. Braithwaite strode back in, beaming with joy.

Mrs. Metcalf followed behind her. "I'm sorry about the way you left the WVS, Phyllis. I think we all appreciated what you did, but perhaps you understand that you weren't the right person for the job of leader."

Mrs. Braithwaite gave her a hearty slap on the shoulder, knocking her forward a step or two. "I couldn't agree more, Myrtle." She laughed a long booming laugh, as if everything was suddenly complete in the best way possible. "And I want to thank you for booting me out, sending me on my own quest. I can heartily recommend it. Little did I know that in searching for my daughter, I'd finally find myself."

The ladies gave another cheer, then someone put on another record, "Singin' in the Rain." All the ladies began dancing their way back to the jumble on the tables.

Mrs. Metcalf was left alone with Mrs. Braithwaite. "I confess that I've been feeling rather sorry about the way things ended between us. We were such very good friends."

"Yes, we were." Mrs. Braithwaite gave her old friend another hearty pat on the shoulder. "And let's see if we can't be friends again."

"I hope you'll stay and help us with the jumble?"

"Of course! Let me know where to begin."

"Right here." She directed her to a table piled high with children's clothes. "We're quite behind." She smiled at Mrs. Braithwaite. "I know you'll be a great help."

"So do I."

And together they both began to laugh.

## 63

The following afternoon, Betty made her way to number 47 Rectory Road. Blanche had come out of the hospital and was staying with her former headmistress. Mrs. Churley's small terraced house was painted white and cheerily adorned with red gingham curtains in its small, evenly spaced windows. Betty knocked tentatively on the door.

Presently it was opened by a young woman, perhaps only a few years older than Betty, who had short, ruggedly chopped brown hair and a delighted look on her face. Bandages on her one leg and a crutch indicated that she was far from recovered, and there was still a large plaster on her cheek, beneath which burn scars covered the side of her face.

"You must be the other Miss Braithwaite," the young woman said softly, a gleam in her brown eyes, gesturing to Betty to come in. "I'm Blanche."

"Yes, that's right. I'm Betty, Betty Braithwaite." She put her hand out to shake, and then, seeing Blanche put a thoroughly bandaged one out for her, pulled back. "Oh, I'm most dreadfully sorry. I didn't think—"

"Don't worry," laughed Blanche. "It'll mend in time. It just makes introductions awkward. Come in and sit down. I'll put the kettle on."

Betty followed her into a small, tidy kitchen with flowered wallpaper and charming dishcloths in different colors: pale green, sky blue, pink. Someone had been cooking earlier, as the yeasty smell of fresh bread filled the room. The wireless was on in the sitting room, the calming sound of BBC voices drifting through as Blanche filled the kettle and put it on the stove.

She was walking with a crutch, able to get about quite well, propping it under her arm when she needed to use both hands for chores such as making the tea.

"It must be hard, getting used to the crutch," Betty said gently.

But Blanche smiled. "At least I can still teach. I was worried they'd stop me, as teaching small children involves a certain amount of running around, but the children in my class were so terribly keen to have me back. They wouldn't have anyone else."

"Of course they want you back! You saved their lives!"

She laughed. "As if they'd remember something as commonplace as that! No, they want me because I sing to them. None of the other teachers do that."

"Singing? What fun! When I was growing up, our teachers only shouted at us to learn our tables. Are you a trained singer?"

Blanche blushed prettily. Even through the bandages, her oval face with large brown eyes was striking. "Oh no, my mother taught me some songs, and now I like to sing them to remember her—bring her back to life." A sadness transformed her eyes.

"She must have been a lovely mum. To go through life singing; that's the right way to live."

"She sang for the troops in the last war. That's where she met Dad." She sat down beside Betty at the kitchen table. "The performers would visit the injured men. He was in a hospital unit in France with a bullet wound in his leg—he never lost the limp. He took a shine to Mum and started writing to her, although she hardly got any of his letters because she was moving around so much. When the war ended, he came home, gave himself time to recover from his wound, then went to see Mum with a ring, only to find her engaged to another man. But it didn't take long for Dad to charm her around. He was the funniest and kindest man you'd ever meet, handsome, too. They thought the world of each other."

The water began to boil, and she went to make the tea.

"They sound like a wonderful pair," Betty said, watching as Blanche eased the tea cozy onto the round, yellow teapot.

"Mum was never the same after Dad died." Blanche returned to the table. "She still had a smile on her face, singing around the house, but she was always looking for something that wasn't there. She pined for him. Not just the humor and friendship, something deeper. She told me how she'd dream she could just reach out and touch him, feel his big hands, his sturdy shoulders, take a deep breath of him again." She paused, as if living through a faded memory. "Well, now she's with him."

Her eyes filled with tears, which she hastily wiped away, and Betty shuffled her chair closer and put an arm around her shoulders.

"I'm sorry," Blanche said, getting out a handkerchief. "I just miss her so much. It's so dreadful to go through all this"—she indicated her missing leg—"without her here. I know that you haven't always been on the best of terms with your mother, but just stop and think about how devastating it would be if something happened to her. The woman who held you when you were tiny, taught you how to live. When your mother dies, it feels as if the earth you stand on collapses beneath you."

She looked at Betty imploringly. "You have to

promise me to spend time with her. You don't know what you're going to miss until they're gone."

Betty held her close as she sobbed silently into a handkerchief, remembering her own words to Mr. Cummerbatch in her early days at MI5. She'd told him that her parents didn't care for her, that she "was fine by herself." A flush came over her. How naive she had been! How very sad as well. Although she had an important job that meant more to her than anything, the reality was that her obsession with work had concealed an emptiness deep inside. Risking her life had been easy because, without love, it was worthless.

She heaved a large sigh. "I always took my mother for granted until my life was in danger. But she came for me, and frankly I'm not at all sure anyone else would have." The arrest of both Baxter and Cummerbatch had thrown the whole operation into a new light for her. The awful truth of the matter was that they had been waiting for her to make a mistake, and when she hadn't, they'd given orders to have her removed—for good. It wasn't flattering, and she'd been a fool to be taken in, but at least she'd come out the other side.

She had her life.

Blanche put an arm around Betty's shoulders. "Your mum certainly was a kind stand-in for my mum. I don't know whether I would have pulled through without her. It was so thoughtful, so selfless of her to be with me through those dark times. She didn't have to be."

"Well, Mum wasn't always like that. I don't know whether it was being drummed out of the village or her adventures in finding me, but she's definitely changed. Perhaps it was a bit of Mr. Norris—funny, I think that by spending so much time together, she's become a little more thoughtful, as he is. He's certainly taken on some of her daring. It's as if they've balanced out each other."

"Do you know, I think you could be right."

"He's such a kind old soul, and they rub along together like a couple of beavers building a dam, one of them strident, the other questioning. They make rather a splendid pair, don't you think?"

"Was it like that with your father?"

Betty uttered a short laugh. "Not at all." She flattened out the creases in her skirt. "He was in charge, and she was always running to keep up. I remember once when she accused him of having an affair, he made it seem that she was losing her mind."

"I can't imagine your mother being taken in by that."

"He's a manipulative man, only looking after himself. I was taken in by him, too, if I'm honest. By the end, he hardly spoke to Mum. They'd sit in silence in the living room, and then he'd go out, without even mentioning it. We'd just hear the front door slam behind him." She paused with the memory. How cruelly he treated her. "There was none of the jollity she has with Mr. Norris."

"War changes people," Blanche said simply. "You were almost killed." A pallor came over her face. "And me, too." She picked up her tea to take a sip, and then put it back down. "You know how it feels when your life is hanging in the balance? As if it could go either way?"

"I do," Betty whispered with the horror of it. "It was horrific."

"Yes, but wasn't it also strangely awakening? Didn't you come out of it feeling renewed? Like the sunshine was on your face for the first time. I find myself reveling in the snug fur of a cat and the taste of hot, sweet tea. I can hardly believe how much of life I notice now."

They sat in silence. Betty absorbed the pale colors of the pretty kitchen, the sun coming in from the garden, the smell of fresh bread, and the sound of the wireless rounding up the daily advance of the war. How easy it was to miss these moments, looking forward or backward instead of just sitting, feeling, experiencing.

## 64.

Mrs. Braithwaite felt useful. She was surprised to find that she enjoyed helping the other Ashcombe ladies, laughing with them, hearing their troubles, offering advice. Although she still felt that she knew what was best, she'd learned to bite her tongue—most of the time.

The village might not be as thrilling as her days in London had been, but it would have to do. And as she stood at a jumble table folding children's pajamas, she remembered her final night at Mr. Norris's house on Shilling Lane and was surprised to feel a sudden yearning, an emptiness.

Enough of that, she steadied herself. It was right for her to be back at her own home, in Ashcombe.

As she walked home after a busy day with the

jumble sale, there was a man standing outside her house. He was older than she, in his late fifties, with pale gray hair and bright gray eyes looking out from a long, kind face. Wearing a suit that looked slightly old-fashioned, albeit well made, he had a slight hunch and carried a thick, worn briefcase.

"Mrs. Braithwaite?" he asked, putting his hand forward.

"Yes," she replied, taking his hand and shaking it with her usual fervor.

"I'm Mr. Simpson, and I'd like to have a word with you in private. It concerns your role in the recent situation in Clapham."

"I told the police and MI5 everything they wanted to know," she said. "I can't think what else you might need."

"But it is **I** who have something for **you**." He smiled, gesturing toward the door.

Intrigued, Mrs. Braithwaite opened the door and led him inside.

"Would you like some tea?" she said, as they sat down in the sitting room.

"No, thank you," he said, getting to the point. "I need to speak to you about your role." He opened his briefcase and handed her a set of papers. "I would like you to have a look at these."

She looked at them, leafing through the first few pages. It was a briefing document from MI5 about a potential leak within the government. Critical war information was somehow getting to the Nazis. It had to be coming from someone who was working closely with—or inside—the War Office.

"Someone needs to stop them," Mr. Simpson said calmly, a vague question hanging in the air.

"Yes, this sort of thing could lose us the war," she replied, still leafing through.

"That's why we need someone thorough on the case."

"Yes, you do," she agreed, absorbed in the details. "How do they know about our air-defense strategy? This is abominable!"

"Do you know why I'm letting you read it?"

"No, I don't," she replied, still reading. "It's very complicated, and no doubt highly confidential."

"We need someone resourceful to get to the bottom of it." He coughed lightly to get her attention.

She looked up.

"And we were thinking of you."

She leaped to her feet, carrying the papers with her. "I couldn't. You see, I live here in Ashcombe, and—"

"We would give you money to move to London."

She looked at him. "Are you offering me a job as a spy?"

"In a manner of speaking, yes." He handed her another sheet of paper, spelling out her role, her mission.

She took it, began reading, then let her hands fall, still clutching the paper. Her mind was spinning with the thrill of her last adventure, how she could hide in plain view, how she had found the courage, the oomph, to infiltrate groups, spy on people, rescue her daughter.

But would she be able to do it all over again? Perhaps she could only do it if it was for Betty— perhaps without the impetus of her daughter she would lose her nerve?

As if reading her mind, Mr. Simpson said, "There's only one way to find out, Mrs. Braithwaite."

She looked up at him, her eyes gleaming with excitement. "Of course I'll do it!" she said.

After all, what else did she have planned for the rest of her life?

## 65

It was dark by the time Mrs. Braithwaite arrived at Mr. Norris's front door a few days later. The occasional raindrop hung in the air, ready to remind the infrequent pedestrian how unpleasant chilly rain could be. Between the rushing clouds, the moon lurked steadily, watching over the city as it toiled around in its own immeasurable chaos.

**Just wait until I tell Mr. Norris about my new job,** she thought to herself. Except that she couldn't tell him, she remembered with a start. It was supposed to be top secret.

Finding her key, she opened the front door, thinking how observant it had been of Mr. Norris to know that she never had any intention of returning it. She chuckled to herself, looking forward to

seeing him. She could at least tell him about Mrs.
Metcalf and the WVS ladies.

But as she pushed open the door, she was met
by a dark, still hallway. She wondered if something
awful had happened to him; it was past his usual
time for getting home from work, and he was, after
all, a man of routine. She'd written to tell him that
she was coming, with the date and the time, although trains being as they were . . .

"Hello, is there anybody at home?" she called
more cheerfully than she felt.

Nothing.

She closed the front door with a huff, and
plonked her suitcases beside the staircase. Then she
switched on the light, checking that the blackout
curtains were pulled across—which, mysteriously,
they were. Mr. Norris must have put them up before going out. How vexing of him not to be here
himself.

**Still,** she thought as she looked around the familiar place, **it was good to be back.** She smiled
to herself as she repositioned the elephants and felt
the curved banister of the staircase, smoothed by
everyday hands over many years, Mr. Norris's especially. It almost felt warm from him or one of the
girls, Betty perhaps. Mrs. Braithwaite had written
to her, too.

Looking into the dark kitchen, with the light off,
she decided to take a little tour of the house, just to
be sure everything was as it should be. She turned

toward the sitting room to begin there. Perhaps she would have a little sit-down after the walk from the station.

Opening the door, she felt the wall for the light switch, and as she turned it on, the place seemed to glow with life and warmth. She looked around at the familiar pictures on the wall, the carriage clock on the mantelpiece ticking away gently, the fresh orange-pink roses in a small vase on the table, the man's shoe sticking out from the bottom of the curtain . . .

Mrs. Braithwaite stopped in her tracks, a great smile coming over her face as she crept toward the curtain. Then, standing right in front of it, she said, as if to herself, "I wonder where everyone could be?"

And with that, she quickly whisked the curtain to the side, making Mr. Norris leap into the air, tripping over his own feet and stumbling into her, laughing.

Mrs. Braithwaite, laughing, too, took his hands and pulled him out as the girls jumped out of their hiding places, shouting, "Surprise!"

Betty was there, looking much healthier and very well rested, ready to give her a hearty hug.

And then there was Cassandra, looking stunning in a gorgeous floral dress.

"Oh, Cassandra, I'm so glad that you stayed in for the evening," Mrs. Braithwaite said with a grin as she put her arm around her.

"Of course I'm here to welcome you home!" Cassandra said, excitement flashing in her eyes. "Who knows when one might be in peril and need Mrs. Braithwaite to save one's life?"

And there, too, was another girl, shyly standing behind on crutches. Betty brought her forward.

Mrs. Braithwaite recognized her eyes, the soft, chestnut curls.

"Blanche, you're here!"

"I wanted to thank you for, well, sharing your love and your family with me." She smiled shyly, and Mrs. Braithwaite put her arms around her.

"You will always be welcome wherever we are. But how did you know that I was coming back?"

"Betty told me." They both grinned, as if they'd had a good time becoming friends—and hopefully not making too many jokes at her expense.

"Where are you staying? I do hope you have someone looking after you at home?"

"It's fine. I'm staying with Mrs. Churley for now."

"You're not overdoing it, are you?"

Blanche grinned. "Well, I'm trying not to. But there **is** a war on."

"We're not the only ones happy to see you back," Betty whispered, glancing across to Mr. Norris, who was busy putting the curtain back in place. "I think there's one person who hasn't been quite himself since you've been gone."

Mr. Norris came over, oblivious to the fact that

they'd been talking about him, and asked Mrs. Braithwaite to come to the kitchen to help him with the food.

"You know, I was thinking," he said as he took an incredibly flat-looking cake out of the larder. "Perhaps now that you're back, you'd like to stay? We have a spare room here, now that Florrie's gone, and it's still available, and—"

"I thought you had a waiting list of people wanting a room?"

"Well, somehow none of them are interested anymore." He gave her a knowing little smile.

She came toward him and took his hands in hers. "I was hoping that you might ask."

He smiled, lowering his eyes with embarrassment. His face was only inches from hers, and she was smiling at him, glowing with pleasure and that feeling that life can give you sometimes, when it seems that everything is exactly as it should be, that all the gaps are being filled in.

Almost.

And then, just as she was thinking that she should move her head forward a little, kiss him, and wondering what he'd do, whether he'd pull away, shocked, not ready, he leaned toward her and kissed her tenderly, the connecting of two separate forces, each equalizing and enhancing the other.

It felt like more than just a kiss.

It felt like a new beginning.

Sometime later, Betty came in to let them know

that everyone was hungry and, although they all knew what was happening in there, they didn't want to have to wait for the end of the war to have the incredibly flat cake.

The rest of the party went very merrily indeed. Blanche was an exceptionally good singer, and with Mr. Norris at the piano, she sang some old favorites, everyone joining in with "Run Rabbit Run" and "The White Cliffs of Dover." Cassandra helped her out, and they even did a nifty little duet of "The Boogie Woogie Bugle Boy of Company B," which was wonderful to dance along to.

At the end of the evening, after everyone had said their good-nights and gone off to bed, Mrs. Braithwaite helped Mr. Norris with the washing up.

"When do you start your new job?" Mr. Norris asked as he plunged the cake plate into the water.

Mrs. Braithwaite froze. "How do you know that I have a new job? I mean, what new job? Why do you ask?"

He turned to her, laughing. "I know because Mr. Simpson knocked on my door as well."

"Well, that wasn't very fair of him to tell you about my job."

"He didn't." Mr. Norris grinned, handing her the cake plate to dry. "But you have just confirmed it, Mrs. Braithwaite."

She was too excited to be cross with him for fooling her into admitting it. "Are we to work together again?"

"I'm afraid I turned him down." Mr. Norris went back to dunking plates into the sink. "You see, the accounts at the law firm need urgent attention. When I finally went back to work, some junior had left them in a complete shambles. It'll take months to sort them out."

Mrs. Braithwaite stopped drying the cake plate and looked at him, scowling. "Don't you want to work with me again?"

He turned to her and grinned, putting the plate down and taking her into his arms. "I'm only joking. Of course I said yes. Why, I can't think of anything better than to be in another rollicking adventure with you, my dear."

She laughed, slapping him with the dishcloth, and they carried on washing and cleaning, until it was all finished—to Mr. Norris's satisfaction—and then, with a lingering, silken kiss, they headed upstairs.

# ACKNOWLEDGMENTS

This is a book about mothers and daughters, their support for each other, their shared lives, their love—our relationship with our mother is one of the most important and unique relationships we'll have in our lives. The enduring life lessons, experiences, and love stay with us, both in our thoughts but also nestling deep within us, embedded in our psychological makeup, as rooted as our DNA. My warmest gratitude goes to my own mother, Joan Cooper, for everything, from her passion for books and history to her warm and loving support. This book is dedicated to you.

The National Archives in London houses a large collection of beautifully preserved MI5 documents from the war years. It was incredible to be able to leaf through the very documents of the era, and these formed the backbone of the world I have created in this book. The meticulous notes made by the special agents, all typed up, neatly documented each member of the fascist organizations, their movements, and their meetings. I would like to acknowledge the highly dangerous work of the MI5 agents during the war, including the small number of female spies. Their activities were of paramount importance to the eventual Allied victory.

My warmest gratitude goes to my phenomenal editor at Crown, Hilary Rubin Teeman. Her dedication to detail and structure, as well as her incredible vision for the book, have made it into the thrilling, thought-provoking read it is today: thank you so much for all your work and expertise. My thanks also go to Molly Stern, Annsley Rosner, David Drake, Elena Giavaldi, and Jillian Buckley, with a special mention to Lisa Erickson and Christine Johnston for their immense help with marketing and publicity.

My magnificent agent, Alexandra Machinist at ICM, combines editorial wisdom, publishing instinct, and immense charm in a truly spellbinding way. Thank you for your razor-sharp guidance and expertise.

Special gratitude goes to Karolina Sutton, my brilliant and distinguished agent at Curtis Brown in London: thank you for your tremendous skill and support. Huge thanks also go to Sophie Baker, my dynamic translation rights agent at Curtis Brown in London, and to my publishers around the world.

I'm incredibly fortunate to have the pleasure of meeting other authors and would like to thank the community for its fantastic support and warmth. Massive thanks go to Cathy Kelly, who has become a wonderful friend as well as being an exceptional and inspiring author. Thanks also go to Chris Cleave, Martha Hall Kelly, Beatriz Williams, and Douglas Rogers for their help and support.

After this book became a work-in-progress, a multitude of people helped to see it through. Whole-hearted gratitude goes to my beloved critique group, Barb Boehm, Emmy Nicklin, Christina Keller, and Julia Rocchi, for providing excellent critiques and plenty of wine and warmth to help the process along. Thanks go to my teachers at Johns Hopkins, especially to Mark Farrington, whose intuition for plot, character, and narrative is legendary, and also to Ed Perlman and Michelle Brafman. Other people who added information, personal stories, or helped along the way include: Judy Smathers, Grace Cutler, Debbie Revesz, Anne Baker, Jen Mallard, Jerry Cooper, David Beckley, Seth Weir, Elaine Cobbe, Louise and Charlie Hamilton Stubber, Lorraine Quigley, Annie Cobbe, Breda Corish, Colin Berry, Mary Dallao, Rebecca Hassett, Ingrid Stewart, and the Eagle Valley Book Club. Huge thanks to Cheryl Harnden for her generosity of spirit and wonderful humor—your help and support have been invaluable to me. Immense gratitude also goes to Courtney Brown for her tremendous energy and resourcefulness, as well as her legendary hospitality and unstoppable joie de vivre.

Finally, to my sister, Alison Mussett, thank you for your brilliant ideas and first-class editing. As always, it's wonderful to know that you're always at the end of the phone or email with feedback, opinions, and great ideas. Thank you more than I can say. And lastly, massive thanks go to my family, Lily and Arabella and my wonderful husband, Pat, without whom this book would never have been written.

## ABOUT THE AUTHOR

JENNIFER RYAN is the author of **The Chilbury Ladies' Choir** and lives in the Washington, D.C., area with her husband and their two children. Originally from London, she was previously a non-fiction book editor.